MASTERS OF MIDNIGHT

MASTERS OF MIDNIGHT

WILLIAM J. MANN

MICHAEL THOMAS FORD

SEAN WOLFE

JEFF MANN

KENSINGTON BOOKS
http://www.kensingtonbooks.com

KENSINGTON BOOKS are published by

Kensington Publishing Corp.
850 Third Avenue
New York, NY 10022

All Kensington titles, imprints and distributed lines are available at special quantity discounts for bulk purchases for sales promotion, premiums, fund-raising, educational or institutional use.

Special book excerpts or customized printings can also be created to fit specific needs. For details, write or phone the office of the Kensington Special Sales Manager: Kensington Publishing Corp., 850 Third Avenue, New York, NY, 10022. Attn. Special Sales Department. Phone: 1-800-221-2647.

Kensington and the K logo Reg. U.S. Pat. & TM Off.

ISBN 0-7582-0421-3

First Kensington Trade Paperback Printing: June 2003
10 9 8 7 6 5 4 3 2 1

Printed in the United States of America

Contents

HIS HUNGER

William J. Mann

Jeremy Horne's Journal

May 3—Here there be strange people.

At times I feel as if I'm visiting some foreign country, like Slovakia or Romania—one of those Eastern European countries where the women huddle under shawls while making the Sign of the Cross and the men bluster about things that go bump in the night. I mean, one guy actually went pale—all the blood drained right out of his face, Minter!—when I asked him for directions to Cravenwood.

It's really so bizarre. I have to keep reminding myself that I'm only in Maine, that Boston is just a couple hours away, that just south of here lies Ogunquit—the place where we spent our most wonderful honeymoon. I force myself to remember that these are American citizens and this the 21st century—even if they talk as if their mouths are filled with cloves of garlic and they act as if I'm heading to Castle Dracula itself.

Oh, man, I'm beat. It's been a long day. Right now I'm curled up on my twin bed in Motel 6 ready to crash. There's not much else to do in this little seaside burg. Beautiful scenery, but not a bar or a club—gay or otherwise—anywhere nearby. The TV doesn't even get HBO! But as I promised you, sweets, I will write you every step of the way, especially since my cell phone zonked out just north of Kittery. What is it about small towns and cellular towers?

And the place I'm heading for doesn't even have electricity!

Maybe you're right. Maybe all this will turn out fine. It just might make a great article, after all. Do you think for the *Globe*'s Sunday magazine? "Local Writer Seeks the Truth of his Father's Disappearance." Plus, it's got all of the elements that editors orgasm over. Boy grows up abandoned by father, fucked up by his unsolved disappearing act. Boy goes off in search of Dad in some forlorn outpost, trying to fill that empty hole in his soul left by his wayward father. I'll pile on the pathos—editors love that.

I can just hear you telling me to be serious. So I admit that I haven't been all that focused on my career. That's one of the things I love about you, Minter: how ambitious you are. How professional. I wish I could be more like you. I just haven't found the passion for anything the way you have. You love being a photographer. You're so committed to it. I wish I had your discipline.

Maybe writing this piece will do it for me. It's really the only thing that's gotten me interested since that idea I had to market those combination cell phone/car vacuums. But this is even better. It's the personal angle to it, I guess. I admit that my father's disappearance had an impact on me. It wasn't so bad that he left my mother when I was only five for some bimbo. What was worse was that he then had to go and move off to some godforsaken fishing village on the coast of Maine and *then* get caught up into whatever cult it was that swallowed him up. Of course, that gives the story one more juicy angle. Editors love stories about cults. I only wish I knew what this one—

Sorry. I'm back. I thought I heard someone at the door. But no one was there. Except—okay, so maybe all the weird looks from the locals have made me just the teensiest bit jumpy. But I saw something weird out there. A *handprint* on the outside of my door, Minter! In mud.

At least, I think it's mud.

Okay, enough for tonight. I'm going to sleep now. I'll keep writing in this journal as I go along. It will help me put the story together, plus you can read it to help give me advice. And I like writing it to you, Minter. This is the first time we've been apart for so long, and—well, maybe I sound like a goofy romantic fool, but I'm going to crunch up my pillow next to me and imagine it's you. Good night, babe.

* * *

May 4—Okay, so here's my first encounter with one of the natives who actually lives in Cravensport. This is how it went:

"Uh, hello, my name is Jeremy Horne and I'm looking for the Cravenwood mansion."

He was a fisherman. All leathery face and black grimy hands, big bushy eyebrows and white hair growing in tufts out of his ears. He gave me the once-over and said, "Get on with ya."

"Excuse me?"

"I suppose yuah one of them repawters from Bahston."

I had to admit I was.

"Thought ya wuh done with us yeahs ago. It's quiet up heah now. It's all ovah, all that nonsense. Why are you heah to staht things up agin?"

Now, Minter, I had no idea what he was talking about. Part of the problem, I'll admit, was that Maine accent of his, which I doubt I'm doing justice in my attempts at transliteration. But what "all that nonsense" was certainly raised my suspicions—I mean, you just don't say things like that to a reporter and expect him to go away—so I held my ground. "All that nonsense" was *precisely* why I was there, and if I was going to prove my worth as a journalist then I had better push harder.

"Well," I tried explaining, "what I'm here for is to find out what happened to my father. He lived here for a while in the late 1960s. He ran an antique shop. Maybe you knew him. Phillip—"

"I don't remembuh no one from back then," the fisherman said. "Cravensport has been destroyed. Wiped out. All on account of all that craziness the Craven family got inta. They useta run the fishing fleets heah but then they let 'em all go to hell. Which is where I 'spect all of them Cravens have gone too!"

"Are they all dead? Everyone in the family?"

"All but the crazy Mr. Bartholomew. Lives over theah in that fallin' down rat trap he calls home, with not even electricity or indoor plumbin'. And he's not talkin' to no one."

Now, you know, Minter, that I was prepared for this. Remember that call I made to the retired sheriff of Cravensport? He had told me all about this Mr. Bartholomew Craven—how he lived in an 18th-century manor that had never been hooked up to any modern conveniences. So I couldn't call Mr. Craven to let him know I was coming, because there wasn't a phone. I couldn't fax him or e-mail him either. Best I could try, the sheriff said, was writing him, in care of Cravenwood.

I have no idea whether or not Bartholomew Craven ever received my letter. I wonder if it's come back to me since I've been away. I expect you'd leave a message for me on my voice mail if it did. I'll check at a pay phone in the village later.

Anyway, old Jonah Salt wasn't going to be of any more help so I thanked him and headed back to my car. I didn't need directions to the place, I discovered: as soon as I rounded the bend in the road, what's looming down at me from the top of a craggy hill but Cravenwood. It had to be the place. I doubted this little village had more than one gargantuan old house, boarded up and gloomy, with bats hanging from its eaves. I'm not kidding, Minter. *Bats.* Like the frigging Addams Family or something.

So I drove up the long winding driveway that led to the old place. Of course, at the top, there was a rusted old iron gate, padlocked and with a sign: NO TRESPASSING. So I got out of my car and went up to the gate, taking hold and peering through the bars. And I swear—this is no lie, babe—just then it started to thunder. Up until then it had been a clear day, but suddenly the sky went black and it started to pour. Huge lightning and monstrous thunder. It will make for a great lead to my story, don't you think?

May 4 (cont.)—Okay, I'm back. As the storm only got worse, I headed over to the inn where I'm staying. I decided to have lunch in their coffeeshop. I sat there for more than an hour, eating a crispy omelet and drinking three cups of strong joe, writing in my journal. The lady who owns the inn was very nice. She noticed me and came over to my table. She introduced herself as Mrs. Haskell, and said they didn't get many out-of-town faces anymore.

"Why's that?" I asked her. "The Maine coastline up here is so beautiful."

"Yes," she admitted. "But there's not much here to do. So many people have moved away. I keep trying to get the town to promote tourism as a replacement for the depressed fishing industry. But, well . . . they're not very interested."

"Is it because of—well, what happened with the Craven family?"

She looked at me. She's an interesting lady, Mrs. Haskell. You'd like her, Minter. She's the kind of woman you'd like to photograph. I can see you doing a whole show just of her. She must be fiftysomething, but she's still really beautiful. Auburn hair touched with gray. And in her eyes there's a certain gentleness, but strength too, and a lot of wisdom. She's seen a lot with those eyes, I could tell.

Anyway, she sat down with me after I told her about my father. She knew him, Minter! Not well, but she remembered him. How he came to town and opened that antique shop with his wife. "She was very beautiful," Mrs. Haskell said of my father's wife. "She turned many heads in town."

I thought of how much my mother had hated Dad's wife. Megan— that was the wife's name—had disappeared, too. Mom always blamed Megan for stealing my dad, but what I resented most about her was the fact that it was probably her idea to head up here to Maine, and if they hadn't done that, my father would probably still be around today.

"It was a bad time for all of us in this town," Mrs. Haskell told me. "I'm sorry about your father."

"I just want to know what happened to him," I told her. "I've wanted to know all my life."

She smiled at me with sympathy. "I can understand your feelings. But some things—some things are better left as mysteries. Do you ever think that the pain of discovery might be even worse than the pain of the unknown?"

"No," I told her definitively. "I'd rather know. Not knowing is hell."

"In most cases, I'd agree with you."

"What happened in this town thirty years ago?" I asked her forcefully, leaning across the table. I suddenly began telling her everything my early investigations had uncovered. You know all about it, Minter. I've shared all the grisly details with you. A series of unsolved murders—one in this very inn. Men with their bodies mangled, women with their throats slit. And my father, in the midst of what the sheriff would only call "some kind of cult," disappearing forever one dark and foggy night.

Mrs. Haskell's eyes brimmed with tears. "I know about all that," she said. "I lived through it."

"What was the cult?"

"It wasn't a cult."

"Then what was it?"

"Go back to Boston," she said.

It was the same admonition all of the locals had been telling me ever since I'd arrived. But Mrs. Haskell said it kindly, and she reached over to take my hand in hers.

I told her I was going nowhere, not until I finally had some answers. "I want to talk to Mr. Bartholomew Craven," I said. "That's why I came up here. Everything points to that family and to that house."

She didn't deny my charges. She offered only an observation. "People are terrified of him."

"With reason?" I asked.

She shook her head. "He is sad and lonely. That's all. An old man who has lived beyond his time. Everyone he loved is gone."

"But he was apparently involved in this cult, or whatever it was that sucked my father in and brought about his disappearance."

She said nothing. How much more she knew, I couldn't tell. All she repeated was, "He's a sad and lonely old man."

"What was it?" I asked. "What happened here? What were so many of the townspeople involved in? If not a cult, what? The deaths that happened here in town—were they part of some kind of ritualistic sacrifice?"

"It was all so long ago. Why bring it all up? It won't bring your father back."

"The police have given up trying to solve these murders and disappearances from thirty years ago. My father. His wife. And so many others." I flipped open my notebook and began reading the names I'd collected. "Paul Patrick, his body ripped apart. Mr. Bain, the former innkeeper of this very establishment, found mutilated in an upper room. Donna Landers, her throat torn open and left to die in the woods. A policeman, Kenneth Davenport, with his head crushed and every bone in his body broken. And Margaret Everly—she disappeared for weeks, only to be discovered with her memory gone and half the blood drained out of her body."

Well, you should have seen Mrs. Haskell react to that, Minter. Her hand flew up to her neck and she gripped it tightly, as if from some old, half-forgotten habit. It looked as if she were covering something there. Her face grew ashen and she said she had things to do, that she couldn't talk to me anymore, that I really should take her advice and drop the whole matter. Then she hurried away.

Leaving the inn as the rain began to let up, I asked one of the waitresses Mrs. Haskell's first name. You guessed it, Minter. Margaret.

She was part of it, too. I bet everyone in town over a certain age was part of it. Whether they want to remember it or not. That's why they don't want me nosing around. They don't want me to discover their culpability.

It's only made me more determined to get to the truth. So I drove up to Cravenwood again, and tried to find some way past the gate. It was impossible. The rain threatened to kick up again, so I decided to put it off until tomorrow. I'm back in my room now and feel pretty sleepy. So I'll just bid you a fond good night, sweets. I'll call you tomorrow. I hope you and Ralph are cuddling up a storm. Just tell him to keep his snout off my pillow. And no drooling! I miss you both!

May 5, 3:15 a.m.—Minter, I need to write just to steady my nerves. I had a nightmare. Man, it was awful. I feel so nelly admitting how freaked out I am right now, but when you get to read this journal you'll see how much my handwriting is shaking. I'd call you but it's so late and you've probably turned the phone over to voice mail anyway. Oh, man, I wish you were here.

So this is what happened. I woke up because I thought I heard a noise. It sounded like a dog. In my half-sleep I thought it was Ralph and I tried telling him to calm down. But this growling sound only got louder, and for a half-instant I thought I was home and Ralph had detected an intruder. I sat up, put the light on, and realized I was at the inn. The growling stopped, so I got up, took a pee, and put on the television just to remind myself I was still in the 21st century. I watched ten minutes of an *I Love Lucy* rerun—the one where they're in the shack by the railroad tracks and the vibrations keep moving Lucy and Ricky's bed. It made me laugh so I felt better and turned the light off again.

Now here's what's so weird, Minter. I don't think I fell back asleep.

Of course I must have, for what happened next couldn't have been real. I heard the growling again. I sat up in the dark, and at the foot of my bed were these two red eyes. I shouted out, fumbling for the lamp, which, of course, I knocked over onto the floor. I jumped out of bed and ran to the window and pulled open the curtains. There, in the moonlight that suddenly filled the room, I saw a wolf—not a dog, Minter, but a *wolf*—a huge creature, with big red eyes. I screamed. The thing leapt up onto my bed, and on the floor I saw a dead man in a pool of blood. I know it was blood—it was so real, Minter. The moonlight was reflecting off it.

But then there came banging at my door. Someone was shouting to me, asking if I was okay, but I couldn't answer. I just kept my eyes glued on the creature that was salivating on my bed. Finally the door opened—a security guard with a passkey—and the wall switch was thrown on, bringing light to the room. There was no wolf on my bed, no dead man on the floor, no blood.

I felt quite embarrassed, as you can imagine, Minter. But now, sitting here writing this, I find I can't get back in that bed. I can't switch off the lights. I feel certain this is the very same room Mr. Bain was killed in all those years ago. I keep telling myself it was a dream, a stupid hallucination brought about by all these crazy superstitious villagers. But I don't know, Minter. I just can't wait for the sun to come up.

May 5—It really is beautiful here, babe. I'm sitting on a rock at the beach below the cliffs. The spray from the waves that crash all around me is cool but invigorating, making me forget about my stupid dream last night. I'm thinking about how our first anniversary is coming up in a couple of months, and how I'd like to go back to Ogunquit with you. We could sit on rocks like this, looking out over the ocean. I wish you were here, Minter.

It was so good to hear your voice this morning. Did I wake you up? You said no, but I wonder. I hope your shoot goes okay today. Drag queens can be impossible. I wonder how many retakes they'll demand? And of course, they'll want you to fix up their boobs with PhotoShop. You sounded kind of frazzled when I spoke to you so I didn't go into too many details about my dream or about all the weirdness up here. You'll learn all about it when you read this journal.

More and more I'm convinced you're right, though. This will make a great personal interest piece. If not for the *Globe* then for some place else. I can just see the magazine art directors loving it—I mean, here I am on a rocky coastline with some gothic mansion reputed to be haunted looming above me. Hey—you ought to do the photography for it! Maybe I'll suggest it when I talk to you tonight and you can join me this weekend. I'd love to have you up here with me. Everything's better when we're together. You could bring Ralph, too. The inn accepts pets.

This could be the direction I've been looking for, Minter. I admit I've been kind of a wanderer all my life. I never could decide on what kind of a career I wanted. I've tried lots of different things—some things that I've never even told you about. Like I tried working as a publicist for a ballet company a few years ago. I'd never even *been* to the ballet. Then I got my real estate license. I showed six thousand houses but sold none. I hated it. So I became a traffic reporter at a radio station.

But it always came back to writing. I know I never went to journalism school the way you went to photography school, Minter, but I think this is what I want to do. Write stories. In college my best grades were always in English, and I was editor of my high school newspaper. Working at the radio station I used to watch the news reporters type up the stories they'd read on the air. It was so inspiring to me. That's what I want to do: tell really interesting stories.

So I'm not going to leave here until I've gotten to the truth of this old town's mystery. As much to give my life some direction as to learn about my father. Maybe the two things are tied up together. Maybe that's why I've always been kind of aimless. You've changed me, sweets. You've given me a direction and I'm going to show you what I can do.

I've determined that the only way past that NO TRESPASSING gate is to come up from the cliff side. Cravenwood stands on a huge expanse right at the top of the cliff, overlooking the ocean. I can approach from behind, and maybe find the old man lurking around somewhere. He apparently doesn't live at the main house, which is all boarded up anyway. That much I learned from the lady at the post office this morning. He lives in a smaller house on the estate, deep in the woods. The post office lady told me he picked up his mail irregularly—no mailman could make the trek all the way up that hill, she said—but that his box was currently empty. So I'm assuming he got my letter. What good that will do, I'm not sure. But at least he's hopefully expecting me.

So wish me luck, babe. I'm going to find a path among the rocks and scale the side of the cliff. Good thing we took that mountain climbing class last fall in Colorado. This isn't nearly as steep or as tall, but it's still a little daunting. You'd be so proud of how butch I'm being.

Okay, here I go. Keep your cool with the drag queens, Minter. I love you!

May 5 (cont.)—I'm in his house, Minter! I'm writing by candlelight. What a story I have for you!

So I made it up the cliff without too many problems. If I looked down and saw the drop below me, my knees went a little weak, but I managed okay. Only once did I slip, but there were a lot of tree limbs and brush growing out the sides of the cliff that I was able to easily steady myself. I'd say it took about twenty minutes to scale the side. Not bad, huh?

It was probably about ten-fifteen, ten-thirty. I headed toward Cravenwood, which from this side looked less creepy and more simply run down, battered by decades of sea wind and salt air. Most of the windows were boarded over, except for the ones highest in the tower. It looks like a Newport mansion, only completely run down. It's too bad, because it's a fabulous house.

I have to admit my first thought was about my father. I wondered if he'd ever been in that house, if it was here that whatever happened to him happened. I couldn't stop thinking about him, in fact. I felt his presence—as if he were nearby—oh, I don't know. It was odd. Hard to describe.

I know I haven't talked to you about my father much, Minter, except to say that I've long been obsessed in finding out what happened to him. Truth is, I hardly remember him. I remember a few little things—

nice things, like going to the zoo and riding in the way-back part of his bumpy old station wagon. And sharing our birthmarks—you know that little purple splotch on my chest that looks kind of like a dragonfly? Well, my dad had one, too, in just about the same place as I do, and I remember feeling pretty special because it was something we shared.

But Dad apparently had other special people in his life. He began having an affair with Megan when I was just four or five. I guess that's where he'd go when he didn't come home at night. It was a rotten thing to do to a little kid, abandoning me like he did—but my mother (as you know all too well) is not an easy woman to live with. I remember once how she threw a frying pan at him. While she was frying eggs in it! Maybe that's when she found out about the affair. I don't know.

My dad was kind of a wanderer like me. It was in his blood, I suppose, the same way it's always been for me. He jumped from job to job, too. Starting an antique shop in Maine was just the sort of thing he'd do. And he'd probably have left it, too, eventually—if whatever happened to him hadn't happened.

Mr. Craven said that my father was a good man. That meant a lot for me to hear. I mean—

Okay, so I'm getting ahead of myself. Yes, I met Mr. Bartholomew Craven. And really, Minter, he's really such a nice old guy. Mrs. Haskell was right. He's just lonely. He was thrilled when he realized I'd actually come to see him—and he's asked me to stay the night! I think it'll be kind of fun, what with there being no modern conveniences. I have to pee in a bucket in an outhouse, Minter! You'd be freaking out not having running water! I told Mr. Craven about you—I think he might be gay—at least he didn't flinch when I described you as my lover. I told him about the time we went camping and you insisted on bringing a battery-powered hair dryer with you. He got a good laugh out of that one.

Not that it started out so pleasantly, though. Let me back up. There I was, wandering around the boarded-up mansion, when I got the distinct sensation that someone was watching me. You know how that is. You feel eyes on the back of your head and you keep turning around quickly, looking behind you. A wind had kicked up, and there on top of the cliffs, with the salty air sharp in my nostrils, I sensed I was not alone.

I heard a twig snap behind me. I glanced off toward the woods and
saw a figure there, a tall, hulking figure of a man. It disappeared into
the trees so quickly that I immediately convinced myself it had been
an illusion, a play of the morning sun against the leaves. I tried to forget it, but thoughts of my dream returned, and I couldn't shake the
feeling that someone was watching me.

I looked up. I could make out nothing in the windows of the tower. I
snuck around to the courtyard and peered through slats in the boards
that covered the windows into a large, empty parlor. There was no sign
of life, no evidence of anyone who might live in such a foreboding place.

That's when the hands gripped me by the shoulders from behind.

"Hey!" I shouted, struggling to turn around. But the grip was unbelievable, holding me firmly in place. I smelled something rancid. Whoever
held me had the foulest breath I'd ever encountered. It grunted as I
continued to try to twist out of its hold. Finally I slipped free, turning
to face it.

It was a man, but barely so—surely the creature that had been lurking in the woods. He was tall, with a wide shoulder span, but he was
slumped over, as if his back had been broken and never correctly
healed. His face was mangled, with deep purple scars. There was only a
left eye, his right socket grotesquely empty. His nose was crushed into
pulpy folds of flesh, and his mouth was twisted and off-center. His hair
was black and uncombed, and his clothes were equally as dark, torn
and soiled. Looking up at him, I couldn't speak.

"Leave me alone," I finally said. "I didn't mean to trespass. I'm just
looking for Mr. Craven. He's expecting me."

The man-thing growled. He studied me with his beady one eye, tilting his misshapen head as he did so. He grunted again, then pointed in
the direction of the woods.

"Look, like I said, if I'm trespassing, I'm sorry. I just didn't know
how to get up here to see Mr. Craven. He has no telephone—"

The beast made another sound in his throat, more insistent this
time, pointing again toward the woods.

He was a deaf-mute, I suddenly realized. He was reading my lips and
trying to tell me something.

"Is he there? In the woods?"

The deaf-mute made a rough sound of affirmation.

I thought this very strange, you can be sure of that. No way was I wandering into the woods with some hulk who'd nearly split my collarbone in half. But then he withdrew an envelope from his shirt pocket. It was brittle and flaking. On its face was written my name, Jeremy Horne, in a spidery handwriting of an earlier time. I opened it and unfolded the old yellowed parchment inside.

My dear Mister Horne,

Should you arrive to visit as your letter to me suggests, I hope you will forgive me for not being able to greet you myself. I am consumed with writing the history of the Craven family, a vocation which demands my full and undivided attention every day from early morning until dusk. I humbly request that you allow my manservant, Hare, to escort you to my home, where, if you are so kind as to wait for me, I will be most glad to entertain you come sunset. Please have no apprehension of trusting Hare, for, despite his rather frightening appearance, he is a gentle soul and utterly devoted to me.

With kindest regards and a welcome to Cravenwood,
I am,
Yours sincerely,
Bartholomew Craven

I looked up into the beastly face hovering over me. "I—I could come back later," I suggested, "if he's busy—"

Hare made a ferocious sound, gripping my upper arm. He pointed again, but not toward the woods this time. Rather, he was directing my attention to an automobile parked on the side of the house. It was an old black model, some kind of ancient Ford, vintage 1935. I surmised quickly that what Hare was trying to tell me was that wherever Mr. Craven lived, I'd need to get there by car, and that I could make the trip either now or never. I swallowed, telling myself that all this simply added great color to my eventual story. Mr. Craven had said not to fear Hare.

But should I be fearing Mr. Craven?

I followed Hare to the car. He opened the back door for me and I slid inside. The interior was perfectly restored, with gleaming new leather. Odd that I should think of my father again in such a moment, but maybe not. My father had loved cars, and one of my few memories is of him restoring an old Mustang. He would've loved this car.

Hare walked back around and slipped in behind the wheel. As he started the ignition, I glanced at my watch. It was only a little after eleven o'clock; I was facing the prospect of twiddling my thumbs for practically the entire day as I waited for Mr. Craven to finish up with his writing project. Oh, well, maybe I could snoop around the place, pick up some clues as to what happened here thirty years ago, what sort of cult they were all a part of. That was, if Hare wasn't constantly breathing his rancid breath down my neck.

Turns out, he didn't hang around long at all. We drove through the woods for about half a mile, finally stopping at a much older house than the boarded-up mansion. This one looked Georgian, with broken columns lining a cracked portico. The house was in terrible disrepair, with the surrounding trees having grown nearly through it. Ivy obscured most of the windows and the branch of a large oak had imbedded itself into the roof. Hare unlocked the front door with a rusty old-fashioned key and gestured for me to enter. I did so, looking around at the dark, cobwebbed interior. Then Hare closed the door behind me and disappeared.

"Hare?" I called—ridiculously, of course, since he was deaf. I tried the knob of the door. It was locked. He had locked me inside the house!

I panicked, Minter. Can you blame me? I began to beat on the door with my fists, convinced I'd been tricked, that I was about to suffer the same fate as my father, whatever that had been. I turned and ran to an inner door, finding it was locked as well. I ran to the top of a flight of stairs, only to find my way barred there by another secured door. A door with a grated window leading into the basement was likewise bolted. I was confined to the small parlor, and in the dusty darkness I could hear the rustling of bat wings.

"The window," I said to myself. A large picture window, cross-hatched with panes of old lead-plated glass, looked out into the woods. Ivy crept up much of it, but I could still see freedom beyond. I would smash the glass, I would break free—.

But I couldn't, Minter! Try as hard as I might, I couldn't even scratch the glass. Might it have been that the panes of wood that held the glass in place were too resilient? Or might there be something— something unexplainable—that made the glass unbreakable?

I flopped down into a frayed armchair, out of breath. I'm pretty strong, Minter. You know that. I work out at the gym four times a week. But I was useless against that old glass and wood. *Useless!*

I looked back down at Mr. Craven's letter. I had kept it in the pocket of my jacket. He asked me to wait for him until sunset. I could do nothing but trust him, to give him the benefit of the doubt.

But he'd sure as hell have some explaining to do when I saw him! I mean, you don't just lock your guests in! What if there was a fire? What if I got sick and needed medical attention? What if I had to take a pee?

Which, I suddenly realized, I did. And not a bathroom anywhere.

I tried to distract myself. Maybe there was something in this room I could discover about my father's disappearance. Whatever nastiness he'd gotten involved with concerned the Cravens. That much the old sheriff had been sure of. "We could never pin anything on them," he'd told me. "But all the mysterious things that happened in town, all the deaths, had some link back to that family."

I stood up from the filthy old chair and walked over to the bookcase built into the wall. I scanned the titles of the moldy volumes that rested there, draped in cobwebs. Histories of New England with publishing dates from the early nineteenth century. Books on whaling, on the great shipping fleets of Maine. And then—my breath literally caught in my throat, Minter—books on sorcery! Witchcraft. Spells and incantations. A set of volumes on the I Ching. One book was even called *Practical Satanism.*

Is this what my father had faced? I flipped through the volumes. Hideous pictures of witches being burned at the stake and incubi slipping into the darkness to seduce their unsuspecting victims. There was nothing particular to this place, however, nothing about Cravenwood or the Craven family, nothing to connect my father. . . .

Just then I heard a sound. I glanced around, only to see the inner door close once more. I heard the latch slide into place on the other side. Hare had been in the room; he had snuck in so quietly I hadn't heard him. The stench of his foul breath lingered—as did a tray of food placed upon a table. Steaming rice and expertly seared pork loins, freshly steamed snap peas and carrots. A bottle of spring water and a carafe of wine. And, at the foot of the table, a chamber pot.

I looked closer at the meal. Another note from Mr. Craven rested against the carafe of wine.

My dear Sir,

In my absence, please accept this meal with my kindest regards. Please feel free to make yourself at home and enjoy any of the books from my library. And given my singular lack of modern conveniences, please accommodate yourself with my rather quaint tool of centuries past. Hare will take care of everything. I look forward to joining you this evening.

With anticipation of our eventual meeting,
I am, yours sincerely,
B. Craven

I couldn't resist laughing. Using that chamber pot to relieve myself took a little getting used to, but I sure felt better afterward, Minter. Then I replaced the lid and set it against the far wall, turning my attention to the food. My fear had largely evaporated at this point; I was dealing with an eccentric writer, that was all. But his invitation to enjoy the books from his library—*Practical Satanism*, perhaps—still left me a little unnerved.

I must have dozed off after lunch, flipping through a history of the town, my eyelids growing heavy as I read about Isaac Craven, sea captain, who'd founded the place back in 1690. . . .

I opened my eyes suddenly. How long had I been sleeping? It was the strangest sleep, Minter. I kept hearing music, a tinkly kind of sound, like from an old music box, and it felt as if I were moving down long, winding, cobwebbed corridors. I can't remember all the specifics of the dream, but it felt as if I were on a mission: searching for something, something I knew was at the end of the corridor, as I moved down this way and then that, finally leading to a door, I think, a door that I opened—

And I saw standing in front of me a very old man.

"Mr. Horne," he said.

I was too surprised to say anything in reply. The room was now dark, lit by dozens of candles offering their flickering light.

"I'm sorry if I awoke you. You must have dozed off. I do apologize for keeping you waiting so long."

"Mr.—Craven?"

"Yes, my good man. Bartholomew Craven, and I welcome you to Cravenwood."

I stood up. "Mr. Craven, I appreciate your hospitality, but having me locked in here—"

"Locked? But you were not locked in, my good sir."

"I was! I couldn't leave this room."

Mr. Craven studied me carefully, giving me time to do the same to him. He was indeed very old, with a gray pallor to his deeply lined skin that gave it nearly the same look and texture of the dry, flaking parchment he used for his letters. His cheekbones were high, giving a hollow look to his face, and his eyes were deepset and brown. His dark suit was well pressed and tailored, but somewhat frayed and tattered. His hair was white and wispy, what was left of it.

He walked suddenly to the front door and opened it quite effortlessly. "You see?" he asked. "It is not locked."

"But it was!"

He gave me a confused expression. "I can't see why Hare would lock you in. How dangerous that would be. Perhaps he did so accidentally. I shall speak with him."

I narrowed my eyes at him. I wasn't sure he was speaking the truth.

He raised his eyebrows imploringly. "But there was no harm, then? You enjoyed your lunch, I see. And I do apologize for my lack of modern facilities." He grinned, nodding at the chamber pot. "I shall show you later where there is an outhouse in the back courtyard. It might be a bit more preferable than this."

I wasn't sure I could trust him, but I wasn't going to waste any more time trying to prove or disprove the door being locked. I had questions I wanted answered. Things I wanted to know.

"Why do you live this way, Mr. Craven?" I asked. "Without electricity? Plumbing? A telephone?"

"I am a creature of the past," he told me. "I have never felt comfortable with modern technology. I prefer to think I am living in another time. The eighteenth century, perhaps, when this house was first built."

I said nothing, just looked around the room.

"You find me eccentric," he was saying. "I suppose I am. But I prefer it this way. Just myself, and my books, and my writing, and—"

He was distracted by a sound behind him.

"And of course, Hare," Mr. Craven said, gesturing for the beastly servant to enter. He emerged from the shadows with a bottle of wine and one glass on a tray. He set it down and proceeded to uncork the bottle.

"May I offer you some wine? It is a very good vintage."

I nodded (you know how much I love good wine, Minter) and Mr. Craven gestured to Hare, who poured me a glass. He handed it to Mr. Craven who passed it over to me.

"Aren't you joining me?" I asked.

He smiled. "No. I never drink . . . wine." He walked over to a sideboard and withdrew a small bottle and a sherry glass. "I prefer port." He poured himself some of the thick red liquid.

Hare had disappeared back into the shadows. That suited me fine; the guy creeped me out. He had locked me in here, I was sure of that—but whatever devious reasons he had for doing so, I wasn't sure. Still, I wouldn't press the issue with Mr. Craven; I'd just ask my questions and get out of there.

We shared a toast. "To your first visit to our fair estate," Mr. Craven said.

I sipped the wine. "It's—magnificent," I told him. It really was, Minter. Like nothing I'd ever tasted.

"It is very old," Mr. Craven told me. "More than a hundred years. I have several still in the wine cellar."

"That's amazing."

"The Craven family have always been connouseurs." He eyed me over his glass of port. "But you didn't come here to ask me about wine."

"No." I steeled myself. "Mr. Craven, I want to find out what happened to my father."

"Yes. You mentioned that in your letter."

"Did you know him?"

"Oh, yes. A good man. He really tried to make a go with his antique shop."

"What happened to him, Mr. Craven? Do you have any idea?"

"The police could never uncover any clues to his disappearance."

"But what about you, Mr. Craven? I was told you knew him. I was told you knew both him and his wife, that they were often guests of yours."

He smiled at me. "That is true. And did your police informants suggest we were all part of a cult?"

I hesitated. "Yes," I said finally. "They did."

"And did they say what kind of cult?"

"No."

"I wish I could tell you that we were—oh, I don't know, what cults are out there? Hare Krishnas? Branch Davidians? Moonies?" He laughed. "You see, I *do* manage to keep up with news of the modern world to some degree. Hare brings me a newspaper from the village occasionally." He looked at me kindly. "But I know of no cult that your father and his wife belonged to. I'm sorry, Mr. Horne. I don't know what happened to him."

I sighed. "But it was around the time of all sorts of unsolved murders . . ."

"It must be difficult," he said. "Not knowing what happened. I suppose all sorts of ideas would start to fester in your mind. You look for any connection, any link, anything to help you understand why your father walked out on you."

I looked up at him. First I was angry, Minter. Angry that he would suggest that. But there was something in his old eyes, babe—something kind and compassionate and wise. I found myself unable to look away from him.

"I lost my father at a young age, too," Mr. Craven said. "Oh, not in a physical sense. But he was cold and domineering. He didn't approve of the choices I made in life. I used to imagine that my real father had been a pirate, and he had just gone away and that someday he would return. I was able to create all sorts of stories about him that way in my imagination."

I was still unable to take my eyes off him.

"Are you married, Mr. Horne?" he asked me suddenly. "I don't see a ring."

"Uh—" I finally averted my eyes from his face, looking down at my hands. "No, I'm not married."

"But attached, though?"

I nodded. "Yes. I'm attached."

"And not to a woman," he said, which, as you can imagine, Minter, shocked the stuffing right out of me.

"No," I admitted. "To a man. How did you know?"

Mr. Craven smiled. "I have been blessed with intuition. It rarely fails me. More wine?"

I held out my glass for a refill. It was so good, already giving me a soft, happy glow. I was starting to warm to Mr. Craven. And my gaydar was definitely beginning to hum.

"Would you like to see his picture?" I asked, suddenly wanting—almost needing—to take him into my confidence, to share with him some intimate parts of my life. Why I felt that way, who knows? The wine? All I know is I wanted to show him your picture, Minter.

Mr. Craven was beaming. "Yes, certainly. I'd love to see what he looks like."

I withdrew my wallet and flipped open to your photo. I noticed the way the old man gazed at it, the way his thin, cracked lips slightly parted.

"What is his name?" Mr. Craven asked, not looking up at me.

"Minter." I watched as he raised questioning eyes to me. I laughed. "Yes, an odd name. It was his mother's maiden name. His parents gave it to him as a middle name, and he liked it better than his first."

"Which is?"

"Irwin."

Mr. Craven smiled.

"Well, he *is* a striking young man." He paused, lifting his eyes toward the ceiling for a moment, pressing his fingertips together. He returned his eyes to mine. "Might I show you something? In the upstairs corridor?"

I was curious, so I nodded, following him as he led me out of the parlor and up the staircase, holding a candelabra out in front of him to give us light. The doorknob at the top of the stairs, locked earlier, turned easily in his hand, and we walked into a dark dusty hallway. He paused about halfway down the length, lifting the candelabra to illuminate a portrait.

"This was my friend," he said. "My kinsman and my friend."

I strained my eyes to make out the portrait in the candlelight. It was of a handsome young man, dark, with large eyes and full lips. I knew right away what had made Mr. Craven think of it.

The portrait looked nearly identical to you, Minter!

"It's remarkable," I said.

"Isn't it? They could be twins."

I looked closer at the painting. There was no doubt about it. But even more curious than the resemblance was the fact that the man was dressed in clothing of centuries past. His hair, too, was pulled back, styled in the way I'd seen in drawings of the signers of the Declaration of Independence. Over two hundred years ago! Mr. Craven was old, but come on, this was ridiculous!

I was denied the opportunity to point it out to him, however, by a sudden and horrendous clap of thunder. It sure storms often in these parts, Minter. And what storms they are! This one pounded against the house without so much as a gale of warning. Lightning crashed, illuminating the corridor. Mr. Craven headed quickly back down the stairs to find Hare, giving him commands without uttering any sound: just moving his lips, I supposed, because Hare was, after all, deaf. The rain came then, hard against the roof.

"I shouldn't take up any more of your time, Mr. Craven," I said. "If that's all you truly know about my father—"

"But you can't leave in a storm like this," he said. "I insist you spend the night. Getting back through the woods in such a torrential downpour would be far too treacherous."

"No, really, I—"

"Besides, I don't know when Hare will be back to drive you. I've sent him on an errand. Something urgent I just remembered."

He was looking me in the eyes again. I'm not sure what came over me, Minter, but suddenly the idea of staying overnight in this creepy old house just seemed fun. It was like it was the best offer I'd had in ages. Funny, isn't it? I guess we need to get out more, babe.

But I have to admit it's been kind of cool. The thunder and lighting kept on for some time, and Mr. Craven and I sat in front of the fire. He kept drinking his port and I nearly polished off that bottle of wine all by myself. I've got a pretty good buzz going, but nothing where I can't think straight. I mean, I've written all this down, haven't I?

Mr. Craven remembered only a few more things about my father. He was a good man, hardworking, and he had a beautiful wife. Where they might have gone he couldn't imagine.

"It was a bad time here," he said. "You mentioned the murders. Who could blame them for leaving?"

"And so there's nothing to the sheriff's theory of some kind of cult? Nothing at all?"

He smiled kindly over at me. "There was no cult I ever knew of."

So I've hit a dead end. I was so certain that Mr. Craven held some answer, but I guess he doesn't. He can't be lying. His eyes are so sincere. I like him, Minter. I trust him.

It's past midnight now and the storm still comes and goes. I'm finally getting sleepy. Mr. Craven led me to a room that seems freshly cleaned and aired out, as if he'd been expecting me to stay all along. There's a chamber pot in the room and a basin with a jug of water. He lit some candles, and in their light I can see that the bed linens, although old, have been freshly laundered and are of a very high quality. I wish you were here with me in this bed, Minter. It's very comfortable and for some reason I'm very horny. I'll call you tomorrow when I leave here, lover. What a day it's been. Suddenly I'm so sleepy. It's as if

May 6, 3:15 a.m.—Weirdness, Minter. I must have fallen asleep as I was writing. Just zonked right out. And now, at the very same time that I was awakened last night, I've seen something else unexplainable. There was a noise outside my window that startled me awake. The storm was over and the night was still. But I was sure I heard the sound of something crying. Something not human—

I leapt out of bed and looked out the window. Below, entering through a back door of the house, awash in moonlight, I spied Hare. And in his arms he carried a struggling, kicking, mooing calf. A calf! They disappeared inside the house below.

Bizarre, isn't? I want to write this down because I have the strangest feeling that if I don't, I won't remember it in the morning. Now I'm so sleepy again, Minter, I'm not sure that I

May 6, 5:45 a.m.—It's only now that I find I finally have the strength to write again. Could that wine have given me the most peculiar hangover of my life? I saw things, Minter. Things that I—

Okay, let me try to collect my thoughts. I must have fallen asleep once more as I wrote in this journal. It was right after I saw Hare carry the calf into the house. And I was right: I had indeed forgotten about it until I read what I had written in here.

I fell asleep in some kind of deep stupor. But then I woke up—at least, I think I did—maybe it was a dream—oh, Minter, I don't know! I remember leaving my room and walking down the corridor. I was looking for something. I don't know what. A bathroom, maybe? It was like I was sleepwalking.

I turned the corner and entered into this room. There was an old canopy bed and a small table with a vanity. A woman's room, but covered in dust and cobwebs. I just stood there, in the middle of the room, looking around. Why had I come there? I think, if I had been sleepwalking, I awoke a little at that point, because I remember thinking I shouldn't be walking around so late at night without Mr. Craven's permission.

And then I heard a sound. The creaking of a door. Off in the shadows of the room, a partition in the wall slid back, and a woman emerged. She was like nothing I've ever seen before, Minter. Tall, dark, beautiful—but something wasn't right about her. She was pale, and there was something burning in her eyes, something wild, like an animal—

A hungry animal.

"Who are you?" I called out.

She came toward me. Her arms were outstretched. She wore a sheer white gown, and I could see her breasts through it. I backed away from her. She touched me. She opened her mouth as if she'd kiss me—

And then I must have blacked out. It *must* have been a dream, Minter. That's the only way to explain it. An alcohol-induced dream. I remember other scattered images—Mr. Craven was in the dream, too. He was telling the woman to leave me alone, that I wasn't hers, that I would be no good to her—

Next thing I knew I was back here, in bed. I got up to write this all down, because again, I feel if I don't that I won't remember it in the morning.

You always say we should keep a dream journal, Minter. Right beside the bed so we can write them down while they're still fresh. You say they can teach us things, our dreams. Well, what do you make of this one?

I'm afraid you might think I'm just being my usual hysterical self, drinking too much and getting all caught up in fancy daydreams. But I swear these dreams felt so real, so authentic. I can't help but think about those books on witchcraft downstairs. You're always so rational, Minter. You don't believe any of those ghost stories we watch on the Sci-Fi Channel. No such things as alien abductions or near-death experiences or communicating with the dead. I find all that stuff fascinating. I have ever since I was a kid and I was an expert on horror lore, gleaned from watching all the Universal and Hammer fright flicks. Dracula, Frankenstein, the Mummy, the Wolfman . . . *"Even a man who is pure at heart, and says his prayers by night, may become a wolf when the wolfbane blooms and the autumn moon is bright . . ."*

What sense would you bring to these experiences I've had? Oh, right now, Minter, I'd give anything for your logical, skeptical mind. I'm a dreamer; I've always known that. Truth has mattered less to me than fantasy or imagination. But that has meant no career, no direction, and no boyfriend who's lasted longer than a few weeks—until you, Minter.

So I think I'm at a turning point. Whatever's happening here is meant to teach me something. I'm here to discover something about myself. Something about my own truth. About my direction in life. Whether my experiences have been the stuff of dreams or the cold facts of reality, they are meant to show me the way. I believe that. I have come here not only to find my father, but my fate.

May 7, 11:15 a.m.—Another note from Mr. Craven this morning, this one left propped outside my door. He apologized for not being able to join me for breakfast, but said Hare would bring me food in the parlor downstairs. And something else, too, Minter—he wrote that if I waited for him to finish his work today, he'd give me some information he'd "just remembered" about my father. Well, that was sure incentive enough to keep me hanging around this strange old place for a few more hours.

Breakfast was surprisingly good. Scrambled eggs and bacon and freshly baked bread, brought in to me on a silver platter by a shuffling, silent Hare. Was he the cook, too? I hadn't seen any other servant so far. The coffee was hot and strong, which went a long way toward banishing that hangover and those strange dreams. But thinking about them again, Minter, I admit they still unnerve me.

So I decided to wander around the grounds a bit. No locked doors today. It's a gorgeous spring day here. Birds in the trees are chattering back and forth like excited schoolchildren in a playground. The sun is warm and all the leaves have popped, bright green, fresh and new. I can hear the crash of the surf at the bottom of the cliffs. How I wish you were here to experience all this with me, sweets.

Exploring through the woods that lead back up to the main house, I stumbled across a small graveyard. At least I think it was a graveyard. Crooked slabs of concrete marked about a dozen plots, but there were no names etched into the faces. I had a distinct chill standing there, and it wasn't from the sea wind that swept in from the cliffs.

I could have left, Minter. I could have kept walking through the woods, found my way back to town, gotten in my car and driven away. I could be on my way home to you right now, Minter. But I came back to this house. Somehow I just couldn't leave. Sure, it's because of the carrot Mr. Craven has dangled in front of me: more information about my father. But it's more than that.

I just have to see him again. I have to look again into those deepset dark eyes of his. I can't explain it. I just can't wait to see him again. I am transfixed by him, utterly in his thrall. My quest for answers, about whether I can believe in my way of seeing the world, is all tied up with him. He holds the answers I seek. I cannot explain it any more than that. I just know it is true.

* * *

May 7, 10:35 p.m.—Mr. Craven kept me waiting until after sunset. He was most gracious in his apologies, saying his work had simply overtaken him, and insisted I have dinner with him. Before I could say anything, Hare had wheeled in a tray of lamb chops and roasted potatoes, and I agreed. It was excellent. Mr. Craven didn't eat any of it, though, saying he wasn't hungry. "Well, not for lamb, anyhow," he said with a smile.

He just sat there drinking his port while I feasted. Every time I'd try to bring up my father and ask him what he had remembered, he'd change the subject. He seemed fascinated about our lives, Minter. An older gay man living vicariously through the details of a younger generation, I suppose. Though I have to admit he didn't seem quite so old tonight. There was a little more spring in his step, more color in his wizened old cheeks.

"Where did the two of you meet?" he asked.

I laughed. "At a bar, actually. I suppose we both thought it was just going to be yet another one-night stand, but fate had its own ideas."

"Ah, fate." Mr. Craven rubbed his hands together as he watched me eat. "And did you court him? Bring him flowers?"

"Yeah, sure. Especially in the beginning. You know, when things are all hot and heavy . . ."

"Hot and heavy," Mr. Craven repeated.

"You know what I mean."

He arched an eyebrow at me. "So is it no longer 'hot and heavy' then?"

I blushed. "Well, I suppose it still is. We've only been together ten months. This is actually the first time we've been apart any length of time."

"You must think of him often, then."

I nodded. "Yeah. I do."

"Think of him now."

"Huh?"

"Think of him now so that I may see the look on your face."

It was an odd request, but I complied. I must have smiled, for Mr. Craven seemed pleased.

"I can see him in my mind's eye," he said dreamily, "mounted upon his horse."

I looked at him quizzically. "How do you know he rides?"

"Well, of course he rides. He's always loved to ride."

I raised my eyebrows in bemusement. "Are you psychic, Mr. Craven?"

He didn't answer me. He stood and began walking around the room, touching things. A vase. An old lamp. A candestick. The spines of the books on the shelves. "He loved to ride, and he loved to dance. Oh, what a wonderful dancer he was—"

He was no longer talking about you, Minter. His mind was far away. "Mr. Craven," I asked, trying to be compassionate, "are you thinking about your friend? The one in the portrait?"

He turned to me with wide eyes, seeming shaken out of his reverie. He had no answer for me. His lips were tight against his teeth.

"His name was Jebediah," he said at last.

"Was he your lover?"

Mr. Craven's face went dark. He turned away from me and stared out the window. In the distance dogs began to howl. It gave me the creeps.

"He was," the old man answered. "Until a she-devil arrived to take him away from me."

"I'm sorry."

He turned back to face me. He was smiling now. "But enough of the past. The past is gone. I must live for now. For today. Tell me more about Minter—"

"Mr. Craven," I interrupted, "please. You promised to reveal something about my father. Something you said that you'd remembered."

He looked at me. And as I looked back, Minter, I swear he seemed to be growing younger in front of my eyes. His hair was still white and his face still lined, but his jaw was now firmer, his cheeks less hollow. He carried himself with greater strength and determination than he had even when he first came into the room. It was the strangest thing to observe.

"Your father," he spoke. "Yes, your father. He was a good man."

"You've already told me that."

"He was a good man who was caught up in events beyond his control. You shouldn't blame him for disappearing on you. That's what I wanted to tell you. He was powerless to stop what happened."

"Mr. Craven, I'm not following you . . ."

"That is all you need to know."

"What do you mean that's all I need to know?" I felt myself suddenly get angry. All the warm feelings I'd been experiencing for him dissipated. I felt tricked, manipulated. "This is what you told me to wait all day to hear? This is what you remembered?"

He smiled shrewdly at me. "Is it not enough, Jeremy?"

It was the first time he'd called me Jeremy. Before that, it was always "Mr. Horne." I'm not sure why it stopped me, but it did. In that moment I felt the same chill that I'd felt out in the graveyard.

"No," I managed to say. "It's not enough. If you have details, Mr. Craven, I'd like to hear them."

He approached me. If my writing is shaky, Minter, it's because I'm terrified just remembering the moment. There was something about his eyes, so dark, so deep. He came within inches of my face, and his breath was rank. Up close, he looked still younger: the lines were disappearing on his skin almost as I watched. He smiled, revealing gleaming white teeth.

"You don't want details, Jeremy," he said in a deliberate whisper. "Details are the stuff of nightmares. The way of madness. Of ruin. Details warp your mind. They curdle your thoughts. Destroy your hopes. Abandon your soul to its darkest fears."

I held my ground. "In details lie the truth."

"And is it truth you seek above all else, Jeremy? Above everything?"

"Yes," I said, my voice shaking. "Truth is what I came here to find."

"Not only about your father."

I stared at him. "No, not only about him."

Mr. Craven smiled. "You want to know the truth about yourself, too. Why you have been so aimless all your life. Why you have never found your calling, so to speak."

It was eerie, how much he knew.

"Is it so obvious?" I asked. "My life?"

"Minter is successful, is he not? You feel inferior."

I bristled. "No. No, I—Minter is very encouraging of me—my writing aspirations—"

"You are terrified of his leaving you. Throwing you over for someone else. Someone who has a direction in life. Someone who is superior to you."

"No—no, I—"

"You say you seek truth, but you stand there in denial of it. Is truth really what you seek, Jeremy Horne?"

I was unable to reply.

"Is that not right?" he asked. "Above all else, you want truth?"

"Yes," I answered. "I want truth."

A slow, thin grin spread across his face. "And would you trade truth over love, Jeremy?"

"I don't know what you're asking."

"Truth over love. How can I be more plain that that? The truth you seek, in exchange for love." He smiled. "Minter's love, for example."

In that moment I knew utter terror. What did he mean? He was crazy. He was spouting nonsense, but suddenly I detected that in his ravings lay some kind of malice. His gentlemanly demeanor was a mask. The locals were right to fear him. I tried to recall Mrs. Haskell's admonition that he was just a sad, lonely man—but in his sadness and loneliness, he had become bitter. Malicious. And quite possibly dangerous.

"Thank you for dinner, Mr. Craven, but I find I must leave now," I said crisply, turning and heading for the door.

Just then it began to thunder. The crash shook the house so much that vases tottered on the shelves. I stopped. This was too weird. The rain pummeled the roof. The wind began howling through the eaves.

"Oh, but you can't leave in such a storm," Mr. Craven said, an echo of the night before, the gentility and hospitality suddenly returning to his voice. "The road through the woods will be impossible."

"I'll manage," I said, resuming my stride toward the door.

"But I must insist," Mr. Craven said, and there, all at once from the shadows, was Hare, his big hulking form standing between me and the door.

I felt Mr. Craven's hand on my shoulder. It was ice cold.

"What kind of a host would I be if I were to let my guest go out in weather like this? Your room upstairs is waiting for you."

I turned around slowly to face him. He beamed a warm smile at me, gesturing with his hand toward the stairs.

I couldn't move. I was caught in his eyes. I could say nothing. I just found my strength and began to walk in the direction of the stairs.

I'm back in my room now, Minter. I'm trapped here. He won't let me leave. The door is locked from the other side. There's no escape. The drop from the window is too steep. I'm trapped!

I had come here seeking truth. I had thought that here were the answers I'd been looking for all my life. I had convinced myself this was my destiny, my fate—

But what kind of fate is it?

Once again I've let dreams and fancies cloud my judgment. I'm sorry, Minter. How disappointed you'd be in me. I'll get out of here in the morning. He doesn't want to be charged with kidnapping. He's got to let me out then. He'll let me out to use the outhouse or something, and I'll make a run for it. I'll smash through a window, use a candlestick as a weapon this time if I need to—

And maybe I'm simply being melodramatic yet again. I just don't know anymore. But I know I'm not going to sleep. I'm going to stay awake all night. There's no way I can close my eyes now.

May 8, 6:02 a.m.—At last the sun is starting to break through the night. Why is it so difficult for me to write? My mind keeps wanting to slip away, to forget—and the pen is so heavy in my hand. But write I must—

The wounds on my neck are throbbing. The flesh is torn, bright red.

Proof, Minter. Proof that what I've seen is real. You can't explain these wounds away with any of your logic, any of your damned rational assessment, the way you do when we're watching *Unexplained Mysteries* or whatever show like it. I have been attacked, Minter. It was not my imagination. Stop thinking that it was!

"He is not yours!" Mr. Craven's voice had echoed through the room. "He is not yours!"

The woman was sobbing. "He looks so much like Phillip! Please! You must give him to me!"

My father's name . . . she had used my father's name . . .

Where was that? When did that happen? Had I fallen asleep as I'd tried so hard not to do? I remember images . . . my door opening, the soft tinkling music—the woman's room, yes, the same place I'd been the previous night. And the same woman—.

Mr. Craven had laughed at her.

"Go ahead," he said. "Take him if you want him so much. You will see."

No. I can't allow myself to remember what happened next. My mind pushes the thought away. It was too horrible.

But I've got to. For you, Minter. I've got to record what's happened to me. There must be a record. And you've got to believe!!

Her teeth. So sharp and long. And she came forward as if to kiss me, and I felt such revulsion for her. She punctured my neck with her teeth. The pain was excrutiating. The bile rose in my throat as she lapped at my blood, and I vomited right there, all over her. There are still stains on my shirt. That was no dream. No hallucination.

The creature screamed. She pulled back from me, and Mr. Craven laughed.

I fell to the floor, gripping my neck. I felt warm blood ooze through my fingers. I retched again, and spewed the last of my lamb dinner all over the floor.

"Come to me!" she cried. "Come to me, I command you!"

I answered her only with a dry heave.

Mr. Craven's laughter filled the room.

"You see?" he said. "I told you he was not for you!"

"But he is Phillip's son!"

"And like Phillip, he is mine," Mr. Craven told her, and the woman shrieked.

I can't write anymore. I can't

May 8, 9:30 a.m.—With the sun shining through my windows, I can finally think more clearly. My strength is slowly returning so that I might plan my escape.

That was no dream. And so I know now that my father met his fate here in this house. The woman knew him. And Mr. Craven's chilling words:

And like Phillip, he is mine.

I inspected my wounds in the mirror. They are healing quickly, far more quickly than they should be.

Vampires. In the haze of last night, I understood what they were.

There are such things. That's what old Edward van Sloan, playing old Van Helsing, had said at the end of *Dracula*. He was right. *There are such things!!*

This journal is not the ranting of a madman, Minter, even though I fear that even now, even after all I've written, you still might insist on thinking so. You trivialize my dreams. You demean my imagination. But I was right, my love. This place has confirmed to me that my truth is real. Coming here I did indeed discover my destiny—but is that destiny my death?

At least I am safe now. While the sun shines, I am safe. And if I am to escape, it must be now. But how?

My door is locked. There is no way out of this room. No breakfast served this day. And there's no one to hear me if I tried to call. Hare's deaf, and besides, he's under Craven's power.

Yet perhaps I could reason with him. Tell him he doesn't want to be party to a kidnapping. Or worse. As soon as I get out—and Minter, for the record, I *am* getting out—I'll report Craven. I'll bring the police back here and fuck them if they don't believe me when I tell them they'll need crucifixes and wooden stakes instead of guns. They'll find out soon enough.

What had Craven done to my father? He must have had him in his power. That's the cult! The cult of the vampire! My father's fate—it must have been hideous.

But it won't be mine, Minter! I swear!

May 8, 4:45 p.m.—My hopes have faded, my love. My desperate attempt to escape backfired. So I am keeping this journal as a record. Writing it all down so that if I do not make it out of here, you will know what happened to me, Minter. I'll find a way to secure it. Hide it. You'll get it somehow. You must! And then you must believe! You must put aside all you have been taught and you must believe!

Yes, Minter, what he said to me is true. I do fear you leaving me. I do fear you will tire of my aimless ways, my dreams, my flights of fancy. You will leave me unless I can become something else, someone better, someone with direction—

And yet what does it matter now? My dreams have led me to ruin. I will never see your face again, my love, and you will remember me as a lost soul who wandered off one night, never to return.

I dread dusk, which draws closer with every tick of the old clock. What I am about to write may be my last entry, my love. It will seem unbelievable, totally fantastic. But believe it, Minter. I want you to know what happened to me. I didn't leave you of my own free will! I am destroyed by a devil! I am powerless against him!

I thought I was home free. I really did. I figured that even though Hare couldn't hear my calls, he'd *feel* them. I began to bang on the door, rattle the knob, stomp my feet on the floor. I kept at this for fifteen, twenty minutes, feeling the vibrations shudder through the old wood of the house. Finally I heard the heavy shuffling of Hare on the stairs. I began pounding on the door even harder.

I heard the key in the lock. The old door creaked open enough for Hare to look inside. His single pulpy eye glared at me.

"I'm sick," I said, enunciating the words clearly so that he'd be sure to read them correctly. "I'm sick and I need a bathroom. Please, Hare! Show me some mercy!"

He grunted.

"Look at me, Hare." The stains were still on my shirt. "Please don't leave me here like a sick animal in a cage!"

He hesitated, making a low, gurgling sound in his throat. Then he pushed the door forward roughly and took ahold of my wrist. He pulled me out into the corridor and shoved me toward the stairs.

Hare's stronger than I am, I knew that much. But I took a chance that I was faster. I'd been a cross-country star in college, after all. So as soon as we were near the bottom of the stairs, I made a break for it. That was my first mistake. In my eagerness to get away, I was rash. Why didn't I wait until we were outside at the outhouse?

Oh, sure, I proved faster than Hare. His lumbering stride was no match for my swift sprint across the parlor. But the front door was locked—of course it was—and the heavy iron candlestick only bounced off the glass of the window. Hare was only a few feet from me by then, snarling and salivating, his massive hands reaching for me. I eluded him, dodging behind a chair as he lunged. The big hulk went sprawling to the floor. I ran deeper into the house, slamming doors behind me and locking them when I could. There had to be a way out somewhere!

But the door leading outside from the old eighteenth-century kitchen was locked too. I was left standing there among old copper pots and pans hung on hooks around an ancient hearth. I lifted one of the largest pots from its place, intending it as a weapon. The glass here proved similarly invulnerable to my swing, so I merely held the pan in front of me, waiting for Hare, who I could hear stumbling and growling his way through the house toward me.

That's when I spotted the door to the cellar. It was standing open. I had no idea if there was any way out from there, but perhaps it would offer me a place to hide. Better to chance the unknown than face a certain pummeling by Hare.

So I hurried down the steps, still carrying the copper pan in case I needed it. Immediately I was hit by the thick, fruity smell of old soil. It was a damp, dark place, constructed with stone in some places, with rotting wooden posts and earth in others. The ceiling was low and the corridors narrow. Yes, there were hiding places here. But for how long? Hare would know all of them. He would trap me down here. Kill me, probably.

The only light came from small windows cut into the earth. Even if the glass was breakable, the windows were too small for me to crawl through. I paused at one point, crouching behind an old rolltop desk to listen for Hare. There was no sound of him following me. In fact, as I strained to hear, I detected his footsteps above. He was in the parlor. He hadn't pursued me into the cellar.

I took a moment to breathe, to think. What would I do now? Had I made my situation worse? What if night fell and I was still down here, trapped in utter darkness? What might Mr. Craven do to me then?

I leaned against the desk and the weight of my hands caused the top to roll upward. Inside were revealed several old, flaking newspapers. I looked at the dates. 1969.

My eyes quickly scanned the faded type.

LOCAL COUPLE MISSING

I lifted the newspaper and held it toward the faint light of the window. Two photographs. I recognized them.

My father—the same photo I'd kept for years, the only photo I had

of him, in fact. Handsome, smiling, his broad shoulders extrending beyond the frame.

And the woman—his wife—Megan—

I gasped.

I saw immediately it was the creature who had attacked me, who
had tasted my blood.

He looks so much like Phillip! Please! You must give him to me!

My hand went instinctively to my neck. The wounds there were
nearly healed.

He had made her into a thing like himself. My father's wife. So
what had happened to my father?

Without even knowing why, I suddenly took several steps down the
corridor. Ahead of me light flickered. Candlelight. I followed its tremu-
lous dance without any conscious thought. I turned into a small room.
There, in the middle of the floor, a candelabra set atop it, rested a
plain wooden coffin.

I didn't hesitate removing the candelabra or lifting the lid. I felt no
fear, only a deep repugnance as I stared down at her face, sleeping
peacefully. She was beautiful, no doubt about that. But she was also
dead, and her face shouldn't have been soft and supple. It should
have been sunken and rotten, her eyes eaten by maggots. I tried to
summon compassion for her, but could find none. This thing drank
my blood.

I left her exposed as I hurried back to the rolltop desk. I tipped it on
its side, disturbing its contents and making a loud bang as it crashed
against the wall. I didn't care if Hare sensed the vibrations or not. What
I needed to do had to be done quickly. I had no time to lose. I gripped
the leg of the desk and with all my might pressed down on it. After a
second or two of hesitation, the wood snapped off in my hands, in a
perfect pointed break. I grabbed the copper pot with my free hand and
returned to the coffin.

I looked down at her. Her eyes were now open, returning my gaze,
though her body remained immobile.

"You took my father away," I whispered.

I positioned the wood just above her left breast. With my other
hand, I lifted the pan and swung it in an arc through the air. I brought

it down on the tool I was using to pierce her heart, and it made a loud clanging noise on contact.

That's when I felt the pity. That's when the tears flowed for me, dripping down my face as I kept pounding that stake into her heart. My tears fell upon her cheeks, and I could see why my father had loved her, why he had preferred her to my mother. She was a gentle soul, turned into this thing against her will. Her eyes opened and closed as I killed her, but she made no sound, just shuddered with each thrust of the wood gouging deeper into her flesh. There was surprisingly little blood. Nothing like you see in the movies. It was over in less than a minute. For a while she kept twitching, little spasms of her arms or her legs, but soon enough she was still. Her skin went gray, then a deep shade of blue.

I stood back to catch my breath. Why hadn't Hare stopped me? Why hadn't he rushed down here to protect her, as surely he'd been ordered to do?

It struck me then why he hadn't pursued me down here. *He wanted me to kill them.* He was as much a prisoner of this place as I was.

"Leave the stake," I whispered to myself, remembering some folklore from some old Dracula chronicle. You have to leave the creature impaled or else it comes back to life—unless, of course, you cut off the head. And as numb as I might be feeling, I hadn't the stomach to attempt that.

Or the time.

I returned to the desk and broke off another leg.

I had another coffin to find.

I walked a few feet until the corridor emerged into a much larger room. A stone staircase led back up into the house. This was Craven's sanctuary. His coffin was far more ornate, set up on a pedestal, but with the same candelabra ablaze on top.

Then I noticed the smell. Faint at first, then thick and pungent, threatening to choke me. In the flickering candlelight I struggled to find the source of the odor. I nearly tripped over it, straining my eyes to look down at the floor.

Dead animals, piled in a heap. Calves mostly. There were four, maybe five of them. And a deer. Its glassy black eyes were still open, glaring up at me.

All at once I understood why they were here. Hare had brought them for his master to feast upon. Not their flesh—no baked veal or broiled vension for him. Instead he fed off their warm blood, sipped from their veins as they still lived, kicking and screaming. Their bodies looked deflated, as if they were rugs, animal skins thrown carelessly upon the earthen floor.

I looked over at the coffin and thought of the monster sleeping inside.

Surely Hare would stop me now. Surely he wouldn't just allow me to kill his master the way I'd killed the female. He might even be waiting in the shadows, ready to pounce.

But there was no sound, no disturbance, as I lifted the candelabra from the coffin and set it on the dusty floor. I gripped the lid of the casket. I paused, filled once again with that chill that had come over me before. I took a deep breath and raised the lid, the creaking of old hinges echoing against the stone walls. I looked down. There he was. Bartholomew Craven.

Except not the old man I had met. This was a young, handsome, attractive man. I couldn't take my eyes from him. He was beautiful. He quite literally took my breath away.

His hair was black, his skin smooth, his lips full. I stared down at him. I felt frozen, unable to think, let alone move. Even asleep—or dead—he had some power over me, the same magnetic pull that had kept me in this house these past few days. I realized standing there, looking down at him, that such was his power: the allure, the magnetism, the enticement of the senses. That is what gives the vampire his strength. I *wanted* him, Minter. Standing there, looking down at him in his coffin, with a stake in my hand ready to kill him, I wanted him. *Sexually.* I wanted to kiss him, make love to him, not pound a stake through his heart.

I screamed out, trying to break the spell. I forced the broken desk leg up and into the air, aiming it at his chest.

And then his eyes opened.

I gasped. His body didn't move, not so much as a shudder, but his eyes were open and looking at me. Such dark eyes. Such beautiful eyes.

I couldn't do it, Minter. I started to cry then, looking down at him, because I knew I had lost. I dropped the wood to the floor, let the copper pan fall with a clatter. I backed away from the coffin, covering my face with my hands. I began to sob.

That's when I felt an arm around me. A gentle, reassuring arm. It was Hare. He pulled me close to him and held me in his arms, my nose pressed into his musty, torn coat. He led me slowly up the stairs and back up to my room, where he brought me some food and some water, tenderly touching my face once more before securing me again in my prison. Yes, he must have wanted me to kill Craven. He must want to escape as much as I do. But we are both prisoners. Both trapped.

I will get this to you somehow, my love. Somehow you will read this journal and know what happened to me. For I fear we shall never see each other again, Minter. I expect this will be my last night alive. Know that I love you forever, and that no matter what happens to me here in this house of blood, that will always be true.

May 9, 1:30 a.m.—I am still alive. And while I live, there is still hope.

But what I am about to write, Minter, fills me with shame. Forgive me, sweets. Forgive and try to understand.

As expected, I received a summons after sunset to meet Mr. Craven downstairs. Hare came for me, and I pleaded with him, encouraged by the compassion he had shown earlier. But there was none of it in evidence now, and he just grunted at me, pointing at the stairs. This time he stayed close behind me, but I was cooperative. I knew running would be pointless.

Mr. Craven waited in the parlor.

In the candlelight he looked even more handsome than I remembered. He smiled at me, a dazzling smile, filled with the whitest teeth I'd ever seen. His body had filled out, with magnificent shoulders and a small waist, and the clothes he wore were expertly tailored to reveal his impressive taper. He shook my hand firmly, and his touch was no longer icy. It was warm. And just that simple touch from him was enough to plump up my cock, though I fought the feeling. Fought it hard.

"I trust you enjoyed your little tour of the house this afternoon," he said.

"It was informative," I replied, holding my ground, not wanting to look directly into his eyes. "At least I finally got the answers I came here looking for."

"Really? You mean to say you've learned all you need to know?"

"All that I care to."

He smiled, lifting the glass top of the decanter of port. "Will you join me?"

I said nothing, so he poured me a glass and handed it over to me. I accepted it. He poured himself a glass as well and we drank. Thick and rich.

"It's my only weakness," Craven said. "A good port."

"But it's not port that's given you such a youthful glow," I said, daring him to admit the truth.

He just beamed. "Why, thank you, Jeremy."

"But why animals? Why not some girl from the village?" I smirked, raising an eyebrow. "Or some boy?"

Mr. Craven sighed, looking out the window. "You think me a monster. You think of me as some devil who takes delight in death."

"I saw what you did to my father's wife. What you made her."

He looked over at me, pained. "I had no other choice. She found me—she was a threat—"

"The animals must have been just for her sustenance in the beginning, for she was still young and beautiful. You didn't let her go hungry as you did yourself."

His eyes reflected sadness. "I could not condemn her, cause her any more suffering, than I already had."

There actually seemed to be some guilt in his words, some measure of accountability. The truth became plain. "You loved her, didn't you?" I asked.

"I have never discriminated in love. Men, women—"

"But in loving her, you turned her into something vile."

Again I saw the pain and guilt on his face. "You did her a great favor. You have given her the peace that I never could."

"And my father? Did you make him into some undead thing too just so you could have his wife?"

"Oh, no. Your father was fortunate. He escaped that fate." He smiled sadly. "Though whether he would have thought himself fortunate is unlikely."

"What do you mean?"

He set his glass down on the table and took a deep breath, pressing his hands together in front of him as if he were at prayer. "For more than thirty years, Jeremy," he said thoughtfully, "I have gone hungry. I learned to ignore the urge, to suppress the desire that ate away at my soul. Too much harm had come to this village because of me. So much death and misery to my family, my friends, all because of the curse the she-devil cast upon me when she stole Jebediah away. I wanted no more death, no more suffering. So I stayed here, away from all human contact, with Hare as my only companion." He drew close to me, letting his hands fall upon my shoulders. "Then you arrived at my door."

I just stared up at him, into those compelling dark eyes.

"You, with your talk of love," he continued. "You rekindled something in me, Jeremy. Something dormant. Something too long forgotten."

I felt the swelling in my loins again. He was so close I could see the tiny red veins in his eyes. I could smell his breath, no longer rancid but sweet. His warm hand came up to caress my cheek. I wanted him to kiss me, to drink my blood if he must—anything, just to have him.

"Do you feel it, too, Jeremy?" he asked. "The desire that lives between us?"

I tried to deny it. I managed to move my head away, breaking eye contact.

"No," I said hoarsely. "I feel nothing for you."

"But you do not tell the truth," he said, his hand dropping to my crotch and pressing against the fabric of my pants. My erection only lengthened and hardened. Mr. Craven laughed gently. "Oh, Jeremy, the truth is evident. Why do you fight it?"

"Because . . ."

"Because of Minter?"

"Yes!" I shouted. "And because of what you are!"

"What I am? Tell me what that is, Jeremy. What am I?"

"A—"

"Say it, Jeremy."

I couldn't.

"I'll tell you what I am, Jeremy," Mr. Craven said, moving still closer and turning my face gently into his gaze again. "I am the man of your dreams. Of your deepest, most profound yearnings. I am the man you dreamed of when you were a young boy, the man you hoped was out there waiting for you, when the stirrings of lust were just beginning to take root down deep in your soul. I am the man you have looked for every night since, searching for me in the darkest corners of your world. I am the man you see in those deep and roiling dreams, when you awaken flushed and aroused, unable to explain the sensations to the man lying beside you, a poor substitute for me."

I could say nothing in defense. What he said was true. Oh, God, I'm sorry, Minter. Really I am.

He kissed me. And it was the most erotic kiss I have ever known. I submitted without any further struggle, my lips surrendering to his, my heart pounding in my ears, my mind floating somewhere outside myself. Consciousness was gone. There was only lust, carnal lust. Sensations I cannot describe here. He eased me down onto the daybed, and his hands explored my body. And when his lips moved down my neck and I felt his teeth puncture my throat, I orgasmed in my pants without even touching myself.

I don't remember much of the immedate aftermath. I know I lay there dreamily, aware of him in the room, moving about. He finally sat beside me and stroked my cheek, bring me back to clarity.

"Tell me about your life in Boston, my love," he said softly.

"My life is only with you," I said, not even aware of the words until they were spoken.

He smiled. How gorgeous he was, sitting there in the candlelight. "Of course, my love. I am your life now. But tell me. Tell me about Boston. Where do you live there?"

"The South End," I managed to say. "It's the . . . the gay neighborhood."

"Ah, so there are many like you there."

"Yes. Many gay men."

"What street exactly? What is your address there?"

"Why?" I asked. "Why do you want to know?"

Mr. Craven looked at me with kind reproach. "My love, such things needn't trouble you now."

"Clarendon Street," I said. "At the corner of Columbus."

"Clarendon at Columbus," he repeated to himself, as if memorizing the words. "Do you enjoy living there?"

"Yes. Well, I did . . . before you . . ."

"And Minter? Does Minter enjoy living there?"

It was like a stab into my heart when he said your name. I couldn't answer at first, so he asked the question again.

"Yes," I said. "Minter likes living there."

"And what do you do? Where do you go?"

"What do you mean?"

"He enjoys riding. And he takes pictures. What else does he like?"

"Well . . . we go out sometimes. Dancing."

"Dancing. But of course. How he loved to dance."

"And the gym . . . we work out, play basketball, swim . . ."

"Yes. Athletics. Yes, I can do athletics." He was looking at me with wide eyes. "And a dog. You have a dog, yes? Does Minter love this dog?"

Thinking of Ralph shook me up again. "Why are you asking me all this?"

Craven kissed my forehead. "Enough talk for now. You should rest, my love." He ran his hand down my face. I held it there, not wanting him to take it away. Ever. But he stood up. "Hare. Help Mr. Horne up the stairs. He should rest."

"No, I'm not tired," I said, but once on my feet, my knees buckled, and Hare had to hold me up under my armpits.

"Take him upstairs," Mr. Craven said brusquely, dismissing us. I felt horribly rejected, and had to fight back the tears as we headed back up the stairs.

In my room, once again Hare was gentle, looking at me with compassionate eyes. He handed me a cold damp towel to press against the wounds on my throat.

Sitting here now, some sense has returned to me. I know I am under his control, but I also know that I need to escape. The daylight hours offer my only hope. Only then will his power over me weaken enough. I will try again with Hare while Craven is in his coffin. I'm not sure I will ever get home, Minter, but while I still live, even with his marks on my neck, I can still hope.

＊ ＊ ＊

May 9—Part of me wants to protect him now. Part of me wants to stand guard outside the door to the cellar and beat off any who might try to hurt him.

But another part of me wants nothing more than to plunge a stake right through his centuries-old heart.

And what of Hare? The same complex emotions must run through him, for my door was left unlocked this morning. Or maybe it's simply that, with Craven's oversize hickey now prominent on my neck, Hare figures I'm powerless to run away.

Am I?

I'm writing now in the parlor. The front door is not locked. But I haven't left. I still may, of course. Yet what would leaving accomplish? I know enough of the lore to understand that Craven could merely summon me back anytime he wanted to. No, it's better that I stay, at least until I can figure out what the next step is.

I suppose I could go to the police. Bring them back here, show them Craven in his coffin, show them the wounds on my neck.

But I'm not going to do that. Whether it's Craven's power over me or something else that stops me, I'm not sure. I just know I'm not going to the police.

I've got to handle Craven myself.

My love.

The man of my dreams.

May 9 (continued)—Minter, I know it's difficult to understand, loving a vampire. I can't rightly explain it myself. But I *do* love him. Not that I don't love you. I do, with all my heart. But as the afternoon goes on, I'm filled with such a sense of excitement to see him again. Such passion. Really, Minter, he's all I can think of. Maybe I should just end this journal. Why send it to you? What's the point? You'd never understand, and it might just hurt you. Better for you to think me dead, I suppose. How can I explain the change—the *glorious* change—that has come over my life?

＊ ＊ ＊

May 9, 5:45 p.m.—It's almost time! I can barely control my excitement. Soon he'll be walking up those stairs and he'll take me into his arms—

May 10—It's a few seconds past midnight, and the echoing of the clock as it chimes through the house drives me mad. I've got to find a way of getting this to you, Minter. For your own safety!

He appeared as soon as the shadows had deepened into blackness. I was there, waiting for him. But he did not greet me. He walked past me as if I were invisible, and gave no answer to my protests of love. He was engrossed in studying road maps that Hare had left for him.

"I've waited for you," I said, reaching out to him. "I didn't run away. I could have. But I waited—"

"Of course you did," he said indifferently, still studying the maps.

He was wearing blue jeans that fit him superbly, shaping his high, incredible ass over powerful thighs. A brand-new white T-shirt was stretched across his muscular chest, his biceps straining at the sleeves. His dark hair had been cut short, and his skin was golden and glowing. He looked just like a contemporary urban gay man.

That's when it hit me. His questions about Boston—

About *you*, Minter—

"You're leaving here, aren't you?" I asked.

"It's no concern of yours," he said, not even looking at me.

Hare entered the room then, carrying two suitcases. He set them down on the floor and looked up at his master.

"Very good, Hare," Craven said. "Put them in the car. I think I'll drive rather than fly." He smiled, finally looking at me. "Bats have such a difficult time carrying heavy luggage. Such little claws, you know."

I said nothing, just stared at him.

"A joke, Jeremy. I made a joke."

"Don't leave me," I said.

What a pitiful thing I had become. I detested myself standing there. All I could think of was that he was leaving me, that I was losing him. Nothing else. Nothing that I *should* have been thinking at the time, and that shames me, Minter, it really does.

"It's Minter you want, isn't it? Because of his resemblance to Jebediah . . ."

Craven's dark eyes danced as they looked at me. "Yes, Jeremy. It's Minter I want."

"He won't want you. He loves me."

"Well, I had no trouble turning *your* fancy, now did I?"

The full horror hit me. "You can't do this to Minter!"

He laughed. "Yes, Jeremy, I can. That's what you need to understand if you are to have any peace. I *can* do it, and I *will*."

"But he's not Jebediah. He's Minter. Irwin Minter. He's not from some century long ago. He's not some old dead forgotten creature like you. He's living. He's alive. He's a photographer, a modern guy, twenty-six, full of life—"

"Full of life." Craven snorted. "A life you expected to share with him."

I began to cry. "Yes. Yes, I did."

"I can give him a life you never could. Eternal life, as they say."

"No," I moaned.

He drew close to me, grabbing my filthy shirt in his hand. Being so near to him made me weak. I longed for his hard muscular body, for his full, red lips. But he had only contempt for me.

"Let me tell you what will happen to your beloved Minter," he said, and I could see cruelty shining from his eyes, a cruelty engendered by loss and grief, by sorrow and bitterness. "I remember the first day I awoke with the curse. I remember the strange sensation of understanding what it felt like to be dead. To live within a dead shell of a body, a walking, thinking corpse where vital organs were now irrelevant, where such simple functions as eating and excreting were forever changed. But most of all I knew the hunger—the overwhelming urge for the taste of warm blood in my throat. It replaced the sexual urge, but not the desire for love. Imagine that, Jeremy. To have love and death so inextricably woven together."

"You have a conscience," I said, trying to argue with him. "I saw it last night. When you said the people of this village had suffered too much. That's why you suppressed your urge for so long—for thirty years—ever since the tragedies your friends and family suffered because of you—"

"A conscience? Yes, I have a conscience. It is the devil that haunts me always. It's what has kept me prisoner here for thirty years. But am I never to know love?"

"You can love *me*," I offered. "Leave Minter alone."

Craven looked at me shrewdly. "Do you offer yourself out of your desire for me or out of your love for Minter?"

I couldn't lie to him, nor can I lie to you. Of course I wanted to save you, Minter, but that was not the overwhelming motivation I felt. I wanted him. And still do. That's what's so horrible, so shameful, about all of this.

He saw the answer on my face. "I don't want your kind of love," Craven said to me. "I could have had that easily anytime in the many decades that I've walked with this curse. My plan is different now. I will meet Minter as a man. A man who will be there to comfort him when you fail to return. In time, he will love me with the kind of feeling that the two of you share now. Then I will make him mine for eternity."

He moved toward the door. I couldn't let him leave. Suddenly I lunged at him, tearing away my shirt to reveal the wounds on my neck. I scratched them open, releasing a fresh flow of bright red blood. Craven saw it, all at once snarling and salivating like a dog.

"How long did you deprive yourself of this?" I shouted. "Too long! Take my blood! Drink!"

Craven gripped me hard by the shoulders and glared down at me with furious yellow eyes. "How dare you tempt me in this way?"

"You want me as much as I want you," I said.

He growled and almost pulled away, but then he swung back at me, baring his fangs and sinking them deep down into my bloody neck. Oh, the sensation—it was exquisite. The sharpness of his teeth, the lapping of his tongue—I orgasmed once more as I stood there in his embrace. He drank long and voraciously, to the point where I could feel my very life flowing out of myself and into him. My head grew light, my senses became dulled. But tonight he cared not a whit for my pleasure, as he had the last time. Tonight it was all about him.

Holding me around the waist with one hand, he reached up with his other and tore his T-shirt, revealing perfectly chiseled pectorals. He pressed my face close to them. Now it was his turn to draw blood, and with a sharp fingernail he opened a vein in his neck. What flowed from his body was my own blood, and it was my own blood that I was forced to drink. As he held me tight, the warm blood coating my throat as I swallowed, I could feel him shudder against me, his own shattering climax. Then he dropped me, spent, to the floor. I lost all consciousness.

I awoke in my room. How long I have been here I do not know.

The house is quiet. There is nothing but the wind outside my window and the low, constant crash of the surf.

I have lost him. The chiming of the clock drives me mad. I cover my ears and try to force sleep upon myself. I hope I never awaken. I am nothing without him.

May 10, 10:05 a.m.—He hasn't gone. He's still here!

I knew it as soon as I opened my eyes this morning. He never left last night as he'd been planning to do. I know it, for somehow, in my mind's eye, I can see him, sleeping in his coffin, his torn T-shirt stained with my blood.

And I can see more, too. So much more.

I see him tall and handsome and young, but not because he has gorged himself with blood. I see him as he was, two centuries ago, a young man flushed with life. I can see into his mind now, into his very past.

He's with Minter—Jebediah—

They're both on horses, riding fast, the wind in their hair. They're laughing. It's their last day together: I know this somehow. Tomorrow each will be betrothed to women, as their families demand. Yet there is no sadness, no heaviness in Craven's heart. He assumes his friendship with Jebediah will continue, that nothing will change. He loves his bride, he loves Jebediah: there is no reason he should not have both of them. *I have never discriminated in love.*

But now I see *her:* the she-devil he spoke of. A beautiful blond woman with the cadence of the French West Indies in her voice. Is she Craven's bride? Perhaps, but this is not the woman he had loved. He may have dallied with her, toyed with her affections . . . but he has not loved her. In revenge, she has prevented Jebediah from coming to Craven—Jebediah is dead, that's what it is, Jebediah is *dead!* I see him now, bleeding on the earth. Dear God, Minter, it is you! *It is you!*

"I killed him," Craven is saying, standing over his body, the smoking gun still in his hand and tears falling from his cheeks. "She made me do it. The witch! She has set a curse upon us all! Everyone I love will die!"

I see her again in all her fury: her eyes popping, her mouth in a terrible snarl. "I curse you, Bartholomew Craven!" And then the giant bat—it flies into the room to attack him. I feel the pain at my own throat. I feel his life slip away.

We are linked now. Yes, that's what it is. Our minds, our spirits—I can see his past, read his thoughts, feel the coldness of his grave. I shudder now against the confinement of his coffin. I can see him there, glutted with my blood. I can see him last night, too, stumbling across the room, Hare helping him to a chair. He was drunk, bloated, unable to move.

So I have succeeded: I have kept him here with me.

But with the linking of our souls has come something else: clarity. Oh, how pathetic I have been. I do not love him. I love *you*, Minter, and the liberation of knowing that once again is exhilarating. Worse than any physical confinement has been the emotional imprisonment—the brainwashing, if you will, the utter lie that was foisted upon me. Take my blood, take my body—but my love, my soul, *that* was the most despicable theft of all. To think that I professed love for such a monster.

And yet—what am I now? My body feels different. The sensations around me are new. Sound is unfamilar, and I see with new eyes. The very touch of my hand to pen and paper is like nothing I have before experienced. I have changed, Minter—we have shared each other's blood, Craven and I—and that has made me nearly his equal, his peer. Perhaps it will allow me to fight him now, Minter. Perhaps it will allow me to save you.

For tonight when he awakens, there will be no stopping him. He will leave this place. He will show up in Boston under an assumed name. He will be there for you when word reaches you of my death. He will try to win your love, Minter. He will be successful. And then he will turn you into the same sort of undead monster he is, and has been all these centuries.

I will not let that happen. I make that vow, Minter! I care not what happens to me anymore. All that matters is saving you from the fate he has planned.

But there is only one way I can stop him. Only one way. And I will do it, Minter. I will not fail.

May 10, 4:55 p.m.—All is ready, my love. I am here, waiting beside his coffin. Hare is nowhere to be found. Even if he arrives, he will not stop me. For what I plan, none of them could suspect. I will be successful, my love. There is only one way to fight Bartholomew Craven—and I will do it!

May 11—(blank)

May 12—I've been unable to write, but I'm going to try. I must get it down. What happened needs to be recorded, and I'm not sure what condition I'll be in tomorrow. How much will I remember? How much will make sense?

I hope you can read my handwriting, Minter. I'm so weak. I can't hold the pen very well. It keeps falling from my fingers. I've lost a lot more blood . . . and I was already down several quarts.

So I was there, waiting for him, when he rose from his coffin.

"What are you doing here?" he snarled.

"Waiting for you," I said.

He glowered over me. "You mean nothing to me. Do you understand? It's Minter I want. My Jebediah!"

Everything was riding on how good an actor I could be. How believable, how mesmerizing. But I had the power now. *His* power. The power of seduction.

"Please!" I gripped his arm, loathing myself for this display. "Let me satisfy you again. Please, drink my blood as you did last night!"

He shoved me away from him. "You will not tempt me again."

Hare had come down the stone staircase then and was watching helplessly. He seemed to be taking great pity on me. Who'd have thought?

"Please!" I begged, following Craven like some pitiful dog. I was utterly convincing. "What will become of me?"

He spun on me. "Don't you see? I don't care. Hare might drop you from the cliffs, or maybe he'll just let you starve to death down here. I have ceased caring about your fate. I am off to find what I have denied myself too long."

He pulled the torn, bloodied T-shirt from his torso and revealed a physique even more magnificent than the day before. My blood had given him that. And despite myself, I felt the lust take hold of my mind once more. He still had that hold over me. That's why I couldn't have killed him as he slept. It would have been impossible. That's why this was the only way—the only way to save you, Minter, my love.

I wouldn't look at him as he pulled on a clean shirt, offered to him by Hare. "Please," I said, "you will need sustenance for your journey. Take mine!"

He laughed. "I don't *need* sustenance. If I did, I'd never have made it for those thirty years, sober and alone. Yet *had* I tasted blood, drunk of it regularly, I would never have become the hideous old creature you first encountered."

"Then drink again from me now," I said. "You look magnificent, but there are many gay men who look just as good in Boston. Have you ever thought of that? Drink from me, and make yourself even *more* spectacular, so that Minter will be unable to resist your beauty."

He narrowed his dark hypnotic eyes at me. "And why are you so eager to sacrifice yourself so that I might win Minter?"

I managed to hold his gaze without breaking. "Because if I can't have you, I want eternal life. I want you to drain my blood. I want to become as you are."

He smiled in fascination. "You are a brave young man, bargaining with me."

"I am faced with either eternal death or eternal life. Those are the only two options I can possibly hope for now. I can never go back to my life as it was. Am I not right?"

He studied me for several moments. "Are you saying that you would go willingly to an eternity of darkness, of never seeing the sun again, of spending your days as a corpse in a coffin? You would accept that life with conscious choice, when even I myself fought the witch who made me thus, and forever rued the curse she placed upon me?"

"I'd choose it, yes—over dying here of starvation, over being flung from the cliffs like some unwanted rag doll."

Craven laughed. "You observed that I had a conscience. You were right. Very well, Jeremy Horne. You shall know the life of the vampire."

What happened next is hazy, a blur of motion. Craven bent forward and took me in his arms, and I thrilled once more at his touch. But just as his teeth punctured the raw skin on my neck, I heard a shout from behind—but who could it be? There was no one else, no one but Hare—

And Hare was mute!

"No! You will not have him! Not my son!"

There was a sudden struggle, as Craven was grabbed from behind, taken unawares. It only served to drive his teeth deeper into my neck, and like some crazed dog, he could not let go, not stop drinking, even as he began to be pummeled from behind. I couldn't see what was happening, couldn't comprehend—

Until suddenly Craven's fangs were ripped backward from my throat as he clutched his chest in pain, and I saw the wooden stake burst through his white T-shirt, driven in from behind.

I fell to my knees, staggered by the assault and the sudden loss of blood. I watched as Craven screamed, twisting from side to side, trying to pull the wood from his body. But he was growing weaker—and older—with every effort, and finally he collapsed onto the earthen floor, twitching and shuddering. I watched him die. I watched him turn into an old, old man. His mouth kept opening and closing for several seconds after he died.

I looked up weakly. Standing over him was Hare.

"Why?" I asked, barely able to talk.

He stooped down beside me. Then he pulled down his soiled shirt to reveal his chest. There, in nearly the same place as mine, was a birthmark in the shape of a dragonfly.

How he had become so disfigured I will likely never know. Trying to fight off Craven, before he was turned into his slave? It doesn't matter now. He spoke not another word after his outburst, and I suspect he won't ever again. He just picked me up in his arms and carried me like a baby up to my room. My *father*, Minter. I had found my father. The reason I had come here.

I'm afraid writing this has used up the last of my strength, sweets. It is time for me to close my eyes now.

Just remember that I love you.

May 13—Craven was right. It *is* an odd sensation, being dead. It takes some getting used to. It's not horrible. Just different.

I've learned so much in just a few short hours. For example: I'm not sure where the myth started that says a vampire does not cast a reflection in a mirror. It's a lie. I'm looking in a mirror right now and see myself quite plainly. My pallor isn't very good, and the dark circles under my eyes don't make me very happy, but there's no doubt that the face staring back at me is me.

Oh, yes, and there's no problem with crucifixes, either. Probably an old story started by the Church to make themselves feel important. I found one in Craven's drawer. I picked it up, turned it over, held it in front of my face. It's just an object, nothing more.

But the hunger is real—Craven was right again about that. It's like feeling horny, only stronger. It's like feeling horny when you haven't had sex in weeks, not even any jacking off.

I know you're going to be surprised by the change in me, sweets. But I *had* to do it, and when you read this, you'll understand. If I was to fight Craven for your love, it had to be on an even playing field. I figured if you were going to spend eternity as the walking undead with anyone, it was going to be me. Hare—my father—just made it all easier. I never would have expected that. Brilliant move on his part. Took Craven right out of the competition.

Though if he'd have been just a little quicker, maybe I wouldn't have died. But then I wouldn't be a vampire either, and I'm kind of liking this new existence. Maybe I'll change my mind when I have to climb into that stinky old coffin, but I just drained a calf that Dad brought me, and man, I'm already looking better. Beats a week in the gym any day! Steroids have nothing on a little calf's blood.

I just called you. You thought I was calling from a telephone. But I don't need a telephone to call you, sweets! Not anymore. It's so cool how I can make your phone ring from so far away. I never knew vampires could do that. You sounded so happy to hear from me. So relieved. You said you'd been worried about me, unable to reach me at the inn. You said you missed me.

And oh, baby, how I miss you. In ways I couldn't imagine possible.

You're going to like the change in me, I think, once you get used to it. Being a vampire tends to give one some direction in life. I can do so much. Imagine the trips we can take, Minter! Imagine what we can get people to do for us! You can still take photos, sweets: I suspect if vampires can cast reflections in mirrors, we can be photographed, too. We're still flesh, after all: dead flesh, but flesh nonetheless.

And just think how you'll be able to control your subjects! No more fussy diva drag queens!

Oh, baby—I'm coming home! I can't wait to see you. I'm leaving tonight. I'll be there before sunrise. *Have* to be, you know.

A joke, Minter!

And when I see you—oh man!—I can't wait to take you in my arms and kiss you! Kiss you as I've never kissed you before. Make love to you like you won't believe. Believe me, you have never experienced an orgasm like I'm going to give you.

I used to worry you would leave me. I used to think I had no power over that eventuality. I thought you were the stronger one, superior to me. How wrong I was. Your logic, Minter, has no power next to my dreams. Not anymore.

I think I'll let you read this after it's all done. It'll be better that way. After I bring you back up here and you've had a chance to meet my dad and get used to everything. You know, like how it feels to be dead.

You'll like Dad. He's got a gruff exterior but a heart of gold. And he takes such good care of me, just like he'll take care of you. It's just what I always wanted, Minter. My father, you, eternal life—

You know, Craven was wrong about one thing. He said I had to choose between love and truth. But he was wrong.

I can have both.

For eternity.

I'm coming home, my love. Get ready! I'm coming home!

Sting

Michael Thomas Ford

Chapter One

"As you can see, our information systems fall somewhere between the Luddite and the Amish."

Ben Hodge laughed. It was the first time he'd laughed since arriving in Downing the day before, or perhaps even since deciding to leave New York in February. Maybe, he thought, even since the night before Trey's death.

"We've got a computer, and we're linked to the big library in Cedar Creek, of course, but you probably won't get many requests for inter-library loans. Mostly people come in for the new Stephen King and Jackie Collins titles."

Martha Abraham spoke with the still, soft voice of a woman who had been a librarian for most of her 72 years. With quick, intelligent eyes peering out from behind thick bifocals and a body that appeared to be nothing more than twigs held together by sheer force of will, she reminded Ben of a hummingbird.

"And that's about it," Martha said as they returned to the front desk from their tour of the library. It hadn't taken long. The Downing Public Library was comprised of just three rooms: the central stacks holding the collection of fiction and nonfiction, a smaller children's room, and the librarian's tiny office. The latter was tucked behind the library's long wooden counter, under which the tools of the librarian's trade—

checkout slips, rubber stamps, pencils, reference materials, and assorted candies for the infrequent young patron—were housed.

"You're sure you want to do this?" Martha looked at Ben, her dark eyes fixed on his face.

Ben looked around the small library and nodded. "I'm sure," he said, sounding more confident than he felt.

"Then here you go," Martha said, taking a ring of three keys out of her dress pocket and handing them to Ben. "Big one's for the front door, medium one's for the office, and no one remembers what the small one is for but it's always been on that ring and I'm not about to break that particular chain."

Ben smiled as he closed his hand around the keys. *Another Ozark superstition*, he thought to himself.

"And now I am officially retired," said Martha. "If you'll excuse me, there's a garden waiting for me to attend to it. If you need me for anything, my number's on your desk."

With a simple wave of her hand, Martha left the library without another glance. When the door had shut behind her, Ben took another look around. He sighed. It was all his now. He held the keys up, watching them swing from his finger, the light from the library's many windows glinting off the well-worn metal. What was it about keys that seemed so magical?

They open doors, he told himself. *They open doors to new adventures.* Unexpectedly, he saw an image of himself standing in front of a door, holding a similar set of keys. They were the keys to the apartment he and Trey had moved into a year after meeting at a book signing, both of them standing in the rain for an hour to get Drayton Leister's signature on his new novel. A casual conversation had turned into coffee, which had turned into dinner, which had turned into a night of lovemaking, which had turned into three years together.

He forced himself to stop thinking about it. He'd left New York to escape those memories, to leave them behind in the congested streets that smelled more and more like death to him and the crowds of people that filled the city like shades, the life drained from them by the demands of living in such a place. It was a city that ate its residents, and he'd been lucky to escape.

He walked through the stacks, investigating the library's holdings more carefully. The contents of a library's shelves were in many ways a reflection of its patrons' lives. A good librarian picked and chose based on what he or she knew of the people who walked through the doors. He'd done as much in his job as the director of one of the New York Public Library's many smaller offspring. He was curious to see what Martha Abraham's choices could tell him about his new home.

As Martha had promised, there were the usual suspects, including King, Collins, Grisham, Straub, and pretty much every novel ever selected by Oprah for her book club. But he also found some surprises: a complete collection, in hardcover, of every book ever written by Shirley Jackson; Angela Carter's *The Burning Boat*; Tarcher Debitt's wonderful first novel, *Under the Rabbit Moon*. These were unexpected discoveries, books he might expect to find in a library (such as his old place of employment) with resources to spend on titles considered less than necessary to a collection, not in a place like Downing.

Then again, he was still surprised that Downing itself existed. When he'd first discovered the ad for a librarian in the employment section at the back of *Library Journal,* he'd had to go to an atlas to find out exactly where Downing, Arkansas, was. Even then he'd had difficulty. Tucked into the mountains like a dollar bill hidden in the pocket of a winter coat, Downing was easily missed. He'd scanned three maps before locating it in the northwest corner of the state, a tiny dot surrounded by the Ozarks National Forest and a group of lakes.

Now, looking at the books whose spines stared out at him with long, thin faces, he still wasn't quite convinced that Downing was real, or that he himself was actually there. But he was. His belongings, still in their cardboard boxes, were sitting in the little house he'd rented in town. His apartment on New York's Upper West Side was probably already inhabited by new tenants. His job was, he knew, already filled. His former assistant, an ambitious Columbia graduate with big plans and family connections, had been only too happy to move into his office and begin putting her stamp on the library's collection.

In short, there was nothing for him to go back to, even if he'd wanted to. He knew people thought he was mad. His friends had tried to talk him out of the move, as had his boss at the library. Even his dry cleaner, when told that Ben was relocating to Arkansas, had looked at him strangely and said, "Is that in America?"

It was that very aspect of the place—its ability to be overlooked by the rest of the world—that appealed to him. He could get lost there, become forgotten. *Or at least forget*, he thought. That would be enough.

He was interrupted in his browsing of the shelves by the sound of the front door opening. Thinking it was Martha returning to give him some piece of information she'd neglected to pass along, he waited for her to appear. Instead, he was surprised to see a man walk into the room. Tall, with a stocky build, he appeared to be in his mid-30s. His dark hair was cut short and he was clean-shaven. He wore faded khaki work pants and a blue shirt, the sleeves rolled up to reveal his forearms.

"Is Martha here?" he asked when he saw Ben.

The man's voice was soft and pleasant, a rich tenor holding the faint traces of the accent that Ben had already come to recognize as being unique to the area. It was, he thought, much less harsh than the strangled New Jersey and New York speech that had filled his ears for so long.

"I'm afraid Martha has retired," Ben said, walking forward and holding out his hand. "I'm Ben Hodge, the new librarian."

The man looked at Ben's outstretched hand for a moment, as if unsure whether to believe him or not. Then he looked up at Ben and said, "Titus Durham."

With no handshake apparently in the offing, Ben retracted his hand. "Is there something I can help you with?" he asked.

Titus shook his head. Walking past Ben, he went directly to one of the shelves. After only a moment's search, he removed one of the books and returned to the front desk, where Ben still stood. He handed the book he'd selected to Ben.

"Cottington's *Beekeeper's Handbook*," Ben said, looking at the cover. He looked at Titus. "You raise bees?" he asked.

"Some," Titus answered.

Ben waited for an elaboration. When none came, he took the book with him as he went behind the desk. Opening the back cover, he removed the checkout slip that was tucked into the pocket and looked at it. Nearly every line was filled, each one with Titus Durham's name.

"Looks like this is one of your favorites," Ben remarked as he stamped the new due date on the slip and on the pocket. Putting the slip into the file beneath the desk, he handed the book to Titus. "You're my first customer," he said cheerfully.

Titus answered him with a nod, then turned and walked out of the room. Ben watched him go, listening for the sound of the door closing.

"Welcome to Downing," he said, sighing.

Chapter Two

It was hot, too hot for sleeping. Ben kicked off the single sheet that covered his body and swung his legs over the side of the bed. He'd been tossing for hours, trying to get to sleep. The clock on his nightstand read 2:47.

He'd gone to bed wearing his boxers and a T-shirt. Now the T-shirt lay in a heap on the floor, tossed there shortly after midnight in an attempt to cool his flushed skin. It had done little good. A film of sweat covered him, matting the hair on his chest and making him feel even more uncomfortable, as if he'd gone to sleep fresh from a five-mile run without the benefit of showering.

He stood and walked to the window. The white curtains on either side of it hung limply, no breeze passing through the screen to move them. It was as if the world had died. Outside, the moon was a pale sliver in the sky, and even the stars seemed dimmed. The faint calls of nightbirds drifted through the night.

If he were still in New York, Ben thought, he would be surrounded by the sounds of taxis and snatches of conversations rising up from the street below his window. The city would be shrouded in the perpetual twilight that seemed to emanate from the very stones of its buildings, keeping it forever poised between night and day. And there would be the familiar rattling of the old air-conditioner in the bedroom, the one that always seemed on the brink of failure but which managed to exude enough of its chilly breath to ward off the worst of the summer heat.

The new house felt strange. He didn't yet know the sounds of its sleep, and the paths to the bathroom and downstairs to the kitchen had yet to be burned into his subconscious so that he could traverse them while only half awake if he needed to pee or get a drink of water. Even the smells were different, the scent of his old apartment replaced by those of the mountains, of pine and dirt and water.

If he were still in New York, he thought too, he would return to bed and slip beneath the sheet again. Trey would turn in his sleep and slide a hand across his chest. Still sleepy, he might even continue south, his fingers following the trail of hair leading to Ben's crotch, then wrapping around his cock. If he were still in New York. And if Trey were still alive.

He had placed an armchair next to the bedroom window. He'd brought very few things from the apartment, from *their* apartment, but the armchair had been one of the items he'd been unable to part with. It had been Trey's favorite reading chair. A large, overstuffed chair covered in worn velvet the color of faded grass, it had seemed out of place in whatever room they'd placed it. But as soon as Ben had set it beside the window in his new home, intending to move it later when the boxes were unpacked, it had finally looked at peace with itself.

Now he sat in it. The velvet felt soft against his bare skin, and the smell of Trey surrounded him immediately, a combination of aftershave, paint, and turpentine that had always seemed to cling to him no matter how many showers he took. Closing his eyes, Ben breathed deeply. An image of Trey came to him immediately. He was seated in the chair, a book in his lap. His dark eyes looked up at Ben in surprise, his mouth opening in a smile as he saw that Ben was walking toward him nude.

Ben stopped in front of the chair, his cock level with Trey's chin. Reaching out, he put his hand behind Trey's head and pulled him forward. Trey obliged, his lips opening and surrounding the head of Ben's dick, sucking gently. In moments Ben was hard and Trey's mouth was sliding down the length of him, his nose pressing against Ben's stomach.

Ben pumped his hips slowly, feeling the warmth of Trey's mouth around him. Trey ran his tongue along the underside of Ben's cock, teasing him. Ben responded by thrusting harder, deeper, until every inch of him was buried deep in Trey's throat. He was going to come.

Then he heard the buzzing. At first he thought it was Trey humming. He felt tiny flickers of movement on his dick, which he took to be Trey's tongue attempting to finish him off. But then the movements became sharper, more intense. The buzzing increased.

He looked down. Emerging from Trey's mouth was the head of a bee, its antennae twitching curiously. Ben watched as it slipped from between Trey's lips, the yellow-and-black-banded body contrasting with the whiteness of his skin. The bee's feet pricked his skin as it walked, and he watched as its abdomen moved rhythmically up and down. There was, he knew, a stinger embedded in its end, and he prayed that it wouldn't pierce his flesh.

The bee was followed by another, and then another. Ben watched, unable to move, as they emerged from between his lover's lips. Even worse, he could feel them inside Trey's mouth. His head was full of them. They were pushing against his teeth, covering his tongue. And for every one that found its way out, more were pushing up from his throat.

Ben pulled his dick out of Trey's mouth, backing away. Trey fell back against the chair. Bees swarmed from his lips and nose, covering his face in a blanket of striped bodies and buzzing wings. Trey's hands hung limply at his sides, his head lolled to one side. His cheeks pulsed as the bees moved behind them, his lips opening and closing in silent screams.

Ben looked down and saw that several bees still clung to his now-limp dick. His skin was still smeared with traces of Trey's spit, and the bees were stuck in it. They were buzzing angrily as they fought against the sticky prison, and Ben knew that at any moment they would sting. He moved to brush them away, and as he did one of them plunged itself into him.

"No!" he screamed, as pain burst through his body.

He sat up, his heart racing and the image of Trey dissolving into the darkness. He was in his bedroom, alone. There were no bees. There was no Trey. He was seated in the chair by the window. He had fallen asleep.

He looked at the clock. 4:23. Well, he hadn't fallen asleep for long. Just long enough for the nightmare to come. He rubbed his forehead, trying to banish the images from his mind. He knew that morning would push them back, but morning was still several hours away. For now they lingered, trying to lure him back into unconsciousness so that they could grow stronger.

He stood up quickly, before sleep could overcome him again, and made his way through the darkened hallway and down the stairs to the kitchen. There, he filled the tea kettle from the sink, lit the stove with one of the matches from the box he'd found in a drawer, and put the water on to boil. It seemed like an antiquated procedure, one long ago replaced with a few pushes of the buttons on a microwave, but going through the motions brought him some degree of comfort. It was what people did, he imagined, in times of trouble. They made coffee.

When the water was ready, he poured it into a cup and added some of the instant coffee he'd picked up at the small grocery in town. There had been nothing fresh-ground, and he hadn't wanted to draw even more attention to himself by asking for the nearest Starbucks. Besides, he wasn't all that fond of coffee anyway, not really. Coffee had been another of Trey's things, like Cary Grant movies and sushi. Ben had grown accustomed to them over time, had even learned to enjoy them. But without Trey's enthusiasm for them to feed his own, they had lost much of their appeal.

He stirred the coffee listlessly. The smell suddenly made his stomach knot up. Taking the cup to the sink, he poured the coffee down the drain, following it with a long blast of water. The rest of the jar he tossed into the trash. Opening the refrigerator, he removed a carton of orange juice and poured himself some of that instead. He took a large swallow, letting the acidic liquid coat his mouth and throat, washing away any stray traces of the coffee.

Putting the empty glass in the sink, he leaned against the counter and suddenly found himself crying. Why had he come here? Why had he ever thought that leaving New York would mean leaving behind the memories? All he'd done was carry them with him, packed them up along with the dishes and towels, the books and the paintings. They hadn't remained behind in the apartment, like the jar of pickles he'd forgotten to clear out of the refrigerator or the stain on the living room rug where he and Trey had spilled a bottle of red wine while making love. They'd traveled, unbroken, across 1500 miles, and now they were unwrapping themselves, one by one, and returning to him in nightmare fantasies.

He took a deep breath, calming the sobbing, and looked out the window over the sink. The sun was coming up, a narrow line of gold thickening in the east. The darkness, fleeing back to its burrow, was growing thinner. The world was waking up again. Seeing the dawn, Ben felt the heaviness in his chest lift a little.

Then his gaze moved to the corner of the window. There, suspended in the perfect filigree of a spider's web, hung a bee. Its body was wrapped round in silk, its wings and legs tethered by the impossibly delicate bonds of death. Only its head remained free, the hollow eyes staring out at nothing. And from its nether end its stinger, small and sharp and full of poison, protruded from the wrappings.

He watched the bee for a moment, half expecting it to spring to life and free itself. When it didn't, he looked once more at the rising sun and felt the weariness of the night begin to fade.

Chapter Three

The basement was, not surprisingly, dusty and strung with cobwebs. As Ben wiped away the tattered strips of spider silk that hung from the joists supporting the enormous weight of the bookshelves above, he thought that perhaps venturing into the underbelly of the library wasn't the best idea he'd ever had. He kept glancing up, alert for tiny scurrying shadows, and pulling the collar of his shirt closed in case a clumsy arachnid happened to fall from its hiding place and tumble onto his body.

It was, however, cool in the basement, much cooler than in the upstairs rooms, and that was a relief. Without the benefit of air-conditioning, the library was suffering in the afternoon heat. The old fan Ben had found in the office closet—a rattling Zephyr Airkooler whose badge was stamped 1942—was doing its best to move air through the building, but even with its valiant efforts it was still unbearably warm. Wilting in the oven-like confines of his office, and bored with organizing the checkout system for the third time that day, Ben had gotten the notion to inspect the contents of the library's nether realms, an area Martha had neglected to include on her tour of the place.

Now he saw why it had been left off the itinerary. Small, dark, and musty, the cellar contained little of interest. An ancient typewriter, almost certainly acquired at the same time as the fan wheezing away on the counter upstairs, sat in one corner atop a wheeled table whose one missing caster caused it to lurch to the left. Stacks of newspapers, neatly bundled but nonetheless in the last stages of decay, were piled against one wall. Ben glanced at the date on the topmost one—November 17, 1958—and made a mental note to find someone to cart the whole lot away before it managed to spontaneously combust in the summer heat.

There were also some books. Several cartons of them were placed at seemingly random points in the room. It reminded Ben of an exhibit he'd once seen at the Museum of Modern Art, an installation in which the artist—a thin, bearded man the *New Yorker* described as "the savior of conceptual art," and who later died of a heroin overdose in a famous rock star's hotel bathroom—had filled an entire gallery with boxes of books that had at one time or another been banned. Visitors were encouraged to pick books at random and open them, thereby freeing them from the tyranny of censorship. The books, however, had each been glued shut, rendering them useless. As Ben remembered it, the whole thing was supposed to have been a statement on the sadness of having a treasure trove of thoughts so close at hand yet so unavailable. His only lasting memory of the experience, though, was of a well-dressed Manhattan socialite desperately clawing at the unyielding cover of Alice Walker's *The Color Purple* with her manicured nails while saying to her bemused husband, "Harold, I just don't *get* it."

The books in the library's basement were, he assumed, ones that had been weeded out of the main collection due to either their unpopularity, deteriorating condition, or irrelevance in the face of more current scientific discovery. Such discards were common in all libraries. He himself had held annual purgings, offering the unwanted volumes to collectors, curiosity seekers, and generally anyone who was willing to pay a dollar for a copy of *Valley of the Dolls* whose spine was weakened to the point of inefficacy, or perhaps an edition of Edward Gorey's *The Curious Sofa* in which someone had blacked out potentially offensive parts of the illustrations with Magic Marker.

The graveyard of the Downing Public Library, unfortunately, appeared to hold nothing even that interesting. A quick inventory of the nearest box revealed several Nancy Drew mysteries whose covers had been torn off, half a dozen novels from the 1930s and 40s whose titles

Ben didn't recognize, a fly-fishing manual, some outdated encyclope-
dias and, inexplicably, a Sears Christmas catalog from 1974. The other
boxes appeared similarly loaded, and further exploration was deemed
unnecessary.

Ben was turning to go back up the stairs when he happened to notice another box. Like the others, it was an old produce box—in this
instance for Boy-O-Boy Lettuce. Unlike the others, however, its top
was sealed shut with several shimmering lines of packing tape. It had
also been placed in the farthest corner, where it was almost completely
concealed by the shadows.

Intrigued by the box's special handling, Ben went for a closer look.
Finding the edge of the tape with his fingernail, he pulled back one of
the strips. The others followed quickly after, and he opened the box.
Inside he found more books. Unlike those in the other boxes, however,
these had been neatly stacked.

He picked one up and looked at the cover. *"Witchcraft of the Ozark
Mountains,"* he read out loud. "Interesting."

He put the book down and looked at what else was in the box, tak-
ing each book out and examining the cover before setting it aside.
Soon an odd collection was assembled on the floor. In addition to the
witchcraft book, the box yielded up *Riddles of the Devil: Hexes and
Curses in American Folk Magic*; *Poppets, Talismans, and Charms*;
Banishing the Dark; *Haints and Haunts of the Ozarks*; and *Dreaming
Demons: The Downing Child Killings and the Search for a Monster*.
This last title particularly interested Ben, as did the remaining books,
of which there appeared to be two dozen or so. But rather than sit in
the basement, taking them out one at a time, he decided to take the
box and its macabre contents upstairs.

Putting the books he'd already removed back into the box, he
picked it up and carried it up the steps. Shutting the cellar door, he
continued to his office, where he deposited the box on his desk. His
shirt bore several streaks of dirt, but he ignored these as he sat down to
explore the contents of the strange box more closely.

Once again he removed *Dreaming Demons*. This time he opened
the cover and read the description printed on the book's jacket flap.
"In the summer of 1932, the children of Downing, Arkansas, seemed
to be under attack by something murderous," he read. "It began with

the death of thirteen-year-old Jacob Brewer, found in the woods with his head severed from his body. What at first was blamed on an attack by a bear or mountain lion quickly took on a far more sinister air when a second boy, nine-year-old Dylan Whitemore, was discovered dead in his bed, his body drained of all blood and bizarre symbols carved into his flesh. Soon talk turned from a maddened animal to something more sinister. And as three more children were killed in the course of a month, the tiny community rippled with rumors of devil worship, magic, and creatures of legend."

There was more, most of it having to do with the investigation into the killings and the resulting effects on the town and its inhabitants. Ben read through the description with increasing interest. He was surprised, when he reached the end, to discover that the murders—which ultimately numbered seven—had never been officially solved by the police. The town, however, had ultimately meted out its own brand of justice, blaming the horrific murders on one John Rullins, an unemployed tinker who some said had turned to witchcraft in an attempt to reverse his failed fortunes. "Rullins, convicted without the benefit of judge or jury," the book's description concluded, "himself became the final victim when a mob first stoned him to death and then burned his body in a desperate attempt to bring the summer of evil to its grisly end."

Ben turned from the jacket to the title page of the book. It had been written by someone called Wallace Pyle Blackwood, and published by the University of Arkansas Press in 1979. Ben turned to the back flap, hoping he would find a little information about the author. He was rewarded with a photo and a brief bio. "Wallace Pyle Blackwood, a graduate of Short Mountain College, is the librarian at Downing Public Library in Downing, Arkansas," he read. "Twenty-two years old at the time of the Downing child killings, he knew all of the victims."

Ben put the book down on his desk and stared at it. The idea of something so grotesque happening in a quiet little town like Downing was unthinkable. Certainly murder wasn't limited to big cities, and he was well aware that unbelievable things happened on a regular basis. Mothers drowned their children in bathtubs. People set one another on fire. Entire groups poisoned themselves in the belief that they would be rescued by alien saviors. These things did happen. But something about the child killings—and the town's way of putting an end to them—was particularly brutal.

Equally puzzling was why the book had been included in the box along with the other occult titles. Why had they all been hidden away in the basement? And where had such a peculiar assortment of books come from in the first place? They weren't exactly the kinds of books he expected to find in a collection like the one housed in the Downing Public Library, even if one of them had been written by its former librarian.

Martha. Martha would be able to provide some answers. She was also old enough that she likely remembered the killings herself. He would have to ask her about them. Picking up the phone, Ben looked at the number she'd scribbled on a piece of paper and began to dial. But before he could complete the call, he was interrupted by the appearance of a boy in the doorway. He appeared to be about nine years old, with red hair and a face dotted with freckles.

"Can I help you?" Ben asked, setting the phone down.

The boy nodded. "I'm looking for something to read," he said shyly.

Ben nodded. "Then you've come to the right place," he said as he stood up. "Come with me. I bet we can find something for you."

As he walked out of the office to help the boy, he took one last look at the book on his desk. The mystery could wait a little longer.

"Have you ever met a guy named Harry Potter?" he asked the boy as he led him to the stacks.

Chapter Four

"Wally Blackwood. Now there's a name I haven't heard in a long time."

Martha Abraham poured some more wine into Ben's glass. They were seated at the table in her kitchen, picking over what was left of the roast chicken Martha had made for dinner. Martha refilled her own glass and took a sip before continuing.

"I meant to clear out all those old books of Wally's," she told Ben. "All the other garbage in that cellar, too. I guess I just forgot."

"You knew Wally then?" Ben asked.

"Of course I did," answered Martha. "Learned most of what I know from him. He was the librarian before me."

"What happened to him?"

Martha grew quiet, and a pensive look passed over her face. She sighed. "He died," she said finally. "Shortly after the publication of his book."

"I'm sorry," Ben said. "I didn't mean to bring up unpleasant memories."

Martha waved a hand at him. "It's all right," she said. "It just all seems so long ago now. Reminds me that *I'm* getting old."

"If you don't mind me asking, why did you put those books down in the cellar?"

"Wally was interested in some very—unusual—subjects," said Martha.

"Those books of his upset a number of our patrons. I felt it would be best to remove them from the stacks." She hesitated, looking at Ben. "I know what you're thinking," she continued. "A librarian should never censor her own collection. Perhaps you're right. But Downing isn't entirely like other places. There are some deep wounds here, and they need time to heal."

"You mean the child killings," Ben said carefully. He'd been trying to find a graceful way to bring up the subject of Wallace Blackwood's book, and now that Martha had provided an opening, he took it.

Martha nodded. "There's not a family here who wasn't affected in some way by those events," she explained. "If it wasn't one of their own children who was killed, it was kin of some kind."

"But that was more than seventy years ago," Ben said. "Surely people can talk about it now."

"People here don't *talk* much about anything," Martha told him. "When Wally published that book, well, it reopened some doors that should have stayed shut."

"Have you read the book?" asked Ben.

"Oh, yes," said Martha. "For Wally's sake I read it."

"And do you agree with him that John Rullins was the victim of some overactive imaginations, that people were looking for someone to blame the tragedy on?"

"Who can say?" Martha replied. "Was he possessed by demons? Was he practicing some kind of evil magic? I don't believe in such things. But did he do it? Did he kill those children? The people who killed him thought so. My father thought so."

"Your father?" said Ben.

Martha nodded. Then she stood up and went into the living room. When she returned, she was carrying an old photo album, which she placed on the table in front of Ben. Opening it to the first page, she pointed to a faded sepia photograph. It depicted a group of young boys dressed in old-fashioned baseball uniforms, some of them holding bats and gloves. Behind them a man stood, his handsome face stern yet kind as he peered out from beneath his cap. His hand was on the shoulder of a small boy standing in front of him.

"The Downing Rockets," Martha said. "Every family in town had a boy on the team that year." She pointed to a tall boy in the back row, his chest thrust proudly out and his hair neatly plastered against his head. "Jacob Brewer," she said.

"The first one killed," Ben said.

Martha nodded. She moved her finger to another boy. "Dylan Whitemore," she told Ben. "Arthur Rikes. Michael Privet. George Jenkins. Leyton Settles."

Ben recognized the names. They were the boys who had died in the summer of 1932. He looked at each of their faces as Martha pointed to them. Each one looked back at him, filled with happiness.

Martha's finger came to rest on the man with his hand on the boy's shoulder. "My father," she said quietly. "He was the coach. And my brother," she added, gently brushing the face of the boy. "He was the seventh."

"I don't remember seeing the name Abraham in the book," said Ben, confused.

"Abraham was my husband's name," explained Martha. "My family name was Garvey."

"Garvey," Ben repeated, thinking about what he'd read in Wallace Blackwood's book. "Milton Garvey. He was the one found—"

"Hanging in a tree in our backyard," Martha said, completing his sentence. "Yes. I was the one who discovered him. I was seven years old. I woke up in the middle of the night. I still don't know why. I heard something, or had a nightmare. I called for my mother. When she didn't answer, I got up to go to her room. That's when I looked out the window and saw Milt."

Martha stopped speaking and sat, holding her wineglass in her hands and staring down into it. Ben could only imagine what she was thinking, what memories were running through her head. He had similar memories of his own, memories he was trying very hard to keep at bay. He felt guilty about making Martha relive her past.

"He looked like he'd been crucified," Martha said, her voice soft and distant. "His arms had been lashed to the branches. He reminded me of the statue of Christ that hung in our church. Only his eyes were gone and his belly had been ripped open. He was eight years old."

When she looked up at Ben, her eyes were misty. "My father was a good man," she said. "He never lifted a hand against any living creature. But he was the first one to pick up a stone and bring it down on John Rullins's head."

Ben looked away. "I should never have asked," he said apologetically.

"You asked me if I think John Rullins committed those murders," Martha said, her voice growing stronger. She paused a moment before continuing. "I don't know. But I do know that after he was killed they stopped, and that's good enough."

The ritual sacrifice, Ben thought to himself.

Martha drained her glass. "I didn't mean to get so serious," she said. "You must think you've settled yourself in the midst of a horde of mad people."

"Not at all," Ben answered. "But I can see now why you thought it best to remove that book from the shelves."

"Wallace would have killed me if he'd been alive," Martha said. "He was so proud of that book. Spent most of his life writing it."

"Why was he so interested in it?" Ben asked her.

Martha shook her head. "I don't know, really," she said. "I think perhaps because he knew all the boys from the library."

"Were any of them his family?"

"No," said Martha. "Wally had no family. Didn't grow up in Downing, either."

"What brought him here?" Ben asked.

"The library," Martha explained. "There wasn't exactly a lot of call for librarians back then. When Wally heard about the job here, he took it."

"And he never married?" said Ben.

"The library was his whole life," Martha said. "The library and the people who came to it. It was everything to him. The murders devastated him. I think that book was his attempt at understanding them."

"What about those other books?" Ben inquired. "The ones in the box."

"Wally was always a little obsessed with the occult," Martha told him. "He was particularly fascinated with local superstitions and folklore. The Ozarks have a long history of supernatural occurrences. Witchcraft. Hauntings. That sort of thing. Wally read everything he could find about it."

"He sounds like an interesting man," Ben remarked.

"He was," Martha said. "A bit strange, but very interesting. It was impossible not to like him."

"You mentioned one of the murdered boys was named Settles," said Ben. "A boy named Settles came into the library a few days ago. Red-haired kid. Lots of freckles. Is that the same family?"

Martha nodded. "Steven Settles," she said. "Leyton Settles was the brother of his great-grandfather. He was my brother's best friend."

"Steven seems like a nice kid," said Ben. "I just wish I could get more of the kids to come in. Apart from Steven and Titus Durham, I haven't seen anyone all week."

"Titus," Martha said, smiling. "Come in for his bee books, did he?"

Ben nodded. "Is that all he ever checks out?"

"I tried to get him to branch out," answered Martha. "Lord knows I tried. He always took the books I suggested and brought them back a few days later, unopened. Finally I gave up."

"Why bees?" asked Ben. "Is he . . ." He hesitated, searching for the right word.

"Special?" Martha suggested. "No, I don't think so. He's just quiet. Always has been, ever since he was a boy. Keeps to himself. He and Wally were always close. I know he grieved terribly when Wally died. Didn't come into the library for months."

Ben leaned back in his chair. "Well, I certainly appreciate the information," he said. "And the dinner. It was amazing."

"It was my pleasure," said Martha. "What with Jerry gone almost seven years now, I don't get many chances to cook for anyone. You'll have to come again next week. I'll make my pot roast."

"I'd like that," Ben said.

"What about you?" Martha asked as she shut the photo album and started to clear away the dishes. "Any family?"

"My mother died several years ago," Ben said. "And my father lives in a retirement home in Florida. I don't have any brothers or sisters."

"Never married?" said Martha.

Ben thought about the question. Was what he and Trey had had together a marriage? It had certainly felt like one. They'd shared a home, a life, a love. But would Martha understand it if he told her? He thought somehow that she would. Yet telling her the truth would mean telling her all of the truth, and that was something he wasn't ready for. Not yet.

"No," Ben answered as he helped her clear away the empty wine glasses. "I've never been married."

Chapter Five

"How'd you like it?"

Ben took the book that Steven Settles had placed on the counter and returned the checkout slip to the pocket in the back.

"It was okay," the boy replied. "Better than the movie."

"They always are, Steven," Ben told him. "You ready for another one?"

Steven grinned, the picket fence of his teeth broken by a single black hole where he'd recently lost an incisor in a run-in with a baseball. Ben had been wrong about the boy's age, miscalculating by nearly two years. Anticipating his eleventh birthday in less than a week (when he hoped to receive either a Sony Playstation or a mountain bike), Steven was simply slight of stature.

"Let's see if we can't find volume two of Mr. Potter's adventures," said Ben. He found it difficult to believe that there was still a child on the planet—even in tiny Downing, Arkansas—who had yet to discover the Harry Potter books. Yet Steven had been completely surprised to learn that the movie, which he'd seen five times, had its origins in the printed word.

Now, four days after leaving the library with the first Potter adventure in his hands, he was back for more. *My first repeat customer,* Ben thought as he located the book and handed it to Steven.

"It's longer than the first one," Steven said doubtfully as Ben walked him back to the checkout desk.

"You'll be fine," Ben reassured him. "And this time you'll know the story *before* the movie comes out."

He was stamping the book's slip when a shadow fell across the desk. Looking up, he was surprised to see Titus Durham standing in the doorway. Titus looked at Steven, who smiled at him, and then at Ben. He nodded a greeting and slid the book in his hands across the desk.

"Right on time," Ben said cheerfully. "Another day and I would have had to charge you a quarter."

Titus nodded again, still not saying anything, and retreated into the stacks. Ben looked at Steven, who shrugged.

"Do you know him?" Ben asked the boy.

Steven nodded. "I know *everybody* around here," he said. "It's hard not to."

Ben laughed. "I guess it would be," he said.

"He doesn't talk much," Steven continued. "Lives over by Drowned Girl Pond."

"Drowned Girl Pond?" Ben repeated. "It's really called that?"

"That's what we call it," Steven answered. "The kids, I mean. This girl drowned in it a long time ago—before I was born."

"Got you," Ben said. "I guess you guys don't swim there much."

"Sure we do," Steven replied, looking at him. "Why wouldn't we?"

"Well, you know," said Ben. "Because of the girl and . . . never mind."

Steven shook his head in a gesture suggesting that all adults were completely out of their minds.

"Hey, shrimpy, you done feeding your head?"

A teenage boy had walked into the library. Dressed in well-worn jeans and a Motorhead T-shirt, he carried himself with the air of some-one who wanted to make it perfectly clear that he was there only be-cause necessity demanded it. Books, his attitude declared, were not his thing.

"My brother, Darren," Steven said to Ben. "I've got to go."

Ben waved at the older boy, who replied with a curt nod. Steven waved his goodbye, and the two of them walked out, Darren's arm around Steven's shoulder in a protective gesture, as if the books might at any moment leap from the shelves in attack. Ben watched them go, wondering if Darren had ever read more than a comic book or a *Playboy*.

"Nice kid."

Ben gave a start, the voice surprising him. Titus Durham was standing in front of the desk. He'd brought two books with him.

"Steven?" said Ben as he pulled the books toward him. "Yes, he is."

He looked at the books Titus had chosen: *The Silent Song: Communication in the Hive* and *The Bee's Year*. "More bees," he remarked.

"Martha ordered them for me," Titus said, as if that explained everything.

"Looks like you're the only one who's ever checked them out," Ben said, looking at the checkout slip and, as with the man's previous selections, seeing Titus's name on nearly every line. "I guess there's not much call for bee books in Downing."

"Probably not," agreed Titus as he picked up his books. "Thank you."

Titus left. As he walked away, Ben wanted to call to him to come back. There were things he wanted to ask Titus, things he wanted to know. Something about the man intrigued him.

You could follow him. The thought came to him unexpectedly, as if someone else had spoken it. Ben dismissed the notion immediately. He couldn't just follow Titus. He had to stay in the library. *Why?* asked the same voice. *No one is going to come in.*

That, Ben thought, was most likely true. His two regulars—Steven and Titus—had both made their appearances for the day. The chances of anyone else coming in were highly unlikely. *Besides,* said the voice, *you won't be gone long.*

Before he could talk himself out of it, Ben grabbed the keys from his desk and went after Titus. Locking the library door out of habit, he glanced up the street, where he saw Titus walking at a surprisingly quick pace down the sidewalk. Starting after him, Ben tried to appear as if he were simply taking an afternoon stroll through town.

He tailed Titus, keeping a safe distance between them in case Titus happened to turn around, and manufacturing a story he could use to explain his presence if actually confronted. He was, he decided, familiarizing himself with the area. It was a poor excuse, he knew, and he hoped he wouldn't have to use it.

Titus, however, showed no sign of going anywhere but forward. He passed swiftly by the row of stores that constituted Main Street: the grocery, bank, post office, hardware store, video store, and diner. He continued on past the school, finally veering from his straightforward course when he came to the dirt road that intersected the paved one just past Downing's lone gas station.

Ben almost gave up his pursuit at that point. Following someone on Main Street was one thing, an act that could potentially be attributed to sheer accident. But following someone on a dirt road that led nowhere was something else altogether. If Titus discovered him walking along behind him, how would he explain himself?

Still, he found himself turning and continuing his journey. As Titus walked, more slowly now that he was off the main street, Ben lingered behind, keeping to the side of the road in the event that he had to dart into the trees that lined each side like sentries. Now that they were on what seemed to be the only road going in that particular direction, the possibility of losing sight of Titus became less of a concern. All he had to do, he thought, was keep walking until he came to something— most likely Titus's house.

After twenty minutes, Ben found himself passing a large pond. *Drowned Girl Pond*, he thought as he looked at the smooth black glass of the water's surface. Picturing Steven and his friends jumping into that water, splashing in it and laughing, made him shudder. He imagined the girl who had given the pond its name floating in its depths, her pale eyes staring up through the grass and mud to watch the bodies of the living moving above her. Would she reach up with her cold hands to try and drag them down? He looked away from the pond, concentrating on Titus's retreating back.

As he'd expected, another five minutes of walking brought him to a house. As he came over a low rise in the road, he was just in time to see Titus enter the front door and close it behind him. Ben stood in the long grass, looking at the house. It was an old farmhouse, its white paint peeling from years in the sun, its windows dark eyes in its weary face. Yet despite its age, it appeared to be well cared for. The lawn

around it, what there was of it, was cut short, and Ben could see a corner of a garden in the backyard.

Keeping to the grass, he walked along the side of the house until he
could see more of the rear. There, the rest of the garden came into
view, a long, narrow bed filled with plants. And beyond the garden, Ben
saw a row of white boxes placed in a semicircle. There were seven of
them, each about four feet high.

Beehives, he thought. So, Titus did keep bees.

His thoughts were interrupted by the opening of the house's rear
door. Titus emerged. He walked toward the hives. When he reached
them, he removed the top from one and reached inside.

He's not wearing any protection, Ben thought, horrified. *He's going
to get stung.*

He watched, his heart beating, as Titus removed his hand from the
hive. Ben could see that his fist and forearm were covered in a sticky
mess of honey. And in the honey something moved. Ben knew that it
was the bees. They coated Titus's flesh. He could see some of them
flying around the man's body. Surely he was getting stung. Yet Titus
held his hand up, looking at it and not moving.

Then he turned his head and looked directly at the spot where Ben
stood. Ben felt his heart stop, and he gasped. Could Titus see him? He
didn't see how it was possible. He stood, frozen, waiting for Titus to
say or do something.

Finally, Titus turned away again, returning his attention to the hive
and to the bees that now flew around him in a thick cloud. Ben
breathed more easily. It was as if with Titus's gaze removed from him
he could move again. Although part of him wanted to stay to see what
Titus was doing, a stronger part of him told him to leave. Giving Titus
a final glance, he turned and made his way quickly back to the road.
And once he was there, he began to run.

Chapter Six

He was trying to escape sleep. He knew ultimately he would lose the battle, but he was attempting it anyway. It made him feel better, at least, fighting it as hard as he could. Then, when he did succumb to his body's demand for rest and the nightmares came again, he wouldn't blame himself, at least not as much.

Ben poured himself another cup of coffee and resumed unpacking the box. He'd worked his way through most of the living room already. Only three boxes remained. He was working on them slowly, taking his time. It was only just after midnight, and dawn seemed an eternity away.

He reached into the box and removed an item wrapped in the now-familiar white newsprint in which he'd swaddled his belongings. The stuff was piled around him in crumpled drifts, a rustling paper sea in which he and the box had become an island. It was amazing how much of the paper there was. It was amazing, too, how much stuff he *had*. He couldn't remember packing so much, and some of the items he scarcely recognized as his own.

The wooden monkey, for example, with its red fez and look of surprise. Where the hell had *that* come from? He couldn't recall buying it, and he was sure it hadn't been a gift. But there it was, sitting on his coffee table waiting for him to find it a place in his new home. He must have packed it, taken it from wherever it had sat in the New York apartment and tucked it into the moving box along with the other odds and ends of his life. But looking at it didn't bring back a single memory.

He unwrapped the item in his hands. It was a framed photograph, himself and Trey standing on a beach, smiling in Hawaii. They'd gone there to escape the bleakness of a New York February. It had been Trey's idea, a last-minute decision. Ben still recalled how Trey had burst into the apartment, snow from an unexpected storm dusting his hair and his coat. "Pack a bag," he'd said. "We're going to Hawaii." Ben had been making dinner. He'd thought Trey was joking until his lover showed him the tickets, picked up from a travel agent friend on his way home from work. Two hours later, they'd been on a plane, the spaghetti on the stove back in their apartment still waiting in its pot of now-cold water.

Ben put the photo on the coffee table beside the monkey. It was too soon. He couldn't think about such things. He wasn't ready to remember those times. Not now that they were gone forever.

He closed his eyes, then opened them quickly as the soothing voice of sleep whispered in his ear. He had to stay awake. He feared that if he slept, the dreams would begin. The dream about Titus Durham and the bees. He'd had it first the night after following Titus to his home. In it he'd been once again hiding in the grass, watching as Titus approached the hives and removed the top from one. Only this time when he reached inside, Titus pulled out not an arm covered with honey but an arm covered with blood. It ran thickly through his fingers, dripping from them in heavy threads. And in the blood the bees squirmed. Ben could hear their buzzing, the frantic beating of their wings as they tried to escape. Some fell, exhausted, to the ground, where they died. Others, stronger or perhaps angrier, pierced the bloody flesh of Titus's arm with their stingers.

Ben had woken from the dream unable to breathe. He'd lain in his bed, staring up at the ceiling and trying to force air into his chest. His body had been unwilling to comply, and he'd felt the weight of the hot air in the room pressing down on him until finally, with an enormous effort, he'd willed his throat open and taken a breath. He'd spent the remainder of the night with the lamp on, not stirring from his bed until the first light of morning had slipped over his windowsill and created a pool of safety for him to stand in.

The dream had returned the next night, playing out in exactly the same way. Ben had forced himself to wake more quickly, pushing through the thick blanket of his dreams to consciousness before he saw too much. Still, he had been frightened, and again he'd lain in the protective light of the bedside table lamp, half afraid that the bulb would somehow go out before the sun came to replace it.

It was stupid, he knew. It was only a dream, a dream birthed in his own feelings of embarrassment at having followed Titus home and spied on him. But coupled with the dream he'd had about Trey, it was enough to make him fearful of putting his head on the pillow again. He knew the two were connected, had become entangled in his thoughts. There had been no blood in the hives behind Titus's house. But there had been blood—lots of blood—in that other room, on that other night.

He had to get out of the house. He felt the picture of himself and Trey behind him, Trey's eyes looking out, begging for him to turn around. Standing up, he slipped in the wrapping paper that scattered like leaves beneath his feet. Catching himself, he ran from the room, from the picture and the memories. He needed air. That would keep him awake.

He left the house, not knowing where he would go. He just needed to be walking, moving, thinking about something else. He made his way down the driveway and onto the sidewalk, forcing his feet to carry him forward. He walked without purpose or direction, simply following the ribbon of cement.

He'd left without thinking to bring a flashlight, but the moon, only a few days from fullness, cast its silver glow on the world. Ben moved through the summer night as if through water, passing the houses and shops that slept deeply. Only occasionally was there a lighted window or the brief electric flicker of a television screen to crack the darkness. The town had gone to sleep, the air rustling gently as if it were no less than the collective breath of bodies at rest.

Ben himself entered a kind of waking sleep, a dreamy state in which he walked without thinking. His mind, clouded by the competing forces of the coffee and the need of his body to lose itself in several blissful hours of slumber, had responded by summoning forth a series of completely unrelated thoughts. They flashed across the screen of his mind like colored scarves pulled one after another from a magician's sleeve, each one hanging in the air for a moment before being replaced by the next. And like the magician's scarves, he sensed vaguely that they were nothing but distraction, something meant to draw his attention from the sleight-of-hand that was going on elsewhere, unobserved.

Trey, his skin already brown after only two days in the sun. Bees circling a hive. Boys splashing in a pond. A hand covered in something wet. A door swinging open. Blood. Oh, so much blood. Where had it come from? He saw it spreading over the surface of the water in a filmy cloud. The boys, not seeing it, continued to splash one another, their laughing faces streaked now with red. But still they laughed, their voices filling the air even as the water around them darkened.

Ben stopped, shaking his head to clear it of the thoughts. Where was he? He looked around. He was standing on a dirt road. Turning, he saw that it stretched behind him into blackness. How far had he walked? He had no idea. But he knew that home was behind him. He saw his own footprints leading back, into the open mouth of the night. All he had to do was follow them.

He was turning to go when he heard the sound of water. It was faint, coming to him on the air. He paused, listening, and heard it again. It was behind him, further down the road. It was then that he knew where he was. He was on the road that led to Titus Durham's house. Beyond him, waiting in the darkness, was Drowned Girl Pond. It was the pond's voice he heard.

He turned and walked toward it, not sure why but doing it nonetheless. Now that he knew where he was, he moved more quickly, as if he'd reached his destination. The moon's light revealed the next several yards of road before him, even as the night swallowed up that which he'd already traveled. And soon he saw, glinting in the field to his left, the surface of the pond. The moon played lightly on it, gilding the water with silver and admiring its own reflection.

Ben stopped at the edge of the road. He could see the pond before him, but he feared leaving the path. It was his way back. But he stood and watched, waiting for something to happen.

It was then that he saw that there was someone standing at the edge of the water. At first it was only a shadow, something slightly darker than the night around it. Then a figure stepped out into the circle of light cast by the moon. It was a man. He was naked, his skin shining white.

Titus, Ben thought. Even in the darkness he recognized the man's features. Titus stood silently, looking out at the surface of the pond. The contours of his body, the lines and planes of his chest and torso, were limned in moon-glow. His arms hung at his sides.

As Ben watched, Titus lifted his hands and looked at them. The fingers appeared darker, stained. Titus brought them to his face, pressing his mouth against them. After a moment, he pulled away again. The darkness was smeared on his lips.

Honey, Ben thought suddenly. *It's only honey.*

Titus held his hands to the sky, gazing up at the moon. Stepping forward, he entered the water. Ben saw a ripple streak the surface, breaking the moon into pieces as it moved across the pond. Titus continued to walk, his body disappearing into the water as if he were melting into it. Slowly he was consumed, the water rising past his calves, then his knees. Ben watched as it reached for Titus's cock, then slid over the mounds of his ass and up his back. A few more steps and all that remained visible was the bare chest of the man, his hands and face still raised to the heavens. He looked like someone entering into baptism, pausing before God and asking for forgiveness.

Titus sank beneath the surface then, his stained hands lingering all alone for a moment, reaching up from the depths of the water. Then they too were gone, and the pond was still once more. Ben waited for Titus to come up for air, to emerge from the water. When a long minute had passed and there was no sign of him, he began to worry. Hesitating only a moment, he stepped into the grass.

As he did, the pond broke open and Titus came up, his head pushing through. Ben stopped. Swimming to the edge, his arms arcing gracefully in the light, Titus emerged from the water. His hands and face had been washed clean, and his body shone. Without pause, he walked forward into the night, disappearing into the trees and leaving Ben looking at the place where he had been and wondering if this was yet another dream.

Chapter Seven

Ben spread the paper open on the desk and looked at the photograph on the front page. A young man in a football uniform looked out at him from beneath the headline LOCAL YOUTH FOUND DEAD AFTER SEARCH. The article accompanying the photograph provided details.

CREAVERTON, AR. Paul Mickerley, 17, was reported missing two days ago when he failed to come home after a party at a friend's house. His body was found yesterday when dogs provided by the state police drew searchers' attention to an unused cemetery holding the bodies of the town's original settlers. Mickerley, a starting quarterback for the Creaverton Bandits football team, was described by his family as a "carefree boy with everything to live for."

"I don't know why this happened to him," Mickerley's mother, Justine Fuller, said as she emerged from the county morgue, where she'd just identified her son. "I don't understand." Her feelings were echoed by her ex-husband, Randall Mickerley, who appeared dazed as he answered reporters' questions. "Paul never did nothing to anybody," he said. "I can't believe he's gone."

The elder Mickerley's statement caused some to speculate that his son's death involved foul play. Creaverton Police Chief Harris Finch, however, deflected the suggestion. "From all appearances, Paul Mickerley died of natural causes. What those causes were, exactly, has not yet been determined."

According to sources, Mickerley's body was discovered propped up against a tombstone. There was no sign of struggle, and no apparent wounds to his body. "It could have been drugs," suggested one officer involved with the search. "Or maybe a heart attack or something like that."

Whatever the cause of Paul Mickerley's death, he is being mourned by those who knew him. A memorial has already been scheduled for Thursday at Holy Oak Gospel Church, and the family asks that any donations be sent directly to the church.

Ben folded the paper and turned it over so that Paul Mickerley's face wasn't staring up at him. He didn't need any more ghosts in his life. He felt sorry for the kid's parents, almost more sorry than he did for the boy himself. At least he wouldn't have to live with the pain. But his mother and father would. They would live with it for the rest of their lives, wondering how they might have prevented their son's death. That, Ben knew, was worse than dying itself.

"Sad, isn't it?"

Titus Durham had come into the library without Ben even hearing him. Now he stood in front of the desk, his eyes cast in the direction of the newspaper.

"Yes," said Ben. "It is sad."

Titus looked up, his eyes meeting Ben's. Ben attempted to avert his gaze, but found himself looking into Titus's eyes. They were brown, deep brown, the color of earth, and they held infinite sadness. How had he never noticed before? he wondered. Trey had had eyes like that.

"Why do you think he did it?" Titus asked.

"Who?" said Ben, not understanding.

"The boy," Titus replied. "Why do you think he did it?"

"I don't know that he did," answered Ben. "Someone else might have killed him."

Titus surprised Ben by laughing softly. "Not around here," he said simply.

"Why would he kill himself?" said Ben. "From all accounts, he was perfectly happy."

Titus nodded. "From all accounts," he repeated thoughtfully. "Then again, who ever really knows what someone else is thinking, what's happening inside. Who really knows what eats people alive when they're all by themselves."

Ben didn't say anything. Titus had never spoken so much at once, and he didn't know what to think of this sudden turn of events. Titus, however, didn't seem to notice. He continued to talk.

"My grandmother used to talk about the ghosts that roamed the woods in these parts," he said. "Scared me half to death with her stories. But she was wrong. It's not the ghosts in the woods you have to fear; it's the ghosts in your head. They're the ones that keep you up at night, the ones whose voices wake you from your dreams. Those are the voices that boy heard, the ones that made him do what he did."

He looked at Ben. "What is it you're afraid of?" he asked.

Ben shook his head. "I don't know," he said.

"Dying?" said Titus.

"No," Ben answered. "I'm not afraid of dying."

"Being alone?" Titus suggested. "Being alone with yourself?"

He had come closer while he was talking, leaning across the counter so that his face was separated from Ben's by only a short distance. Ben could feel his breath, warm from his mouth, against his skin.

"Sometimes," he said quietly. "Sometimes that's what I'm afraid of."

Titus nodded. "That's the most frightening, isn't it?" he said. "I know."

Ben didn't reply. His heart had begun to beat more quickly, and he could feel a fluttering in his stomach. It took him a moment to recognize it for what it was—desire. He wanted to reach out to Titus, to pull him close. He wanted to taste the lips that were so close to his.

"I saw you," he said. "At the pond. I saw you."

Something in Titus's eyes wavered. He looked into Ben's face.

"You were beautiful," said Ben. "In the moonlight. In the water." Titus pulled away. "I should go," he said.

"No," said Ben, reaching out and grabbing his arm. "No. Please."

Titus looked at Ben's hand where it held onto the sleeve of his shirt, his fingers gripping the material tightly. Ben relaxed his hold, but didn't let go entirely. Then he let his hand drift down to Titus's wrist, trailing his fingers through the hair that covered his forearm and coming to rest lightly on top of Titus's hand.

"I want you to stay," Ben said.

Titus closed his eyes for a moment. When he opened them again, he leaned in and kissed Ben. He was gentle at first, his mouth soft. Then his tongue entered Ben's mouth, more insistently. His hand went to Ben's neck, pulling him closer. Ben felt the counter pressing against his stomach.

"Back here," he said breathlessly, nodding at the door of his office.

Titus came around the desk, and Ben led him into the small room, shutting the door behind them. Immediately, Titus pushed him against the closed door, pressing his body close against Ben's and kissing him again. Ben felt himself growing hard as Titus ran his mouth over his neck, biting gently. He placed his hand between Titus's legs, squeezing softly. Titus groaned, pushing himself into Ben's hand.

Fumbling with the buckle of Titus's belt, Ben sank to his knees. Titus leaned against the door as Ben, his fingers shaking, unzipped him and freed his cock. Taking the head of Titus's dick into his mouth, Ben pulled his own pants open and began stroking himself slowly. He slid as much of Titus as he could into his throat, taking in the taste and smell of him. He encircled Titus's balls with his fingers, squeezing gently.

Titus was moving in and out of his throat, thrusting deeply. His cock, slick with Ben's spit, slid easily over Ben's lips. Ben let his tongue trace the length of it as it retreated, sucking on the full head for a moment before Titus reversed direction and entered him once more. He lost himself in the rhythm, the emptying and filling of his mouth.

His own cock was wet with the sticky precursor of his approaching climax, and his fingers worked the length of his dick. It had been a long time since he'd come, even by himself. He felt the tightening in his balls that signaled his closeness. He felt, too, Titus growing thicker in his mouth. Then there was a sudden throb, followed by an explosion of heat over his tongue. Titus pushed forward, driving himself deep, and came again, the bittersweet taste of cum filling Ben's throat.

With his nose buried in the soft hair of Titus's belly, Ben allowed himself the release he desperately needed. His cock twitched fiercely as he came, his load spattering the floor between Titus's feet with milky wetness. Three times Ben's body convulsed, and three times he felt the pulse of his dick in his hand, until finally the blissful shaking subsided.

Reluctantly, he let Titus's cock slip from his lips and looked up. Titus was looking down at him, his eyes dark.

"I should have gone," he said, his hands caressing Ben's face. "I should have gone while I still had a chance."

Chapter Eight

He couldn't get the taste of Titus out of his mouth.

Ben took another drink of whiskey. He'd had three glasses already, and still his tongue burned with the memory of what had happened in the library that morning. He closed his eyes, and immediately his mouth filled with the musky taste of Titus's cock, the warm sweetness of his cum rising up and breaking through the oakiness of the whiskey. He breathed in, the scent of sweat and need and desire surrounding him as if he weren't in his own bedroom but once again kneeling on the floor of his office. He could feel the insistent prodding of Titus's dickhead at the back of his throat, forcing its way farther in. He could smell his balls as they nudged his lips.

He opened his eyes. He had to think about something else. He'd been replaying his encounter with Titus over and over in his head all day. He'd gotten nothing done at the library, the hours there passing in a dreamy haze as he'd sat in his office chair, remembering how he'd felt looking up into Titus's face, how he'd swallowed his load eagerly and immediately wanted more.

Now, seated in the chair in his room, the whiskey bottle on the floor beside him, his need was almost unbearable. His cock, hard in his pants, ached for attention. Yet he knew somehow that getting himself off wouldn't satisfy his craving. He needed the touch of flesh on flesh.

He needed the release he could only get when Titus once more used him for his pleasure.

He stood up, the room swimming slightly. He was, he knew, very close to being drunk. But something was forbidding the alcohol to have its way with him. Something more powerful kept it at bay, the same thing that caused him to see Titus's face whenever he closed his eyes, that made him remember the pleasure he'd experienced in their brief encounter. Ben wanted, for the first time in a week, to sleep. He saw his bed, only a few feet from him, and he yearned for its comfort. Instead, he found himself leaving the room and walking unsteadily down the stairs to his door.

He knew where he was going. By now the way was familiar to him, even in the night. As the whiskey sang softly to him, calling him to sleep, something deeper urged him on. He kept moving forward, the desire in his heart growing stronger with each step he took, first down the sidewalk and then down the dirt road that led to Drowned Girl Pond and then to the white farmhouse with its peeling paint.

This time he went directly to the door and knocked. When a minute later the door was opened and Titus looked out, Ben resisted the urge to fall into his arms.

"You shouldn't be here," Titus said. "Go."

Ben, puzzled, shook his head. "But I came to you," he said. "I want you." The words came of their own accord, surprising him with their directness.

Titus shook his head. "You don't know what it is you ask," he said. "Please, go before you lose more than you already have."

He moved to shut the door, but Ben reached out and grabbed his hand. At his touch, Titus closed his eyes, as if the contact caused him pain.

"Let me in," said Ben. "I want to be here. I want to be with you."

Titus opened his eyes and looked into Ben's face. "I've already taken too much from you," he whispered.

Ben stepped forward, putting his other hand on Titus's chest. "I want you," he said, leaning in and trying to kiss Titus.

Titus turned his head, Ben's kiss landing on his cheek. Ben put his hands on either side of Titus's face and turned him back to face him.

Then he pressed his mouth against Titus's. For a moment Titus resisted. Then his lips parted and he drew Ben's tongue into his mouth.

Ben ran one hand down Titus's body, slipping it between his legs. Titus was hard, his prick pushing against the fabric of his pants. Ben squeezed it tightly. Titus pulled him inside the house, shutting the door behind them.

Ben took little notice of the house as Titus led him up a stairway to the second floor. Down a hallway, a door led into a bedroom. Titus drew him into the room and to the bed that was pushed against one wall. A single candle sitting on a bureau filled the room with pale light.

The mattress groaned as Ben sat on the edge of the bed. Titus, standing a few feet away, looked down at Ben. Moving slowly, he unbuttoned his shirt and let it fall from his shoulders onto the floor. His pants followed, Titus stepping out of them and pushing them aside with his foot. He stood before Ben naked, his cock jutting out from between his legs.

"Is this what you want?" he asked, his voice soft.

Ben nodded. Seeing Titus there before him, the desire that had taunted him all day quickened. He reached out to touch him. But Titus grabbed his wrists, holding them tightly in his fingers. Pressing forward, he pushed Ben back onto the bed, then climbed on top of him, straddling his waist so that he was leaning over Ben, his cock stretched out along Ben's stomach.

"Do you know what it is you want?" Titus asked him.

"You," Ben said. He could feel the heaviness of Titus's cock on him, the weight of his balls where they rested against his own imprisoned dick.

"You don't know what it is you ask," said Titus. "No idea of the price you might yet pay."

"I don't care," Ben said.

Titus shut his eyes. When he opened them, the gentleness that had been there, the worry, was gone. In its place was the dark light of passion. He bent down and kissed Ben, hard, his teeth biting at Ben's lip. Ben, groaning, pushed up against him.

Titus reached for Ben's shirt. Pulling roughly, he ripped it open, the buttons flying onto the floor. Ben's chest lay exposed to him. Titus moved forward, sliding his cock and balls over Ben's skin until the head of his dick rested on Ben's lips. Ben licked at it greedily, hoping Titus would give him more. But Titus taunted him, keeping his cock just out of reach.

"Please," Ben said breathlessly. "Give it to me."

In answer, Titus moved back down his body until he was standing beside the bed. Then he undid Ben's pants and pulled them off, leaving him naked. Ben's cock rested in the soft hair of his stomach.

Titus crawled back onto the bed, putting his hands beneath Ben's legs and lifting them up as he pushed forward. His head lowered towards Ben's cock, and Ben waited to feel the warmth of a mouth surround him. But Titus dipped passed Ben's dick and pressed into the space between the parted cheeks of his ass. A moment later, his tongue fluttered against Ben's asshole.

Ben moaned, closing his eyes as Titus's tongue entered him. He felt Titus's nose pressing against his balls as the other man's mouth worked over his opening, his tongue making warm, wet circles on Ben's skin. Titus pushed inside and retreated, gently easing Ben open.

Several times Ben thought he might come. Titus brought him close, then pulled away at the last moment, letting Ben's desire ebb a little before beginning again. Ben's balls, already aching, longed for release, but Titus teased them relentlessly.

Lifting his head from between Ben's legs, Titus knelt and looked down on him. Wordlessly, he positioned the head of his cock where his tongue had been moments before. Then he was inside, the thickness of him spreading Ben's hole even wider. Ben gasped at the invasion, his hands gripping the sheets as he tried to breathe.

Titus didn't wait for him. Pressing forward, he buried his cock in Ben's ass. Heat ripped through Ben's belly as Titus pulled back and slammed in again. All Ben could do was give in. He waited for the next thrust, trying to open to it. Again the pain came, a kind of delicious thrill that rippled through him.

His thoughts swirled in his head like a cyclone, images passing by and disappearing again as he lost himself in the rapture of the moment. Trey's face. Titus disappearing into the water. A dark cloud of tiny, buzzing things circling overhead. They all swirled around him, moving more and more quickly as Titus continued to piston in and out of him.

Then, just as Ben was picked up by the rush and carried to its highest point, Titus pulled out. Ben felt himself falling, the whirlwind that had lifted him gone and his body once more heavy with the weight of disappointment as he tumbled down through darkness.

He opened his eyes to save himself. Titus was on the floor, kneeling. His face was cupped in his hands. After a moment, he looked up.

"I won't do it," he said, speaking to himself and not to Ben.

Ben scrambled off the bed and knelt beside Titus. When he tried to touch him, Titus pushed him away roughly, so that Ben sprawled on the floor.

"I don't understand," Ben said.

Titus shook his head. "No," he said. "You don't."

"What did I do?" asked Ben.

"You did nothing," said Titus sadly. "Nothing at all."

"Then why—" Ben started to say.

"The funeral is tomorrow," Titus said, interrupting him. "For the Mickerley boy. Go to it. You'll find some answers there."

Ben stared at him, not comprehending. "What does the Mickerley boy have to do with this?"

"Go tomorrow," Titus said again.

Titus made no move to stand up. Ben hesitated for a moment, wanting him to say something else. Then he gathered up his clothes and pulled them on. His shirt, the buttons gone, hung open, but he didn't care. Giving Titus a final look, he left the bedroom and stumbled down the stairs to the front door.

Chapter Nine

The interior of the Holy Oak Gospel Church was packed. Ben took one of the few empty seats in a pew toward the back, sliding into it quietly and exchanging a nod with the sad-faced woman nearest to him. Dressed in black, she had the look of someone who had been crying for some time and no longer cared whether anyone knew it or not. He understood the feeling all too well, but he wasn't there to mourn.

He didn't really know why he was there. He'd left Titus's house the night before and gone home, trying to make sense of what had occurred between them. He didn't understand what had caused Titus to stop his lovemaking, or why he had insisted that Ben attend the funeral of Paul Mickerley. It was an absurd request, and one that Ben had intended to ignore completely right up to the moment he'd found himself pulling into the church parking lot.

He didn't like funerals. In truth, he'd only been to two—his paternal grandmother's when he was eight and then Trey's. That was enough. He'd been relieved when his father had decided against a funeral for Ben's mother. He didn't like being among the dead, even if it was to mark their passing. Excuses for public grief, he called them, opportunities for the assembled to let everyone know just how sad they were. He preferred to do his mourning in private, where only he had to deal with the embarrassment of the tears.

He had arrived late, and the service was well underway. At the front of the church a casket was placed on a table. It was open, and Ben avoided looking at the face of the dead boy inside. He knew what death looked like. It was an absence of spirit, a hollowness that no amount of makeup or embalming fluid could fill. Even the most beautiful corpses were still just shells, the material that had animated them having been extinguished at the moment of death.

Adding to his discomfort, the church stank of roses. They had been placed in enormous quantity around the sanctuary, bundles of red and pink and white that he knew were meant to suggest rebirth but which to him signified a vain attempt at erasing the smell of decay. *Ring around the rosy,* he thought grimly. *A pocket full of posies. Ashes. Ashes. We all fall down.* The childhood rhyme came to him, its words so sweet on the surface but so chilling underneath with their references to the horrors of bubonic plague, when the residents of afflicted cities carried flower petals in their pockets to ward off the stench of decaying corpses in the city streets. *We all fall down,* he thought again. *We all fall down.*

"Paul was my best friend."

Ben's attention turned to the speaker standing at the front of the room. It was a teenage boy. He was wearing jeans and a Creaverton Bandits varsity jacket, as were a great many of the young men scattered throughout the church. *Paul's football team,* Ben thought. Of course they would be here.

"We always talked about what we'd do when we finally got out of here," the boy continued. "You know, when we became famous football players and all."

A trickle of laughter greeted his remark, and the boy smiled self-consciously, as if he'd only been half joking and didn't like his secret dream being mocked. He glanced at the coffin.

"This shouldn't have happened," he said, his voice quavering. He began to sob, and a moment later he was joined by two of his teammates, who put their arms around him much as they might in a huddle on the field. They stood that way for a minute, until the moment was broken by the appearance of the minister, who had been sitting quietly in the front pew.

"I think these young men express what we're all feeling," he said, facing the congregation. "This *should* never have happened. But in his wisdom, God allowed it to happen. Why? We might never know. Maybe it's not for us to know. We are, after all, only the creations of his will."

Fuck you, Ben thought angrily. He wanted to stand up, to tell the minister that God was a big fucking joke, and that shitty things happened to people because the world was a shitty place. He wanted to tell everyone assembled that they *should* be crying, that they should be totally pissed off because what happened to Paul Mickerley was going to happen to them eventually and there was nothing they could do about it.

Instead, he sat quietly and nodded politely while the pastor continued to talk. Ben distracted himself by looking at the church's stained-glass windows. A series of them lined each side of the sanctuary, their colored pieces lit up by the sun that, defying tradition, had chosen to show up in place of the rain that was, if you chose to believe every Hollywood depiction of a burial, supposed to accompany every such occasion. Ben examined the images rendered in bits of color. The windows depicted the life of Christ, each one a different scene. They began with a window showing his birth, a single brilliant star set into a field of blue above a traditional nativity tableau, and ended with a vision of the crucifixion complete with mourners at the foot of the cross.

The window Ben found the most compelling, however, showed Jesus with several of his disciples. His hand touched the brow of one of them, and above the anointed one's head a flame danced. *The bestowing of the spirit*, thought Ben, digging into the recesses of memory for the explanation. He remembered it from a Sunday school lesson he'd sat through years ago, when he was not much more than five or six. His teacher, Mrs. Barnard, had described it for them using a series of cutout figures that she'd affixed to a black flannel-covered board.

As she'd explained it, Jesus had touched his followers and given to them the gift of eternal life. Ben, however, had thought that the figures merely looked as if their hair was on fire. When he said as much, he'd been rewarded with a look that suggested that not only would he not receive any cookies during the post-class snack time, but also that if Jesus himself were present Ben would almost certainly be in for a spanking.

Despite the experience, he found the image of the Holy Spirit appearing as a flame above the heads of the redeemed a fascinating one. Equally fascinating was the belief that someone could be given eternal life. That one had always amazed him. Once it had even comforted him, offering as it did the hope that there was something awaiting him after death. But he no longer believed that, no longer *wanted* to believe it. Reincarnation he could handle, but everlasting life, even in a place as glorious as the heaven Mrs. Barnard had described for her class, interested him not at all.

Something in the air around him shifted, and suddenly he was aware of people standing up. The service had apparently come to an end, and the mourners were preparing to leave. Ben stood with them, not sure what to do next. He allowed himself to be swept into the tide of people leaving the church, and a minute later found himself standing on the steps. He stepped to one side, allowing people to file past him.

"Are you going to the cemetery?" a man standing nearby asked him.

Ben shook his head. "I don't think so," he said.

The man nodded. "How did you know Paul?"

Ben thought for a moment. He hadn't counted on being asked such a question, and he wasn't certain how to respond. The truth, of course, was that he hadn't known Paul Mickerley at all. But to admit as much to someone at his funeral seemed inappropriate.

"I'm a librarian," he said finally. It was hardly an answer, but at least it was the truth. "And you?"

"I work for the police department," the man replied. "I was one of the guys who went to get him."

"I'm sorry," Ben said automatically. "That must have been difficult."

"No kid should die like that," the man answered, as if Ben had been referring to Paul's death, and not to the experience of having to put his body in a bag and seal it shut.

"Do they know what happened yet?" Ben asked him.

The man shook his head. "No fucking clue," he said. "Not one damn clue. How he got into that graveyard is a total mystery."

"The graveyard," Ben said. "That's not where they're burying him, is it?"

"Christ, no," the man said. "Not that one. No one has been buried in that place in over a hundred years."

"Where exactly is it?" asked Ben.

"Up in the hills," answered the man, nodding in the general direction of the area west of the church. "On old Cold Creek Road."

Ben nodded, as if he knew exactly where the man was describing. Then he excused himself, leaving the police officer to join the rest of the people filing into cars and heading for the burial.

Getting into his own car, he left the church parking lot and turned in the opposite direction of the funeral procession. For some reason, he wanted to see the place where Paul Mickerley had died. He'd learned nothing at the funeral, at least nothing he could imagine was responsible for Titus's behavior the night before. Perhaps, he thought, the answers he was looking for lay elsewhere, and the place where Paul Mickerley died seemed as likely a spot as any to begin looking.

Finding Cold Creek Road was easy. Getting to the end of it was not. A twisting, turning path that wound through the hills, it clearly had not been regularly traveled in many years. Its dirt track was badly rutted in places, and several times Ben almost turned around. But something urged him on, and finally he found himself arriving at what he recognized, even in its disrepair, as a cemetery.

In front of it was a foundation of stone. A few broken timbers remained standing from the rocks, but the whole of it was overgrown with creepers and trees that had sprung up from the rotting wood. Ben walked past the remains of what he assumed had been a church and entered the graveyard. Many of the stones were broken, jagged teeth rising from the green mouth of the earth. Many more were so worn by wind and rain and time that the names on them had been obscured.

Still, some remained readable. Ben stooped and looked at one. MARY PATIENCE OSBOURNE, it read. 1846–1869. INTO GOD'S HANDS WE DELIVER YOU. A crude carving of an angel adorned the stone, its expression one of passive watchfulness. Ben stood and continued his walk through the garden of the dead.

Finding the place where Paul Mickerley had been discovered was also not difficult. Yellow ribbons of police tape remained affixed to the trees on either side, their torn ends fluttering in the faint breeze. The grass around the site had been trampled flat by many feet, and the ghostly sheen of powder dusted one of the tombstones, indicating, Ben assumed, the stone against which Mickerley's body had been placed.

He knelt in the grass and looked at the stone. The top had been broken, a piece removed like a bite taken from a cookie. What remained was covered with a thin layer of moss that filled much of the carving, making the inscription difficult to read. Ben could just make out the rough shape of a skull at the top of the stone, its eyes round and its teeth mossy. Part of it was gone, removed along with the bit of missing stone, so that the skull had only one eye.

The dates on the stone were 1812–1832, and below these was written NO MORE TO ROAM. The name was more difficult to decipher. Ben could make out some of the letters—an A, a C, some Es. These were followed by a P, what looked like an L, and a pair of Os. The rest was covered in moss. With his fingers, Ben pulled at it, removing the bits of green from the letters. It flaked away easily, revealing the name little by little.

"Wallace Pyle Blackwood," Ben read when he was finished. He stared at it. "Wallace Pyle Blackwood," he repeated as what he was seeing began to sink in.

Chapter Ten

"Why did you send me there?"

Ben stood in the backyard of Titus's house. He'd come there directly from the old cemetery. Titus was standing by his hives, preparing to remove the top from one of them.

"Let's go inside," Titus said. "This isn't the place."

"Not until you tell me what's going on," Ben demanded. "Why did you send me to that funeral? And why is Wallace Blackwood's name on that gravestone?"

"Please," said Titus. "Inside."

Ben hesitated. He was angry, and afraid, and he did not want to be alone with Titus inside his house. He didn't know what to think, or what to believe.

Ignoring Ben's hesitation, Titus walked toward the door. After a moment, Ben followed him. They entered the house's kitchen, where Titus sat down at the table. Ben remained standing.

"I didn't want any of this to happen," said Titus.

"Any of what?" asked Ben. "Sleeping with me? What?"

Titus looked at him. His eyes looked tired. "What do you know of vampires?" he asked.

Ben shrugged. "They suck blood. Who the fuck cares?"

"Wallace Blackwood was a vampire," said Titus.

Ben stared at him. "A vampire," he repeated.

Titus nodded. "That was his grave that you saw. His first grave. His most recent one is not marked."

"I saw his *name* on that stone," Ben said. "But that wasn't the same Wallace Blackwood. That's not possible."

"It is possible," replied Titus. "And yes, that was the very Wallace Blackwood who formerly occupied your position."

Ben laughed. "Okay," he said. "I'll be leaving now. Because *you* are nuts. I don't know what happened here the other night, but it's over now. So let's just both forget about it, okay? I'll be seeing you."

He turned to leave, one hand on the handle of the door.

"He's come back," Titus said. "That's who you saw swimming in the pond the other night, not me."

Ben froze.

"Wallace Blackwood. He's come back. Not in the same form, but he's back. He killed that boy. He'll come for you."

Ben turned. "What kind of sick game is this?" he asked, growing angry. He walked toward the table. "Do you get off on this? Is that it? You like seducing guys and then playing with their heads?"

"I wish I were playing," said Titus. "But this is no game. It's very real. Wallace Blackwood killed that boy."

"How do you know that?" Ben asked.

"Because he killed me once," Titus answered.

Ben said nothing, looking at Titus's face. The man seemed perfectly ordinary. Not at all like a crazy person, Ben thought. But what he was saying was completely unbelievable. Surely he must be mad.

"In 1832, Wallace Blackwood died for the first time," said Titus. "He rose again several nights later when the virus in his blood grew strong enough to revive him. Half mad, he lived in the hills, feeding on whatever came his way. The Creaverton Demon they called him, and they weren't much mistaken. No one but his victims ever saw him, but he claimed many lives. These deaths were blamed on many things: bears, Indians, accidents, even witchcraft. Yet no witch could do what Wallace Blackwood did. Nor could any demon. Only the living dead could kill like that, draining his catch of their blood and casting them aside like empty husks for the earth to reclaim."

Titus's voice had taken on a weary quality to it, as if he were telling a story he had long ago tired of. Although Ben still thought he was delusional, or worse, he sat in the chair opposite him and listened as Titus continued.

"After a time, he came again to reside among the living. He made his home among them, and none of them knew what he really was. He'd learned to fill their heads with memories, with remembrances of things that had never happened, people who had never lived. They believed he'd always been among them. And when he took from them, they looked elsewhere for explanations."

Titus looked at Ben. "You asked Martha Abraham about him, didn't you?"

Ben nodded.

"And what did she say?"

"She said Wally came here during the Depression," he said.

Titus nodded. "Still he clouds their minds," he said. "His power is very strong. No doubt they remember little of the events of that summer."

"1932?" Ben asked.

"Yes," answered Titus. "That summer, Blackwood grew hungry. The sickness in him had grown stronger, and he sought to quench it with the blood of children."

"Blackwood?" said Ben. "What about John Rullins?"

Titus gave a small laugh. "John Rullins knew nothing of it," he said. "Blackwood made them all think it was the tinker who did his work."

"How do you know all of this?" Ben asked.

"Because I helped him," said Titus softly. "I helped him kill."

"You couldn't have," said Ben. "You weren't even alive then."

"No," Titus said. "I wasn't alive. Blackwood killed me seven years before. Nonetheless, I was walking the earth, and I helped him murder those children."

Ben rubbed his eyes with his hands. "Maybe I'm the one going crazy," he said. "I need to get out of here."

He started to rise, but Titus caught his wrist. His grip was stronger than Ben remembered it, and no matter how hard he tried to pull away, Titus's grip remained firm.

"Let me go," Ben said, growing fearful.

"It won't matter," Titus told him. "You can't run now. All you can do is listen."

Ben struggled for another moment. Then, realizing that he would never be able to pull away, he sat. Titus released his wrist and Ben rubbed it, soothing the burning skin.

"There is much about the world that you don't know," said Titus. "The sickness that keeps Blackwood and myself alive is one of them. I pray that you never know it."

"What is this sickness you keep talking about?" Ben asked. "You said Blackwood was a vampire."

"Yes," said Titus. "He is. As am I."

"You?" repeated Ben. "You're a vampire?"

"Yes," Titus said. "I have the sickness."

"Then why can you walk around in the sunshine?" Ben asked. "Vampires can't do that."

Titus smiled. "Neither can we tolerate the touch of holy water or the sign of the cross, right?"

"Right," Ben said decisively.

"Superstitions," said Titus. "Lies, most of them created by the old ones to make their prey think they could protect themselves. But none of it is true."

"Of course not," Ben said. "Just like none of this bullshit you're feeding me is."

"What would you have me do to prove myself to you?" asked Titus. "Drain your blood and make you like me? Would that satisfy you?"

Ben looked at him nervously. He didn't know how to reply. Every ounce of common sense he had was telling him that Titus was lying. Yet another part of him believed, or at least wanted to believe, that he was speaking the truth.

"I had my chance to infect you," said Titus. "Last night. I could have done it then."

"Last night?" Ben said. "What, when you were fucking me?"

Titus nodded. "I was tempted," he said. "It would have allowed us to be together, much as Wallace wanted me to be with him forever."

"You and Wallace were lovers?" Ben asked him.

"Why do you think I helped him kill?" answered Titus. "I loved him. I believed his lies. But I was young. I didn't understand then what the sickness could do. When I saw what he was truly made of, I destroyed him."

"You killed him? But Martha said he died of—" He paused. He couldn't remember what Martha had said was the cause of Wally's death.

"She didn't say how he died, did she?" asked Titus.

Ben searched his memory, trying to recall any explanation Martha might have given him. Finally, he shook his head in defeat. "No," he said. "She didn't. She just said he died after his book came out."

"Yes, the book," Titus said. "His masterpiece. If only I'd known about it beforehand, I might have stopped him."

"Stopped him?" said Ben. "From what? Publishing it?"

"Reviving the lies," Titus said. "Planting the seed of doubt in the minds of the town once more."

"I don't understand," said Ben.

"He was planning on trying again," said Titus. "He thought enough time had passed. The book was meant to rekindle the sparks of fear, so that when the killings began again people would remember John Rullins and once again find someone to blame."

"But the book claimed that Rullins was innocent," Ben said. "Blackwood blamed his death on mob hysteria."

"That was Wallace's vanity," said Titus. "He could never stand that Rullins got the credit for the killings, even though it spared him. Still, he knew that people would be looking for a human explanation for what he had planned, and that the memory of Rullins would lead them to another monster."

"They'd think that someone read the book and decided to recreate the crimes," said Ben, understanding.

"Yes," Titus replied. "It was a good plan."

"But you stopped him?" said Ben. "How?"

"There are ways of killing the undead," Titus explained. "I used one of them. But my work was not complete, because now he's returned."

"How do you know that?" asked Ben.

"I can sense him in the world," Titus said. "And I know his hand when I see it."

"Paul Mickerley," Ben said. "Why did he leave his body where it could be found?"

"Again, vanity," said Titus. "To announce his return. To stir up fear. He feeds on that as much as on the blood of those he takes."

Ben hesitated before speaking. "Let's assume I believe any of this," he said finally. "Let's assume I actually believe that you and Wallace Blackwood are both vampires. If he killed so many people, why should I believe you haven't?"

"I have," answered Titus. "Before I understood what I am, I killed too. But not in many years."

"How is that possible?" Ben asked. "Don't you need blood to live?"

"Only to stay young," said Titus. "I no longer wish to be young at that price. I have found a way to fight the sickness."

"How?" Ben asked, curious despite his skepticism.

Titus stood up. "Come with me," he said. "I'll show you."

Chapter Eleven

"Isn't she beautiful?" Titus asked. "Her name is *Apis mellifera ligustica*. The Italian honey bee."

He held up the jar so that Ben could see the bee inside. It clung to the glass, its antennae in constant motion. Its golden abdomen was ringed with five bands of darker brown. When Titus set the jar down, the bee buzzed angrily.

"She's a worker," Titus told Ben. "Her lifespan is only about two to three weeks in the summer. She works tirelessly, flying out in search of food to bring back to the hive for her queen. Then she dies."

Ben looked around the room Titus had brought him to. It was in a small barn-like structure behind the house, past the collection of hives. The walls were lined with shelves, which in turn were lined with row upon row of tiny glass bottles. In each one a bee waited.

"Do you know anything about bees?" asked Titus.

Ben shook his head. "Only that they make honey," he replied, eyeing the collection of bottles nervously.

"That is the least interesting thing about them," said Titus.

"I'm sure it is," Ben said. "Can I ask what you're doing with them?"

Titus smiled. "I don't blame you for being afraid of them," he said. "Most people are."

He picked up a pair of tweezers from the workbench and unscrewed the lid to the jar he'd been looking at. Reaching inside, he deftly pinned the bee between the blades of the tweezers and lifted it out. The bee buzzed loudly, its trapped legs flailing.

"What are you doing?" Ben asked.

"The bee's sting is generally incorrectly referred to as its stinger," Titus said, ignoring the question. "But the instrument and its action are more rightly called by the same name. It does what it is."

Rolling up the sleeve of his shirt, he placed the bee against his skin near his wrist. Ben watched, horrified, as he pressed the insect down. Its abdomen tapped against Titus's skin several times, then stayed in one position. Titus closed his eyes.

"The sting is barbed," he said. "Edged like a saw blade. It tears through the flesh, and because of its teeth it sticks in the body of its victim."

The bee was struggling. Titus released it from the tweezers' hold and it walked away, crawling up his arm for a space of several inches before suddenly falling to the workbench.

"When either the bee or the victim pulls away, the sting is torn from the bee's body, taking with it the poison sac," said Titus, his eyes still closed. "The sac remains attached to the sting, pumping poison into the wound for a minute or longer. The design is perfect, except for one thing." He opened his eyes and looked at Ben. "The bee that gives up its sting must die as a result."

Ben glanced at the bee that had fallen onto the workbench. It was still, neither its antennae nor its legs moving. Titus picked it up and looked at it, an expression of sadness on his face.

"She gives up her life," he said softly, "in order that I might live."

"I don't understand," Ben said. "What do these bees have to do with you being a . . . with you being sick?"

"Do you know what a vampire is?" Titus asked him.

Ben shrugged. "A creature that drinks blood in order to live forever," he said.

"In part that's true," said Titus. "But it's not the whole story. I'm afraid we can thank the storytellers for turning the sickness into something more romantic than it really is."

"Then what is it exactly?" Ben asked him.

Titus leaned against the workbench. "A virus," he said. "A virus very much like any other that causes sickness. Only in this case, the end effect is eternal life."

"That sounds more like a cure to me," remarked Ben.

"A cure that comes with a great price," Titus said. "The virus keeps the organs alive, but to do so it destroys the red blood cells at an alarming rate. In order to replenish them, the vampire must drink the blood of its victims."

"And if it doesn't drink?" asked Ben.

"It dies," said Titus. "Or, more accurately, it begins the process of decaying. But even this takes many years to complete. In the meantime, the vampire exists as a kind of animated corpse."

"The living dead," Ben said.

Titus nodded. "Yes, the living dead."

"And the people who are bitten?" Ben said. "Do they become vampires too?"

"Not if they are completely drained," said Titus. "If there is no blood in them, the virus has nothing to live off of and it dies along with its new host. But if the body is not drained, then the virus takes hold and multiplies quickly. That's what happened to me. It's why Blackwood drained all the others."

"I still don't understand what the bees have to do with it," said Ben.

Titus rubbed the spot on his wrist where the bee had stung him. A red welt had appeared. "When a bee stings and its venom enters the body, the body responds by attacking the foreign antigens. It's a kind of war, pitting the body's defenses against the invaders. The same virus that causes the sickness and keeps the organs alive also attacks the venom. As long as it's busy battling the antigens, it can't destroy the red blood cells."

"Whatever happened to vampires just being dead bodies inhabited by evil?" Ben asked. "You make it sound like a medical condition."

"It is," answered Titus. "It's not magic. I used to think it was. Wallace wanted me to think it was. But it's not, although it does eventually provide the vampire with certain powers as a result of its work."

"How did you think of doing this?" Ben asked.

"I read an article," replied Titus.

"An article," Ben repeated.

"Again, it wasn't magic," said Titus. "I didn't find some ancient book of spells or a gypsy herbal remedy for the affliction. I read an article about people with MS being treated with bee stings. In the bodies of people with MS, the cells that are supposed to defend the body actually attack it, interrupting the pathways that send messages from the brain to the muscles. When stung, the body reacts by fighting the bee venom instead. While it's doing that, the communication pathways function more or less normally, allowing the patient a brief period of relief from pain."

"This is completely insane," said Ben after a moment. "First you want me to believe that you're a vampire, and that Wallace Blackwood was a vampire too. Now you want me to believe that somehow stinging yourself with bees keeps you from needing to drink blood?"

"I know how it must sound," Titus said.

"How it must *sound*?" Ben exclaimed. "I'll tell you how it sounds. It sounds totally fucking ridiculous."

"What do you want me to tell you?" Titus asked. "Do you want me to tell you that we all live in coffins? Do you want me to tell you that we're poor tortured souls who can never find rest? Do you want me to tell you that my life is like an Anne Rice novel? Would you believe me then?"

"No," Ben snapped. "I wouldn't believe you. I wouldn't believe you if you suddenly turned into a bat and flapped out of here. I wouldn't believe you if you had pointy teeth and a black cape."

Titus stared at him silently for a moment. "You're a fool," he said finally. "And I'm a bigger fool for thinking I could trust you."

"I should go," said Ben.

Titus nodded.

Ben turned around. The doorway of the shed was filled with the golden light of afternoon. Behind him, Titus stood in the shadows, surrounded by the jars of bees. For a moment, Ben almost went back to him. Then he walked forward, heading as quickly as he could for the light.

Chapter Twelve

Vampires. Ben laughed. How could Titus ever have thought he would believe such a story? It was ridiculous. And all that nonsense about the bees—what had that been about? What kind of twisted person stung himself with bees?

A *freak*, Ben told himself. *That's who.*

He was in the library. *Where he belonged*, he reminded himself. He'd spent too much time away from the place in the past few days, too much time chasing after nothing. It was time he got back to his job.

"Hey, Mr. Hodge? Where would I find more of those Edward Eager books?" Steven Settles popped his head out from behind the bookshelf he was scanning. He'd come in an hour earlier, returning the books he'd checked out on his previous visit and anxious for more.

"In the second row," Ben called out to him. "First shelf."

Steven retreated into the children's room, a moment later calling out, "I found them!"

So much for quiet, thought Ben. But he didn't care. He was pleased to have Steven around, both because watching the boy's interest in reading blossom was rewarding and also because it made the library feel less lonely.

"Which one should I read?" Steven asked him, coming up to the desk with three books in his hand. "*Half Magic, The Time Garden,* or *Knight's Castle?*"

"*Half Magic* is my favorite," Ben replied. "I'd take that one."

Steven nodded. "I'll put these back," he said, leaving the chosen book on the counter and taking the others back to the children's room.

Ben picked up the book. He'd first read *Half Magic* when he was about Steven's age. He'd been enchanted by the story of four siblings who discovered a magic talisman that granted their wishes. The trick was that it only gave them half of what they wished for, so they had to figure out how to wish properly. Their bumbling attempts at mastering the art made the book a great read.

Back then, Ben had wished that he too could find a magic talisman. Now, though, the idea of magic made him uneasy. Even though he didn't believe Titus's tales of vampirism and bizarre cures, the notion of anything supernatural occurring in the world was unpleasant to think about.

"I hope this one's as good as *Magic By the Lake*," said Steven, coming back to sign out the book.

"It's better," Ben reassured him, taking the checkout card from the rear of the book and filing it away.

A honk sounded outside the library, and Steven looked toward the door. "That's Darren," he said.

"How come he never checks out any books?" Ben asked.

Steven blushed a little. "He says only fags read books," he said.

"Oh, really?" said Ben. "Well, you tell him that only morons *don't* read books."

Steven laughed. "I'll see you later," he said happily, running for the door.

When he was gone, Ben went back to his office and sat at his desk. The box of books he'd brought up from the cellar still sat on the floor next to his chair. Reaching inside, he brought out *Dreaming Demons*. He flipped open the cover and looked at Wallace Blackwood's photograph on the back flap. A handsome middle-aged face looked back at him. But how old would Blackwood have been at the time of publication? he wondered. Surely in his late 60s or early 70s. Yet the man in the photo looked a good twenty years younger than that.

"It's probably just an old photo," Ben said. He'd met more than one author whose appearance in person made his or her author photo look like it had been snipped from the pages of a high school yearbook. Most likely Wallace Blackwood had just been vain.

He put the book down and looked in the box again. This time he took out *Haints and Haunts of the Ozarks*. The title had intrigued him the first time he'd seen it, and he wanted to look at the book more closely. Opening it, he read part of the introduction.

"No region other than perhaps the Catskill Mountains of Washington Irving's imagination have housed so many goblins as the Ozark Mountains," he read. "Its woods and dells are home to spirits, imps, and beasts whose nightmarish countenances and evil intentions would rouse even Rip Van Winkle from his dreams, such is their power to inspire horror."

Ben flipped through the book, looking at the chapter headings. The author, Sadie Filkins Ransome, had apparently collected every Ozark legend she could lay her hands on and detailed them in her book. She'd also gotten someone to illustrate it with black and white drawings, most of which featured people running from one strange creature or another.

Ben was going to put the book away when he flipped by an illustration that caught his eye. Locating it again, he looked at the drawing more closely. It depicted a hideous-looking creature standing in a cemetery. It was dressed in the remains of once-elegant clothes, the scraps hanging from its skeletal frame like ribbons. Its nails and hair were long and dirty, and its eyes were hollow and spectral. Its arms were raised in a crooked gesture.

He looked at the page opposite the drawing. "Some of the earliest reports of strange goings-on in the Ozarks came from early settlers, who reported that from time to time they would find graves disturbed and their inhabitants missing. Days, weeks, and even months later, loved ones of the missing would report receiving visits from the dead, who demanded that they be fed. When refused, the dead would become violent, often attacking the living and attempting to bite them. At least 17 fatalities in early communities were attributed to these creatures, which came to be known as Death Puppets due to their ungainly way of moving, as if they were being controlled by unseen hands that animated their limbs."

Ben looked at the drawing again. The creature did indeed look as if it were engaged in some kind of gruesome dance. He could just imagine it twitching as it moved, its arms and legs thrashing about in mindless motions, like a spider in its death throes.

He continued to read. "The greatest number of deaths attributed to Death Puppets occurred in the remote community of Dunbart, in the northwest part of the state. There, a total of nine deaths were blamed on the creatures before they were eventually rounded up and destroyed in 1832, reportedly by setting them afire.

"While the parallels between the Death Puppets and the vampires of Old Europe are clear and obvious, it is interesting to note that residents of the area regarded the Death Puppets as being very different. Their resurrection and subsequent penchant for violence was believed not to be merely a thirst for blood but the result of some kind of curse on the afflicted families, a punishment for improper or impure behavior. Communities experiencing torment by a Death Puppet sometimes allegedly took revenge not only on the creature itself but on its family as well. Undocumented reports tell of men, women, and even children being killed by townspeople as penance, or perhaps as sacrifice, in an attempt at breaking the curse and bringing an end to the Death Puppet risings."

Ben shut the book and pushed it away from him. "They're all insane," he said. "Every last one of them."

He knew the book was simply a collection of folklore, and not a history book. Still, the fact that someone would come up with something as horrific as the Death Puppets was disturbing. *Maybe Martha was right*, he thought. *Maybe I have landed in the middle of a bunch of crazies.*

He picked the book up and dropped it unceremoniously into the box with the others, following it with *Dreaming Demons.* He was beginning to understand why Martha had removed all of Wallace's personal collection from the library shelves. The books were sick, filled with weird images and even weirder ideas. Heaven forbid someone should read them and believe the crap in them.

Someone like Titus, he thought. Yes, that was probably what had happened. Titus had read those books and dreamed up a whole story about vampires and curses and whatever the fuck else was rolling around inside his head. Maybe he and Wallace *had* been lovers, and this was his way of dealing with the man's death.

But if Titus and Wallace had been lovers, he thought, *Titus couldn't have been more than twelve or thirteen at the time.* Suddenly it all became clear to him. If Titus had been involved with Blackwood in that

way, perhaps he'd seen the older man's obsession with the dead boys
from the 1932 killings as some kind of threat. Maybe he'd been an-
gered by it, even angry enough to kill Wallace.

It made sense. If Titus had been the victim of a pedophile, he
would likely have looked for a way to deal with what had happened to
him. It was a classic response to abuse, inventing a far-fetched explanation to avoid dealing with what had really happened. Ben had read
stories about such people, people who claimed to have been abducted
by aliens, used in Satanic rituals, or even utilized in secret government
experiments—anything to avoid confronting the horrible things that
had been done to them.

Such people, he knew, were to be pitied. Yet sometimes their delu-
sions simply spread their misery to others, infecting the people around
them and continuing the hurt and pain. Sometimes, innocent people
became caught in the snare of lies, people who paid dearly for stumbling into those traps.

He brushed the thought away. There was no time to entertain it.
What mattered was that he had found the root of Titus Durham's behavior. He was sure of it.

But what about the other boy? The question stopped him cold. *What
about Paul Mickerley?*

Yes, what about Paul Mickerley? Who had killed him? And what
about the name on the tombstone? Why had it matched Blackwood's?

The answer to the second question escaped him. But the answer to
the first was apparent and chilling. Had Titus killed Paul Mickerley? Is
that why he'd told Ben to go to the funeral, as a way of confessing? Ben
didn't want to think so, but everything pointed to that as the answer.
Paul had been a handsome young man. Perhaps Titus, seeing him
somewhere, had become obsessed with him. Perhaps it had triggered
memories of his own abuse at the hands of Wallace Blackwood, memories that had caused him to kill.

I had my chance. The words came back to Ben with chilling clarity.
He could hear Titus speaking them, his voice heavy with regret. *I could
have done it then.* Titus had said that his shame came from having entertained the thought of harming Ben. But now Ben saw that wasn't
true.

He was going to kill me, he thought.

Chapter Thirteen

Ben tried the knob for the third time. It was locked. He resisted trying it again and moved to the windows. Pushing the locks shut, he made sure they were secure. Then he drew the curtains over the panes, closing the house in. He went to the kitchen and did the same there, locking the back door and testing each window to make sure it couldn't be opened. *They could always be smashed,* he thought with some small concern, but he would be sure to hear the noise.

Upstairs he went from room to room, first checking the closets and behind the doors and then shutting up the windows. He saved the bedroom for last. There, he left the windows open. It was too hot, for one thing. Besides, there were no trees or trellises outside for someone to climb up. A ladder would have to be used. Although he was certain he would hear someone attempting such a thing, he placed several empty glasses on the windowsill. If someone tried to enter, no matter how stealthily, the glasses would fall to the floor and shatter, giving him enough time to grab the baseball bat he'd placed next to the bed.

The last thing he did was shut and lock his own bedroom door. It had a sliding bolt on it, one that could only be opened from the inside, so there was no way an intruder could enter without using violent force. Once he was certain the house was as safe as he could make it, he got into bed. He hesitated a moment, then turned off the light. The moon, still bright, filled the room with enough light to see by.

Pulling the sheet up, Ben stared at the door, as if at any moment he expected to hear fists pounding on it, demanding entry.

"Just relax," he told himself. "He can't get in."

He didn't really think that Titus would come after him. Still, he wasn't taking any chances. If Titus had killed both Wallace Blackwood and Paul Mickerley—and more and more Ben was believing that he had—then he was likely capable of anything. Tomorrow, he told himself, he would go to the police and tell them what he knew.

He continued to watch the door until his eyes grew weary and his head began to nod against his chest. Several times he forced himself awake, but shortly after one o'clock he began to snore softly.

"Ben."

The voice rippled across the surface of his dreams. Ben turned in his sleep.

"Ben."

His eyes fluttered. Someone was calling him. He heard the voice as if through water, faint and distorted.

"Ben, wake up."

Ben struggled to swim up from the depths of slumber. Someone was tapping at the door. No, someone was drumming his fingers on the door, the rhythmic motions filling the room with muffled retorts. Suddenly, the noise seemed to be coming from all around him.

Rain. The word came to him from somewhere inside his thoughts. *It's raining.* He listened. Yes, that's what it was. Rain was falling on the roof above his head. That was all. It was a reassuring sound, steady and gentle. Having declared that all was well with the world, sleep pulled heavily at his mind, trying to drag him under again.

But he resisted. Someone had called him. He'd heard it. Someone was in the room, speaking his name. It hadn't been just the rain. He tried to get his dream-clouded eyes to open and focus on the world around him.

When he did, he saw that his bedroom door was open. Someone was standing in it, a black place in the shadows cast by the dresser and the bed. He sat up, suddenly frightened, and reached for the bat. His fingers searched, finding nothing.

"A storm is passing through."

The figure detached itself from the shadows and moved forward into the light. As moonlight fell across its face, Ben felt his heart jump in his chest.

"Trey?" he said, his voice a whisper.

The figure walked to the window, looking out at the moon and the rain. Then it sat in the chair facing the bed. It certainly looked like Trey. Ben stared at him. There was the face he remembered so clearly, the soft eyes, the full mouth, and the nose, slightly turned up at the end. Trey smiled. "I've missed you," he said.

Ben rubbed his eyes. Was he awake, or was this yet another dream? It seemed real enough. He could hear the rain, smell it on the breeze that came through the window. He could smell something else as well, the scent of earth or wood. He couldn't quite place it.

"How are you here?" asked Ben.

Trey laughed, the rich sound rolling over Ben and making his skin prickle in recognition. How many times had Trey laughed like that with him? He'd missed that sound so much, longed to hear it so many times since Trey's death.

"I brought you something," said Trey.

Ben looked at the item that Trey held out in his hands. Trey was wearing a white T-shirt, and when he extended his hands Ben saw the scars on his wrists. He looked away.

"It's all right," said Trey. "I'm whole again."

Ben looked into his face. Surely he was dreaming. But if he was, he hoped never to wake up. He looked down again. Trey was holding out a shoebox.

"This is for you," he said.

Ben recognized the shoebox. It had sat for many months on the floor of their bedroom closet in New York. But Ben had thrown it out when he'd moved, tossed it along with some worn-out shoes and back issues of the *New Yorker* into the apartment's trash chute, listened as it slid down to the bowels of the basement and landed with a soft thud. He'd been glad to be rid of it.

"No." He shook his head, staring at his lover in confusion.

"You need to remember," Trey said gently. "For me."

"I don't want it," Ben said.

"Remember," Trey said, setting the box on the nightstand and getting out of the chair.

"Where are you going?" Ben asked.

"I can't stay," said Trey.

Ben tried to pull the sheets off of himself, but they had become entangled in his legs. He pulled at them frantically, attempting to get out of the bed.

"Goodbye, Ben," Trey said.

Ben looked up. Trey was fading. Already Ben could see the pattern of the wallpaper behind him.

"No!" he cried. "No."

Trey grew fainter and fainter, finally dissolving into nothingness just as Ben managed to free himself from the sheets and jump out of bed. At the last moment, Ben's foot caught in the sheets again and he fell to the floor.

He awoke with a start, his head spinning and a throbbing pain in his side. He was on the floor, looking up at the ceiling. But how long had he been there? He wasn't sure. Had he just woken up, and had Trey indeed been nothing but a trick of his imagination? Or had he lain there for some time, knocked out by the fall?

You were dreaming, he told himself. *Of course you were dreaming. Trey wasn't here.*

He sat up. It was still night, and it was indeed raining. The rain was coming down harder now, striking the roof in a quick patter. The wind had changed direction, and some of the rain was being blown into the room. Ben could feel it hitting his skin, and there was a small damp patch on the floor beneath the window.

Standing up, he went and pulled the window closed. The rain tapped against the glass, protesting loudly. Ben straightened the curtains and turned to get back into bed.

The shoebox was on the nightstand, just where Trey had left it. Ben stared at it, cold fingers of fear stroking the back of his neck. How had it gotten there? Not by his hand. He'd destroyed the box, he was sure of it.

Maybe you didn't, he told himself. *Maybe you only* think *you did. But maybe you packed it along with your sweaters and your ties.*

He looked at the box again. Maybe he *had* saved it after all. He glanced at the bedroom door. It was still locked from the inside. No one could have gotten in. But in his dream, it had been open.

Because you imagined it all, he admonished himself. *Trey wasn't here.*

He touched the shoebox hesitantly, stroking the surface with his fingers. It was real. He wasn't imagining it. Turning on the light, he picked the box up and sat in the chair. He held the box in his hands for a long time before removing the top.

Inside were newspaper clippings. They had begun to yellow. Looking at them, Ben felt a sense of dread filling him. He didn't want to look at them. He'd read them all a thousand times each, trying to make sense of what had happened. He didn't want to relive that again.

Yet he found himself picking up the first clipping and looking at it. PREP SCHOOL MATH TEACHER ACCUSED OF MOLESTING STUDENT, the headline read. Beneath it, a picture of Trey. Ben read the text, reciting most of it from memory.

> A popular math teacher at prestigious Cole Academy was arrested today after a student accused him of making sexual advances during after-school tutoring sessions. Trey Middleman, 33, was picked up by police without incident while exiting the school. His accuser, an unnamed 16-year-old, alleges that Middleman exposed himself and suggested that the boy could receive a passing grade in the class if he performed oral sex on him.

Ben put the clipping down. He knew the rest. The mention of Trey's "homosexual partner," the suggestion that there might be more than one "victim," the quotes from concerned parents expressing their fears that a gay teacher might be preying on their sons.

He knew, too, the name of the unnamed 16-year-old. Peter Ellis Lipton. Pete. He had been one of Trey's favorite students, a nice kid with a great sense of humor. Then something had changed. Pete had become sullen, withdrawn. His grades had plummeted. Trey discovered that Pete's parents, stars in the firmament of New York society, were divorcing. He took Pete under his wing, offering to help him with his studies after school.

And then came the accusation of molestation. Trey had been stunned. Of course he hadn't done it, would never have thought of doing such a thing. But Pete's father and mother, reuniting for the battle over their son's innocence, had pulled strings in the DA's office and ensured that the case was given top priority. Charges were quickly filed, and Trey had found himself facing a lengthy and very public trial.

Ben riffled through the collection of articles, looking for one near the bottom. He knew what those would say as well, in headlines even bigger than the ones announcing Trey's arrest. He found one and unfolded it. ACCUSED PREP SCHOOL MOLESTER COMMITS SUICIDE.

He didn't need to read the article. He'd been the one to find Trey, the evening before his first scheduled court appearance. Ben had opened the bathroom door to tell Trey that dinner was ready. He'd found his lover resting in a sea of pink. His wrists, held below the water, had been neatly slashed. The blood had long since drained from his body, and Trey's head had fallen to one side, resting on his shoulder. The razor blade, a red thread glistening on its edge, sat neatly on the edge of the tub.

There had been no note, no last declaration of innocence or plea for forgiveness. This, more than anything, seemed to enrage those who had already convicted Trey of the crime. It was as if he had robbed them of their rage, taken away their chance to sacrifice him by doing it himself. Even Ben and Trey's friends hadn't understood. "Why would he do something like that if he was innocent?" one had asked.

Ben understood why, but he still blamed himself for not saving Trey, for not loving him enough to somehow make facing the ordeal of a trial endurable. If he'd just been a little stronger, he thought, things might have ended differently. Instead, his lover was dead and he was alone with his guilt.

He crumpled the article up and dropped it into the shoebox. Had he really brought the box of memories with him? It didn't matter. What mattered was that they had returned. But why, he wondered, had Trey told him to remember? Why would he want to stir those ghosts from their graves?

So that you can redeem yourself, a voice in his mind answered. *To give you another chance.*

Ben looked at the shoebox. That was it. He understood now. He hadn't been able to save Trey. But perhaps he could save someone else, someone else who was innocent of any crime. Someone Titus Durham wanted to kill.

Chapter Fourteen

"Mr. Hodge? I'm Harris Finch."

Ben stood and took the officer's extended hand. He was seated in the police chief's office, a small room at the rear of the Creaverton police station.

"Can I get you some coffee? A doughnut?"

Ben shook his head. "No, thank you."

"You said that you have some information about the Paul Mickerley case," the officer said, sitting down.

"I think I might," Ben answered. The chief was looking at him expectantly, and suddenly he wasn't sure that he could tell him what he knew, at least not without editing it somewhat to leave out the more outrageous parts.

"There's a man," Ben began. "His name is Titus Durham. I think he might have something to do with the boy's death."

Officer Finch wrote something on a pad on his desk. "What makes you think Mr. Durham is involved?"

"He said some things that make me think he is," said Ben.

"Things?" the officer said. "What kind of things?"

Ben hesitated. "He told me that Paul Mickerley was killed by a man named Wallace Blackwood," he said. "But Wallace Blackwood died more than twenty years ago."

"Blackwood," the chief repeated. "Why does that name sound familiar?"

"It's the name on the gravestone that Paul Mickerley was found near," Ben said.

Officer Finch eyed him cooly. "And how would you know that?" he inquired.

"I went there," said Ben. "Titus told me to."

"He told you to go to the cemetery?" the officer asked.

Ben nodded.

"May I ask why?"

"I believe he wants to be found out," Ben said. "I believe he needs help."

The chief put his pen down. "Mr. Hodge, the graves in that cemetery are nearly two hundred years old. How could Titus Durham have killed someone who was dead centuries before he was even born?"

"He didn't kill that Wallace Blackwood," Ben said. "He killed another one, the one who was the librarian in Downing. They must have the same name. I think placing the boy's body on the grave was supposed to be symbolic."

"That's where I know the name from," the chief said. "Blackwood. Wrote a book about the Downing child murders."

"Yes," Ben said, relieved that the officer was connecting his story to actual events and people. "That's him."

"You think Mr. Durham murdered Mr. Blackwood?" asked the officer.

"I think he did," Ben replied. "And I think he murdered Paul Mickerley and put him in that cemetery."

"Why would he do that?"

"Because he thinks Wallace Blackwood was responsible for the Downing child murders," said Ben. "He's obsessed with the idea. I think he killed Paul Mickerley as a way of getting revenge on Blackwood."

"Revenge?" the officer said. "Revenge for what?"

Ben paused before answering. "I think he was molested by Wallace Blackwood," he said. "I think this is his way of dealing with what happened to him."

The chief sat back in his chair and sighed deeply. "Mr. Hodge, do you know how this sounds?"

"Yes," Ben said. "I do. But I believe it's the truth. I think Titus Durham was molested by Wallace Blackwood when he was a boy, and that first he killed Blackwood and now he's recreating the crimes he thinks Blackwood committed."

The police officer looked at him without saying anything. Ben met his gaze. *If you think this story is unbelievable, you should hear the one Titus gave me,* he thought. He tried to imagine what Harris Finch would say if he was told that vampires were mixed up in the case he was investigating.

"Let me ask you something," Ben said after a minute. "Do you know yet how the boy died?"

The chief hesitated.

"His blood was drained somehow, wasn't it?" asked Ben.

Finch gave a start. "How did you know about that?" he asked. "Nobody was told that."

"Titus Durham believes that he's a vampire," Ben said, watching the expression on the officer's face go from one of surprise to one of outright shock.

"There wasn't a drop of blood in that boy," said the chief softly. "Not one. The coroner had never seen anything like it."

"Talk to Titus Durham," Ben said. "Ask him about it."

The chief nodded. "I will," he said. "But I still don't understand why Durham would tell you any of this."

Ben shrugged. "I'm new in town," he said. "He saw me regularly at the library. I think he's a very disturbed man."

Finch nodded. "Well, thank you for coming in, Mr. Hodge. I'm sure you and I will be speaking again. I'll need to get an official statement from you if this leads to anything."

"You can reach me at the Downing Public Library," Ben told him as he stood up to go.

"Oh, and Mr. Hodge?"

Ben turned around.

"If you see Mr. Durham before we do, don't do anything foolish."

It's too late for that, Ben thought as he walked out of the chief's office.

He left the police station and got into his car. Once inside, he breathed a sigh of relief. The weight that had been bearing down on him for days had been lifted, at least a little. Now that someone else knew about Titus, Ben didn't feel all alone. Hopefully the police would deal with the matter quickly and he wouldn't have to worry about Titus Durham anymore. Then he could get back to starting his new life in Downing.

He drove to the library. What, he wondered, would happen to Titus now? Surely the police would speak to him as soon as possible. But what then? Would he be taken into custody? Would he admit to his crimes? And if he did, what would become of him? The man was clearly insane. What would happen if he told investigators that he was a vampire who needed to sting himself with bees in order to keep from killing?

That's not your concern, Ben told himself. *You did what you had to do.* That, at least, was true. And he was proud of himself for doing what he'd done. Maybe if someone had done the same when Pete Lipton had manufactured his lies against Trey, things would have ended very differently. How ironic, Ben thought, that his life had been irreparably changed by a boy whose claims of impropriety were nothing but fantasies designed to get the attention of his parents and now he was helping stop a man whose own mistreatment had led him to abuse others in the most tragic way possible and create even more elaborate fantasies to cover up his actions.

It was one of life's neat little surprises, he thought bitterly as he parked his car in front of the library and got out. But if he could save another young man from the fate suffered by Paul Mickerley, perhaps it was worth it.

"It's about time you got here."

Steven Settles stood up, brushing off the seat of his pants. He'd been sitting on the library steps. "I've been waiting *forever*," he said dramatically.

"Sorry," Ben apologized, giving Steven a smile. The sight of the boy cheered him considerably, and he was glad Steven was there. If nothing else, it was a distraction from his more depressing thoughts.

"You were right about *Half Magic*," Steven said as Ben unlocked the library doors and they went inside. "I really liked the part where they wished for something exciting to happen and the house caught fire."

As Steven ran to the children's room and started browsing the shelves, Ben turned the lights on and went into his office. Sitting on his desk was a Miracle Whip jar. It was filled with bees. They were climbing the sides, crawling over one another as they looked for a way out. Their buzzing filled the room.

"What's that noise?"

Ben whirled around, half expecting to see Titus standing behind him. Instead, he found Steven there, a book in his hand.

"It's nothing," Ben said, putting his hand on the boy's shoulder and steering him out of the room. "Just some bees that got in through the window. But you need to leave so that I can clear them out."

"But I haven't checked out the book," Steven protested.

"That's okay," said Ben. "I trust you."

He led Steven to the library doors and walked him out. As the two of them stood on the steps, a police car drove by slowly. Ben watched it roll past. As it did, a figure in the back turned and he saw Titus's face through the glass. He looked directly at Ben and Steven for a moment, and then the car was gone, leaving Ben with the sound of buzzing in his head.

Chapter Fifteen

"How did Wally die?"

Martha Abraham repeated the question that Ben had just asked her. They were seated in the chairs on her screened-in porch, sipping gin and tonic. Beyond the screens, fireflies flickered in the gathering dusk, their lights sparking as they flew among the flowers in Martha's garden.

"Do you remember?" asked Ben.

Martha gave a little laugh. "Isn't that funny?" she said. "I can't say as I do."

"Was there a funeral?" Ben inquired.

"No," answered Martha. "Now that you mention it, there wasn't. I believe his body was sent back to his family."

"But last time we spoke you said he had no family," Ben reminded her.

"Well, it was sent *somewhere*," said Martha. "I forget where. Why are you suddenly so interested in what happened to Wally?"

"Just curious," Ben answered. "I've been reading his book."

"Best to let that hour in Downing history rest in peace," said Martha.

"I understand it was painful," Ben said. "But I find it interesting."

Martha took a sip of her gin and tonic before answering. "Curiosity's what killed the cat," she said firmly. "It doesn't do to spend too much time dwelling on such things as what happened here that summer. Look what it did to those boys over in West Memphis."

"The West Memphis Three?" said Ben. "You mean those teenagers who were convicted of killing the three little boys?"

"They didn't just kill them," Martha said, her voice filled with simmering anger. "They sacrificed them. Satanic worship."

"Actually," said Ben, "there was no evidence of that at all. In fact, most people believe those boys were innocent and that the father of one of the victims committed the murders."

"They found Wally's book at the leader's house," Martha countered. "He'd studied it. Underlined whole passages." She looked at Ben. "They used that book as an instruction manual."

Ben didn't reply. Clearly Martha had her opinions on the guilt of the three young men who had been the victims of the West Memphis witch hunt. Arguing with her wasn't going to help him get any of the answers he was looking for.

"I don't know why people are so fascinated by evil," said Martha, sounding less agitated than she had a moment before. "They should turn their backs on it, not study it like a painting, looking for the meaning."

That's why you hid all of Wally's books in the basement, Ben thought. *You thought that if you buried them, people would forget.*

"Wally was a good man," said Martha. "But he spent too much time in the dark. I think in the end it's what killed him." Her voice had taken on a slight slur, as if the alcohol in her drink had finally taken command of her thoughts. Ben looked at her. She was staring out at the yard, a look of sadness on her face.

"I'm thinking of holding a weekly story hour at the library," Ben said, trying to change the subject. "I'd love it if you would help out. You know, come read to the kids."

Martha nodded, as if she'd only half heard what he'd said. Ben started to speak again when suddenly a shout broke the silence of the evening.

"Steven!" It was a young man's voice, loud and annoyed.

His call was joined by that of a woman. "Stevie?" she called, her cry a question instead of a command. "Stevie? Where are you?"

Ben saw two figures approaching the house, walking quickly down the sidewalk. From time to time they stopped and called again, their voices filling the air.

"Who is it?" Martha asked. "Can you see who it is?"

"No," answered Ben. "Wait here. I'll go ask."

He left the porch, the screen door banging shut behind him as he jogged across the lawn toward the two figures. When he reached them, he recognized one as Darren Settles.

"Is something wrong?" he asked.

The woman with Darren turned to him. She appeared distraught, and she looked at Ben with frightened eyes. "Stevie," she said. "My son."

"We can't find him," Darren clarified. "He went to the store to pick up some milk, and he never came home. That was two hours ago."

"He probably just got distracted," Ben said calmly. "I'm sure he's around somewhere."

"Stevie always comes right home," Mrs. Settles said. "He's a good boy."

"I know he is," Ben replied, smiling and patting her arm. "And I'm sure we'll find him. I'll help you look."

He ran back to Martha, who was now standing in the doorway of her porch, watching the proceedings as well as she could in the gloom.

"Steven Settles is missing," Ben told her. "I'm going to go help look for him."

Martha nodded. "Probably just playing with his friends," she said.

"That's what I think," said Ben. "I'll let you know when we find him."

He returned to Darren and Mrs. Settles. They continued calling Steven's name, and several other people joined them on the sidewalk. Ben recognized most of them from his walks through town, although he didn't know their names.

"Who was the last person to see the boy?" asked one of the men.

"Frank did," replied a woman.

A man Ben recognized as the owner of the town's small grocery store stepped forward. "He bought half a gallon of milk," he said. "Told him to get it home to his ma soon as he could so's it wouldn't get warm. That was a couple of hours ago."

The first man nodded. "We'll split up," he said. "Groups of two. We can cover more ground that way."

The party broke into pairs, and Ben found himself standing with Darren Settles. The teenager looked at him with an expression indicating that he would have to take what he was stuck with. "Come on," he said, walking away.

Ben followed him. Darren marched ahead, calling out his brother's name.

"Maybe we should be a little more methodical about this," Ben suggested.

Darren turned and looked at him. "Huh?" he said.

"Instead of just running around yelling, maybe we should try to figure out which way Steven would have walked home. Chances are, we'll find him somewhere between the store and your house."

Darren stared at him for a moment, then nodded. He pointed to the corner. "Store's there," he said. "Our house is a couple of blocks the other direction."

Ben nodded and walked in the direction of the store. When they reached it, he waited for Darren to take the lead. But the boy hung back, as if he were suddenly afraid of going back to his house.

"This way?" Ben asked, pointing.

Darren nodded. Ben began walking. "Steven!" he called out. "Steven, can you hear me?"

They walked for two blocks, calling out to the missing boy and receiving no answer. They could hear Steven's name being shouted by the other groups, rising into the night sky and floating over the roofs of the houses.

He's got to be here somewhere, Ben thought. *He couldn't have just disappeared.*

They walked another block, pausing at each house to call out. When they were almost to the end, Darren suddenly pointed to one of the porches.

"There he is!" he said excitedly. "Sitting on our steps!"

Ben looked in the direction in which Darren was pointing. He saw a house set back from the street, and on its front steps the figure of a small boy sat.

"Steven!" Darren cried out happily. "Mom! I found Stevie! He's home!"

Darren ran toward the steps, with Ben close behind him.

"Stevie!" Darren said happily as they reached the steps. "Why didn't you answer us?"

Steven made no reply. Darren reached out for him. "Stevie?"

As Darren's fingers touched his brother's chest, Stevie's head rolled to the side. It tumbled to the porch and continued down the steps, coming to rest at Darren's feet. The rest of Stevie's body remained seated on the steps. Between his legs sat a bottle of milk. His hands were still resting on either side.

Chapter Sixteen

"I don't understand what's going on."

Ben looked across the desk at Harris Finch. The police chief rubbed his eyes. He looked exhausted.

"I thought you guys brought Titus Durham in this morning," said Ben.

"We did bring him in," Finch replied. "In fact, he's still here. But not for long now."

Ben shook his head. "If he's here, then who killed Steven Settles?"

"That's what we'd like to know," the officer said. He looked at Ben with a tired expression.

"What?" said Ben. "Why are you looking at me like that?"

"Mr. Hodge, what can you tell me about these?"

Finch pushed something across the desk to Ben. It was a large envelope. Ben took it and opened it, emptying the contents out onto the desk. It was a pile of newspaper clippings. Ben recognized them immediately.

"Where did you get these?" he asked in disbelief.

"Someone mailed them to the station," Finch answered. "They arrived this afternoon."

Ben stared at the clippings. It wasn't possible that they were there. They were sitting in the shoebox in his bedroom. He was certain of it.

"Is it true that you and Mr. Middleman were—partners?" asked the officer.

Ben nodded. "Yes," he said quietly.

Finch leaned forward. "One of my men said he spoke to you at the funeral of Paul Mickerley," he said. "He said you asked him for directions to the old cemetery."

"I just asked him where it was," Ben said wearily.

The chief nodded. "That doesn't explain why you were there in the first place," he said. "You didn't know the boy."

Ben sighed. "I told you," he said. "Titus told me to go to the funeral. No, I didn't know Paul Mickerley."

"You just went because this man you suspected of killing Wallace Blackwood told you to?" said the officer.

"I didn't suspect him then," Ben said defensively. "It wasn't until after I saw the name on the gravestone."

"Right," Finch said. "The gravestone. I checked that out too. There's no stone for anyone called Wallace Blackwood up there. The stone the Mickerley boy was found leaning against was too faded to read."

"No," Ben said. "I saw it. I read the name. It was Wallace Pyle Blackwood. I read it plain as day."

The officer handed Ben another piece of paper.

"What's this?" asked Ben, looking at it.

"The death certificate for Wallace Pyle Blackwood," the chief informed him. "December 21, 1979. He died of congestive heart failure. He wasn't murdered, by Mr. Durham or anyone else."

Ben read over the certificate. It confirmed what Finch had just told him.

"Mr. Hodge, I'm going to ask you again, what do you know about the deaths of Paul Mickerley and Steven Settles?"

"Just what I already told you," replied Ben.

Chief Finch looked at him for a long time, not speaking. Ben sat in his chair, staring at the pile of newspaper clippings and the death certificate for Wallace Blackwood.

"You know what I think?" the officer said finally.

Ben looked up. Finch was eyeing him coldly. "I think what happened to you and Mr. Middleman did something to you. I think you came here to run away from it, but instead of getting away you came face-to-face with your demons. Then I think you read Wallace Black-wood's book and you got some funny ideas. That's what I think."

"I would never do something like that," Ben said.

The chief nodded. "Sometimes we do things we never thought we would," he said. "Especially when we're not in our right minds."

Ben looked at him and laughed. "You think *I'm* crazy?" he said.

"All I'm saying is that sometimes our minds do strange things to us," answered Finch.

"I didn't kill Paul Mickerley and Steven Settles," Ben told him. "For Christ's sake, I'm the one who helped *find* Steven."

"I didn't say you're the one who did it," the officer said. "I'm saying you seem to know an awful lot about it, and there are a lot of things that don't make sense here."

"I told you what happened," said Ben. "Titus Durham is the one you should be talking to."

"Maybe so," Chief Finch said. "All the same, I'm going to keep you here tonight while we check a few details."

"What?" Ben exclaimed. "You can't just keep me here."

"I could book you on suspicion of murder," the officer told him. "But I'd prefer not to. Now, you can stay here voluntarily or we can do it the hard way. It's up to you."

Ben started to protest, then stopped. He knew that anything he said would just make him appear guilty. The best thing to do, he told himself, was to cooperate.

"Okay," he said quietly. "I'll stay."

Finch nodded. "Thank you," he said, standing up. "Why don't you come with me."

Ben stood up. The chief motioned for him to walk in front of him. He followed behind as Ben walked down a short hallway to another door. Finch took a key from the ring on his belt and slipped it into the lock. He turned the key and the door opened onto another hallway. This one contained cells, two on each side.

"It's not the Hilton," said Finch as he opened one of the cells, "but I think you'll be all right for the night. I'll be in to check on you later."

Ben entered the cell and the officer slid the door shut again, locking it. When Finch had left, he turned and surveyed his accommodations for the night. The cell contained very little—a bed, a sink, and an exposed toilet. Ben went to the bed and sat down, the springs groaning wearily.

How had this happened? How had he ended up in jail when Titus was free? All he'd done was try to stop the killings. But now Steven was dead too. In the rush of the night's events, that realization hadn't even had time to sink in. Now he thought about the little boy, his head torn from his body. What kind of monster could do such a thing?

He began to cry. Maybe he *was* going crazy. Maybe somehow he *was* responsible for everything that was happening. Harris Finch had looked at him the way he would look at a wild animal that couldn't help itself. Was that what he had become?

No, he told himself. *No, it isn't possible.* He knew he hadn't killed Paul Mickerley or Steven Settles. Someone else had. The same person who had sent the newspaper clippings to the police. Titus Durham. But how would Titus have known about the clippings to begin with?

He must have gotten into the house, Ben thought. *The same way he got into the library and left the jar of bees on your desk. He's trying to make you believe you're losing your mind.*

He stretched out on the bed. The mattress, thin and filled with hard lumps, did little to protect him from the springs poking into his back. He didn't care, though. Despite his situation, he was tired. His mind ached with the effort of trying to find his way out of the maze he was wandering in. He just wanted to sleep, to forget about it all for a few hours.

That didn't seem possible. Although he closed his eyes, his thoughts continued at breakneck speed, jumping from one thing to the next. In addition, the harsh flourescent light of the cell glowed relentlessly, shining even through the protection of his eyelids. He placed his hands over his face, trying to block it out. But he couldn't block out the scenes playing over and over in his head: Steven Settles's head falling from his body, the look of anguish that passed over his mother's face when she ran to her boy, the officer asking him to come to the station for what he thought would be routine questioning. They rolled in an endless loop, taunting him until finally, worn out, Ben faded into a kind of half sleep.

Chapter Seventeen

"Dance with me."

Ben opened his eyes. He was in darkness. Where was he? Jail. He was in jail. But someone had turned off the lights. The cell had been plunged into blackness. No, not quite blackness. There was light. Pale light. Silver light. It was coming from a window set high in the wall, a narrow sliver of window that revealed a tiny piece of the night sky.

"Dance with me."

He sat up. Someone was in the cell with him. *Not someone,* he thought. *Something.* It was standing near the door, outlined by the moon. Its arms were raised above its head at an impossible angle, the hands dangling. Ben could see long-nailed fingers moving slowly in the shadows.

"Who are you?" he asked.

He received a laugh in response. Then the figure moved toward him, lurching and swaying drunkenly. As it grew closer, he smelled a familiar scent—earth and leaves and rotting things—the smell of death. The figure stopped a few feet from the bed. Ben looked into its face and had to force himself not to scream.

Its eyes were pale orbs in its withered face. Bits of its skin hung in tatters, and its mouth was filled with teeth like needles. Its hair hung loosely about its shoulders, tangled and snarled with twigs and small bones.

"Won't you dance with me?" it asked. It spun around, teetering precariously on its spindly legs, its arms flying out like broken wings. A horrible, thin laugh poured from its throat. When it came to a stop again it cocked its head. "Don't you recognize me?"

Ben couldn't take his eyes off the creature. "The Death Puppets," he said, recalling the illustration he'd seen in one of Wallace's books.

The thing clapped its clawlike hands together like a child. "A quaint name, don't you think?" it asked. "And really, it was *they* who were *our* puppets."

It waved its arms around and hopped from foot to foot, like a marionette moving on unseen strings. The sight filled Ben with fear, and he licked his lips, trying to muster the strength to call for help. Before he could, the thing was beside him, bending close to his face and holding one of its wicked nails to his lips.

"It won't do you any good," it said. "They won't hear you. No one would hear you."

Ben tried to avert his eyes. The creature pulled back. "You hurt me," it said. "I thought you would be glad to see me again."

Ben looked at it, not understanding. The creature laughed. Then it began to spin again. As it did, its appearance changed. Its arms straightened, its hair grew short, and its faced transformed from that of a dead thing to the handsome, smiling face of Trey. The spinning stilled, and Trey stood before Ben.

"Hello, lover," he said.

Ben shook his head. "No," he said. "It's not you."

Trey laughed, the creature's voice coming from his lips. "I suppose you can't be fooled twice," he said. He stopped laughing and looked at Ben, who stared at him in wonder. "I'm sorry to disappoint you, especially after our tender reunion."

"What are you?" said Ben.

"What are you? Who are you? So many questions," Trey said. He turned his back on Ben. "It's asking so many questions that got you into this mess, isn't it?"

"This is just a dream," Ben told himself. "Just like the other night."

Trey whirled around, changing as he did back into the twisted form of the Death Puppet. "I'm afraid it's not," it said. "A nightmare, perhaps, but I assure you that you're very much awake."

"Are you Titus?" Ben asked.

The creature snarled. "You insult me," it said. "Do you think that fool could take such forms as I take? Do you think he has such power?" It strode forward once more, standing full in the moonlight so that Ben could see it clearly. "Do you really not know me?" it asked.

Ben stared at it for a moment, thinking. "Blackwood," he said. "You're Wallace Blackwood."

"Very good," the thing said, its torn mouth twisting up in some semblance of a smile.

"Then you are alive," said Ben. "Titus was right."

"Hardly *alive*," replied Blackwood. "But risen, yes. I'm afraid young Mr. Durham wasn't as skilled as he thought he was."

"And it was you who came to me?" asked Ben.

"One of my better glamours, I think," Blackwood told him. "Even better than the one you saw at the pond."

"And you killed those boys?"

"Questions, questions, questions," said Blackwood impatiently. "Yes, I killed the boys. Delicious they were." He paused, as if remembering the taste of an exquisite dinner. "The innocent are so sweet. I'd almost forgotten."

"Titus didn't lie then," Ben said, more to himself than to Blackwood. "You did kill those children in 1932."

"Oh, yes. But not on my own. Did Titus tell you how he helped me? Did he tell you how he held them down while I drank? Did he tell you how he covered their mouths to muffle their screams?"

"He said he didn't understand what you were doing," answered Ben.

Blackwood laughed. "Did he? I'm afraid that isn't quite true. He knew very well what he was doing, just as he knew what he was asking when he begged me to make him what I am."

"He's not like you now," said Ben.

"No," Blackwood said. "He's not. He's turned his back on his gifts, denied himself in a foolish attempt at redemption."

"Why are you doing this?" Ben asked.

"Why?" repeated Blackwood in a mocking tone. "Why embrace eternity? Why live forever?"

"You aren't alive," said Ben, surprised at his boldness.

"What is life?" Blackwood asked him. "The filling of the lungs? The beating of the heart? No. Life is seeing the passing of centuries, the rise and fall of countries. Life is seeing something you desire and possessing it the next moment. Life is seeing the world come to an end. You have no conception of what life truly is."

"Maybe I don't want to," Ben told him.

"I think perhaps you do," Blackwood countered. He knelt by the side of the bed, his dead eyes looking into Ben's. "I think you would welcome my gifts."

As Ben watched, Blackwood transformed once more into Trey. Gone were the shriveled skin and broken teeth, replaced by smooth flesh and Trey's smiling eyes.

"We could be together again," he said gently as he reached up to touch Ben's face.

Ben flinched, but when he felt warm, soft skin caressing him, he found himself relaxing. He could feel Trey's breath on his face.

"I love you," said Trey. "And I forgive you."

Ben felt tears forming in his eyes. How many nights had he lain awake, willing to trade everything just to hear those words? How often had he begged for another chance to hold Trey in his arms? He reached out with trembling hands and touched Trey's face.

"Let me give this to you," said Trey, leaning in.

Ben shut his eyes as Trey kissed him. Their lips met, and Ben felt himself surrounded by a familiar warmth, a security and safeness he hadn't felt since Trey's death.

"Accept the gift," Trey whispered, moving his mouth down Ben's neck.

Ben felt the pressure of Trey's teeth against his skin, a sharp prick of pain followed by a flood of heat. He was aware of a dimming of his senses, a dark embrace of calm that made him forget everything.

And then, cutting through it all, came the smell of rot. It filled his nose, gagging him, and suddenly he was awake once more. He pushed against Trey, sending his lover stumbling backward. Trey looked up at him, his mouth bloodied. Ben put his hand to his neck and it came away wet and sticky.

"Fool," Trey hissed as his features collapsed into the corrupt patchwork of skin and bone that was Blackwood's real countenance. "You could have had everything."

Ben grabbed the sheet from his bed, tearing off a strip and holding it to his bleeding neck. Watching him, Blackwood laughed cruelly.

"That was your only chance for survival," he said. "Now that you have refused me, you are as good as dead. When you've served my purposes, then I will come to finish you."

He stood up, backing away into the shadows. Ben watched him, his fingers trembling and fighting the urge to retch. The smell of Blackwood was all around him, choking him like smoke. His throat, filled with the taste of death, ached as he tried to breathe.

And then it was gone. He choked as fresh air entered his lungs. When he was able to breathe freely again, he looked into the corner of the cell. Where Blackwood had been, there was only moonlight and shadow.

Chapter Eighteen

"You're free to go."

Harris Finch opened the door to the cell as Ben sat up, rubbing the sleep from his eyes. Somehow, despite the horror of the night before, he'd fallen asleep. Now it was daytime, and the shadows of the cell had been replaced by the clear light of a summer morning. Ben got up, stretched, and walked out of the cell, Finch standing aside to let him pass. He followed Ben to the end of the hall and through the station. At the front door, he stopped.

"Don't go too far, Mr. Hodge," he said. "This isn't over yet."

Ben nodded, not saying anything. Then he went to his car, started it, and drove with great relief out of the parking lot. He wanted to put as much distance as possible between himself and the cell in which he'd spent the night. The memory of Blackwood's kiss still lingered in his memory, the putrid smell threatening to envelop him at any moment.

Had it all really happened? He wanted to believe that it hadn't, that he'd dreamed up the creature that had visited him in the jail. But he knew that it had been all too real, that he'd come face-to-face with something that shouldn't be possible, something that had been birthed in the darkest recesses of the world. A vampire. The word still made him cringe, conjuring up images of the goth kids who had roamed his New York neighborhood, their eyes heavily made up, their faces pale as snow. He and Trey had laughed at their earnestness, imagining them sitting in dreary clubs listening to the drone of electronica music while they longed to be more interesting than they really were. Pretenders they were, children playing at dress-up, creating new identities out of fishnet and velvet.

But they had no idea how mistaken they were. The vampire he'd faced the night before had been nothing like them. Blackwood may have spoken with a human voice, but he was anything but human. He had been once, Ben knew, but now he was nothing but a shell, a crumbling cocoon of skin and bone filled with unnameable evil that animated his limbs. He promised life, but he lied.

Was Titus like him? Ben wondered. Beneath his skin, was he nothing but blackness and rot and pain? Or had he really somehow escaped Blackwood's fate, fighting the decay of his mind and soul? Ben remembered how it had felt in Titus's arms, how he'd longed to stay in them forever. Had that been a trick of the mind, like Blackwood's transformation into Trey? Had it been nothing more than his imagination?

He didn't believe it. Despite his recent doubts about Titus, he wanted to believe that he'd been wrong. It gave him some small hope that everything would turn out all right, that somehow what was happening to him could be stopped.

He needed to go to him, he knew that. It was the only way. But would Titus turn him away? Knowing that Ben had betrayed him, would he now turn his back in turn? There was only one way for him to find out.

He drove quickly through town, not wanting to stop or be seen in case word of his suspected involvement in the killings had gotten out. But the streets were empty, even in the bright light of day. *They're frightened,* he thought as he passed by the houses with closed windows and doors. *They're afraid it's happening again.*

Turning onto the dirt road, he sped past Drowned Girl Pond, averting his eyes from its dark gaze. A minute later he pulled into the driveway of Titus's house. He turned off the engine and sat, looking at the windows. Was Titus watching him from behind them? He resisted the urge to turn the car around, opening the door and stepping out before he could change his mind.

As he approached the house, the door opened and Titus stepped out onto the porch. Ben stopped, waiting for him to say something. Titus watched him, not speaking.

"I saw him," Ben said finally. "Blackwood. He came to me last night."

Titus nodded. "I smell him on you."

Ben shivered at the thought. He recalled the effect that Blackwood's stench had had on him. Was that how Titus felt now, repulsed by his presence?

"I'm sorry," said Ben. "For not believing you."

"You don't need to be sorry," Titus replied. "Come in."

He turned and walked into the house, leaving the door open. Ben followed, entering the coolness of the house as if entering a sanctuary. Already he felt safer, as if Blackwood could not touch him as long as he was in the house with Titus. He shut the door behind him with relief.

Titus was standing near the stairs. He motioned for Ben to follow him. "Come," he said. "We'll wash his smell from you."

They went upstairs to Titus's bedroom. Titus left Ben there for a moment while he went into the bathroom. He returned with a white metal basin and several towels, all of which he set on the floor.

Standing, he slowly unbuttoned Ben's shirt, slipping it from his shoulders and dropping it on the floor. Then he undid his belt and the buttons of his pants, sliding them down. Ben stepped out of his shoes and allowed Titus to remove the rest.

When Ben was naked, Titus knelt and placed a cake of soap in the basin of water. He worked it into a lather, releasing the scent of lavender into the air. Then he dipped a cloth into the water and wrung it out.

Without speaking, he stood and began to wash Ben, beginning with his neck and shoulders. His strong fingers worked the soapy water into Ben's skin, kneading firmly as he moved over Ben's back. Then he refreshed the cloth and started washing Ben's chest. The water turned the hair on Ben's body into wet whorls as Titus scrubbed away the odor of decay, replacing it with the soothing scent of lavender. Ben felt himself relaxing as he was cleaned, the feelings of anxiety turning into ones of peace. He lifted his arms, and Titus washed beneath them. The soap trickled down Ben's sides, and Titus followed it with his hands, running them over Ben's body as he chased the water with the cloth.

He continued down, washing Ben's legs and feet. Then Ben felt the warm cloth pressed into the crack of his ass. Titus's fingers worked their way in, parting Ben's cheeks and teasing his hole for a moment before retreating. A moment later, his cock and balls were surrounded by warmth as Titus cupped them in his hand and washed them too.

Ben felt himself becoming hard as Titus washed his dick, the soapy water sliding easily over the length of his rapidly-growing shaft. Then the cloth was gone, replaced by the softness of Titus's mouth. Ben groaned as Titus took him in. His hands moved to Titus's head, guiding him.

Titus's fingers pulled at Ben's balls as he sucked, his tongue teasing the head of Ben's cock. Ben thrust against him, sliding deep into Titus's throat for a moment before pulling out. He fucked Titus's mouth slowly, savoring the long, warm pull that surrounded him each time he moved in and out.

Ben was close, but before the first small quakes of release could grow stronger and carry him over the edge, Titus stood up. Turning Ben around, he pushed him over the foot of the bed, so that Ben landed on his stomach. Behind him, he heard the sounds of Titus removing his clothes. Then Titus was between his legs, urging him forward.

Ben got on his knees, turning to see Titus climbing onto the bed behind him. Titus's hands gripped the mounds of his ass, spreading them, and then Ben felt a drizzle of warmth as Titus spit. A single finger plunged into Ben's hole, working it open. Ben shut his eyes, readying himself for what he knew would come next, and when Titus entered him in one fierce thrust, he let out a small cry of pain that quickly turned to a whimper of joy.

Titus fucked him hard, his thick tool repeatedly pounding Ben's ass. Ben could feel his own cock slapping against his stomach with each thrust. He reached between his legs, grasping himself and matching the rhythm of Titus's movements. Each time Titus entered him, Ben pushed down on his balls, driving Titus as deep as possible inside him.

Soon, Titus began to moan, and Ben felt the dick inside him thicken. A moment later his ass was filled with a burst of heat. He closed his eyes as his own climax ripped through him, covering his hand with thick blasts of cum. He continued to jack off as Titus came again, still fucking him. He could feel Titus trembling as his muscles were seized with the force of the explosion. Then Titus fell forward, pushing himself even deeper into Ben as they both collapsed on the bed.

They lay like that for some time, Ben relishing the feeling of Titus's body pressed against his, Titus's mouth gently kissing his neck. Then they turned on their sides. Titus slipped an arm around Ben, holding him close. And Ben, suddenly more tired than he'd been in a long time, surrendered to the warmth of the sun coming through the window, the softness of the bed, and the strength of Titus's embrace.

When he awoke again, it was night and he was alone. He reached for Titus, but the place where he'd been was empty. He noticed, too, that the air was filled with the smell of burning wood. Shadows danced wildly on the walls around him.

Fire, he thought. *Something is on fire.*

He sat up, suddenly very much awake. Looking toward the window, he saw Titus standing there. He was staring out into the yard. His face was illuminated by an ugly glow.

"He's burning them," said Titus quietly.

Ben got up and joined him at the window. In the yard, the hives were ablaze. Each one burned like a small pyre, the flames leaping up gleefully as they consumed the wooden boxes. Thick smoke swirled up to the sky, the tendrils from each fire joining together to form a black cloud that blotted out the stars.

And in the midst of the inferno, Blackwood danced. His twisted figure whirled in the haze of ash and fire, celebrating his triumph. Ben and Titus watched him as he performed his fantastic ballet, his body moving to the music of destruction.

Chapter Nineteen

They let the hives burn. By the time Ben and Titus dressed and got into the backyard, they were mostly gone anyway. What remained was a smouldering mess of charred wood held together by melted wax in which the bodies of the bees had become fixed, drowned in their own honey. Titus walked from hive to hive, touching each one tenderly. There was no sign of Blackwood.

"Where do you think he is?" Ben asked.

"Gone," Titus said. "Off to do more evil work."

Ben looked around at the ruined hives. "What will happen now?" he asked Titus.

"Without the bees, the sickness will grow stronger in me," he said.

"Can't we just get new bees?" Ben said.

Titus shook his head. "It will take time," he replied. "More time than we have. Than I have."

"Then what do we do?" asked Ben, fearful of hearing the answer.

"I must find Blackwood," Titus said. "Find him and end this."

Ben looked around helplessly. There had to be something that would help them. But with the bees gone, he knew that Titus would begin to grow hungry. And when he did, he would need blood. *If only he had another hive,* Ben thought miserably. Even a wild one would probably be enough. But where would they find such a thing? They needed to find an old hollow tree or a . . . barn. A thought came to him. He turned around, looking at the small shed that still stood, intact, beyond the blackened hives. *He forgot about the shed,* he thought happily.

"Titus," he said, pointing. "Are there still some bees in there?"

Titus nodded. "Yes," he answered. "A few in the jars."

The two of them exchanged glances, then ran toward the shed. Ben said a silent prayer that Blackwood had failed to notice the building, that they wouldn't find the jars smashed and the floor littered with bits of glass and the dead bodies of bees.

Titus flung open the door and turned on the lone bulb that hung in the center of the room. Ben glanced around. The jars were still on the shelves. "They're safe," he said.

Titus went to the shelves and took down two jars, which he brought back to the workbench. The bees inside were moving. Ben could hear their humming, more frantic than usual.

"They know what happened," said Titus. "They can smell the deaths of their brethren and of their queens."

"How many do you have in here?" Ben asked.

Titus surveyed the shelves. "Enough for several days," he said. "But I have to establish new hives soon. These few will not last."

"We need to leave here," Ben said. "We need to get someplace safe. We have to—"

He stopped speaking as he saw Titus shake his head.

"What?" he asked.

"I can't just leave," Titus said. "Not until Blackwood is destroyed. If he's allowed to survive, he will keep on killing."

Ben began to protest, but stopped himself before he spoke. He knew Titus was right. They could run as far from Downing as was possible, but Blackwood would still be there, waiting in the darkness to take the lives of anyone he chose.

"He must be found," said Titus. "It's time for this to be over."

"How do we find him?" Ben asked.

"He will need to feed soon," said Titus. "He needs blood to grow stronger."

"He could find victims anywhere," Ben said helplessly. "Anyone in town would do for his purposes."

"He prefers the blood of the grieving," said Titus. "It's like wine to him."

"Darren Settles," Ben said. "He'll go after Steven's brother. We have to get to him first."

The two men left the shed and hurried to Ben's car. Within minutes they were pulling up to the Settles house. Getting out, they ran to the front door and knocked on it. When a moment later it opened to reveal the distraught face of Mrs. Settles, Ben began speaking.

"Is Darren here?" he asked.

Mrs. Settles nodded. "Yes," she said anxiously. "Why?"

"He's in danger," Ben explained. "From the man who killed Steven."

"Stevie?" Mrs. Settles said, her brow knit up in confusion. "You know who killed Stevie?"

"Yes," Ben said. "Can we speak to Darren?"

"He's in his room," Mrs. Settles said. "Upstairs."

Ben and Titus entered the house and went up the stairs. Mrs. Settles followed them. "I don't understand," she said.

"Which room is it?" asked Titus when they came to the second floor.

"At the end," said Mrs. Settles.

Ben reached the closed door to Darren's room and knocked. There was no answer. Trying the handle, he pushed the door open. Immediately, the overwhelming smell of blood filled his nose. He gagged, turning to retch as Titus entered the room behind him.

Darren Settles was on his bed, stretched out as if in sleep. His hands were folded on his stomach. Where his heart should have been, a gaping hole yawned in his chest. The ribs, splintered and shiny with blood and muscle, stuck up from the ripped flesh like fingers. His innards stained the bedsheets, great chunks of meat spread out on the blood-soaked quilt. The walls, too, were spattered with blood, wet roses covering the paper with their grisly pattern.

"Don't come in here," Ben said, suddenly remembering Mrs. Settles. "Don't look at it."

"Oh, I've already seen it," Mrs. Settles said softly.

Ben looked up at her as Titus turned around, his fingers red with blood from where he'd touched the boy's mutilated body. Mrs. Settles regarded them with amused detachment, a small smile playing across her face. "Isn't it beautiful?" she asked.

"Blackwood," Titus said, his voice harsh.

Mrs. Settles laughed. "You've grown weak," she said as her features morphed into those of Wallace Blackwood. "I remember when a simple trick like that would never have worked on you."

Ben staggered back, away from the walking corpse that now stood in Darren Settles's bedroom doorway. In his haste, he tripped on the bed, falling against the boy's body. When he righted himself, he found he was covered in blood and bits of Darren's flesh. He wiped his hands on his pants, trying to get rid of the stuff.

Blackwood, watching him, laughed happily. "What wonderful evidence those stains will make," he said.

Ben looked at him, not understanding.

"The police," Titus said. "They're coming."

As proof of his statement, Ben heard the sound of sirens outside the house. Blackwood smiled, his lips cracking obscenely. "I think soon you will have company," he said. "I'm sorry I won't be here to see what transpires."

He disappeared into the hallway. Ben glanced at Titus, looking for direction.

"Let him go," said Titus.

The sound of the sirens grew louder. Then they heard the sound of voices at the door.

"Police!" shouted a male voice.

Ben looked at Darren, noticing for the first time that his eyes were open, as if the terror he'd experienced at the moment of his death had frozen them that way, fixed forever on the face of the thing that had killed him. Ben wondered what had become of Mrs. Settles. Undoubtedly her body was elsewhere in the house, equally ravaged.

"We have to go," said Titus, snapping Ben out of his trance.

"Where?" Ben asked.

Titus pointed to the bedroom's lone window. Going to it, he opened it and looked out. "Jump," he told Ben.

Ben looked out. The ground seemed impossibly far beneath them. He hesitated.

"They're coming," Titus said behind him.

Ben heard the footsteps on the stairs. In a moment there would be men coming into the room, men who would believe that he and Titus had killed Darren Settles and his mother. He put one knee on the window ledge, feeling himself tip forward. He followed it with his other foot, so that he was perched on the edge. Then he let go and tumbled into nothingness.

Chapter Twenty

The pain in Ben's leg was getting worse. As he limped along behind Titus, he longed to stop for a moment. He would even welcome being caught by the police. At least he wouldn't be running for his life then. *No, your life would probably be over,* he reminded himself.

"Where are we going?" he asked, wincing as a stab of pain sliced through his knee. He'd landed on it when he'd jumped, and it was moving with an odd clicking sensation. Titus seemed to take no notice of his injury, however, moving quickly through the streets.

"To the library," Titus answered. "Do you have the key?"

Ben felt in the pocket of his pants. "Yes," he said. "I have it."

He could still see the faint flashing of the police car lights several blocks behind them, the sky around them turning alternately red and white. The officers were certain to have found the bodies. What would they do next? he wondered. Where would they look for the killers? *For us,* he thought. *Where will they look for us?*

He knew that he and Titus must be the prime suspects in the crimes. After what had happened during the past few days, their names would be foremost in the minds of the police. Ben suspected, too, that Blackwood may have worked some of his evil magic on them. The vampire seemed to possess powers that Titus didn't.

They reached the library and Ben took the keys from his pocket. His hand shook as he unlocked the door and let Titus in, following behind him and securing the bolt so that anyone else attempting to get in would have at least that minor difficulty to contend with. It might, Ben thought, provide them with a few extra seconds in which to escape.

Titus went into the main room, not bothering to turn the lights on. "Blackwood!" he called out, his voice trembling with rage. "Show yourself!"

"What makes you think he came here?" asked Ben, glancing around nervously.

"This was where he began his work," said Titus, turning around in a circle as he peered into the shadows.

"The boys," Ben said. "This is where he would first see them."

"Yes," said Titus. "He would befriend them, gain their trust, so that when the time came to take them they wouldn't fear him. Not at first."

The realization of what Blackwood had done stunned Ben. He had pretended to care about the children he'd killed. They'd gone to him willingly, seeing him as someone they could believe in. And in turn, he'd torn their souls to pieces, throwing away their bodies like spoiled fruit.

"You judge me too harshly."

Ben drew closer to Titus as Blackwood emerged from the darkness of the children's room. Instead of inhabiting the horrific form of the Death Puppet, he looked as he did when the photograph on his book jacket had been taken. He reached for a light switch and flipped it on, flooding the room with light.

"That's better," he said. "Now we can see things as they really are."

Ben stared at his face. It was the face of a man in his middle years. His hair was neatly cut, and he wore small, round glasses that magnified the size of his eyes. He was dressed in brown pants and a white shirt, the collar and cuffs neatly starched. When he moved, it was with neither the ungainly gait of the Death Puppet nor the smooth movements of a man confident in his powers. Instead, it was with the slightly stiff walk of a man whose body was beginning to slow down.

"You see," he said, directing his comments to Ben, "I am not such a horrible creature as you imagine me to be."

"That isn't your true form," Ben said, trying to control his emotions.

Blackwood smiled. "Perhaps not now," he replied. "But it was then, when the things Titus accuses me of took place."

"Accuses you of?" Titus said. "There's no doubt that you killed."

"As did you!" Blackwood shot back. "As do we all!"

Titus looked away as Ben tried to meet his gaze. "What's he talking about?" asked Ben. "There are more of you?"

Blackwood laughed harshly. "Indeed there are more. Dozens more. Perhaps even hundreds. Hidden in the woods and mountains. Living openly among you. We are not the first, nor shall we be the last."

"There will be one less when I am done with you," Titus told him.

Blackwood smiled and nodded his head. "We shall see about that," he said. "Already the people come for you. Already they are remembering John Rullins and pairing his name with yours."

"Why did you come back here?" asked Titus. "With the whole world at your disposal, why did you return?"

"This is the place of my greatest achievement," Blackwood said, gesturing at the library. Then he looked directly at Titus. "And of my greatest failure." He paused. "You could have been magnificent," he said. "You could have surpassed me in power. But you turned your back on it. You betrayed me."

"I betrayed nothing," Titus said.

Blackwood walked toward him. Ben saw Titus stiffen as the vampire approached, his eyes watching Blackwood warily. Blackwood stopped in front of them. Reaching out, he ran his finger down Titus's cheek.

"Do you remember how it felt to lie in my arms?" he asked. "Do you remember how our bodies moved against one another, how our mouths hungered for the taste of one another?"

Titus said nothing. Blackwood looked wounded. "You don't remember?" he asked, his voice teasing. "But you told me that you would always love me, that you would do anything for me."

Titus grabbed hold of Blackwood's wrist and twisted it sharply. With a scream of rage, he pushed the vampire forward and into one of the stacks. It fell backward, showering them with books as they tumbled to the ground. Blackwood let out a furious hiss.

"It's time to finish what I failed to do the last time we met," Titus said.

Blackwood's free hand went to Titus's throat, the fingers wrapping around it tightly. Ben saw the nails begin to bite into the skin, and blood welled up from beneath them. Blackwood seemed to gain strength from the sight and feel of the blood. He struggled against Titus's hold, slowly bringing his pinned wrist up and taking hold with that hand as well.

Ben knew that Titus, despite his strength, was going to be over-powered. He was tired and weakened from running. Blackwood had the strength of desperation to aid him. He had nothing to lose, and he knew it. He also had his hatred of Titus to power his body.

Do something, Ben thought. *Help him.* But what could he do? He'd already proven that he was no match for Blackwood. He had no pow-ers, no magic with which to attack the vampire.

Suddenly he recalled the book in which he'd read about the Death Puppets. They had been killed, he remembered. But how? The details escaped him. He hadn't been interested in such things then.

The book, however, was still in the box beside his desk. As Titus and Blackwood continued to struggle, Ben ran to his office. Switching on the light, he opened the box and looked for the book. When he had it in his hands, he raced to locate the illustration of the Death Puppet. Behind him, he heard the grunts and muttered curses that accompanied the fight between Blackwood and Titus. Time, he knew, was running out.

He fumbled with the pages, flipping through them until he found the drawing. Forcing himself not to look at it, he scanned the page op-posite it. "A total of nine deaths were blamed on the creatures before they were eventually rounded up and destroyed," he read. "Reportedly by setting them afire."

Fire. That was the answer. He threw the book down and stood up, looking around the room for anything he could use against Blackwood. Opening his desk drawer, he found a box of matches that Martha had left there. These he held tightly in his hand as he ran back to the great room. There, he found Blackwood on top of Titus, their positions re-versed. The wounds on Titus's neck were bleeding freely, and Blackwood was bending down, his snake-like tongue extended toward the blood.

Frantic, he ran at Blackwood and smashed into him with all his might. The vampire slid sideways, falling off of Titus. Ben opened the box of matches in his hand and struck one. It flared to life, and he held it out toward Blackwood.

The vampire laughed. "You poor, brave boy," he said. "Trying to save him."

As he spoke, his face changed, becoming younger. A moment later, Trey looked up at Ben. "You couldn't save me," he said. "What makes you think you can save anyone now?"

Ben stared into Trey's eyes, mesmerized. The flame burned down the thin spine of the match, scorching his fingers and going out. He didn't even notice as Blackwood's hands closed around his throat.

"I'll suck your eyes from your skull," the vampire said as all the air fled from Ben's lungs.

Ben began to black out, his consciousness dimming quickly as Blackwood choked him. Then he felt a violent wrenching as he was pulled from the creature's grip.

Titus stood over Blackwood. He was holding in his hand a can of some kind. "Give me the matches," he ordered Ben.

Ben did as he was told. Titus took one of them and lit it. Holding it in one hand, he pointed the can at it and pressed a button on its top. A faint mist burst from the nozzle. When it touched the match's flame, it bloomed into a cloud of fire. The cloud streamed at Blackwood's face and surrounded it.

The vampire uttered a shriek of pain and tried to shield its face from the fire. But it was too late. The flames clung greedily to his clothes and hair. Blackwood staggered to his feet, the flames spreading wildly over his body. He beat at them uselessly with his hands, screaming. As he turned first one way and then another, the flames reached out and caught hold of the things he touched. Tongues of fire leaped from the open pages of books, and the old wood of the shelves quickly followed.

Ben and Titus moved toward the door as the library became a crucible kindled by the whirling dervish of fire that Blackwood had been transformed into. It seemed to ignite with ferocious eagerness, as if the books themselves had been waiting for the chance to devour the thing that had once used them for its unholy purposes. Blackwood danced in the hellish ruins of the collection, writhing in agony as his tortured body transformed into a myriad of shapes before settling once more into the twisted form of the Death Puppet.

Titus looked down at the can in his hand. It was furniture polish, an old can that Ben had found in a desk drawer and used to remove the dust of summer from the library's tables. Titus tossed it into the flames, where it exploded in a shower of sparks.

"Will he die?" Ben asked.

Titus nodded. "This time he will," he said.

The fire was crawling up the walls of the library. Thick smoke already filled the room. Titus grabbed Ben's hand and led him to the door and out into the warm night.

"Where are we going now?" asked Ben.

Titus gripped his hand more tightly. "Home," he said as he started to walk.

Chapter Twenty-one

The walk back to the house was slow and difficult. Ben's leg was aching, and each step brought fresh pain. Even with Titus's help, Ben wasn't sure he would make it.

"Are you sure that Blackwood's dead?" he asked Titus.

"I believe he is, yes," Titus answered.

"You sound almost disappointed," remarked Ben, hearing a note of sadness in Titus's voice.

"He didn't start out a wicked man," Titus said. "Once he was like you or I. But he allowed the sickness to distort his mind. He believed its promises, and it made him something terrible."

"He didn't have to let it," Ben said, the pain in this leg making him angry at what seemed like a defense of the monster they'd just destroyed.

"You can't imagine its power," Titus said. "It surrounds you with its voice, fills your dreams with its lies until you want nothing more than to give in."

"Then why didn't you?" said Ben.

"I did, for a time," Titus replied.

"But you changed," Ben reminded him.

"Yes," Titus said softly. "I changed."

Finally they reached the farmhouse. Titus helped Ben inside and up the stairs to the bedroom. Ben collapsed onto the bed, welcoming its embrace. Although the smell of the burned hives still lingered in the air, he felt safe. Blackwood was dead, and it was over.

Titus sat on the edge of the bed and looked down at Ben. Seeing the expression on his face, Ben grew worried. "What's the matter?" he asked.

"Blackwood was right," Titus said. "They will come for us."

"So we'll run," Ben said. "We'll get in the car and leave."

Titus shook his head. "Running will only stop them for a short time," he said.

"Why can't you use some of those mind tricks?" Ben asked. "The ones Blackwood used on me and everyone else?"

"Perhaps I could do that," Titus answered. "But that would protect only me. You would still be vulnerable."

Ben stared at him. "I don't understand," he said. "Why?"

Titus took a deep breath. "The powers we develop work only for us," he explained. "They are designed to fool, not to protect. We can use them only to benefit ourselves, not to help others."

Ben looked into his eyes. He knew Titus was telling the truth. He could tell by the worry that was clouding Titus's face, by the concern in his gaze.

"Then make me one," he said. "Make me like you."

Titus shut his eyes. "I can't do that," he said.

Ben sat up, taking Titus's hand. "You can," he said. "I know you can. Blackwood made you, didn't he? Why can't you do the same?"

Titus opened his eyes. They were wet with tears. "I promised myself I would never do to anyone what Blackwood did to me," he said.

"But I want you to," Ben insisted. "That way we can be together." He leaned in and kissed Titus gently on the mouth. "Forever," he added.

"You have no idea what you're asking," Titus said. "You're asking for death."

"I know," Ben replied. "But I'll be with you. And we can use the bees to keep from becoming like Blackwood."

Titus gripped his hand tightly. "Think about what you're asking me to do," he said. "Think about what it will mean."

"Never dying," said Ben.

"Yes," Titus said. "Never dying. Seeing centuries pass, civilizations disappear, people grow old and wither away while you stay the same."

Ben thought about what Titus was saying. It was similar to what Blackwood had said to him in the jail cell, only instead of sounding wonderful, now it sounded horrible. The idea of remaining alive forever seemed fantastic at first, especially if he could spend that time with Titus. But what would he be giving up in return?

"Do you see now?" Titus asked. "I am nothing more than the watchman for death, the witness to every one of the world's endings. I don't possess the gift of eternal life—I am damned to be here when all else is gone."

Ben did understand, and the realization broke his heart. Tears slipped from his eyes and down his cheeks as he pressed his face against Titus's chest and wept. Titus put his arms around Ben and held him tightly.

The sound of voices coming from outside made Ben pull away. Titus left him sitting on the bed while he left the room. A minute later he reappeared. "They've come," he said.

"The police?" Ben asked. He hadn't heard any sirens, but perhaps they'd turned them off so as not to alert Titus and Ben to their arrival.

"No," Titus said. "Not the police. The others."

Ben brought his injured leg over the side of the bed and sat up. Standing, he hobbled toward the door. "I want to see them," he told Titus.

Titus helped him down the hall to the front of the house, where Ben looked out a window. The front yard was crowded with perhaps two dozen people. Their faces were filled with anger as they stood looking at the front door. Many of them carried flashlights, which they shined up at the windows, searching for any signs of life.

"Up there!" a woman shouted as her light flashed on Ben's face.

He let the curtain fall and stepped back into the hall, as if somehow that would hide him from the crowd. Turning to Titus, he thought feverishly, trying not to succumb to the panic he felt building inside him.

"What do we do?" he asked.

"I could destroy them," said Titus.

Ben shook his head. "No," he said. "Then you would be no better than Blackwood."

"It would save us," said Titus.

"Only for a short time," Ben told him. "It's like you said—then others would be after us."

"What other choice is there?" Titus asked him.

Ben closed his eyes, calming himself. He imagined Trey in the bathtub, his life swirling around him in pink clouds. He had been unable to do anything to save his lover. He hadn't been given the chance. But now he had been given a second opportunity, a chance to redeem himself.

"There's another way," Ben said, opening his eyes and looking at Titus. "I can give them what they want."

Titus shook his head slowly as the meaning of Ben's words sank in. "No," he said.

"Yes," countered Ben.

He walked to the stairs and descended them as quickly as he could. Titus followed, grabbing Ben by the arm. "You can't do this," he pleaded.

Ben reached up and stroked Titus's face. Then he kissed him gently. "Go," he said. "Out the back door. There are others like Blackwood. Find them and destroy them."

"You can't do this," said Titus again. "Not because of me."

"Go," said Ben.

He released Titus and walked toward the front door of the house. Outside, the crowd was yelling for those inside to come out. Some of them were banging on the door.

Ben turned. Titus was still standing there, watching him with a look of loss and pain on his face. Then he turned away and ran to the kitchen. Ben heard the sound of the screen door opening.

He went to the front door. Pausing there, he opened a drawer in the small table that sat in the hallway. Searching among its contents, he located a box of matches and a pocketknife among the bits of string and pencils needing sharpening. These he took out.

Opening the knife's blade, he ran it across his palm. Blood immediately began to run. He looked at it for a moment before wiping it across his face and coating his other hand in it. Then he opened the box of matches and, with bloodstained fingers, struck one against the side. It flared to life. He looked at the cheerful flame for a moment, then held it to the curtains that covered the windows on either side of the door. As the fire took hold and began to burn, he opened the door and walked onto the porch.

The crowd surrounding the house stopped their movements and looked at him. Ben stared out at their faces, at the fear and rage in their eyes. Had John Rullins seen such faces when they'd come for him? Had he looked up into eyes filled with hatred and understood what was about to happen to him?

Ben understood. He faced the people of Downing and held up his hands.

"I killed him," he said. He laughed. "I killed all of them."

Behind him, the fire was taking hold of the house, moving from the curtains to the wallpaper. He could feel its heat against his back. Soon, he knew, the whole thing would become an oven, burning away all that was inside. They would look for remains of Titus's body, but they would find nothing but ashes.

"I killed your children!" Ben shouted.

He wondered if Titus was watching. He hoped not. As the first figures moved up the steps and reached for him, he hoped that Titus was running, running through the darkness with the jars of bees in his hands.

Bradon's Bite

Sean Wolfe

Prologue

"Is there anything else I can get you, Mr. Suazo?"
The flight attendant smiled as he handed Bradon his second vodka and tonic. He was a striking man, if a little young to be the ranking first-class attendant on a transnational flight. Bradon guessed him to be in his mid-thirties, even though he looked much younger. Not quite masculine enough to be handsome exactly, but elegantly poised and professional. His brown hair was gelled and spiked with bleached-blond tips. His eyes were a piercing blue-gray and lined with long, thick brown eyelashes. When he smiled, twin dimples graced either side of his thin, pink lips.

Despite the persistent buzz of his own internal alarm system, Bradon couldn't control the fluttering he felt in his stomach when he looked at Daniel.

"A cigarette would be just perfect," Bradon said.

"I'm sorry, sir, but all Delta Airlines flights are non-smoking flights. It's federal law."

"Yes, I know." Bradon smiled and set his glass at the upper right corner of his tray table. "I was kidding. I'm just not a fan of air travel, that's all."

"I understand," Daniel said, and smiled back. "I wear the patch myself, just to get me through these longer flights," he said, and tapped his upper arm. "Unfortunately, it's going to be a very long trip, and

170

Sean Wolfe

we've barely lifted off. Hopefully that drink will help a little. I'll be sure to keep them coming."

"Yes, I'm sure it will. Thank you."

"My pleasure, sir," Daniel said, and moved on to attend the next row of passengers behind him.

Bradon took a long drink of his vodka before diluting it with the sparkling tonic. Then he leaned back in his seat and closed his eyes. Not so much because he was tired, but because he did not want the tears to fall. The last thing he needed after the most hectic and horrible week of his young life was to fall apart now, after he'd taken such drastic measures to move on. No, falling apart now was out of the question, and so he took a cool, deep breath of pressurized and filtered oxygen, opened his eyes and swallowed the last of his drink.

"I think that little fairy likes you," the overweight man sitting next to him said.

Bradon grumbled to himself and rolled his head to the right, so that he stared out the window into the dark night.

The overweight man had been sweating and trying to engage him in ignorant banter from the moment he'd squeezed himself into the aisle seat next to Bradon. He'd introduced himself as Ted, then accidentally passed gas with the effort of forcing his oversized ass into the tiny seat. A nasty, almost visible stench hovered around a three-foot radius of the man, and instantly warmed any cool air that was directed out of the tiny air-conditioning vent above them.

"They're everywhere now. Can't even go to the supermarket without bumping into them."

"Them?"

"You know. The fags."

"Mmm-hmm," Bradon said and sat up straight in his chair. "I'd be careful who you say something like that to."

"Ah, they don't mind. They're used to it. Prancing around like little princesses all the time, making a big deal of the fact that they do the nasty with each other. It's disrespectful, that's what it is."

"Disrespectful?"

"Hell, yes. They should keep it in the bedroom, not be openly coming on to unsuspecting young studs like you and me."

"So Daniel was coming on to you, too?"

"Fuck no. I'd snap his neck in two, and he knows it. He knows I'm a big ladies man. Did you see that broad with the French braids? The little blond gal near the back. I'd give my left nut for a chance with a broad like that," Ted wheezed.

Bradon said nothing, but scowled at the fat man and raised his empty glass for Daniel to refill.

"Another vodka and tonic, Mr. Suazo?"

"Yes, please. No ice this time, if you don't mind."

"Certainly. Is there anything else I can get for you?"

Ted snorted and nudged Bradon's arm.

"No, I'm fine, thank you. But, Daniel, would you happen to know anything about the attendant in the back section of the plane. The blonde with the braids?"

"Pamela?" Daniel asked, not completely successful in hiding his disappointment.

"Yes, I believe that was her name."

"I'm sorry, I don't know very much about her. We've only worked a few shifts together."

"I see. Well, Daniel, to be very honest with you, I'm not really interested in Pamela at all. I would very much like, however, to wrap you into my arms and kiss you until you're breathless. Pamela isn't really my type, you see. But my friend here, Ted, was just relaying to me that he'd be willing to perform a most painful act of self-mutilation in order to do with Pamela exactly what I'd like to do with you."

The fat man choked on his drink and spit a mouthful of it onto the back of the seat in front of him.

"You have obviously had more than enough to drink," Daniel said sternly. He removed the cup from Ted's shaking hand and tossed the almost full drink into the trashcan a few feet away. "You're cut off, Mr. Carlton. You've been told more than once on previous trips about your sexual comments toward our female attendants. One more word out of you about how fiercely you would enjoy yourself with the pleasures of any of my crew's body, and I will have you arrested and escorted off the plane the minute we land."

As he struggled to regain his composure, Ted put his hands up in a gesture of surrender. "Okay, okay. I was just trying to make a little lighthearted conversation. No need to get your panties all in a wad."

"Nothing about you is light, Mr. Carlton. I'm sure Mrs. Carlton would not be pleased to hear of how horribly you've been conducting yourself on this trip all alone, either. Don't think for a moment I won't tell her how horribly you've behaved the next time she accompanies you on one of these little business trips."

"Oh, really, there's no need to . . ."

"Are you quite certain?"

"Yes, I'm sorry. I promise. Not another word."

"All right, then. Is there is anything else I can get you, Mr. Suazo?"

"No, thank you, Daniel. I'm fine. Actually, I'd rather enjoy that kiss I mentioned earlier, but I'd hate for you to get all aggressive on me like you did with Ted, here."

Daniel smiled, then leaned across the massive bulk of Ted Carlton's body and kissed Bradon on the mouth. "Come on to the back of the plane after we've finished serving beverages. I'll switch areas with Pamela and we can be alone for a few minutes then."

"I'll do that," Bradon said, and pulled Daniel closer to him for a final kiss.

"What'd you go and do a thing like that for?" Ted whined as Daniel pulled the curtain in front of them closed. "You kissed him."

"Yes, I did. And in a few moments I'll probably be doing much more than that with him."

"You're a fag!"

"Certifiably."

"I should have known. You pretty boys are all alike with your hundred-dollar haircuts and your fancy clothes and expensive jewelry. And I can tell you pluck your eyebrows, too. Don't think that one got past me. Those big blue eyes are faker than a wooden penny, and I'll bet you spent half your parents' fortune to get those cheekbones and that jaw-line done. But, to each his own, I suppose. But that Daniel pansy better not try any of that fancy stuff with me, or I'll beat him to a pulp. And don't you go getting all limp-wrist on me, either."

"Oh, I think you can count on that."

About ten minutes later, Daniel's voice came over the intercom, calling Pamela to the front of the aircraft. As she passed their aisle, Ted reached out and pinched her on the ass. Pamela yelped and slapped his shoulder.

"Mr. Carlton! You've been warned about that kind of behavior before," she said as she slapped his shoulder again and walked off. She seemed more concerned about why she was being called to the front of the plane than she was about Ted's little pinch on the ass. She stumbled forward toward the cabin.

Ted snorted a phlegm-filled chuckle and began coughing again. "She would never admit it, but she really does have a thing for me. Did you see the way she caressed my shoulder as she left?"

"She slapped you."

"Oh, that was for your benefit. She has to maintain that professional image in front of other passengers."

"Sounds like she was pretty serious to me."

"Nah. Underneath that tough exterior, she's a little pussycat. Get it? *Pussycat*?"

"I don't think that's very appropriate."

"Lighten up, man. She's a stewardess, for chrissakes. Coffee, tea or me? Everyone knows the real reason a girl gets into this line of work. You don't really think they make enough money *legitimately* to survive, do you?"

Bradon arched his brows.

"They all supplement their income." Ted smiled, revealing uneven rows of yellow-stained teeth and a gray tongue. He grabbed his crotch and squeezed it grotesquely as he nudged Bradon in the arm again. "Know what I mean?"

"No, I'm afraid I do not."

Ted tried to raise his hips suggestively, but was lodged tightly in the seat. He took a deep breath and smiled again. "Let's just say our little Pamela serves up a little more than just soda and chips from time to time. I'm wearing her down, slowly. One of these days she's going to come around and jump on the old Ted Carlton train. And once she gets a taste of Big Daddy, she'll be begging me for more. That tongue of hers will be way too busy licking my lollipop to be worrying about smarting off to me like that."

"Yes, I'm sure she'd be quite interested in hearing that."

"Nah. There's no sense in getting her all worked up again. She's gotta save some of that energy up for when I smack that tight little ass of hers and pull her down onto my . . ."

Bradon grabbed Ted's arm and squeezed it tightly. "You are a vulgar pig, Mr. Carlton, and you are wearing my nerves dangerously thin. Perhaps shutting that rotting little mouth of yours for the duration of this trip might be prudent."

"You're hurting my arm," Ted moaned.

Bradon squeezed even harder and leaned in a couple of inches closer. He squinted his eyes into piercing narrow slits. From this close, the stench caused Bradon's stomach to churn. "I really do not want to have to take this to the next level, Mr. Carlton. It would be a much less painful trip for you if you just nod your head right now to show me that you understand me."

Large beads of sweat popped out across Carlton's forehead and ran down his face.

"Mr. Carlton? Ted?" Bradon's voice lowered to a deep bass whisper that was barely audible. "Nod your head very slowly to let me know that you hear me."

Ted nodded his head very slowly, and tried unsuccessfully to produce enough saliva to swallow.

"One more word out of that stinking little trap of yours, and I will kill you. I will sink my teeth into that fat neck and rip it apart until there is nothing left of you but a bloody, dripping carcass. Am I making myself perfectly clear?"

A tear formed in Ted's eyes and fell down his cheek as Bradon tightened his grip and held his gaze.

"Your head is not moving, Ted."

Ted nodded his head and began weeping.

"You will stop crying this instant, Ted. When I release your arm, you will not remember this conversation. And you will not say another word to me the remainder of this trip. Do you understand me?"

"Yes."

"Good. I can tell just by looking at you that you would be quite tough, and not the least bit palatable. I prefer not wasting my time with killing you. I'm going to let go of your arm now, and return to my drink and the comfort of my solitude. I want you to apologize to Pamela for insulting her with your disgusting comments, and then I want you not to say another word the rest of the flight. Will you do that for me, Ted?"

Ted nodded again.

"Fine," Bradon said, releasing his grip on Ted's arm. He leaned back in his seat and closed his eyes. A couple of minutes later he heard Ted call Pamela over and apologize for his behavior.

When Pamela mumbled her acceptance, Bradon allowed his mind to drift for the first time in over a week. In just over three hours he would be landing in San Francisco a new man. He'd left Bradon Lugo far behind him in Boston, with his dead father.

Bradon Suazo was a new man. A different man. A better man. He was his mother's son now, and taking her name would give Bradon the strength to move ahead and survive. Bradon Lugo had been weak and had always lived in the shadow of his father. He had relied on the half-truths and the unspoken lies Victor Lugo dispensed at will.

He'd believed them all, too. With all his heart he'd believed the stories, the fantasies, the mythical love story of Rachel Suazo and Victor Lugo. He'd believed he was the very special product of an incomparable passion and boundless love.

How foolish he'd been.

There was nothing truthful about Victor Lugo. His was a world of lies, craftily designed and meticulously told. Victor hadn't told a truthful word in decades, possibly centuries. Each day was lived in preparation for the next deception.

But Bradon had put an end to all the lies, all the deceit. He took a deep breath and laid back in the farthest reclining position on the seat and closed his eyes. In a few more hours, he would arrive in his new home. Boston, and every grimy, despicable memory of his youth there, would become distant memories.

"Mr. Suazo, I have a few free minutes. If you want to come back with me, I can show you the galley."

Bradon opened his eyes and looked into the smiling face of the cute flight attendant.

"Call me Bradon," he said, and stood up to follow Daniel to the back of the plane.

When they reached the back section of the plane, Daniel whispered that this was where they kept the cups and snacks and extra pillows and blankets. He turned around to face Bradon, and when he did, Bradon leaned in so that his full body pushed gently against Daniel's until Daniel was walking backward blindly. He stopped only when his back abutted the lavatory door.

"I can't go in there with you," he whispered.

"Of course you can," Bradon whispered back, and reached down to open the door. "Why else would you have called me back here?"

"I was thinking we could make out a little in the galley. But the bathroom? Someone will catch us. We won't hear them coming and then they'll try to get in and make a scene."

"No, they won't. They're all otherwise engaged."

Daniel peered around Bradon's shoulders and noticed, that indeed, all the passengers seemed occupied.

"Your heart is beating fast, Daniel," Bradon whispered as he leaned in and kissed the attendant's earlobe. "Are you afraid?"

"Yes, a little."

"Don't be afraid," Bradon said as he opened the restroom door and ushered Daniel inside.

Daniel was panting heavily and gasping for breath as he leaned over the sink and pushed his ass against the hardness straining against Bradon's jeans.

Bradon looked at his reflection in the small mirror above the sink. His black, shiny hair was trendily cut and styled. His bright blue eyes sparkled with excitement. His lips were full and pink. His muscles bulged against the fabric of his clothing. To anyone else, Bradon Suazo would look like the next budding cinematic superstar. But Bradon looked closer into the mirror. His lips weren't quite as pink and supple as they normally were. And his skin was pale. Very pale. He hadn't fed in over a week, and it was beginning to show. He felt the strength and energy drain from his body with every passing hour.

Now was the time to feed. Daniel was perfect, and his for the taking. The young attendant panted even more heavily now, and reached down to drop his trousers to his knees. He humped the back of his ass against Bradon's throbbing crotch.

Bradon moaned with the pleasure and wrapped his arms around Daniel's waist. He ground his pelvis against the supple flesh of Daniel's ass.

"I've never done anything like this before," Daniel managed to whisper between pants.

"No, of that I'm quite sure."

"I want you, Bradon. I want you so badly."

Bradon nibbled on Daniel's earlobe and kissed him softly on the neck. His lips tingled with excitement and hunger as they passed over the thick, throbbing vein running across the length of Daniel's silky smooth neck. His own heart was now racing as quickly as Daniel's, and his cock throbbed painfully against the constraints of his jeans. He closed his eyes and quickly shoved his jeans to the floor in one move.

He pressed his hardness against the smooth, muscular ass in front of him. His flesh was hot and hard against the cool, soft, smooth ass cheeks, and he moaned again. This time his moan sounded desperate and animalistic. His heart raced faster, and he looked up at his reflection in the mirror again. Daniel was bent all the way over the sink, so that Bradon could only see the back of his head. Bradon's own reflection was different now than it had been a couple of minutes earlier. His eyes looked red, and his skin was so pale it looked translucent. He opened his mouth wide and looked at his teeth.

They were there. His two front canine teeth were long and sharp. Bradon moaned and leaned his body against Daniel's.

"I'm sorry, Daniel," Bradon said as he rubbed his naked, hard cock against Daniel's butt and legs. "I don't want to do this. I swear, I don't want to do this."

"It's okay, Bradon," Daniel whispered back encouragingly. "I want you to. I want you inside me."

Bradon began sobbing. He lifted his head from Daniel's back and leaned forward. When his lips touched the supple skin of Daniel's neck, he breathed in, savoring the sweet smell of Daniel's sweat and his cologne. He opened his mouth and pressed his tongue against the warm throbbing flesh.

"I . . . don't . . . want . . ."

"Do it, Bradon. I want you insi—"

Bradon bit down softly into Daniel's neck, just barely enough to pierce the skin. It was enough to startle Daniel, and his body stiffened beneath Bradon's.

"Bradon? What's going on?"

Bradon cried softly, as his fangs sank another quarter of an inch into

Daniel's neck. As the first trickle of warm blood slid across his tongue, he squeezed Daniel tighter beneath him and sucked softly on his throat.

"Ow. That's a little rough, Bradon. It hurts."

Bradon continued sucking for a few seconds, but did not sink his teeth completely into Daniel's neck. If only he could feed for just a couple of seconds, he would be fine. If only he could stop himself before he went too far. Just a few drops were all he needed for right now. He could wait to fully feed until he was safe in San Francisco. He didn't want to kill Daniel. Daniel was a nice kid who'd made the mistake of flirting with Bradon while he was in a weakened state of body and mind.

He drank for a few seconds more, and when he felt Daniel's body begin to quiver and grow limp, he quickly withdrew.

"Daniel?" Bradon cried out as he pulled himself away from the young flight attendant. Daniel's body grew heavy and more limp as it slumped to the toilet seat.

"Oh, Christ," Bradon whimpered as he crumpled to the floor next to Daniel's unconscious body. "No. Please don't let this happen. I didn't drink too much. I swear, I didn't drink too much. Just a little bit. I only needed a little bit. Please don't be dead, Daniel," he said as he gently shook Daniel's body.

"What happened?" Daniel said dazedly as he came to.

"I'm so sorry," Bradon said as he rocked Daniel in his arms. "I didn't mean to . . ."

"Did I faint?"

Bradon choked back a sob and wiped a tear from his eyes. He took a deep breath before answering. "Yes."

Daniel looked down at his trousers, which were still around his ankles. He reached down and touched Bradon's naked thigh beneath him.

"Damn, you must really have been fantastic. I've never fainted before!"

Bradon laughed softly and leaned against the sink.

"I just wish I could remember it. After a fuck that good, it's usually nice if you can recall all the juicy details later, you know what I mean?"

"Yes, I do," Bradon whispered. He stood and helped Daniel do the same. "But trust me, you were fantastic."

"Well, of course I was. Hell, I passed out. How much more fantastic can you be, right? I always did have a flare for the dramatics."

Bradon laughed, and the two young men began getting dressed.

"What the hell is that?" Daniel asked suddenly.

"What?" Bradon asked.

"This mark on my neck." He leaned in closer to the mirror. "Did you give me a fucking hickey? My supervisors will freak when they see this."

"No, I didn't give you a hickey. It's just a scratch. I think you might have knocked against the sink when you passed out. Nothing to worry about. Borrow some of Pamela's foundation and cover it up. No one will notice."

"I hope not. I just got this promotion. The last thing I need is for someone to find me getting screwed in the can on my second trip as ranking attendant."

"Believe me, no one will notice a thing. I promise. Now, should I leave first, or do you want to?"

"I'll go first. Wait about thirty seconds or so before you come out, okay?"

"I will."

"And thanks for a really great time. At least, I guess it was."

"It was fantastic. Thank you."

Daniel opened the door and squeezed himself out into the galley of the plane. Bradon waited a full minute before he opened the door and left the restroom himself. Every passenger was still reading a book or sleeping or working on a computer. No one seemed to notice the two young men having been gone. No one seemed to notice the locked bathroom door. No one seemed to notice that Bradon's face was slightly less pale and slightly more flushed. No one noticed the tiny dried trickle of blood on the corner of his now fully soft and pink lips.

The Boy Vampire

"Tell me again, Daddy," the young boy said anxiously as he struggled to push the heavy chair closer to the kitchen table. After a
couple of minutes, the chair was at a sufficient distance from the edge
of the table, and the young boy took a deep breath before raising his
leg high enough to rest his knee on the padded seat, shoving himself
up to the top of the seat. "Please, Daddy. Just one more time."

"I know what you're doing, son," Victor said, as he pulled the plastic
Ziplock bag from the freezer and laid it carefully in the sink. He waited
until the water turned warm, and then directed the spout so that the
warm water ran over the plastic bag. "This will take about five minutes, and then I have to nuke it for a minute. You know the drill,
Bradon. There's not enough time to go into the story again."

"Five minutes is a long time," Bradon said. "The stories have been
getting shorter, anyway. Pretty soon they'll only last a couple of minutes."

"You're pouting, son. That's not an admirable trait. Especially for a
big five-year-old."

"I'm not pouting. I just want to hear the story."

"But it's time for your feeding. I know you don't like to feed,
Bradon. But it's very important. I've told you before, you will die without the blood. You're trying to manipulate me into letting you skip

today's feeding. It's not going to work. You haven't fed for ten days. That's three days longer than you should go without at your age. You're not a baby anymore, son. You're growing very fast, and you need more and more blood as you grow and get older."

"I'm not going to grow or get older in the next five minutes," Bradon said, and crossed his arms across his chest defiantly. "My food will be ready by the time you finish the story."

"Oh, you have your mother's wit. And her mouth. You're very intelligent for your age, son. Maybe too smart for your own good."

"That's not possible. You're just trying to get out of telling me the story again."

Victor fought the urge to smile. Instead, he turned his back to his son, and turned the Ziplock bag over so the warm water could heat the other side. He sighed and walked slowly across the room to the kitchen table.

"Your mother was an angel, Bradon. A gift from heaven. I knew it the moment I laid eyes on her."

"You were walking along the Charles River, right?" He knew the story by heart, and was determined to fill in the many blanks his father seemed increasingly intent on creating.

"That's correct, son. It was about midnight. A small riverside concert had just let out, and there were several young people walking around the banks of the river. It was dark outside, of course, but your mother's smile and the sparkle in her eyes shined right through the darkness and beckoned me to her."

"It was cold outside, right? And she wasn't wearing a coat."

"That's right, son. It was late August, and the nights were beginning to get a little chilly."

"We're in August now, aren't we, Daddy?"

"Yes," Victor sighed, as he turned his gaze to the darkness outside the kitchen window. "Next week will be the seventh anniversary of the night I met your sweet mother. You'll never know how much I miss her."

"That's not part of the story, Daddy. Stick to the story. I've only got five minutes, remember."

Victor laughed out loud, despite his attempt to the contrary, and ruffled his young son's head. "Rachel Suazo was the most beautiful woman who ever lived."

"Prettier than Alexis Carrington on *Dynasty?*"

"Much. And so much nicer, too."

"Prettier than Heather Locklear?"

"No comparison."

"Wow!" Bradon whispered, and shook his head in disbelief. He'd often brought up lots of pretty girls' names during this part of the story, but he'd never dreamed that his mother could actually have been prettier than Heather Locklear.

"Yes, wow, indeed. I knew the very moment I saw her that I had to have her. She was several yards away from me, but I saw right through the damp morning air and darkness, and I fell in love with Rachel even before we'd said a word to one another."

"And that's when you gave her your coat."

"You know this story better than I do, squirt!"

"Yeah, but you were *there.*"

"I was, indeed. I walked directly up to your mother and she fell madly in love with me instantly."

"Yeah, right. That's not the way the story used to sound when you first started telling it to me."

"Yes, it is!"

Bradon rolled his eyes, and walked over to the sink to check on the bag of blood warming. He used a small stepladder to reach the counter and leaned into the sink so that he could turn the bag over.

Victor smiled as he watched his son preparing his own meal. It was good that he was beginning to get hungry. At his age, going too long without food could quickly become fatal. Though Bradon didn't like to feed, he always came around when the hunger began to get too strong. He was a good boy.

"All she wanted was your coat," Bradon said, and crawled into his father's lap.

"Maybe at first. But it didn't take long for her to come around. I walked her home that morning, and before I left, she gave me her phone number. I called her the next evening, and from that moment on, we were madly in love with one another."

"Why didn't you get married?"

"That's complicated, son. My family was against the relationship from the very beginning. They didn't see Rachel the way I did."

"How did they see Mommy?"

"They saw her as a mortal, and as a threat. But it wasn't just my family. Rachel's parents were not thrilled with our arrangement either."

"Because you're a vampire?"

"No. They never knew that. Rachel didn't even know that until a couple of months into our relationship."

"Why didn't they like you, then?"

"Because I had money. Because I was not Puerto Rican. Because I only came to see Rachel at night, and they were sure I stole her innocence. Because I took their little baby girl away from them."

"Mommy wasn't a little girl. She was nineteen."

"She was still *their* little girl. And they were right, really. I had no right coming in and sweeping her off her feet like I did. But I couldn't help myself. When I finally decided to tell her I was a vampire, I prepared myself for the worst. I had all my bags packed and was ready to flee Boston forever. To run and get away from your mother so that I could never hurt her."

"Where would you have gone?"

"I don't know. I hadn't really thought it out that far in advance. But I never had to leave. When I told your mother I was a vampire, she was a little stunned, but not shocked. She was very smart for her age, just like you. She believed in vampires and ghosts and angels and spirits equally. She understood that we are all a part of the cycle of life."

"So she didn't care that you eat people?"

"We do not eat people, son. You know that. And so did your mother. Flesh is filthy and poisoned. It is only blood that we need for survival. It took your mom a couple of weeks to completely accept who I was. But eventually her love for me proved much stronger than her fear of me. When she finally came back home after spending some time at her parents' house she wrapped her arms around me and wept for a very long time."

"Why was she crying?"

"Loving a vampire is not easy, son. She knew her life was going to be difficult. But she swore her love to me, and promised never to leave me. She only had two conditions of her undying love. Do you remember what they were?"

"That you never feed on her, and you didn't tell her about your feedings."

"That's right. She understood that I was immortal, but she was very adamant about not wanting to become immortal herself. She wanted to live a natural life. So I was never to feed on her, and never to convert her."

"Why didn't Mommy want to live forever?" Bradon asked as he snuggled against his father's chest.

"Because she was smart. A vampire's life is a very difficult one. It's not easy living for centuries."

"Then why did you want to be a vampire?"

"I had no choice. I was born into a long family of vampires."

"So nobody ever bit you?"

"No. But even though I never chose to be a vampire, I am proud of my ancestry and my heritage. We come from an extremely noble line, son. It's all I've ever known. I do not kill for the sake of killing. I kill in order to survive."

"But not all vampires are like that."

"No, that is true. Some vampires were born mortal, but have made a conscious decision to convert to vampirism. Many of those are just hungry for immortality. They are stupid and greedy, and do not realize the painful existence of eternity. Others hunger for violence and the thrill of killing. These people become vampires because the thought of hundreds of lifetimes filled with violence and blood excites them."

"How do they choose to become a vampire?"

"They study vampirism. They know the underground, and they hunt us out. Then they offer themselves to us as a sacrifice. There are many among us who find the idea of mentoring a new convert challenging and exciting."

"And what about you?"

"I find the thought reckless. True vampires are born into it. To bite a human being and allow him to live through the conversion is a horrendous act, and it only results in creating hybrids. Sometimes vampires find a mortal they feel is their soulmate, and they convert that person so they can spend eternity together."

"But you didn't do that with Mommy."

"No, I didn't. I loved and respected your mother too much to do that to her. If she'd wanted to convert, that would have been another story. But she valued her life as a mortal human and wanted to remain that way. She also valued my life for what it was and never asked me to be anything else. I respected her for that and vowed to honor her conditional love."

"That was nice, Daddy."

"Yes, nice and also difficult. But your mother and I grew more in love with one another with every passing day. Her parents hated our relationship and would have nothing to do with us. My parents hated our relationship and warned of the impending doom that would result. They also wanted nothing to do with us. So we were on our own."

"That's sad."

"Not really. We got along just fine. And then when we got word that you were going to enter our lives, we became ecstatic. It was a long and painful pregnancy for your mother, but we were so happy that you were going to join our family."

"And then Mommy died."

Victor lifted Bradon off of his lap and set him on his own chair, then walked over to the sink and removed the now thawed bag of blood. "Yes," he said as he walked with his back to his son over to the microwave. "She died while giving birth to you."

"Did she ever see me?"

"Oh, yes," Victor said as he removed the bag of blood from the microwave. He took a straw from the cabinet above the stove and slid it into the tiny slit at the top of the zippered bag. "She held you in her arms for a couple of minutes right after you were born. You were so tiny cradled against her breasts. Her last words were 'take care of my son.' I promised her I would."

"I wish I could have known her."

"Me too, son. Me too. But you have her heart, Bradon, and her soul. Don't you ever forget that. Your mother was an angel on earth. The best woman to ever live. And now she is an angel in heaven, and she is always with you."

"Is she here right now?"

Victor shivered and looked around the dark kitchen. "Yes, she is, son. She is here right now."

"Good."

"Now drink up," Victor said, as he handed the bag of warmed blood to his young son. "You haven't eaten in over a week. It's time."

"Do I have to?"

"Yes, you do. And then it's time for bed. The sun will be coming up soon."

Bradon took a sip of the blood, and puckered his face in disgust. He looked up from the top of his eyes and saw Victor's disappointment. Then he closed his eyes tightly and drank the remaining pint of blood without pausing to catch his breath.

"That's a good boy. I'm proud of you, son."

Bradon belched loudly, then covered his mouth as his face reddened.

"Come on, kiddo," Victor said as he ruffled Bradon's hair again. "Let's get you downstairs and tucked in."

Over the next two years, Victor began deleting more and more from the story. Once, he had spent hours in front of the fireplace, with Bradon snuggled warmly against his chest as he spun the most magnificent love story in history. Now, he had it scaled down to a little over three minutes, and he told it with his back to his son as he washed the dishes and Bradon cleared the kitchen table.

"You're getting old and lazy, Dad," Bradon said, as he wiped the wooden table clean with a dishrag.

"I'm older than you can imagine, son. But I am not lazy. Why would you say such a thing?"

"You act like I don't remember the story the way you used to tell it."

"I don't know what you're talking about," Victor mumbled, as he stared out the kitchen window and rinsed the suds from a clean plate.

"You're forgetting her."

"That's ridiculous, Bradon. I could never forget your mother. She was the love of my life."

"Then why do you have the story down to under three minutes?"

"Not tonight, Bradon, okay? I'm tired. I don't feel like arguing."

"Me either. So from now on, I'll tell you the story. It wouldn't hurt for you to remember it like I do."

"It would hurt, Bradon. It would hurt very much."

"Too bad. I won't let you forget Mom. I know you don't want to."

"I don't want to forget her, son. I just want to move on. Your mother's death was a very painful time in my life. I don't want to rehash it every single night."

"But you deal with death at least a couple of times a week. Even more than that the past few months."

"It's not the same thing, and you know it. Those people are homeless transients and prostitutes and drug dealers. No one will miss them. And they certainly mean nothing to me. I loved your mother very much."

"I still do."

"She meant the world to me."

"She still does to me."

"You didn't even know her, Bradon."

"So? She lives inside of me. Her heart and her soul are a part of me. Remember? You used to tell me that all the time."

"Yes, I remember. And I never want you to forget it, either. But I simply cannot go on reliving the memory, the pain of your mother's death."

"You'll survive, Dad. You're immortal, remember? So from now on, I will tell the story and you can wash the dishes with your back to me if you want. I don't care. But if you love me, you will listen."

"Of course I love you."

"Good. Starting tomorrow I'll be the storyteller."

"You are way too intelligent for you own good. Or for mine, for that matter. No one should be that smart at your age."

"I can't help it."

"I know. By the way, that reminds me. In two weeks you turn seven. You know what that means."

"I don't want to talk about it."

"That's good, because there's nothing to discuss. Every naturally born vampire executes his first live feeding on his seventh birthday. It's nature's law."

"But I'm only half vampire. I'm also half human."

"You are a vampire, Bradon, and you are my son. On your seventh birthday, we will go out together and you will feed on the live, warm blood of a human. The frozen bags of blood I've been storing for you are no longer sufficient. You're growing dizzy easily and getting weak. It's time for you to become a man."

"At seven years old? What's the hurry? I'll live for eternity, right? I'm sure it can wait another couple of years."

"Damn, you do have your mother's wit. And her tongue."

"Thanks."

"Nevertheless, you will accompany me two weeks from tonight for your first feeding. I will have no more arguments."

"But, Daddy . . ."

"Give it up, Bradon. Don't 'Daddy' me. I won't fall for that childish act. You only act like a child when you're losing a fight. I'm not so old and lazy that I don't know that."

"I don't want to . . ."

"Not another word, Bradon. And if you do not join me on your birthday feeding, I will burn every photo of your mother and forbid her name to be spoken ever again."

"You wouldn't dare!"

"Don't push me on this, Bradon. I'm making you a deal. You agree to start your live feedings at least once a month. It's all you will need for a few more years. Promise me that, and I will listen to your whimsical stories, no matter how long they may be. But I'm warning you, son. This is a one-time offer. I will not bring it up again. Am I making myself understood?"

"Yes, sir."

"Good. I'm tired, now, and the sun will be coming up in a couple of hours. I'm going to bed. I suggest you do the same."

"I'll be down in a few minutes. I just want to finish the chapter I'm reading in my book."

"All right. But don't be too long."

"I won't. I promise."

"I love you, son."

"I love you too, Dad."

Bradon watched as his father dressed and groomed. His dad looked marvelous in his black tuxedo and white, starched shirt. His short, black hair was slicked back and his sideburns were perfectly tapered. His lips were full and pink against the creamy white skin of his smooth face. He hummed and tapped his feet as he looked at himself in the mirror.

"I can't do this," Bradon said, as he zipped up his jeans.

"Of course you can. You just have cold feet. Everyone does their first time."

"No, I really can't do it."

"Bradon, we've talked about this before. You know it is not an option."

"I know, but . . ."

"God damn it!" Victor yelled suddenly, and shoved Bradon down onto the couch. "I'm tired of this childish behavior, Bradon Lugo. We had a deal."

"I thought I could do this, Daddy, but I can't."

Victor grabbed the framed picture of Rachel that graced the fireplace mantel and threw it forcefully against the far wall. The glass faceplate shattered into dozens of pieces, and the wooden frame splintered in every direction.

"No!" Bradon cried out. He stood, ready to run to the broken framed picture that had been his favorite of his mother.

Victor pushed Bradon back to the seat of the sofa and walked briskly to retrieve the torn picture of his dead wife. He held the glossy picture by its corners and ripped it into tiny pieces, and then threw them into the dwindling fire in the brick fireplace. The blaze crackled and sputtered lively for a moment, and then died down again when it had completely consumed the remains of the photo.

Bradon wept loudly and covered his face with his hands.

"Damn it, son. I didn't want to do that. But I wasn't joking. This is not an option. We had a deal. I've listened to your three-hour mini-series of your loving mother every night for the last two weeks. It is time for you to live up to your part of the deal. Your responsibility."

"But that was my favorite picture of her," Bradon sobbed, as he wiped at his wet, red eyes.

"I know. It was my favorite too. But I had to do it, son. And I will not hesitate to do the same thing with every other picture and any other reminders of her if you do not stand up right this second and follow me out that door."

Bradon looked into his father's eyes and saw that he meant what he said. He wiped the last remaining tear from his eyes and stood up slowly.

"That is the Anchor Hotel," Victor whispered to Bradon as he wrapped his arms around his son's shoulders. The hotel was a shabby two-story wooden building in the middle of an old, almost abandoned industrial district near the docks. The once-fluorescent sign that used to announce the hotel's presence now blinked only once every three or four minutes, and only in splotches of lights that still carried some life in them. The only other light for a three-block radius came from behind the shabby yellowish-white curtains of the hotel rooms, and from a blinking low-wattage street lamp that was several feet from the back of the hotel, right on the alley.

"They rent their rooms by the hour. It's always full. Some of the whores rent their rooms by eight-hour blocks and entertain six or seven men a night. Most of the johns are sailors, but not all. They also get a lot of married businessmen who don't want to risk being seen on the other side of town where they actually live."

"It's scary out here," Bradon said, as he hugged himself tighter to his father's side. "I don't like how that light shines through the fog."

Victor laughed and squeezed his son's shoulders. "You will learn to appreciate that hazy light, believe me. It will help you see the prettier whores, and trust me, that will make the experience so much better. A whore is a whore, but the prettier whores always seem to taste so much better."

Bradon sighed and drew his jacket collar closer around his neck. He waited with his father in silence for a few minutes, and then the back door of the hotel's ground floor creaked open. A fat, middle-aged man stumbled out into the darkness and rushed to the new Mercedes that awaited him a full two blocks down on the opposite side of the street.

As the Mercedes roared to life and screeched its way down the street and out of sight, the back door of the hotel closed as noisily as it had opened. A few seconds later a tiny orange glow lit the damp foggy air and a thin trail of smoke drifted up toward the glow of the streetlight. A thin woman, clad in a short skirt and a thin wraparound shawl, strolled leisurely over to the lamp and leaned against it. She took deep drags from the cigarette and held the smoke deep in her lungs for several seconds before blowing it out into the cool night air.

"That's Veronica. I've had my eye on her for a couple of months now. Even spoken with her a couple of times. I told her I wanted to get together with her sometime soon, so she won't be afraid when I approach her. You stay here in the shadows for a few minutes. I will go and speak with her, and then pretend to kiss her neck. She will begin to struggle after a few seconds and then she will go limp in my arms. When I wave you over, you must hurry. The blood is only warm for a few minutes."

"I don't think I can . . ."

"Bradon, this is not the time for doubt or hesitancy. When I wave for you, you will hurry and join me. This is not a request. It is a command. I will not tolerate insubordination. Is that clear?"

"Yes, sir."

"Good. Now stand back behind the shadow here, and wait for my call."

Bradon watched as his father strolled over to the woman. She looked a little startled at first, and then relaxed as Victor got closer to her. She extended her cheek and allowed Victor to kiss her, then accepted a light for her new cigarette. Bradon's heart began to race as he watched his father pull the woman closer to him and fondle her breasts. He thought about running away, but found he could not move.

A moment later Victor handed Veronica a bill, and she tucked it into her bra. She pulled Victor's face closer to hers and kissed him on the lips. Then she laughed and flipped her long blond hair behind her

and tilted her neck to the left. The light of the lamp above them reflected brilliantly off her ivory-white throat.

Even though he was at least twenty feet away, Bradon could see her
thick jugular vein pulsing across her neck. The bluish river of blood
throbbed invitingly around her neck and Bradon couldn't take his eyes
off of it. He watched in fascination as his father kissed Veronica's neck,
causing her to moan and giggle.

And then it happened. She whimpered softly, and began to push
against Victor's body. Her hands flung out wildly, beating uselessly against
Victor's chest and shoulders. Bradon saw the first trickle of blood cas-
cade between his father's lips and down Veronica's slender throat.
Seconds later, she stopped fighting and fell limp against Victor's body.
Victor wrapped her in his arms, pulled her just out of the bright glow
of the street lamp, and laid her on the ground. He sucked on her neck
for a full minute before raising his arm and waving to Bradon to join
him.

Before he had a chance to react, Bradon realized he was rushing toward his father and the unconscious woman. He didn't feel his feet hit
the pavement beneath him, but relished the cool damp breeze that
brushed against his face as he rushed toward his first live meal.

Victor raised his face from the woman's neck just before Bradon
reached them. Blood stained his entire mouth and lips, and dripped
slowly down his chin. He was breathing heavily and his eyes seemed
distant and glossed over.

"Hurry," he said, and quickly moved aside so his son could take his
place. When Bradon hesitated slightly, Victor grabbed him by the arm
and pulled him down to the dying woman's neck. "Feed," he said
roughly.

Bradon dropped to his knees and leaned in closer to the woman's
face. She looked to be in her mid-thirties, and was strikingly beautiful.
Her emerald green eyes were frozen open. For a brief moment he
smelled her sweet perfume mixed with the sweat of sex. And then he
smelled the blood.

Suddenly he was filled with a hunger he'd never known. He leaned a
couple of inches closer to the woman's neck and reached out tenta-
tively with his tongue. He licked at the cold blood that was left drip-

ping from his father's puncture wounds. It was salty and a little bitter, but irresistible nonetheless. Bradon sank his teeth into the same wounds his father had previously made and sucked, drawing several mouthfuls of warm blood from the woman's body. He swallowed it eagerly and began to pant from the effort to drain even more from the lifeless body beneath him.

"That's enough, son," Victor said as he pulled Bradon up from the ground.

Bradon's mouth was dripping with still-warm blood. When he reached up with his hand to wipe it from his face, his tiny fingers came back stained with the thick red lifesource of the dead woman. He leaned forward and vomited a few feet from his father and the dead woman.

Victor stood back and waited for Bradon to finish being sick, and then walked over to him. He chuckled as he pulled Bradon up from the ground and hugged him tightly.

"It's all right, son. It always happens the first time. Nothing to be ashamed of. You just kept at it a little too long. You got a little too much, and the last few swallows were probably already turning sour. That's when you know it's time to stop."

Bradon began to sob, and fell back to the ground. He looked over at the dead woman and cried uncontrollably.

"It's okay," Victor laughed softly. "I cried my first time, too. We all do. Tomorrow you will feel much better, I promise. You did well tonight, Bradon. And now you have enough fresh blood to get you through for about another month."

"I will never do this again," Bradon spat out angrily.

"Yes, you will. You can't imagine it right now, but believe me, you will do this again. About once a month for the next several years, and then gradually you will begin to need it once every couple of weeks."

"I will never do this again," Bradon repeated even more angrily. "And I hate you for making me do it this time."

"Of course you do. But you will feel differently tomorrow."

"I want to go home."

"We will. But first I have to dispose of the body. Wait for me over there by the bushes. I'll only be a few minutes. There's a drainage ditch just a few yards away. Between the dogs and rats and birds, she will be gone in a few days. No one will report her missing. The only people who even knew she was ever alive are her johns, the other whores and the manager of this run-down cockroach-infested dump. She will not be missed."

"I'll miss her," Bradon said as he pulled himself up from the ground and walked slowly over to the bushes to wait for his father.

The hunt became a little easier over the next few months and years, but Bradon never acquired a liking for it. He hunted and fed with his father because he needed warm blood to stay alive. He dreaded the time every month when he knew he would have to accompany his father for a feeding. Many times, he questioned the need to kill the victim. Couldn't they just feed on the humans for a while, and stop before they died? Couldn't they leave them to wake several hours later, wounded and dazed, but still alive?

Victor was adamant about killing the victims and disposing of their bodies. Bradon refused to help him, and waited instead in the dark shadows of the night for his father to accompany him back home.

When Bradon turned ten years old, his hatred for the act of killing and the disgust he felt for his father's hunger and excitement of the kill turned to rebellion. He knew his father was growing weary of his long-winded nightly stories of Rachel, and he spent hours adding more and more details until the tale finally lasted over three hours.

"We made a deal, remember?" he taunted Victor. "If I joined you for feedings once a month, you would listen to my stories of Mom."

"I'm listening," Victor said, even as he ran the vacuum cleaner or cleaned the house obsessively or worked on the backyard deep into the dark mornings.

On his fifteenth birthday, Bradon was told he would need to start feeding and killing on his own. His requirement for fresh blood was increasing to every two or three weeks. Bradon thought about refusing to feed solo, then decided that leaving his father out of these sickly intimate moments of his life might be good. Knowing that Victor so enjoyed the time they spent together on feedings would make the act of exclusion sweeter still.

Though Victor was excited to have his son embarking on solo feeds, he was also a little reluctant to let him do them completely solo, at least for the first few times.

"Something could go wrong, and I can't have you botching things. There are consequences to sloppiness that come with a very high price. Higher than we are capable of paying."

"Fine," Bradon agreed reluctantly.

Bradon chose a cold, rainy September evening for his first solo kill. Victor pleaded with him to wait one more evening, when the skies were clear, but Bradon stubbornly refused. "I'm going tonight, with or without you."

Victor grumbled as he grabbed his raincoat and followed his son into the dark night. He mumbled and complained all the way to the theatre. It was here that Bradon had chosen to claim his first solo victim.

"I don't think anyone is going to come out that door," Victor said after waiting outside the backstage entrance for over an hour.

"You're free to leave if you want."

"Damn it, you're intolerably stubborn."

"There she is," Bradon whispered as the stage door opened.

A petite brunette stopped in the doorway, and opened her umbrella before stepping out into the darkened alley.

"Who is she?" Victor whispered.

"Does it matter?"

"No, not really."

"She's not a prostitute," Bradon said, as he rolled his eyes.

"How do you know?"

"She's an actress. A very good actress. She has the lead role in the play here. I've seen it several times. She plays a very strong character, but I sense that she is quite vulnerable. She never socializes with the rest of the cast, and always leaves the theatre alone."

"Good choice."

"I'm so glad you approve."

"You'd better hurry," Victor said, as he shoved Bradon forward. "She's heading for a car."

Bradon stumbled forward and fell against a plastic trashcan that had been propped against the brick theatre building.

"Who's there?" the woman asked as she turned to face Bradon.

Before he could think of anything to say, Bradon lurched forward and tackled the small woman to the ground. She screamed and swung her umbrella, striking Bradon in the front of his head and knocking him to the ground. She continued to scream as she kicked him in the groin and then turned to run.

Bradon groaned and wriggled painfully on the ground. The woman was several feet away before he realized she was dangerously close to escaping. He saw his father preparing to strike, and jumped to his feet.

"No!" he screamed at his father. "She's mine."

Bradon struggled to his feet despite the wracking pain throbbing though his groin and ran toward the woman. He crashed into her back, knocking her to the ground. She was crying now, and pleading with Bradon not to hurt her. She was much stronger than she looked, and fought valiantly against Bradon's attack. His first attempt at her throat was a complete miss, and he knocked his head against the pavement instead. He was stunned, and for a moment, stopped fighting the woman to grasp his aching head. It was all she needed to struggle to her feet and start running.

"Shit!" Bradon yelled as he ran to catch up with her.

He grabbed her from behind, and this time his fangs found their mark. She whimpered as she fell forward into the graveled pavement. Bradon heard her forehead thump against the ground, and cringed even as he sank his fangs deeper into her throat. The collision with the ground knocked her unconscious, and made the rest of the kill easy. Bradon gnawed clumsily at her throat and drank her blood. When it began to turn sour, he continued anyway.

"That's enough," Victor said, and reached down to pull his son from the dead woman's throat.

"Leave me alone!" Bradon yelled, and thrust his face back into the bloody neck of the actress. He ripped at her neck, pulling the flesh from it and spitting it toward his father.

"Leave me alone," he cried, and dropped himself limply across the dead body underneath him.

Bradon lay across the woman for several minutes. When there were no more tears, he pulled himself up and looked at Victor. His father looked at him with a mixture of pride and pity.

"Now what?" Bradon asked as he wiped the drying blood from his mouth.

"You wait here. I'll get rid of the body."

"No," Bradon answered. "I'll do it. You wait for me at home."

"That's not a good idea, Bradon. You've never done this before."

"Yeah, well I'd never killed anyone before either. But now I have. So I'm all grown up now. I hope you're proud of your son, Daddy."

Victor started to reply, but was stung by his son's reproach.

"Go home," Bradon said as he reached down to pick up the heavy body. "I'll be there shortly."

Home was not a pleasant place for either of the Lugo men after that night. Bradon grew more rebellious and more hateful to his father with every passing week. He hated his father's macho attitude. He hated that his father no longer wanted to talk about Rachel and had grown impatient with Bradon's stories. But most important, he hated the fact that he had to kill people and feed from their blood to survive. It didn't feel right for Bradon. It never felt natural.

His father was never able to understand Bradon's aversion to feeding or to killing. What could be more natural to a vampire than feeding? What could be more right? What could be more exciting than finding a loose whore, tricking her into believing you were desperate for her sex, and then feeding on her blood and eventually killing her?

Soon after his eighteenth birthday, Bradon proclaimed his independence. He no longer needed his father's approval to leave the house or to do as he pleased. He began going to late-night parties and made a few friends, something which was completely foreign to him up until this point in his life.

It was at one of these after-hours parties that Bradon's life changed forever.

"Dude, what's up with that hair?"

Bradon looked up from his seat at the small table and looked into the eyes of the newcomer to his small group of friends.

"Don't mind him," Monica said, pulling long strings of chewing gum from her mouth and sticking small patches of it underneath the table. "He's the village idiot. Just blurts out the first thing that comes to his feeble mind. He has no grace whatsoever." She blew a large bubble with the pink gum, and then picked it from her nose and eyes when it popped.

"She's right," the newcomer said. "I'm Josh. And I am an idiot. I didn't mean to insult your hair. It's just that I thought the Flock Of Seagulls look went out about ten years ago."

"I'm Bradon," he said, and held his hand out.

"God, who the fuck shakes hands anymore?" He pulled Bradon close and gave him a hug. "It's all cool."

Bradon tensed up at the emotional embrace of the hug, and pulled away quickly. He looked again into Josh's eyes, and felt a queasy feeling in his gut. He hadn't drunk anything yet, so he knew it couldn't be alcohol. He hadn't eaten anything all day, so it couldn't be food.

"And speaking of lack of grace," Josh said, "what the fuck is up with all that damned chewing gum, Mon? Is there a Bazooka convention in town, or what?"

"Screw you, Josh," Monica said, as she unwrapped another piece of gum and popped it into her mouth. "You know I'm trying to quit smoking. This is the only thing that helps."

"Girl, you don't have to tell me about oral fixations. You're preaching to the choir with that one."

Bradon looked back and forth from Monica to Josh. He was obviously on the outside of an inside joke, because both of the teenagers were laughing hysterically.

"You're so gross," Monica finally spat out when she caught her breath.

"True. I am one gross fuck. But a damned good cocksucker, you've got to admit that."

"How would I know?"

"You've heard. Everybody has."

"I don't listen to gossip, you know that."

"You're a sick little liar, Monica. You start ninety percent of all rumors out there."

"I do not!"

"Come on, Bradon," Josh said. He grabbed Bradon's hand and pulled him onto the huge dance floor.

"Shouldn't we wait for Monica?" Bradon leaned in toward Josh so that he could be heard over the pounding bass of the sound system.

"Fuck no," Josh yelled back. "Let her find her own man. Tonight you're my man."

"What?"

"I mean, if that's cool with you, that is," Josh said more quietly as he leaned in closer to Bradon. He swayed with the music and pulled his hips tight against Bradon's as he danced. "Loosen up, Bradon. I don't bite. Unless you want me to."

"What the hell does that mean?" Bradon yelled, and pulled away from Josh's tight clutch.

"Chill, dude. I just want to have a good time, that's all. And I want it to be with you."

"What do you mean?"

Josh grabbed Bradon by the waist again, and pulled him closer, until they were pressed against one another's frontsides. Josh danced slowly against Bradon, and after a few moments, Bradon began to sway along with Josh.

"That's what I mean," Josh said. He wrapped his arms around Bradon's neck and leaned up and kissed him on the lips.

Bradon's heart pounded in his chest. He thought he was going to pass out. The music around him grew louder, and the air in the room seemed to double in temperature. When Josh licked at his lower lip as he kissed him, Bradon sucked in his breath and sucked on Josh's probing tongue at the same time.

He got hard instantly, and it didn't take Josh long at all to feel his excitement.

"Right on," Josh said, and reached down and groped Bradon's semi-erect cock through his jeans. "Now, that's what I'm talking about." He kissed Bradon on the lips again.

Bradon broke the kiss after a minute or so. "I . . . don't . . ."

"I don't care. I'm not asking for a longtime commitment or anything. I just wanna get it on with you. You're fucking hot, dude. Even with that silly haircut."

"What's wrong with my hair?" Bradon asked, and then couldn't help but laugh at how silly he sounded. His face was flushed, his heart was racing and he had a raging hard-on in the middle of a huge dance floor. All of this was so new to him. And exciting.

Monica joined Josh and Bradon on the dance floor a couple of minutes later.

"I should've known it. Everyone told me not to bring Bradon to a gay club. They told me I'd lose him."

"What?" Bradon asked.

"Girl, wake up and smell the Starbucks!" Josh yelled. "You're in the middle of the largest gay bar in Boston, and you're the biggest Mary of us all."

"I really don't understand."

"Monica is the biggest fag hag in the Western Hemisphere. You're her new best friend and the only person she can talk about."

"But I'm not gay."

"Of course you're not. Now shut up and suck my dick."

Bradon gasped, and pulled his hand away from Josh's.

"Oh, don't be silly. I was just kidding. I'll suck yours if you want. I'm not a label hag."

"I can't believe this is happening to me again," Monica whined, and stomped her foot. "Every time I get a new boyfriend, you come along and steal him away."

"But I'm not . . ."

"Come on," Josh said. He grabbed Bradon's hand and dragged him farther into the dancing crowd. "This is my favorite song. Let's dance."

Bradon watched Monica walk back to her table, light up a cigarette and order another beer. He shrugged his shoulders and began dancing with Josh. Everywhere around them hundreds of muscular, shirtless guys danced with one another. Bradon got caught up in the moment, and before he could stop himself, he grabbed Josh by the neck, pulled him close and kissed him.

"Now that's what I'm talking about!" Josh said. He took Bradon by the hand and led him outside to the patio.

"Look, I don't know what came over me in there," Bradon said when they were by themselves. "I'm not gay. I've never . . ."

"Shh," Josh said, and leaned in to kiss Bradon again. This time when he licked at Bradon's thick, full lips, Bradon sucked at his tongue eagerly and returned his kisses. "I want you, Bradon," Josh said as he caught his breath.

"I want you, too."

"Can we go back to your place?"

"No!" Bradon said more quickly than he'd intended. "I mean, my dad's there and everything."

"That's cool. We can't go back to my place either. My old lady would freak."

"That's all right. Maybe we should just . . ."

"No. We shouldn't . . . just . . . anything. I know a place where we can go. Come on, follow me."

Bradon accepted Josh's hand and followed him down the steps of the terrace and across the parking lot. There was a park across the street, and Josh led Bradon deep into the heart of it. When they reached an area that was heavily treed, Josh leaned Bradon up against a tree trunk and ripped his shirt off in one yank.

"What the . . ."

"Shh," Josh said, and then dropped to his knees and began unbuckling Bradon's jeans.

"Look, Josh, I really don't think this is a good . . ." A second later his cock was pulled from his boxers and sucked deep into Josh's wet, warm mouth. Bradon got hard instantly, and leaned against the tree as Josh sucked him deeper and deeper into his throat.

"Oh my god," Bradon moaned. "I think I'm gonna . . ."

"Oh no you're not," Josh said as he quickly pulled his mouth from Bradon's swollen cock and stood up. He leaned up and parted Bradon's lips with his tongue.

Bradon could taste himself on Josh's tongue, and his excitement grew with each new kiss. Josh was undressing himself as they kissed, and was soon completely naked. He pulled away from Bradon.

"What'd you stop for?" Bradon pleaded.

"It's my turn now."

"But I've never—"

"Yeah, I know. You've never kissed another dude before tonight either. But you did a damned good job of that, too."

"Really?"

"Yeah, really. So what do you say?" Josh asked. He wiggled his erect cock in front of Bradon.

Bradon knelt on both knees and looked at Josh's swollen member for a moment, and then held it in his hand for another few seconds. Josh leaned against the same tree trunk and moaned as Bradon stroked him. Then, slowly, Bradon stuck out his tongue and licked the head of Josh's cock.

"Oh yeah, man. That's it."

Bradon took a deep breath and then sucked the entire head into his mouth and licked around it as much as he could. His own cock throbbed up and down with his excitement, and before too long, he knew he'd have to stop sucking or he would blow his load right there.

"That's okay," Josh said, catching his breath. "Let's lie down over there, by the park bench."

Bradon followed his new lover to the bench and lay next to him. He cradled Josh in his arms, spooning him from behind. Without thinking, he slid himself into Josh's welcoming ass.

"Oh my god!" Bradon moaned as he felt the heat of Josh's love-making.

"I want you so bad, dude," Josh said.

Bradon slid into and out of Josh slowly and lovingly. His heart raced almost painfully, and he fought to catch his breath. Even though there was a slight breeze, he began to sweat and pant as he drove deeper into Josh. He leaned in and began kissing Josh lightly on the neck. Josh moaned his pleasure and shoved himself deeper onto Bradon's cock.

"That's it, man," Josh said huskily. "Kiss my neck. Fuck my ass."

Bradon picked up his stride and began sliding in deeper and faster. He was wild with desire and excitement. He couldn't get enough of Josh, and began kissing him across his neck, down his back, and then back up to his neck. He tasted the salty sweat of his lover's body.

Josh stopped bucking against him and moaned and whimpered loudly.

Bradon pumped into Josh even harder and continued his kisses across the back of Josh's neck and to the other side. He barely noticed that Josh had stopped bucking back against him. By the time he did, he was seconds from releasing himself.

"That's it, baby. I can't hold out anymore. I'm gonna come," Bradon said a little louder and faster than he'd intended.

He pulled out and shot his load all over Josh's still, cold body.

Halfway through his ejaculation, he looked down and noticed that Josh wasn't moving.

"Josh? Josh, are you okay?"

He turned Josh over onto his back and saw vacant, glossy eyes staring back at him. Blood was trickling from the side of Josh's neck and down his lips and nose.

"What?" Bradon screamed. "No!"

He turned Josh's head to the side. It was then he saw them. Two large puncture wounds right on the jugular vein. Another set about an inch away. He began to cry as he turned Josh's head from side to side. There were identical sets every couple inches apart all the way around his neck and partially down his back.

Bradon wiped frantically at his mouth, and when he pulled his arm back, dark red blood was streaked across his forearm.

"No. Oh, God, no!" Bradon cried, as he cradled Josh in his arms. "What have I done?"

That night, several hours after he'd made love with another man for the first time, Bradon walked into his house. Victor was waiting for him.

"Where have you been?"

"Out," Bradon said, and brushed by his father.

"I was worried about you," Victor said, as he followed his son into the kitchen.

"Well, don't be."

"Son, look at me," Victor said. He turned Bradon around by the shoulders to face him. Blood was still dried and streaked across Bradon's mouth and cheeks. "Oh, son! Good for you. You've been out feeding this evening. I told you it would get easier as time went on, didn't I?"

"Dad, I wasn't out feeding tonight."

"What? I don't understand. The blood . . ."

"I didn't leave the house tonight with the intention of feeding. I went out to have a good time with some friends."

"Friends? What friends? What happened?"

"I met someone, Dad. Someone special. Someone I liked very much."

"Oh, Bradon, this doesn't sound very good."

"No, Dad? Why not? Because you can't stand the thought of me being happy?"

"Son, it's not that. You know that's not true."

"It is true!" Bradon yelled. He stormed out of the kitchen and into the living room, where he stared out the large window.

"Bradon, I want you to be happy. Of course I do. How could you ever think I want anything else?"

"Dad, I fell in love tonight. I was happy for the first time in my life."

"But, Bradon, the blood on your mouth."

"Yeah, apparently it didn't go so well."

"Who was she, son? Where did you meet her?"

"Dad . . ."

"Why didn't you tell me you were seeing someone. I could have prepared you better for dealing with mortals, son. Women are seductresses, and young, handsome men must be mentally prepared for their games. Oh, god, son. I should have seen this coming. I thought you would have learned from the story about your mother and I. Mortal women are nothing but trouble, son. Nothing but trouble."

"His name was Josh, Dad."

Victor stopped pacing and looked at his son. "What? I don't understand."

"I fell in love with another guy, Dad. His name was Josh."

"That's impossible."

"No, it's not. I never knew it was possible either, until tonight."

"Son, you're confused. Something terrible happened tonight, and you're very upset. That's all."

"No, Dad, that's not all."

"Vampire men feed on mortal women."

"Not this vampire man, Dad."

"What are you talking about?"

Bradon jumped to his feet. "I've never liked women, Dad!" he yelled. "Never. I've always despised the taste of female blood. It's sour and rancid in my mouth. I vomit every time I feed on women. Have you not noticed that over the last few years? I hate women, Dad. I like guys. I like the taste of men. I like the feel of men. I like making love to men."

"No, no, no. That is not true. Something terrible happened tonight and you're upset."

"I'm gay, Dad. I don't like women. I like men. I love men. I loved a man named Josh, and tonight when I was making love with him, I bit him. I fed on him and I killed him, Dad. Are you listening to me? Do you have any idea what I'm saying?"

"No, son. I don't. This is not possible."

"It is possible, Dad. I'm gay. I always have been. And you didn't prepare me for that. You didn't let me know it was okay. You didn't let me know I could fall in love and that it could be dangerous. You didn't tell me I could kill someone I love."

"Bradon, you did not love this man you fed on."

"You're not listening to me, Father," Bradon screamed. "I was not feeding on Josh. I was making love with him."

"I don't want to hear any more of this."

"Too bad, Dad. I don't care if you don't want to hear this. I am your son, and you have to listen to this. I am gay, Dad. I loved another guy tonight. For the first time in my life I felt whole and complete and happy. I felt right. And right in the middle of my first time with another man, I bit him, Dad. I wasn't feeding on him. I didn't mean to bite him. I was kissing him and making love to him, and before I knew it I had drunk the life right out of him."

"I'm going to bed now. We can talk about this tomorrow evening."

"No, we can't. There's nothing to talk about. You let me down, Dad. From now on I'm on my own. I'll figure this all out myself. You can figure your life out on your own, and deal with it however you see fit. But this is my life. I'm gay. I will never again feed on women, and I will never again feed with you. Ever. Do you hear me, Dad? Never."

Victor stormed up the stairs. Bradon could hear his father slamming every door as he roamed without purpose from room to room. Bradon

ran downstairs, kicking his father's bedroom door as he passed, and
then slamming his own bedroom door behind him. He flung himself
on his bed and cried himself to sleep.

Bradon and Victor hardly saw one another after that, and they spoke
even less often. Bradon woke just a few short moments after sunset
each night, and showered and shaved before Victor arose. Sometimes
he would fix himself a sandwich or some other light snack. But more
often than not, he rushed out of the house before he heard his father
stirring around his bedroom and the bathroom upstairs. He went out
dancing with Monica a lot, who was happy to have Bradon's attentions
all to herself once again, and seemed none too eager to press Bradon
on what might have happened to Josh.

When he came home in the early hours of the morning, his father
was usually nowhere to be seen. Sometimes Bradon could hear music
coming from behind his father's bedroom door and the drunken slur
of his father's voice trying to sing along with his favorite songs. But
usually the house was heavy with the absence of Victor's presence altogether. After awhile, that was actually preferable to Bradon, and he
retired to bed early enough to avoid running into Victor as he stumbled through the front door increasingly closer to dawn.

It was Monica who introduced Bradon to the magical world of the
Internet. One night, a couple of years after the incident with Josh, and
when Bradon was sure his father would be out late, he asked her to
come over and show him how to browse around.

"It's really boring, actually," she said as she went over the basics
with Bradon, "unless you know exactly what you're looking for."

"I'm not looking for anything in particular," Bradon said, as he watched
over her shoulder. "Just something to kill some time late at night. The bars
are getting to be pretty monotonous. You know what I mean?"

"I know exactly what you mean, sweetie," she said, as she scooted to
one side to allow Bradon a better view. "Voila!"

"Monica! What is that?"

"MaleSex.com. It's the hottest site out there right now."

"But . . . those two guys are . . ."

"Yeah, I know. Fucking fantastic, isn't it?"

"I can't believe they're doing that right on my computer screen."

Just then the computer screen went black, and then blinked a couple of times. When it came back to life, there was an advertisement filling the entire screen.

"Shit!" Monica hissed. "Just when it gets to the juicy part they always cut you off. It's just a teaser, really. If you wanna see the whole show you gotta pay a monthly membership fee."

"How do you know all this shit, Mon?"

"Please. When you have as many gay friends as I do, it's all you know. Sometimes we just sit for hours and watch guys get it on. They even have some sites where you can tell the guys what to do and they perform just for you."

"Well, that might be all right for a couple of times, but it seems like it'd get boring after a while too."

"I suppose," Monica said, and leaned forward to type something else onto the computer. "That's why most people spend the majority of their time in chat rooms."

"Chat rooms? What are they?"

"Sit back and watch," she said, as she quickly went through the process of creating a screen name and profile for Bradon. Ten minutes later they were in the middle of a lively room.

"What does BostonM4M mean?" Bradon asked.

"Boston men for men. It's a chat room for gay men in Boston. Lots of raunchy talk mostly, but sometimes it's a good way to hook up with other guys."

"Why did you call me Exotic9?"

"Because you are exotic looking, sweetie, admit it. And the 9 . . . well, let's just say it will get you some attention."

Just then a window popped up in the upper left corner of the computer screen:

<<BostonSwallower: *Hey Exotic. What's up?*>>

"Told you," Monica said, and smiled as she scooted away from the desk to give Bradon easier access.

"What am I supposed to do?" Bradon asked.

"Talk dirty to him. It's really what most of them are looking for anyway."

"I can't do that."

"Bullshit," Monica said, and leaned forward to type Bradon's response.

<<*Just hard and horny here. U?*>>

"Monica!"

<<**BostonSwallower**: *Same here. Stats? Age?*>>

"He wants to know what you look like and how old you are. Most guys on here are fat old trolls who lie and make up some outrageous profiles. But you don't have to. The truth is better than 99% of anything out there. So go for it. Describe yourself. Leave out the boring part, okay."

Bradon typed out a response and found himself engrossed in the chat room. He became bolder after only a couple of minutes. It didn't take long before he had three or four windows going on at a time.

"Oh shit," Bradon said, as he inhaled deeply and scooted back from the computer.

"What is it?" Monica asked, as she jumped to her feet and shuffled closer to the screen.

"This one wants to come over."

"He sounds yummy. Your dad gonna be home soon?"

"Not for another three or four hours."

"Then what are you waiting for? Invite him over."

"I can't . . ."

"Of course you can. Just give him your address."

"But what if he's . . ."

"Then you curse him out for lying to you, slam the door in his face, and come back down here and start all over again. I'm telling you, some of my friends have hooked up with some really hot guys this way."

"Really?"

"Cross my heart," Monica said, and typed Bradon's address and hit the Send button.

<<**BostonSwallower**: *Kewl. I can be there in 10 mins.*>>

"Oh great," Bradon said as he stood up and paced nervously around the bedroom. "Now what am I supposed to do?"

<<*I'll be here. Am hard, ready and waiting.*>> Monica typed quickly and sent the message before Bradon could stop her. "I'd suggest you get hard."

"Monica!"

"I'll just slip into the closet there. You'll never know I'm there. I can videotape it if you want me to."

"Get out!" Bradon said as he ushered her to the door.

"All right, all right. But call me tomorrow. I want all the juicy details."

It was the first of many such encounters over the next couple of years. Bradon was fascinated with the world of chat rooms. As he became more comfortable navigating the Internet, he found more chat rooms and sites that interested him. He even found a site called InsomniacM4M. With so much activity available to him on his computer, he found himself going out to the bars less and less. He could avoid Victor without ever leaving his house, and that suited Bradon just fine.

Sins of the Father

"Are you sure no one's home?" the young blond boy asked as he tripped over his own feet into the open doorway. "I'd hate to get caught with my pants down around my ankles, you know what I mean. You said you lived with your folks, right?"

"My dad," Bradon corrected. He sniffed the chilly air inside the living room. "But he's not here."

"How do you know?"

"Because I don't smell him."

"Huh?"

Bradon laughed softly and shut the door behind him. "Just kidding. I know he's not here because he works at night. Usually gets home around four-thirty in the morning. Which means," he said, as he looked at the grandfather clock near the stairs, "that we have about two hours for a little fun of our own before he gets here. Do you think that will be enough time?"

"Hell yeah," the blond boy said with a grin. "But why rush it, right?" He leaned forward to kiss Bradon on the lips.

"Right," Bradon said. He pulled the young man closer to him and kissed him long and deep. The kid was an inexperienced kisser, and he thrust his tongue in and out of Bradon's mouth awkwardly.

"Slow down," Bradon said. "What's your name again?"

"Tanner."

"Okay, Tanner, I'll tell you what. Just lie back and relax. Let me do all the work, all right?"

"Sure," Tanner said. "But don't you at least want me to—"

Bradon shoved Tanner backward onto the sofa and leapt on top of him playfully. When Tanner's arms were pinned beneath Bradon's knees, Bradon reached down and licked tenderly at his lips. Tanner tried desperately to arch upward enough to suck Bradon's tongue into his mouth, but Bradon pulled away.

"Remember, let me do the work." He began unbuttoning Tanner's shirt slowly. Beneath him he felt Tanner respond to the aggression as his erection pressed against the back of Bradon's legs. He ripped the rest of the shirt from Tanner's torso and threw it to one side of the couch.

"Fuck, yeah, man," Tanner said, as he sucked in a deep breath.

Bradon looked into his eyes and smiled as he lowered himself to Tanner's chest. Tanner was breathing heavily, and his twin pecs quivered as Bradon got so close that his breath caused the tiny nipples on Tanner's chest to harden. Bradon licked the hard nipples for a moment, then sucked them one at a time into his mouth.

"That's great, man," Tanner gasped, as Bradon sucked harder and then bit on the nipples lightly.

Bradon barely heard Tanner's hoarse moans. His own head was spinning with bright pins of light and a sharp, high-pitched tone that rang in his ears. The salty beads of sweat that dotted Tanner's lightly hairy chest were intoxicating. Bradon was drunk with the taste of this young man. He couldn't get enough. His own arousal grew harder against his jeans as he licked his way down Tanner's smooth, taut stomach.

It had been such a long time since he'd last allowed himself to feel this way with another man. Sure, he'd fed on many men in the five years since Josh, but he'd never allowed himself to feel anything for the men he fed on. It was all about survival.

But this was different. It wasn't love, or anything remotely close to it. It was sex for the sake of sex. Not for love and not for feeding. Just raw sex. As he got closer to reaching the waistline of Tanner's jeans, he began to get short of breath. Just inches away from the thick curly hair that sprouted below Tanner's navel, Bradon inhaled deeply. The sweet musky scent of Tanner's sweat-soaked body and a light trace of his cologne sent Bradon over the edge. He ripped Tanner's jeans from his legs, and leaned down to kiss the bleached white jockey shorts. Tanner's hardness throbbed against the thin cotton material and beckoned Bradon closer.

Bradon licked his lips and lowered his wet mouth to the mound of flesh under the bright white shorts. The buzzing in his ears was more intense now, and he was dizzy as the lights stabbed behind his eyes. He licked and sucked on the wet shorts for several minutes, until the sharp, clean line of Tanner's cock was soaked and clearly visible.

"Do it, man."

Bradon kicked his own jeans from his legs and onto the floor. Then he lowered his head back down into Tanner's lap. He ripped the damp briefs right down the center and threw the tattered underwear across the room. Now Tanner's sweat-shined body was completely naked and thrusting beneath him. Bradon strained to hear Tanner's coarsely moaned words above the screeching noise behind his ears. Then he decided it didn't matter.

He licked at Tanner's swollen shaft for a moment and then sucked gently on the throbbing head. Tanner bucked beneath him, causing his cock to slide deeper into Bradon's mouth. Bradon took a deep breath and swallowed the entire length deep inside his throat.

"Oh, shit, man," Tanner moaned, clutching the sides of the couch.

Bradon was ecstatic with the tastes, the feel, the sounds of Tanner's quivering and moaning body. He tightened his lips and throat around Tanner's hardness and swallowed eagerly as Tanner dripped a salty-sweet drop of pre-cum from the tip of his cock. He reached down to touch his own hard cock, more to ease the rising pressure he felt building up than anything else.

But it was too late. At the slightest touch of his hand, Bradon released five years of pent-up emotions and passion all over Tanner's silky smooth legs and the side of his dad's favorite leather sofa.

"That's it, man. I can't take anymore. I'm gonna—"

"What the fuck is going on?"

Bradon recognized the stern sound of his father's deep baritone voice even above the incessant ringing in his ears. He loosened his grip on Tanner's cock just a second before Tanner sprayed his own sticky fireworks display across his lips and chin.

"Dad . . ." Bradon stammered as he struggled to get to his feet and wipe the evidence of his lovemaking from his lips.

"Oh, shit!" Tanner yelled, and grabbed his jeans from the floor. He hopped to the front door as he struggled to get his legs into his jeans.

"Tanner," Bradon called out softly, but it was too late. Tanner was out the door and halfway down the sidewalk before Bradon had finished wiping the semen from his warm lips.

"What the hell was that all about?"

"I can explain . . ."

"You won't explain anything, you fucking sissy. I'm not stupid. I know what I saw. I don't need anyone to explain anything to me."

"Well, good," Bradon spat out suddenly, as he grabbed his clothes from the floor. "Because I'm tired of trying to explain myself to you. I don't owe you anything. Not a goddammed thing, do you understand me?"

"I will not have my own son talk to me like that."

"Like what, Dad?" Bradon cried, as he tried to wipe the tears from his eyes before his father noticed them. "Like a human being?"

Victor raised his arm and slapped Bradon across the face with the back of his hand. "Don't you ever call me that again. Ever. Or next time I won't stop with a little slap."

Bradon reeled back from the sting of his father's blow. "Call you what?"

"A human being. I will not tolerate your petty belittlement and insults. I am not like you and your precious little mother, dammit. I am a vampire. Do you understand me? A vampire. And I'm damned proud to be one, too. I will not be ridiculed or thought less of because of who I am. I am not ashamed of who I am, like you are. Get that through your thick little head, Bradon. I am proud of who I am."

"So am I, Dad," Bradon said, as he finished buttoning his jeans. "So am I. I am half vampire, but I am also half human. And I'm proud of that. I am also gay, and I am proud of that too. If you think I'm apologizing for any of that, or making excuses for it, you're sadly mistaken."

"That's ridiculous. No one is proud of being gay."

"I am, Dad. I am."

"What's to be proud of? That you're a cocksucker? Or that you take it up the ass? Huh? Is that something to be proud of?"

"You disgust me."

"Excuse me?"

"You heard me. I said you disgust me. You think being gay is all about sex. That is a very small part of being gay, Dad. My being gay has more to do with love. Loving myself and loving other men."

"Shut up. I don't want to hear any more of this."

"Well, too bad. Because I'm not finished talking. All of my life I have tried to please you. I never agreed with what you did and who you claimed to be, but I tried to understand you and make you proud. But when I needed you to understand me and appreciate who I am, you turned your back on me. It was perfectly fine for you to go out and fuck every little two-bit whore you could get your hands on. God only knows what diseases you'd have if you were human. But you have the nerve to get freaked out and act all macho and shit with me because I've had a couple of somewhat meaningful relationships."

"You call that meaningful? With his seed dripping from your pinkened lips?"

"It might have been. It could have been. And Josh was certainly meaningful, and could have been the love of my life. But you didn't prepare me for anything, and I killed him."

"Good riddance."

Bradon slapped the back of his hand across his father's face.

Victor looked up slowly, his eyes red and angry. A low rumble emanated from deep in his throat as he stared at his son.

"I'm sorry, Dad. I didn't mean to . . ."

"Shut up. I want you out of my house. I don't care where you go or what you do. You're over twenty-one now, and so your trust fund is available to you. Take it and leave. And don't ever come back."

"But, Dad . . ."

"I'm through with you, son. I never want to see you again. Take all of your things with you. And take your mother's things as well. I want nothing to remind me of either of you. I should have finished what I started a long time ago."

Tears streamed down Bradon's face as he stood half naked in the middle of his living room. "What? I don't understand."

"Stop crying like a little girl. You've acted like a sissy enough for one night. Hell, you've acted like a sissy enough for a lifetime."

Victor turned and walked downstairs. Bradon could hear him rummaging around in his closet. A few moments later, Victor reappeared.

"Here," he said, as he hurled a thick book across the room at Bradon. "This is yours. Read it and weep. Now your contempt for me can be based on something real. Take it with you when you leave. I don't ever want to see it or you again. I'm going to bed now, Bradon. I don't want to see you or any trace of you when I wake up tomorrow evening. Is that clear?"

Bradon watched as his father turned his back on him and walked downstairs to his bedroom. Large, pain-wracked gulps of breath forced themselves out of his chest as he controlled his urge to cry.

Instead, he sat on the couch and opened the book. It was his father's journal. Bradon slammed the book closed before reading the first page, then gave in to his desire to read it.

She is the most beautiful creature to ever roam the earth. The moonlight dances through her hair as she strolls along the river's shore. Her eyes sparkle like rare and precious diamonds across the blue night, and pierce my heart with their first glance. Be still my beating heart. Surely nothing good can come from this chance upon an angel.

But then she smiles at me, and my knees and my heart betray me. I try to stop my feet from moving, but they, too, work against me. As I approach her, I feel myself growing weaker with each step. From a few feet away I can smell her scent. Sweet, fragrant, ripe. But strangely, I don't want to feed on her. I try to picture in my mind how sweet and warm her blood would be in my mouth. Instead, all I can envision is how soft and cool the skin of her neck would be against the warmth of my hungry lips. Hungry not for her blood, but for her love.

Again I think to myself that nothing good can come from this meeting between angel and vampire. Centuries of folklore tell me this encounter will only bring pain and suffering and disaster. But when she reaches down and wraps her cool, thin fingers in my warm, thick hands, my heart drops inside my stomach, and I find myself speechless.

I warn myself not to fall for this beautiful young human girl. But when she asks me to walk her home, I wrap my arms around her to warm her and follow her lead. At her house, she stops at the front steps and leans up to kiss me.

Soft are her lips, and sweet is her tongue. My heart has never raced so. Her kiss is like a cool summer breeze after a long, hot and humid evening storm.

"Good night, Victor," she whispers to me, and wipes the remaining traces of her sweet taste from my thirsty lips. "I hope to see you again."

I watch as she ascends the stairs and disappears behind the heavy wooden door. I know at once that I am lost to her soul, to her will. Despite everything I know about the consequences of this union, my heart tells me I must follow it. I must see her again. I must love her. I must give myself to her.

As the light in what must be her bedroom dims to darkness, I push my body from her steps. Goodnight, sweet Rachel. You will definitely see me again.

Bradon wiped the tears from his eyes as he read more and more of the familiar story. It had been a long time since he and Victor had sat around the kitchen table talking and remembering Bradon's mother. It was obvious from Victor's writing that he was madly in love with Rachel. The depth of his emotions was a little disconcerting for Bradon to read. It was all so different from the detached and grieving tales he had grown up hearing. Bradon's heart ached for his father, and for the loss he'd suffered.

He read on, page after page, lost in the love story of his mother and father.

I am happy beyond words, beyond expression, beyond belief. My beloved Rachel is nurturing our first child. I never thought it possible for me to love any more than I have loved Rachel over the past couple of years, but right now, as I ponder being a father, I am overwhelmed with love for my wife and my unborn child.

We are alone in this happiness, however. Rachel's family wishes nothing to do with her or with our family. They believe me to be evil and not nearly good enough for their little girl. This even without the benefit of knowing I am a vampire. We both thought it best not to enlighten them with that information. Apparently we were right in our decision. And Mother and Father are no better about any of this. It's easy for them thousands of miles away, on another continent, to think that my relationship with Rachel is doomed for failure. They wish not to meet her, to have anything to do with her or me while I insist on loving and living with a mere mortal. If only I could convince them, to show them, that Rachel is no mere mortal, but an angel from heaven. First, though, I'd have to convince them of heaven, and that is not likely. Instead, they prefer to disown me and my love.

That is fine with me. Together Rachel and I will grow in our love for one another. When our child is born, we will be a complete family. Ready to face the world, with all of its fear and hatred and prejudice. Ready to triumph in a mean and nasty world. Because we love. And above all else, love conquers all.

Bradon took a deep breath and swallowed hard as he read this last entry. To see his father write so eloquently of love and triumph and prejudice was more than he was able to process, especially after the fight they'd just had. How could Victor write of love and triumph over prejudice?

The time has finally come. My son was born into this world early this evening. I cried a river of tears as our eyes locked for the first time. My son, with his little fingers reaching out to me, and his tiny eyes blinking innocently at me, welcomed me with open arms and an open heart. He is the most beautiful son in all the world. In him I see all the hopes, all the dreams, all the possibilities of the union of his mother and me.

I am a little afraid. I have no experience with children who are half vampire and half human. Will my son grow up to be human, and reject his father? Will he grow strong and healthy, with the need to feed on warm, human blood? If so, what will he feel toward me? Will he hate me for bringing him into this world with this need?

Bradon shut the book, and paced around the room for a few moments. It was difficult for him to read about his father's concerns of fear and rejection. How could he be so hypocritical? How could he fear something he so easily doled out to his own son? How could he believe his father had ever worried about being rejected when he was able to reject his own son so effortlessly?

Bradon walked into the kitchen and poured himself a glass of wine. He debated whether or not he should continue reading or stop before he found himself so lost in love for his father that he went begging to him for forgiveness, promising never to desire or feed on another man.

He looked into the living room from the kitchen. The book was lying on the coffee table, beckoning him to read on. He walked into the living room, propped his legs on the coffee table, and picked up the book. He took another sip of wine and read on.

Be still my heart. Do not think with your heart, but with your mind. Do not let the pain of your heart overrule the wisdom of your mind. Rachel loves you with all her soul. She is only a little afraid, and does not mean to hurt you. You must believe this.

I try to believe this, but it is not easy. This evening I woke to find Rachel crying on the sofa. She says she is confused and doesn't know what to do. I sit beside her and wrap my arms around her. I ask her what she is crying for. She tells me her son is not a vampire.

What is this nonsense, I ask. Of course he is a vampire. And he is human. He is the very best of both worlds.

No, Rachel tells me, Bradon is not a vampire. This afternoon she became so distraught over worrying about this that she could not stop herself from taking our son outside, into the deadly, burning sunlight. Rachel was so overcome with worry and fear that Bradon would burn and die, that she brought a knife with her so that she could kill herself when her son ignited before her eyes.

But Bradon did not ignite. He did not burn. When Rachel slid the blanket back from his face, Bradon relished in the warmth of the sunlight and giggled with delight.

"He is not a vampire, Victor," my sweet and lovely wife tells me. "He is a human boy. He has human needs. I don't want him to grow up different than other kids. Not if he doesn't have to."

"Don't be silly," I tell my wife as she sobs against my chest. "Our son is the best of the both of us. He is different from other kids, but that difference makes him very special. He will know the human love and understanding of his human mother, and the knowledge and wisdom of his centuries-old vampire father. Bradon will be unique. He will be special. He will be loved."

Rachel says that she supposes I am right, but I sense that something is different. When I hug her, she doesn't return the embrace, but tightens up in response to my welcoming arms. When I kiss her, she opens her mouth to me, but does not return the kiss as she usually does. When I try to make love with her, she claims she is tired and has a headache.

Something is very different. Something is wrong. My heart is broken and beats erratically and painfully in my chest.

Bradon read and reread that last section three times. He'd stopped crying minutes before, and now was alert and anxious to learn more about himself. What was this about him not being a vampire? Was it really possible that his mother had exposed him to deadly sunlight? If so, what did that mean? He obviously didn't die or wasn't even hurt from it. All his life his father had been adamant about warning him against the sun and the light of day. Hundreds of times he'd been told of the consequences of being reckless and getting caught in the bright light of death. Daylight was a vampire's kryptonite.

So why had he never been told about this particular part of the story?

*   *   *

My life is over.

How can she ever have thought of leaving me. Even worse, how can she ever have thought about taking my only child away from me?

Oh, but to have this burden lifted from me! I am cursed to live in eternal living hell. The memory of what I have done will live with me for the rest of my eternal life. I should have listened to the wisdom of my fathers. I should have known it would never work. I should never have put myself or my son at the risk of betrayal.

Now my dear sweet Rachel is dead. Dead at my very own hands. Surely it is just, though. I could not have let her leave my home, my city, my life. I could not let her steal my son from me, never to see him again. I could not allow her to deny Bradon his destiny.

The pain is unbearable. How will I ever tell my son that I killed his mother? That in a feigned moment of passion, I bit her neck and drained the life from her. That I did not stop at the crucial moment of possible conversion, but drank until her blood was cold and thick in my mouth? How can I ever tell my son that I buried his mother in our own backyard and wept the entire time I dug her grave?

No, I will not. Bradon will never know the truth. In his eyes his mother was a true saint. A woman who loved him with all his heart, and who loved me equally. She was not the mother who wanted to flee with him in the safety of daylight, to deprive him of his father. She was not the mother who intentionally put him at risk of death and tried to deprive him of his vampire heritage. She was not the mother who betrayed him by denying who he is at the heart of his very soul.

Better that she is dead, even if it is at my own hands. As for my son, he will be told every day of the most beautiful love story ever. He will grow up believing his mother loved him more than life itself, and gave the ultimate sacrifice of her own life upon his birth, so that he might live eternally. My son will know that he is a vampire. That he was born of a human mother that loved him very much, and who sacrificed her life so that he might live his to its fullest potential. My son will grow to embrace his vampirism, and will know that his father loves him more than anything else in the world. So much that he, too, offered the ultimate sacrifice for his son. The sacrifice of the one woman who he truly loved, the one woman who stole his heart.

I pray every evening that Rachel's soul forgives me. I pray that Bradon never knows the horrible truth of the madness that overcame his angel of a mother. I pray that he grows up strong and rich in his vampire tradition.

As for me, I live daily with the pain and the loss of my beloved. I would give my own life for things to have worked out better than they did. But I am firm in my resolve that I have done what is right and true. What is in the best interest of my blessed son. I cannot think of myself anymore, but must be strong in my pursuit of Bradon's best interest.

Good night, my sweet Rachel.

Bradon rubbed his eyes and shook his head, hoping that when his head cleared a little, the words on the pages of his father's journal would be different; that they would not spell out the most painful of denials, but instead a familiar beautiful love story.

But they did not, and when he'd shaken his head to the point of pain, the same stabbing truth was scattered across the pages. In his father's own jerky handwriting was the horrible reality that his father had murdered his mother. And not only killed her, but drained her life from her in the one manner that was the most demeaning and in violation of the one stipulation she put on their love.

Bradon was not a vampire. Or at least he was not predisposed to be. His mother had discovered this truth, and had been prepared to save Bradon from an eternal life of pain and bloody killings and feedings. She'd planned on packing up a few valuable possessions and leaving with her newborn son in the safety of daylight, to establish a life for both of them. A life free of vampires and blood and death. A life free of Victor.

What would his life be like now had his mother succeeded? Would he be a normal human young man? Would he be completely free of his need of warm human blood? Would he have developed into a normal, straight young man with a desire to marry and have children? Would he more easily accept his homosexuality and be more well-adjusted?

This he would never know, because his father had robbed him of the opportunity ever to discover his own real self. His father had murdered his mother in a bloody and cowardly manner. His father had lied to him his entire life, and raised him to believe horrible things about himself that might not be true. His father had insisted he was a vampire, and had forced the life of a vampire onto him. But more importantly, his father had taken from him the one person who really knew and understood and loved Bradon.

Bradon trembled with the rage inside of him. He tossed the journal across the room, and when it fell to the ground in pieces, he kicked at it until it was torn into several unrecognizable sheets.

And then, without hesitating, Bradon walked into his father's study. Above the fireplace mantel was a large wooden stake encased in a glass and mahogany display case, lined with a deep blue velvet sheet. The stake was over 500 years old, and had been used to kill Victor's grandfather. It had been in his family for centuries, as a constant reminder of the threat the human species posed to vampires. When Victor insisted on marrying Rachel, Victor's parents had the stake couriered across the Atlantic as a wedding gift. It was the last contact he'd ever had with them.

Bradon opened the display case slowly. His hands trembled and sweat poured from his face. He was almost blinded by the tears as they streamed down his face and across the heavy wooden stake.

He walked slowly and deliberately out the study door and down the stairs to the dark basement where he and his father had separate bedrooms. He could hear Victor snoring inside his room, and he quietly opened the door. He held the massive stake in front of him, careful not to drop it or bang it against anything on the way.

He stood outside his father's casket for several minutes, crying silently. Then he took a deep breath and opened the casket lid. It was dark inside the basement, but dawn was only about half an hour away. Bradon walked over to the heavily draped window and pulled the curtains aside, so that a little light was creeping in through the ground-level windows.

He walked back to his father's casket and looked down onto his father's face. It was pale white and beautifully handsome. Victor's well-plucked eyebrows were arched just slightly, and his thin lips were upturned into a half-smile. He looked very peaceful.

Bradon raised the heavy stake high above his head. Taking a deep breath, he hammered it down into his father's chest, right between the ribcage, with all his strength. Victor's eyes popped wide open. He stared at his son for a brief moment. Bradon twisted the wooden stake deeper into his father's chest as a wave of tears cascaded down his face and fell onto his father's lifeless body.

When he was sure Victor was dead, he walked slowly to his own room, opened his casket and crawled into it. He closed the lid and fell immediately to sleep.

A Bright New Day

"A re you sure you wouldn't like some company tonight," Daniel asked as the last of the passengers departed the plane. "The good thing about working one of these red-eye flights is that they don't book us for another one until a full eighteen hours later. We'd have plenty of time to be together before I have to fly out."

"Thanks," Bradon said, as he leaned in to kiss Daniel on the lips. "But I'm really beat. Besides, I'm moving into a brand-new place. It's not furnished yet or anything. I'd be a terrible host."

"Like I'm worried about that."

"You're very sweet, Daniel. And pretty damn hot in bed, too. At least if that little quickie in the rest room is any indication. Maybe we can take a raincheck?"

"Sure. Here's my card. It has my home and cell phone numbers on there. I fly into San Francisco at least a couple of times a month. Call me. Anytime, really."

"I promise."

Daniel gave Bradon another quick kiss on the cheek and a hug, then scooted him off the plane. As soon as Daniel turned his back, Bradon deposited the card into the nearest wastebasket on his way out of the boarding tunnel.

At four in the morning the airport was empty and it took no time at all to get his luggage and find a cab. It was a short ride into the city, and Bradon was fascinated with the new skyline. It was so different than that of Boston. Already he could tell he was going to enjoy his new home.

"Here you are, sir," the taxi driver said. "At 234 Paris Street. Pretty nice neighborhood. Wouldn't stay out alone after dark for too long, though."

"Thanks. Not bad advice. Here you go," Bradon said and handed the driver a twenty-dollar bill. "Keep the change."

"Thanks, man. That's very generous."

"Don't mention it."

Bradon got out of the backseat and carried his two pieces of luggage up the stairs to his new home. It was an old nineteenth-century Victorian that had been recently renovated. In the two weeks since his father's death, Bradon had scoured the classifieds and the Internet, and had found the place in no time. Over the previous six months he'd become quick chat room buddies with a realtor in San Francisco with the screen name of HotPropertySF. They'd had cyber sex a couple of times, and hit it off really well. Once Bradon decided on the Victorian, he'd sent a message to HotPropertySF. He gave the details of the house and asked the realtor to do whatever it took to secure the sale. A week later, after Bradon paid cash for the house, the realtor was happy to make all the arrangements to prepare the house for Bradon's arrival. And he was personally very excited to finally meet his Internet buddy in person.

A private contractor had already been out and constructed the basement to his specifications. Even his casket had been delivered and set up downstairs in his bedroom. A minimal amount of questions were asked. Apparently the people of San Francisco lived up to their reputation of live and let live with no questions asked. That suited Bradon just fine.

Bradon stood just inside the front doorway and inhaled deeply. The faint smell of fresh paint still lingered, but the house smelled fresh and clean, almost new. Bradon set his luggage down near the front door and walked around the entire house without turning on any lights. He liked the feel and the layout of the house. It felt instantly like home to him, even without the luxury of furniture. That he could get to in the next couple of weeks. There was no rush.

He was tired. He left his suitcases upstairs and walked downstairs into his bedroom. It was large and spacious. The small windows that lined the upper part of the longest wall were draped in a heavy material similar to the lightproof drapes he'd had back in Boston. His casket was in the corner opposite the windows. He walked over to it, opened it and stared inside. No visions of his father's blank and dead face staring back at him. That was a good first sign.

Bradon stripped naked and climbed into the casket. He thought momentarily about closing the lid, then decided against it. The drapes looked to be of finest quality, and he felt sure the sun would not filter in. He'd never slept with his lid open before. The cool, damp air in the basement felt good against his naked skin, and he drifted to sleep in his new home, with the lid to his casket open for the first time.

The next few weeks were spent buying furniture for the house and arranging for daytime deliveries. Bradon was able to shop online for all the furniture during the evenings. He'd sweet-talked HotPropertySF into agreeing to stop by and let the delivery people in at opportune times so they could set the furniture up to his directions. Bradon, of course, would be barricaded behind his locked bedroom door, deep in sleep during the day. He'd made sure the realtor understood that the basement was off bounds to everyone. He could set up what little furniture he needed downstairs by himself in the evenings.

Cabin fever set in soon after his new home was furnished. Bradon found himself getting restless a few short hours after he woke. There were a couple of prime-time television shows he enjoyed, but after eleven p.m., there was absolutely nothing to hold his interest. He didn't want to start going out to the hundreds of bars that San Francisco boasted. At least not yet. He hadn't felt the urge to feed for a couple of weeks, and hoped he could put it off for at least a couple more.

He decided instead to join a gym and get back into his workout routine. Bradon enlisted the help of his only friend in San Francisco again when he decided to look for the right gym. As luck would have it, HotPropertySF was also a workout enthusiast, and was more than happy to recommend the gym he himself patronized.

Bradon had always loved working out, and his well-muscled body was a testament to his dedication. At three or four in the morning there were hardly any exercise fanatics still lingering around, and he was accustomed to having the gym almost to himself.

So, when in the middle of his bench press reps he was interrupted by another male voice, he was caught off guard.

"You're extending your arms just a little too far."

"What?" Bradon groaned as he strained to put the weight-laden bar on the resting arms above his head.

"On your extension. You should never lift the bar so far above your head that your arms are fully extended. You're locking your elbows for a quick second right before your release and descent. That's not good for the elbows."

"Really? I've never heard that before." Bradon sat up and looked at the young man sitting at the bench next to his. He was glad that he was panting already from the workout, because one look at the man made his heart pound loudly in his chest and took his breath away. The guy had short, tousled light blond hair. His eyes were a light brown that bordered on hazel, framed with long, thick eyelashes. His smooth skin was perfectly bronzed and glistened with the sweat of his workout. He was several inches shorter than Bradon, but his body was meticulously muscled and worked to complete, in Bradon's opinion, an overall picture of perfection.

"It's true. I used to be a personal trainer. I wouldn't lie to you."

"I didn't think you would," Bradon stammered, and wiped his hand on his tank top before extending it. "I'm Bradon."

"I thought you might be. At least I was hoping. I'm Kirk," the ex-trainer said, as he shook Bradon's hand. "Kirk Courey. Otherwise known as HotPropertySF."

"Whew!" Bradon said, as he wiped his forehead. "I was beginning to freak a little."

"I have to admit I had an ulterior motive when I recommended this gym. I've been wanting to meet you in person for six months."

"Me too. Sorry it's taken so long. I've been a little preoccupied."

"No problem," Kirk said. "Moving can be a bitch. But you're here now, so, mind if I join you? We could spot one another."

"That'd be great," Bradon said. He laid back down on the padded bench as Kirk walked around to the head of the bench and weight set. Bradon closed his eyes and tried not to look up at Kirk. He knew he couldn't trust himself in situations like this. But Kirk was standing too close to Bradon to avoid it. Bradon could feel the wisp of air blow against his cheek as Kirk's legs planted themselves on either side of Bradon's face. He could smell the musky scent of clean sweat and a trace of soap. He opened his eyes and looked at the muscular legs on either side of his face. They were thick, with silky strands of soft blond hair dotting the thighs seductively.

"You gonna start lifting or just stare at my legs all night?" Kirk asked, chuckling as he lifted the bar from its resting post and held it high above Bradon's chest.

"Sorry," Bradon stuttered, and blushed as he reached for the bar.

"It's okay," Kirk said, as he wedged his legs even closer to Bradon's face, now in a better position to spot the heavy bar. "I just like to embarrass people. Especially guys I find really attractive. It's a fault of mine, I guess. I try to catch them off guard and put them on the defensive right away. Kind of gives me an upper hand."

"You think?" Bradon panted, as he finished his set. "Your turn." He stood up to make room for Kirk to lie on the bench.

"It seems to work well enough, at least so far." Kirk lifted the bar effortlessly over his chest and head, lowering it all the way to his chest and then lifting it back up.

Bradon noticed that he followed his own advice when lifting the bar.

"And what if you're off the mark? What if you pull that stunt and it turns out the guy you're toying with is straight?"

"Guess I'd have to cross that bridge if and when I come to it. Hasn't happened yet. Am I right?"

Bradon blushed. "Yes, you're right."

"Good. Single?"

"What?"

"Are you single or do you have a boyfriend?"

"No, I'm single. No time for a boyfriend."

"Nonsense. Everyone has *time* for a boyfriend. Now, whether or not they really *want* a boyfriend is another story altogether. But time isn't really an issue."

"You're really quite confident, aren't you?" Bradon asked, as he helped direct the bar back to its resting post.

"Hell yeah," Kirk said as he jumped to his feet and flexed his muscles. "Why the hell shouldn't I be?"

"Maybe arrogant would have been a better choice of words," Bradon said as he reached up to take the bar again.

"Nah. Confident is the right word." Kirk straddled Bradon's face even closer than before, and spread his legs wide to get a better stance for spotting. "I'm really not arrogant at all. I mean, I know I look pretty good by most people's standards. But looks only last so long, and then all you've got are your brains and your personality. I like to think that as long as I'm in possession of the whole package, I'll be okay in the end."

"Looks like you've got the whole package to me," Bradon grunted out loud, as he struggled to raise the heavy bar. He was staring directly up the open legs of the flimsy shorts Kirk was wearing. From his vantage point he could see the white cotton pouch of Kirk's jock strap. It was bulging to near capacity, and Bradon found it difficult to concentrate on anything else.

"I can't believe you're staring at my crotch," Kirk said, as he settled the bar into its resting post and walked around to sit on the bench next to Bradon.

"Well, I can't believe you were thrusting it out there in front of my face like that."

"I was spotting you, Bradon."

"Well, I couldn't help it. It's not like I pulled it out and did anything with it."

"Thank God. I mean, I have a reputation. I'm a decent girl."

Both men laughed and continued working out. Having the sexual tension between them out in the open and joked about actually made the workout more tolerable.

"You wanna go grab an early breakfast?" Kirk asked, as they finished up.

Bradon looked at his watch. It was just a few minutes before four o'clock.

"No, I can't really. Maybe we can take a raincheck?" Bradon said, realizing it was the same put-off that he'd used with Daniel.

"Nonsense. Rain checks are only used for people who want to get out of doing something. Either you want to and you will, or you don't want to and you won't."

"I want to. But really, I can't . . ."

"Look, I'm asking you to breakfast for a little bacon and eggs. I'm not asking you to move in and set up house or anything like that. At least not yet. So stop beating around the bush. What is it? Yes or no?"

"Yes."

"Good," Kirk said, and wrapped his arms around Bradon's shoulders. "Now, can I trust you to keep your hands and your eyes to yourself while we shower and get cleaned up, or do we need to take showers separately?"

"I really can't be trusted."

"Fine, I'll go first. You go take a couple of laps around the track. I'm a quick showerer, so I should be done by the time you complete three laps."

"But I don't like running."

"Tough. I don't like being ogled and fondled in the shower."

"But—"

"Go on. I'll be out in ten minutes tops."

Bradon slumped his shoulders, but trotted toward the running track anyway as Kirk disappeared into the locker room.

"So in all the hustle and bustle of the big move, you never did tell me why the big decision to move to San Francisco?" Kirk asked, as he swallowed a piece of English muffin and followed it with a mouthful of fresh-squeezed orange juice. "Not that I'm complaining or anything, mind you."

"I just needed to get away from my past and start all over."

"Bad relationship?"

"Kind of. But not the kind you're thinking of."

"Tell me more."

"I'd rather not. I'd much prefer hearing all about you."

"Boring really," Kirk said, as he devoured the last of his big breakfast. "I've lived in San Francisco for a little over five years now. Moved out here from Iowa. Just knew it would be much easier to come *out* out here. And it was. I fell in love with someone who wasn't ready to be fallen in love with, and we split up about two years ago. Been dating a couple of guys off and on since then, but nothing serious."

"You must have a serious case of insomnia."

"What do you mean?"

"I don't know too many people who get into working out and having breakfast at two or three in the morning."

"Oh, that. Well, I used to be a personal trainer, and I worked normal daytime hours. But I got bored with it. I worked for my dad's real estate company for a year or so, and I really liked it. But I get bored easily, so I stopped doing it full time. I still do it a little on the side, hence the screen name. But for the most part, I sling drinks for all the fags in Castro. For the past year I've been working as a bartender at the Midnight Sun. Have you heard of it?"

"No."

"It's a great place. Tiny little video bar in the middle of Castro. Packed to overcapacity every single night of the week. I wanted a change of pace. Figured I'd give bartending a try. I really love it. The money is good, the tips are fabulous, and it's a great place to meet guys."

"Sounds like a lot of fun. I'm sure you're never short for dates."

"Nah. But to be honest, I don't really date that much. I used to, but then I just got tired of the whole scene. Most of the guys in San Francisco aren't looking for anything real substantial. Mostly just one-night stands, and I'm really not into that very much."

"I see."

"What about you?"

"What about me?"

"What do you do for a living? I know you're single, but don't know why."

"I could tell you, but then I'd have to kill you."

"Ahh, you're a secret agent!"

"I come from old money." Bradon laughed. "Mostly living off my trust fund, but also manage a little of my family's business every now and then." Bradon liked the sound of his own lie, and smiled with satisfaction. "But I hate talking about money and work."

"Fine. Let's talk boyfriends."

"I've never really had one. There were a couple of guys I really liked a lot, but things didn't work out. They were both really short-term kinda things. Nothing serious."

"I don't get that. You're really beautiful, you've got a head on your shoulders, and you're filthy stinking rich. Why would anyone let you go?"

"I'm a little bit difficult to live with."

"Hmph. Who isn't?"

"No, I mean I am *really* difficult to live with. But that's all right. I learned a long time ago that it's okay to be alone. I like it, actually."

"Why would anyone want to live alone if they don't have to?"

"It's just easier. I don't get hurt. And more importantly, I don't hurt anyone else."

"I find it very difficult to believe you could ever hurt a fly. You're so nice and gentle. And so easy to make blush."

"That's all surface stuff."

"Well, I like what I see on the surface. And I'd like to get to know more of the layers, if you'll let me."

"I don't think that's a great idea, Kirk. I like you. You seem very nice. But I really think it's better if we just stop right here."

"I really don't think the eggs were that great. I don't want them to be the last thing I remember about you."

Bradon laughed. "I'm not good for you, Kirk. I know I haven't been up front with you about everything, and so it might be hard to see the reason, but you have to believe me when I tell you that I'm not."

"Like hell I do. I don't believe anything strictly because someone tells me to. I look deeper than the words. I look into the eyes to find the truth. And your eyes are telling me that you're very good for me. Not only that, but you're good, period."

"They lie."

"No they don't. Eyes never lie. I don't know why you have such a bad perception of yourself, but I know what I see. I know what I feel."

Bradon blushed again and looked down at his hands. He glanced at his watch and panicked.

"Oh my god. It's almost five. I have to go."

"Why? What's the rush?"

"I can't explain right now. But I really do have to go." Bradon jumped up from the table.

"Wait, slow down, Cinderella."

"Kirk, I think you're really great. Thanks for breakfast. But I have to go."

Kirk grabbed Bradon by the waist and pulled him close. "Not before I get two things from you."

"Kirk . . ."

"The first is a kiss," Kirk said, as he leaned into Bradon and kissed him tenderly on the lips.

Bradon's knees buckled and he began to tremble as Kirk kissed him. His head spun and the high-pitched noise in the back of his head returned. He kissed Kirk back and sucked the warm tongue into his mouth. Bradon could taste a light trace of the orange juice Kirk had finished earlier and the sweet minty tingle from Kirk's chewing gum. He darted his tongue in and out of Kirk's tepid and welcoming mouth, trying hard to control his breath. When Kirk returned his kisses and probed his tongue inside Bradon's mouth, Bradon thought he would faint.

"The second is that I want your phone number," Kirk said, as he suddenly broke the kiss.

"But I—"

"Neither one of us is leaving until you give me your phone number."

Bradon grabbed the pen from Kirk's hand and hastily scratched his number out on one of the paper napkins from their table. "Call me tomorrow. Anytime after eight p.m."

Kirk took the napkin and folded it into his pocket. He watched as Bradon ran out the door and down the block.

Kirk did call the next evening. And the evening after that, and the evening after that. He and Bradon worked out every morning right after Kirk got off work, and then went to breakfast. Kirk was honest and up front about everything. Every aspect of his life was open to Bradon. And he was equally direct about his feelings for Bradon.

Bradon, on the other hand, was less willing to deal with his feelings for Kirk. He had more to lose, of course, and so was more cautious. When he was with Kirk, he was friendly and polite, but a little reserved. He loved being with Kirk and longed to spend every waking

hour with him. But the realities of his vampirism kept him from opening up. The memory of the consequences of his lust and love for Josh
still haunted him, and he warned himself not to care too much for
Kirk. But as the weeks passed, it became increasingly more difficult to
do that.

One night, about three months into their relationship, Kirk finally
decided he'd had all of Bradon's mysteriousness that he could tolerate.

"Bradon," he said, as he pulled the blankets back to expose Bradon's
naked body, "I want something from you."

Bradon smiled and leaned down to kiss his lover. His cock was already starting to swell even before their kiss was completed.

Kirk kissed him lightly on the lips, then moved down to lick his chin
and nibble playfully on his neck.

Bradon's body was charged with electricity. Every flicker of Kirk's
tongue across Bradon's hardened nipples, every kiss of his warm wet
lips on Bradon's taut stomach, caused Bradon's entire body to quiver.
As Kirk's lips moved down Bradon's body, Bradon caught his breath
and waited anxiously for his cock to be enveloped in the familiar
warmth of Kirk's tight, loving mouth. He closed his eyes and thrust his
hips upward to meet Kirk's always-eager mouth halfway. He felt the
cool breath of Kirk's teasing whistle, the sure sign that, in just a second, he would feel the entire length of his manhood slide slowly into
his lover's warm, wet mouth and deeper into his clutching throat. He
waited eagerly, for this was his favorite part of foreplay with Kirk.

"I said I want something from you," Kirk said, as he stuck his
tongue out and licked the length of Bradon's hardness.

"Go for it," Bradon panted, "it's right there. Take it."

"I want you to be honest with me."

"I am honest. You can have it."

Kirk smiled up at Bradon and sucked just the head of Bradon's en-
gorged cock into his mouth. He sucked on it for a couple of moments,
then let it slip from his lips. He blew on it a little to cool it down.

"That's not what I want," Kirk said, as he gently squeezed Bradon's
balls between his palms.

"Oh god," Bradon moaned, "well it sure is what I want."

Kirk stuck his middle finger in his mouth and sucked on it until it
was wet with his saliva. Then he lowered it between Bradon's legs and

slid it slowly into Bradon's ass. At the same time, he squeezed Bradon's cock by the base and slowly swallowed it deep into his throat again as his finger slid in and out of Bradon's clutching ass.

"Oh, Jesus, man. That's incredible. Don't stop."

Kirk continued for a couple of minutes and then stopped. He looked up at Bradon, whose eyes were closed in ecstasy, and smiled.

"Tell me your secrets, Bradon." He licked the head of Bradon's cock again as he slid a second finger inside his lover's hot ass.

"Please, Kirk, suck my cock some more."

"Will you tell me everything?" Kirk asked, as he licked the circumference of Bradon's swollen rod.

"Yes, everything. I promise. Just keep sucking my dick."

Kirk swallowed the entire length in one deep thrust and shoved both fingers deeper inside Bradon's ass.

Bradon moaned with animal lust, then whispered, "I'm a vampire."

"What?"

"I'm a vampire, Kirk."

Kirk pulled his fingers out of Bradon's quivering ass in one swift move and bit the head of his cock lightly. "That's not fair, Bradon. You promised you would tell me everything. I was doing my part. You can't keep joking around with me. I want the truth."

Bradon sat up in bed with his back against the headboard. "Come here, Kirk. I'll tell you the truth."

Kirk slid up and snuggled against Bradon at the head of the bed. Bradon laid him flat on his back on the bed, and lay on top of him. Both men were hard and their bodies ground against one another in sweaty heat. Bradon leaned down and kissed Kirk on the lips, and Kirk moaned loudly into his mouth. Bradon kissed his way across Kirk's cheek and up to his ear.

"I'm a vampire," he whispered into Kirk's ear.

"Okay."

Bradon kissed and licked his way down Kirk's face and to his throat. He felt Kirk's excitement as the jugular vein throbbed more intensely every time Bradon thrust himself against Kirk's thighs. He took a deep breath before he sank his teeth slowly and deliberately into the side of Kirk's neck.

"Oh Jesus, that feels incredible, Bradon," Kirk moaned, as Bradon flickered his tongue around the open wound and sucked a small amount of blood into his mouth. "What in Christ's name are you doing?" He moaned even louder and rubbed his hardness against Bradon's thrusting hips and abs.

Bradon pulled his mouth from Kirk's neck and looked up into Kirk's eyes. Blood dripped from his lips, and his canine teeth protruded slightly from the rest of his natural teeth. His eyes were as red as the blood he'd sucked from Kirk's neck, and wild with excitement.

"I'm a vampire, Kirk."

"*What the fuck!*" Kirk yelled, and jumped out of bed. He felt his neck, and when his hands met with warm, slimy fluid, he screamed and began crying. He pulled his hands away and looked at the blood that stained them. "No. No, this cannot be happening."

"I'm sorry, Kirk. I wanted to tell you before, really I did," Bradon said as he leaned back against the headboard. He took a couple of deep breaths and closed his eyes to allow himself to calm down and revert out of the active state. "I can't help it. I'm a vampire. I was born one. But I would never hurt you. I swear to God, I would never hurt you."

"Oh yeah? Well, what the hell do you call this?" Kirk screamed and thrust his bloody hands in front of Bradon's face.

"I know, I know. It looks like I hurt you, but I didn't. I promise you, I did not hurt you. It's just a superficial bite, and it will heal with no problem."

"What?" Kirk screeched in a high-pitched cry. "Are you listening to yourself? You fucking bit my neck and sucked my blood."

"I'm sorry. I didn't want to. I never would have done it on my own. I love you, Kirk. I love you with all my heart and soul. I would never have bitten you of my own will. But you begged me to tell you the truth." Bradon pulled the covers around himself.

"No, no, I didn't." Kirk shook his head vigorously.

"Yes, you did. You were sucking my cock and begging me to tell you my deepest secrets. When I told you I was a vampire you didn't believe me. So I had to show you."

"You *bit* me."

"Yes, I bit you to show you I was being honest with you. Believe me, Kirk, it's only a superficial wound and it will be all healed by morning. You'll never know it happened, I promise. Please, come sit down next to me," Bradon said, as he smoothed out the blankets to make room for Kirk.

"I'll know," Kirk moaned and fell limp to the floor. "I'll know."

"I'm sorry."

"So what happens now? How long does it take before I become a vampire?"

"You will never become a vampire, Kirk. I stopped way, way sooner than it would have taken to convert you."

"Convert me?" Kirk looked into Bradon's eyes. "Convert me?"

"That's the proper term for when a mortal loses his soul and begins his eternal life as a vampire."

"Jesus fucking Christ, I cannot believe I am listening to this."

"You wanted the truth, Kirk. I'm giving it to you. The whole lock, stock and barrel."

"You . . . should have . . . told me . . . sooner," Kirk coughed out between sobs. He stood up slowly and began gathering his clothes.

"Baby, please don't go. I don't want you to leave like this."

"Yeah, well, it's not really all about what you want right now, is it?"

"Come on, Kirk. I didn't do anything wrong. I could not have convinced you of the truth without having bitten you. I didn't hurt you. Please, just stay and talk."

"No," Kirk said, as he buttoned his shirt and tucked the tail of it into his jeans. "I'm leaving. I'll call you in a couple of days, when I've had a chance to clear my head a little."

"Kirk . . ."

"Goodbye, Bradon."

Bradon watched as his boyfriend left the bedroom and walked down the stairs. He noted that Kirk hadn't slammed the bedroom door, and neither had he slammed the living room door. He hoped that meant that at least Kirk wasn't furious with him. Perhaps he might understand just a little bit.

He lifted himself from the bed and walked over to the sink. He stared at his reflection in the mirror. A small trickle of dried blood caked around his lips. His canine teeth were just finally starting to recede back into his gum cavity. His eyes now had only a pinkish tint to them, but were changing back to their bright turquoise blue. His skin had felt flushed while he was in the throes of lovemaking with Kirk, and even more so when he'd sunk his teeth into his lover's supple neck. Now, as he looked in the mirror, he noticed it was turning pale again and beginning to feel cold and damp.

He began to cry as he stared at his own reflection staring back at him. Huge, salty tears streamed down his cheeks and onto the counter below him. He cried for several minutes, and when the tears dried up, he rinsed his mouth with warm water and mouthwash.

Then he walked downstairs into his real bedroom, crawled into his casket, and closed the lid.

A week passed with no word from Kirk. Bradon woke up every evening and spent the next several hours watching the mindless late-night TV shows that did little to comfort him. He was depressed and didn't even try to deny the fact. But he was also growing weak. He hadn't fed in over a month, and that was too long to go without fresh blood, even for his limited needs. The tiny copperish taste of Kirk's blood he'd sampled was enough to fuel his hunger and remind him of his need to feed. But he'd refused to indulge. In fact, he'd promised himself that he would never again feed. He knew quite well the significance of the decision, and decided not to participate in any activity that might tempt him to change his mind.

Night after night and morning after morning Bradon sat lifelessly in front of the television set, watching Nick at Night. The old rerun shows of *Let's Make A Deal*, *Mary Hartman, Mary Hartman* and *Gilligan's Island* were just the remedy he needed to commit to his decision of allowing himself to die. Bradon sprawled across the sofa and turned the volume up almost as high as the television set allowed. Even without the high volume, though, he would never have heard the knocks on the front door. He was beyond hearing anything anymore.

"What the hell is that smell?" Kirk asked, as he walked into the living room.

Bradon stared unblinkingly at the bluish tinged pictures on the television.

"Bradon?" Kirk asked, as he noticed the blank stare and the white, pasty expression on his lover's face. "Bradon, what's going on? Why are you sitting alone in the dark?"

Bradon looked away from the television set and let his eyes wander onto the face of the one guy he'd loved enough to be completely open and honest with.

"Jesus Christ, Bradon," Kirk yelled. He ran over to the sofa past discarded bags of potato chips and TV dinner cartons. "Where's the light switch in here, Bradon?"

Bradon looked over his shoulder to the switchplate on the wall behind him.

Kirk rushed over to the switch and flipped it on. Once the room filled with filtered light, it was easy to identify the retched smell he'd first been assaulted with when he'd let himself into the house after not receiving an answer to his increasingly louder knocks. Most of the TV dinner cartons were still half-full of old, molding food. Glasses were overturned and their contents spilled over onto the carpet, sticking to it like glue. Cigarette butts spilled over the sides of overfilled ashtrays and littered the floor area immediately around the coffee table. Kirk didn't even know that Bradon smoked.

"What the hell happened in here?" he asked, as he kicked some trash out of his way and walked back over to where Bradon lay sprawled on the sofa. When there was no response, he sat next to his lover and picked up his hand. "Shit, Bradon, you're as cold as ice. What's wrong, Bradon? What's going on here?"

"I haven't fed," Bradon whispered, as his unseeing eyes glazed past Kirk's own.

"Fuck!" Kirk yelled. He laid Bradon backward onto the sofa. "Are you dying, Bradon? Tell me the truth. Are you dying?"

Bradon nodded his head. "Just leave," he groaned. "Leave and don't ever look back, Kirk."

"Like hell I will," Kirk said. He leaned down closer to Bradon's face and ripped the neck of his shirt open. "Feed," he said through gritted teeth.

"No," Bradon moaned. He turned his face to the side, away from the temptation of the soft, sweet smell of his lover's neck.

"Goddammit, Bradon, bite me. I just went through a week of the most intense soul searching I've ever undergone, and I finally accepted the fact that I love you and I need you in my life. I'm not about to let you die now. So open your goddamn mouth and feed on me."

A giant tear rolled down Bradon's face and he began to cry softly. He shook his head back and forth, trying not to look at Kirk's face.

But Kirk had made up his mind. He was not going to let the only guy he'd ever loved slip away from him. Not now. Not like this. He reached down and gripped Bradon's chin in his hands. "I love you, Bradon. I didn't think I wanted to, after learning that you're a vampire, but I can't help it. I can't choose who I love. But I do love you more strongly than anything I've ever known. And I will not lose you. Please, sit up if you can, and bite my neck."

"No," Bradon said, and pushed Kirk's face away from his own.

"Bradon, stop being stubborn. If you die, I will die, too. I cannot live without you. I swear, I will kill myself if you die right now. Please don't do this. I don't want to die. I don't want to lose you. Bite my neck."

"Give me your arm," Bradon whispered.

"What?" Kirk asked, not sure he'd heard correctly. He noticed Bradon's eyes were clearer, and he slowly moved his arm closer to Bradon's face.

Bradon took Kirk's arm and pulled it closer. He kissed Kirk's fingers and the palm of his hand. He noticed that Kirk was crying softly. And he saw that Kirk truly did want him to live. He drew Kirk's body closer to his own and maneuvered Kirk so that he was lying directly on top of him.

"Bradon, please . . ."

Bradon pulled Kirk's arm to his mouth again, and this time he kissed the tender area on the underside of the wrist. He felt Kirk writhe on top of him and noticed his arousal pressing against his leg. He opened his mouth wide enough to allow his protruding canines to be released. Then he bit down softly into the soft flesh on the underside of Kirk's wrist. His teeth sank effortlessly into the twin river of veins that ran the length of Kirk's arm. A couple of seconds later he tasted the first drop of warm, thick blood on the tip of his tongue. A loud moan escaped his throat, and he sucked eagerly on the warm arm.

"That's it, baby. Drink. Stop in time. I know you can. But drink enough to bring you back to me."

As he sucked hungrily on the wrist of his lover, Bradon felt his skin tingle and begin to warm up. He felt life snaking its way back into his body like a spiderweb taking form in fast motion. The numbing sensation that had overpowered his mind and body faded quickly, and in just over a minute, he felt his own cock spring to life. He ground it against Kirk's and relished the heat and throbbing excitement he felt from his own body and from Kirk's as well.

He sucked on Kirk's wrist for nearly five minutes. When his body was fully alive and wracked with electric shivers, he thrust Kirk's hand from his face and pushed Kirk's body from his own.

Kirk landed on the floor at the foot of the sofa. "Bradon, what's going on? Are you okay?"

"Get away from me," Bradon yelled.

"Bradon?"

"Go into the kitchen and wait for me," Bradon said, as he turned away from his boyfriend.

"What's going . . ."

"Just go," Bradon yelled, and ran into a corner of the room, hiding his face from Kirk.

Kirk walked quickly into the kitchen and sat at the table, waiting for Bradon to join him.

Inside the living room, Bradon turned around so that his back was pressed against the corner of the room. He allowed the strength to ebb from his body and he slumped to the floor. A sharp pain throbbed through his head as he felt the sharp canine teeth retract back into his gums. His heart pounded thick in his chest, so that he felt, rather than heard, its beat behind his temples. He lowered his head into his hands and cried as the last few stabs of pain passed through his body. He licked the last remaining drops of blood from his lips, then wiped them clean with the back of his hands. Then he stood up and walked into the kitchen.

"Are you okay?" Kirk asked, as he jumped up from the chair and rushed toward Bradon.

"Yes, I'm fine. I just didn't want you to see me like that."

"Like what?"

"Changing."

"Bradon . . ."

"Why did you do that?"

"Do what?"

"Offer your blood to me."

"Because I love you, Bradon."

"But I could have killed you."

"No, you couldn't have."

"I could have killed you, Kirk. You had no way of knowing that I wouldn't kill you."

"Yes, I did. I knew in my heart that you would never kill me. The eyes never lie and the heart never betrays you. It's my cardinal rule."

"Your heart wouldn't betray you, Kirk. But how could you be so sure about mine? Especially after the way I lied to you?"

"You didn't lie to me, Bradon. You were right when you said I wouldn't believe you if you tried to tell me any other way than you did."

"But how could you trust me after all I did to you? How could you know one-hundred percent that I wouldn't drain every ounce of life from you? It's what we do, you know. Vampires kill people, Kirk. We kill them and steal their souls. That's how we live forever."

"Yeah, so they tell me. But you're more than that, Bradon. You're more than a vampire. That's only part of who you are."

"I've killed people, Kirk."

Kirk stared deep into Bradon's eyes, then lowered his own to stare at his shuffling feet. He swallowed hard, then looked back into Bradon's eyes. "I don't want to know about that, Bradon. Please don't talk about that part of your life with me."

"But it's true, Kirk. You have to know that I could have killed you. How can you ever trust me? How can you ever know for sure that I won't kill you in the future?"

"Because I know you, Bradon. I know who you are."

"I'm a vampire."

"You're half vampire, Bradon. But you are also half human."

"How do you know that?" Bradon asked, staring wide-eyed into Kirk's eyes.

"On my way out of here last week, I noticed the book on your book-shelf. I'd seen you reading it early in the mornings, after we'd made love and you thought I was asleep. You always cried when you read the book. I knew it was something special. When I ran out of here the other night, I grabbed it on my way. I knew it held some of the answers to my questions that you might not be able or willing to share with me. So I took it and read it from cover to cover."

"But why would you—"

"Because I needed to know who you are at the core. And I found out. Yes, you are part vampire, Bradon. As hard as it is for me to understand and believe that, I know that I have to. If I love you, and I do, then I have to believe that. But you are also half human. And that's the part I'm interested in, baby. That's the part I love."

"You can't love part of me, and not the rest."

"I love all of you. But I believe you can change the part of you that you yourself despise the most. I believe you can stop being a vampire."

"What are you talking about, Kirk?"

"I read your father's journal very carefully. He killed your mother because he was afraid she would steal you away from him. There were several entries that alluded to the fact that he was concerned she would turn you against him and forever condemn you to a life of mortal hell. Why would he say those things if it weren't possible for you to deny your vampirism and become mortal?"

"But . . . I can't change who I am . . . I've been a vampire all my life . . ."

"No, I don't believe that's true," Kirk said. He reached for the journal and began flipping through it. It had been ripped and torn in several pieces. "I could tell from the way it was taped carefully back together that it meant something to you. I could tell it was important." He flipped through much of the beginning, where the pages were more intact, and slowed down when the pages were more tattered and taped together. "From about the middle, since the first entry about your birth, your father made references to a choice. Because you are half human, you had a choice. Your mother knew that, and was ready to help you make that choice. But your father didn't want that to happen, and he killed her before she had a chance to give you one."

Bradon's head was beginning to ache again, and he felt a little dizzy. "That just doesn't make sense," he said, as he shook his head to clear his thoughts. "I've always had a hunger for blood. I have to have it to survive."

"I don't think so. Look here," Kirk said, as he pointed to an early entry from Bradon's father. "*I have heard that this could happen. It is a possible consequence from a mixed marriage. But I have faith that it can be changed.*"

"I don't get it."

"He's talking about your distaste for blood, Bradon. If you read the journal carefully, he'd been preoccupied with it since before you were born. He knew it was possible you might choose not to be a vampire. He eliminated your mother when he considered her a threat, and he forced your feeding on you long before you ever knew you might have a choice about it. When you were a young child, your father told you that you had to have warm blood to survive, and because you didn't know anything other than his words, you believed him. But think about it, Bradon. Why didn't your father ever remarry or get you a nanny? Why did he raise you himself?"

"He loved my mother," Bradon said mechanically.

"You know that is not true, Bradon. He killed your mother when he thought she might interfere with your decision to live as a human or as a vampire. He raised you the way he wanted you to be raised. He forced his beliefs and his way of life on you. You might not remember it now, but you hated the taste of blood when you were young."

"I still don't like it. But I have to have it. I'll die without it."

"I don't think so, Bradon. You have a choice, and it's not too late to make that choice. Your father wrote many times of your mother's heart. He said that, though it was the thing he loved most about her, it was also the one thing that could be the end of him. I don't think he was talking figuratively. I don't think he was being romantic. I think he was being literal. He meant that Rachel's human heart was stronger than his vampire heart, and could, if he allowed her too much freedom with that heart, literally kill him. And if her heart were given too many liberties, it could steal you away from him. How do you think that is possible, Bradon?"

"I don't know."

"You have your mother's heart, Bradon. You have the choice of being a vampire or being human. You can't be both. Not forever."

"How do you know it's not already too late to make that choice?"

"Because you've never been given the opportunity to make it. Your mother was killed before she was able to tell you that you had the choice. Your father went to great measures to make sure you never knew you had a choice."

"But how do you know for sure that I really do have a choice? What if all of this is just a theory? The journal never mentions any choice."

"I just feel it in here," Kirk said, and placed Bradon's hand on his heart. "I read between the lines. And I think you did, too. That's why you killed your father."

"How did you know I killed my father?"

"I didn't really, until now. But I had a hunch. I know how much your mother means to you, and I know that reading about how she really died would be more than you could deal with. Victor killed your mother. He forced his beliefs and his life on you. He hated that you're gay and tried to convince you otherwise. He rejected you. I just know that there came a point where you made a conscious decision not to accept all the crap that he was forcing on you. And knowing that he'd killed your mother made it easier for you to kill him."

"I thought you didn't want to know or talk about the people I've killed."

"I don't. Whatever you did before now, before you knew that you have a choice about your actions and your life, are all in the past. I can't hold you responsible for any of that. I don't know how we're ever going to put that behind us and not think about it, but we will. Somehow we will. But your father was not human, Bradon, and as much as it might hurt for you to hear, he deserved to die. He deserved to be killed."

"It doesn't hurt at all."

"Good. He hurt you, Bradon. He lied to you and made you think and believe that your being a vampire was predestined and the only option. He forced you into feeding on and killing innocent human beings."

Bradon stood up from the table quickly and rushed to the kitchen sink. He leaned over it and vomited. When he was finished, he returned to the table and sat down beside Kirk.

"So what do I do now?" he asked, as he reached for Kirk's hand.

"You make the conscious decision that you have always been rightfully entitled to. But according to everything I've learned, you can only make it once. Think about it very carefully, because once you make it, you can never go back and change it."

"There's nothing to think about. I don't want to be a vampire. I never have."

"I know, baby."

"There's got to be more to it than just saying I don't want to be a vampire. More than just saying I choose to be human."

"Well, I've done a little research over the last week. Some really underground stuff. Articles from several people who have gone through the process and made the decision themselves. According to the articles, the choice is actually a test of faith."

"A test of faith? But I've never been to church in my life. How am I supposed to have faith in something I've never been exposed to?"

"Faith isn't about something you're familiar with, Bradon. It's about believing in yourself, and also in something more than yourself that has no reasonable explanation. Do you believe that you are human? Do you believe that you are much more than just a vampire with a need for human blood?"

"Yes."

"Are you sure? Because if you're not, then this little test could kill you. Kill you more definitely and quickly than a stake through the heart."

"I'm sure."

"You're putting a lot of stock into a theory that I've thrown at you pretty unexpectedly."

"I know. But I believe it. I believe I am more than what my father said I am, and more than what he wanted me to be. I am my mother's son. I have her heart."

"And you're willing to put it all on the line?"

"Yes. If you're right, and I make the right decision, then I will be free of all of the pain and suffering I've been living with my entire life."

"And if I'm wrong?"

"Then still I will be free. Free from a life of eternal hell and misery. Free of the shackles of living inside a skin that is not my own. I want to do this, Kirk. I do."

"All right."

"So, what is this test of faith?"

"Let's go to bed. I want to make love to you."

"That's the test of faith? Making love to you?"

"No. Letting me make love to you. In the three months we've been seeing each other, you've never once given yourself completely to me."

"Oh man, I've heard of desperate pleas before, but this one has to take the cake."

"I'm serious, Bradon. You have to let go of all of your inhibitions and put your trust and faith in someone other than yourself. What better way of showing you're willing to let go of that control and put yourself in someone else's hands?"

Bradon allowed Kirk to take his hand and lead him upstairs to the spare bedroom that he pretended was his whenever Kirk came over. "Okay, baby, but I still think it sounds like just a line to get me to give up my virginity to you."

Kirk squeezed Bradon's hand and led him to the bed. He undressed Bradon first, and then himself. "This is really just the first step of your decision and your leap of faith."

"Ah, now the truth comes out. And so, what is the second step?"

Kirk walked over to the large bay window on the other side of the room and drew the curtains open wide. Then he opened the windows.

"Oh, shit," Bradon said, as he looked down at the clock on the nightstand. It was five-thirty in the morning, and already the dark black of night was turning to an indigo blue. Bradon could already make out the lining of a few scattered morning clouds.

"If you're having doubts, now would be the time to express them," Kirk said, as he lay down next to Bradon on the bed.

Bradon looked at the open window and took a deep breath. "Come here," he said to Kirk, and pulled him closer. He leaned up and pulled Kirk down to meet his kiss. He was still flushed from the feeding a little over an hour ago. But he was sure the heat emanating from his body had nothing to do with the nourishment he'd received. He was hot with desire for the one man he loved more than life itself.

He slipped his tongue inside Kirk's mouth and kissed him long and tenderly. He hoped Kirk could not still taste his own blood inside Bradon's mouth. He broke the kiss, and licked and kissed his way down Kirk's neck. He grew a little short of breath as his lips tickled the throbbing jugular vein that so prominently mapped Kirk's thick, soft neck. He closed his eyes, took a deep breath and continued kissing a trail down past Kirk's collarbone and between his smooth muscular pecs.

Kirk moaned and thrust his hips upward as Bradon licked his way down Kirk's stomach and past his navel.

Bradon opened his mouth and licked the head of his lover's cock. When Kirk moaned even louder, and lightly pressed Bradon's head even lower, Bradon opened his throat and swallowed the entire length of Kirk's swollen member deep inside him. His own dick was throbbing painfully, and when he reached down to stroke it, he found himself on the verge of collapsing. His legs quivered violently and his torso shook with the force of the shock that rocked through his entire body.

"Come here," Kirk whispered. He pulled Bradon from his cock and back up to his mouth. He kissed Bradon passionately for several minutes and eased first one finger and then a second into Bradon's smooth, tight ass.

Bradon returned the kiss and began rocking his body back and forth against the lightning-hot fingers inside him. His breathing became labored and his body began shaking again. He knew he couldn't hold out much longer.

Kirk quickly withdrew his fingers and broke the kiss. He gently placed his hands on Bradon's shoulders and pushed Bradon's body farther down the length of his own. When Bradon's cool, smooth ass touched the hot head of his cock, he whispered, "It's okay, baby. I won't hurt you. Just take it easy."

Bradon took another deep breath, then lowered himself slowly onto Kirk's long, hard cock. It was still slick with his own saliva, and Bradon's ass spread easily as it entered him. He moaned deeply as inch after inch went deeper inside him. The pain quickly turned to pleasure and he was soon thrusting himself backward onto his lover's cock and riding him deliriously.

Kirk let Bradon find his rhythm and then picked up the pace a little. He loved watching Bradon's sweat-slicked body riding his own. He loved seeing Bradon's long, thick cock bouncing up and down between his legs as he rode his cock. He loved looking into Bradon's eyes and seeing pure bliss and complete trust.

He looked toward the window and noticed that the sky was now a lighter shade of blue. He could easily see the leaves of the tree right outside the bedroom window. The air outside smelled fresh and clean, and the birds were beginning to chirp. If ever Bradon were to question his decision to go through with this, it would be now, when so much evidence of life and morning were beginning to present themselves. He did not want to give Bradon that chance to change his mind.

Kirk rolled Bradon onto his back and shoved his cock deeper inside him. As Bradon moaned with pleasure, Kirk leaned down and kissed him on the mouth as he continued thrusting deeper and harder into his clutching ass.

The first rays of warm sunlight splashed across Kirk's back and ass just a moment later. It felt comfortable and assuring and warm and promising. And at the same time, it felt cold and threatening and ominous. The cool morning breeze wrapped more rays of sunshine around his body, and down his ass and between his legs. He felt the warmth envelop his balls, and farther between his legs, he noticed that Bradon's ass and the backs of his legs were also beginning to warm.

Bradon moaned louder as Kirk thrust into him deeper and faster.

Kirk was so wrapped up in his lovemaking and concentrating on not shooting his load inside Bradon's warm, clutching ass, that he failed to notice that Bradon had stopped breathing. He pulled out of Bradon's ass suddenly and aimed his cock away from Bradon's body. It was well after the third shot of his lust that he looked down and saw his lover's white, still, unmoving face and body beneath him.

"Bradon," he whispered in a hoarse pant. "Bradon, please look at me." He caught his breath and let his body fall across Bradon's. He leaned forward and put his ear to Bradon's chest. He couldn't hear a heartbeat; Bradon's chest had no movement. "Oh, God! No, please don't let this happen," he cried out as he held Bradon's still, lifeless body in his arms. "Please wake up, Bradon. You can't die on me. Not here. Not like this."

He shook Bradon's body violently and then fell limp across the cold, white body beneath him. He cried for several minutes, and then leaned up to kiss Bradon's cold, blue lips. He pried the lifeless lips apart and kissed Bradon long and passionately as his tears cascaded down his cheeks and fell onto Bradon's face.

"I love you, Bradon," he cried, as he continued kissing him.

Then there was movement. At first Kirk thought he was imagining it, and that he'd been mistaken. It started out just a twitch in Bradon's upper thighs. Then a jerk in his arms. A moment later his chest began heaving and he was breathing.

"Baby," Kirk cried out. He scooped Bradon into his arms, bringing him into a sitting position at the head of the bed.

Bradon coughed a few times, then slowly opened his eyes. He looked up into Kirk's tear-streaked face and smiled. "Why are you crying?"

Kirk coughed out a laugh, and hugged Bradon tighter to his chest. "Are you okay?" he asked, as he rocked Bradon back and forth.

"Yeah, I'm fine," Bradon said, as he gained his strength and sat up in the bed. "A little sticky, though." He wiped Kirk's cooled semen from his chest and stomach.

Kirk laughed and cried at the same time, and fell limply into Bradon's arms.

"It's okay," Bradon said, hugging Kirk's quivering body closer to his own. "It's over. I'm okay."

"Are you sure?" Kirk asked, looking up into the bright turquoise eyes of his lover.

Bradon looked over at the open window. He stood up and walked over to stand naked in front of it. Warm, fresh sunshine splashed across his body, warming him instantly.

"Yeah," Bradon said. He ran back to the bed and jumped onto it. He smiled when he saw Kirk's cock was already swelling again. "Yeah, I'm sure." He wrapped his body around Kirk's, kissing his sweaty body all over.

Devoured

Jeff Mann

For John, who said, "Of course you can," and
for the gay men and lesbians of Appalachia

ACKNOWLEDGMENTS

Many thanks to Andrew Beierle and John Scognamiglio
for this opportunity to recreate the world and
thus ease my cultural frustration.

"Long live the weeds and the wilderness yet."
—Gerard Manley Hopkins

"Every angel's terrifying."   —Rainer Maria Rilke

". . . it is impossible to overlook the extent to which civiliza-
tion is built up upon a renunciation of instinct, how much it
presupposes precisely the non-satisfaction . . . of powerful
instincts. This 'cultural frustration' dominates the large field
of social relationships between human beings."
—Sigmund Freud

Fog swallows the stars. It rolls in over the dark waters, and the firth breathes and sighs like a lover sleeping at my side. A restless sleep, the sleep of centuries.

I am Derek Maclaine, and this great lapping darkness is the Firth of Forth, a sea inlet just north of Edinburgh, Scotland. Though I miss the mountains of West Virginia, where I have lived for centuries, still it is sweet to be back here, the country of my birth, the country which once was home. It is sweet to cup the firth's cold and salty waves in my cold hand, to watch misty lights blink across the water.

Tonight is May Eve, an ancient holy day dedicated to the new gold-green of spring and to all its appetites. Appetite drives me tonight. Hunger is like that claymore I once carried, the one that slipped between the ribs of Angus's murderers. These are hunger's double edges: that it gives meaning and focus, and that it always returns, the philosopher's eternal recurrence, like the curse of these waves, lapping perpetually, without peace.

Peace is a grave, and that I renounced long ago. Over the black surf I speak these words to myself, to find some sense in appetite, to make some truce with my own insatiability. This is my history, written not in water, but rather in blood, like the contract Faust signed with Mephistopheles. Study the card of the Devil in old Tarot decks, lovers chained naked to the Horned One's dais. I have not sold my soul to the Christians' Satan. Rather, I am in bondage to the beauty of the earth, to the bodies of men.

For a time I walk in this fog drifting in from the sea, drink my fill of dark-cloaked solitude and its lyrics, relish the silence. But thirst always turns me back to the land, to the poetry of the human. Harder to find than the bleaker beauty of sea, of mist, of those pale stars, distant diamond grit visible for a moment, then swallowed by the chill gray. But if human beauty can be found, I am the man to find it. Tonight, when the Old Gods marry and mate, when the blade descends into the chalice and bloom breaks forth across the hills, I will take beauty's blood between my teeth, lapping skin as the sea licks shingle.

The Star Tavern. I have hunted here before, this waterfront pub. The smoke rises from cigarettes, bubbles break in amber pints of ale. Many nights, all I have found worth devouring is the flashing image of a soccer player's thighs on the television screen, and some nights that is enough. We older ones, we can wait. The thirst does not madden us nightly as it once did. We become like Kafka's hunger artists, waiting for the right food—the muscular curve of chest, the enthusiastic and intelligent eye, strong shoulders and furry forearms. Patient, we find strength of purpose in our own starvation, in this trust: that loveliness will return to us.

I will not starve tonight. I have called out over those dark waters, called the Hunter, the Hunted, the Lord of Wild Things, the God of spring's new leaves, of youth's ecstasies. I am his priest, and with this single malt I toast to Him. Light glints in the golden tumbler, and I take the honeyed fire on my tongue, praying for a sacrifice. Let tonight's savior manifest himself.

See how the Scottish night answers. The door of the pub opens, and a young man in his mid-twenties walks in, trailing ribbons of fog. At my elbow he orders Scotch, then shrugs off his black leather jacket, settles at a corner table, rummages through his backpack for a notepad and book, and then begins to read, sipping single malt every other page.

I study him, and, as I have for almost three hundred years, I ponder the mystery of aesthetics. Why do I see beauty in what I do? Why am I fascinated by this sort of man? He resembles Angus a bit, true. But why did I love Angus in the first place? I have a penchant for asking unanswerable questions. It is a habit which keeps me awake. "Only that day dawns to which we are awake," said Thoreau. Yes, I am a scholar of sorts, and good books have helped fill my centuries, though a day's dawning is one pleasure I must miss.

This boy is recompense enough for the loss of sunlight, the way noon made of the waters of Lochbuie a blue-green satin, the way it ignited fields of poppies. His dark hair shines in the firelight, this pub fire flickering on a chilly and foggy spring night. Summer takes its time here, as it did in the mountains of my childhood on the Isle of Mull. I have never been back to Lochbuie, and, as close as I am—the width of Scotland—this time as well I may not have the heart to return. How many times have I come back to Edinburgh, have mused by the firth, or climbed the extinct volcano of Arthur's Seat after midnight to look over the city's lights, to look toward the Hebrides, only to leave Scotland again, my homecoming truncated, unfulfilled? All these decades, and I have never seen Angus's grave.

Tonight, of all nights, I must not think of Angus.

Broad shoulders. Long hair pulled back in a ponytail. What is the book he pores over? *Byron's Poetry.* I almost laugh out loud. Too easy.

"A Byron scholar? We have something in common," I say, standing by his table. "Forgive the interruption. It's just that I don't every day see someone reading the Romantics, especially in a pub devoted to soccer."

His eyes are blue-green, that color of Lochbuie under the spring sun. Those eyes, surprisingly long-lashed, meet mine, and I can tell what he sees he admires.

This is what he sees: a pale man in his mid-thirties, a little over six feet in height, with thick black hair, a close-trimmed beard, a powerful build not quite concealed by his long gray caped coat. Full lips, barely visible beneath the bushy mustache, and moderate cheekbones above the beard line. A steel hoop in the left earlobe. Small round glasses, giving his brown eyes a professorial and harmless look. Faded jeans, black harness-strap boots, a leather wristband, all a little incongruous beside the elegant coat.

He likes my height, he likes my silver-streaked black beard. Good. This one is too pretty to be forced. I want a willing sacrifice tonight, someone eager to be crucified. Already I can taste the rich roses of stigmata.

"Hey, have a seat. You read Byron?" he quizzes. My fang teeth begin to lengthen a bit, and on the sharp point of the right one I cut my tongue.

Seducing the smart ones, I like to take my time. Occasionally I even learn something, despite my distracted heartbeat, my stiffening anticipation. Chest hair, a chestnut brown, curls over the top of his T-shirt. Several days' worth of stubble darkens his cheeks. Shrugging off my coat, I sit in the chair opposite him.

His name is David. He's an American from Palo Alto, an exchange student studying literature at the University of Edinburgh. "Cool coat," he enthuses, stroking the gray wool. "Isn't that called an Inverness?"

"Yes," I reply. "I grew up in the Highlands, and this garment reminds me of my youth. It's an affectation I allow myself during visits to Edinburgh, though in West Virginia, where I spend most of the year, I'd look pretty odd wearing it, except perhaps at Highland games."

"Reminds me of *Dark Shadows*! I used to watch it on the SciFi channel during my undergrad days. Ever watch that? The vampire wore an Inverness."

"Yes," I admit. "I remember Barnabas. He and Byron's heroes have a lot in common."

"You bet!" David says excitedly, sipping his single malt, his eyes gleaming. "So much of this I can relate to myself," he admits, reaching for the book and turning to *Childe Harold's Pilgrimage*. "Here, 'the wandering outlaw of his own dark mind.' Or"—flipping pages—"*The Giaour*, that poor bastard, a mind 'like the Scorpion girt by fire.' I'm glad he killed Hassan and died unrepentant."

What intellectual enthusiasm. Almost as tasty as the way his chest curves against the gray fabric of his T-shirt. "Byron had such a longing for innocence," I point out. " 'She Walks in Beauty,' and all that. Though," I add quietly, "I would change the pronoun." Leaning back in my chair, I stretch my arms above my head, the gesture of an awakening animal. David can catch, at this angle, just a glimpse of the dark barbed wire tattooed around my right biceps and triceps.

Those sea-green eyes widen. I can see the blood pulsing in his neck. Beneath the table I rest my palm on his thigh, then ask, "Childe David, may I buy you another Scotch?" He nods and grins, leaning his other leg into mine. What a feast we shall share.

After his last mouthful of Dalwhinnie, he's ready to leave. Outside the fog is still thick. We walk along the firth for a while, prolonging the delicious anticipation. He misses California, the hills of golden grass, the scent of jasmine, the farmer's markets full of white peaches and avocados. Gay life in Edinburgh is tolerable, he explains, though he prefers big city bars in America like the Eagle, the Green Lantern, and the Lure. "Ah, bars to match your jacket," I joke. " 'He walks in leather, like the night / o'er Scottish seas and starless climes,' or something like that." Despite that jacket, he's shivering now in the spring chill, and, sensing no one else on the street, I wrap my Inverness-winged right arm about him.

"Would you like to come home with me?" he suddenly sighs, his brow creasing with suspense. As if anyone sane would ever say no to such an offer from such a handsome man. "I live just up the hill," he continues shakily, "in the attic apartment of a big home I'm house-sitting for a year."

I pull him closer, touch my lips to his neck briefly, place my left hand on his chest, over his heart. "Lead the way," I whisper, and he does.

A small garden beyond the gray stone wall. Fava beans and goose-berries, blooming potato plants. "I love to grow things," David says, touching the indigo of an early iris spear before leading me past the neatly ordered plants and into the back door. The force that through the green fuse drives the flower drives us tonight. I'd like to see him shirtless in the hot sun, on his knees, troweling up the soil, armpit sweat running down his sides. Instead I will settle, oh so gladly, for the sight of his body bare and sweat-lacquered in candlelight.

Up several flights, to a small odd-angled room under the eaves and overlooking the firth. My night vision is better than most. A narrow bed, a traveler's-sized guitar. A desk, bookcases, laundry piled in one corner. A narrow closet filled with T-shirts, jeans, cowboy boots. A ceramic Green Man hung upon one wall. David slips off his backpack and jacket, then, in a charming gesture of old-fashioned civility, helps me off with my Inverness. As I'd hoped, there are candles positioned about the room, and he lights them one by one. "Uh, I'm a little nervous," he admits—more inadvertent charm—"so let's have just another shot of Scotch. You like Tobermory? It's from the Isle of Mull, sort of hard to find. I save it for special occasions."

Angus. How long I have searched for you in the faces and bodies of other men, in their beards, the hardness of their muscles, the scent of their groins, the softness of their belly hair. Pieces of you. Scattered, like the fragments of the murdered Osiris, the fragments his wife Isis sought around the world. I can never reassemble you, your breath, your life.

"Tobermory? Yes, please," I respond almost inaudibly, browsing the bookcases beside his bed. Amidst a slew of literary titles—Dostoyevsky's *Crime and Punishment, The Greek Anthology, Swann's Way*—certain suggestive anomalies stand out: *The Claiming of Sleeping Beauty, Rough Stuff,* and *Urban Aboriginals.* Just the clues I need.

For a time, sipping our whisky, we stand in silence before the window, where a hemlock, uneasy with breeze, moves its silhouette against the black expanse of the firth and the distant shore. I can hear his frightened heartbeat. How lonely he is. How badly he wants to be loved. How badly he wants to be hurt.

"The fog's lifted," I state matter-of-factly. "Take off your shirt."

David turns to me. His eyes meet mine, then drop in submission. "Uh, okay," he stammers.

I remember that litany of leather bars he chanted longingly down by the water. What he most wants is what I am most prepared to give.

Swigging the last of his Scotch, David pulls his T-shirt over his head, then stands meekly before me in the candlelight, eyes still lowered. Yes, this is the ritual we both want, this room our Beltane altar.

I take another swig of Scotch—the waters of Mull made molten— then step up to him. His chest is as furry as I'd guessed. I run my hands through the dark mat, over the mounds of his pecs, then brush his hard nipples. I tease them a bit, circling and flicking them before abandoning introductory gentleness. Between my thumbs and forefingers I pinch them now, increasing the pressure till he gasps.

"Look at me." He does, his eyes shadowed with fear and ardor. Now I dig in my fingernails and watch as pain transfigures his face, pain replaced by wonder, accompanied by a groan of gratitude. Bending forward, I nuzzle his neck, lick his chin stubble, then part his lips with my tongue. "You like it rough, don't you, Childe David?" I growl, slowly twisting the hard nubs of his nipples. "You're going to hurt tomorrow," I promise, "but that's what we both want." He groans again, more loudly, and, despite himself, pulls away.

I slap him. Just hard enough to shock. "Oh, we haven't even begun," I promise. "By the break of day we'll have found your limits, little Hercules. But for now let's keep you quiet."

From the pile of laundry I retrieve a grimy sock. "Stuff this in your mouth," I order. His hand shakes as he takes it from me. He swallows hard, drops his eyes in shame, then, hesitating only a second, he obeys.

Beautiful. White fabric of the sock against the dark shadow of his beard stubble. I cup his chin and raise his head till our eyes interlock. Robbed now of speech, his moist surprised eyes are doubly expressive, full of what might pass for worship. "Do you like that?" I ask quietly. He nods slowly. "I'm guessing an aficionado like you has several lengths of cotton rope within easy reach of the bed. Show me now. It's time you were restrained."

The drawer of the bedside table is stuffed full of the familiar paraphernalia of sacrifice. What is it about leather, metal and rope that lends a sense of the sacramental to my feasts? Another question without answer, for eroticism is as much a mystery as aestheticism, its proper twin. I only know that I savor the struggles, the helplessness of my lovers as much as I savor their blood. *"Let me see your beauty broken down,"* I hum the Leonard Cohen song, uncoiling some rope, *"as you would do for one you love."*

Angus, tonight I will forget you.

David does not struggle. He's been dreaming of such a night for a long time. No resistance as I tightly knot his wrists behind him, slip off his jeans and briefs, then stretch him out on the bed and knot his ankles together. Now I strip to the waist, sit on the bed's edge and simply watch him, sipping the remainder of my Scotch. His chest rises and falls rapidly, his eyes silently ranging over my muscles, chest pelt, Thor's cross necklace and tattoos. I run my fingers across his torso and down his belly; I grip his penis, which bobs and drips with excitement. He shudders and bucks, and I pull away. "Oh no, not yet. We have all night." I smile, lifting him to a sitting position beside me. I face him, and gently undo the leather cord about his ponytail. The dark hair falls free about his shoulders. "You look like Christ," I whisper, kissing his gagged mouth—taste of sock-musk, scent of whisky. When I lean his head against my left shoulder, I feel a few tears trickle down my tattoo, the face of the Horned God. Moonlight pools on the hardwood floor at our feet. My fangs lengthen and ache.

I want to live this again and again. How I pull his head firmly back by his long hair and lick his neck, restless tides across an eroding beach, my hard fingers again roughly worrying his nipples. How he winces—that delicious muffled sigh—as I sink my teeth.

Mead: think of it. A rich red mead. An intoxicant made from honey. Sweet, but edged with rust, the rough edge of mortality. My mouth is the goblet. I drink to the gods of this earth, to the dark places of fern and larch, the thick heather, the Highland streams purling over time-smoothed stones, to moonlight streaming over his loins as he sinks back against me, faint.

Only a little from the neck. Now I'm licking the sweat which runs down his sides—sweat even in this chill room—and now I take his nipples into my mouth one by one. Licking tenderly, then biting down again, hand over his groaning sock-stuffed mouth, taking mouthfuls of his blood, oh-so-carefully. Childe David. This one is too sweet to kill.

I take a break, leaving him bound on the bed. He rolls over on his side, to take the weight off his aching wrists. Beyond our high window, fog has rolled in again, and I watch it smudge the firth's far shore, swallow the spring stars. Behind me, David groans and pants. He's struggling a little, trying to work his wrists free. Far too tight.

Rolling him over, I slap his buttocks hard, again and again, till the whiteness—of California's white peaches, of bee-tormented apple blossom, of the flower of the bloodroot, oh the bloodroot, blooming in the early West Virginian spring—till the smooth curved whiteness flushes with my handprints. Handprints in prehistoric caves, like an illiterate's autograph: I was here. Then slowly slipping inside my spit-wet finger, sinking my fangs into the reddened cheeks of his ass. I draw in the blood long, goblets full of it. It is so hard to stop, breaking the waxen cloisters of the cells one by one, coaxing out the nectar. Only centuries of hard-won knowledge make me withdraw my fangs in time. Unnatural, really, like pulling out of a man before you explode. But a boy so beautiful: I cannot help but care for him. Weak but thankful, for me he will greet the dawn.

Again I roll him over, slide another finger inside, and now I cover his drooling cock with my mouth, sliding along its stiffness for only a few seconds before tilting my head and breaking the skin with one fang. He shouts as best he can, slams his loins against my face, and—oh, blessed amalgam, the Hunter's gift—floods my mouth with the mingled tastes of semen and of blood. Gulping lava, oak embers, liquid moonstone.

When his pants subside, I move to untie him, but he weakly shakes his head. Understanding, I lift him just far enough to pull back the covers—he's shivering again—and slip him between the sheets. Pulling off my boots and jeans, I slide in beside him, cupping his smooth back with my hairy chest, his smooth buttocks with my hairy groin. With one hand, I push the sock a fraction deeper into his mouth; with the other, I tug absentmindedly on his nipples. After such rigorous abuse, they're no doubt on fire by now, but how I love to torment a pair of hairy tits which already ache. He groans—his cock's hard again—and grinds his ass against my crotch, but if we were to start again, I would surely kill him. It's all I can do not to drink from the fine muscles of his shoulders. "No, no. No more, novice knight. Sleep," I urge, and soon he does.

So warm, the human form. I might as well be curled up by the great fireplace in our family castle on the Isle of Mull. Tonight the flickering hearth I drowse beside is his heart.

Damn you, Angus. Let me love this moment, this bound boy sleeping beside me, his life and death entirely in my hands.

Well before dawn, the birds begin. A warning I have noted for many years. And dawn comes soon in springtime Scotland, so far north we are. I am kissing the back of David's neck when he wakes. It is still too dark for him to notice that the silver in my black beard has been replaced with a touch of red. In Gaelic, Derek means "the red-headed one." It is a name I grow into when I feed, when my several centuries, so eager to catch up with me, for a time give up the chase, when the heat of a youth gives my youth back to me.

Gently I tug the sock out of his mouth. He licks his dry lips, works his aching jaw, then looks up at me with silent happiness. "Derek. It's been so long since . . ."

"I can tell." I smile. "I'm delighted to have been your Beltane priest." Rising, I loosen the ropes about his wrists and ankles, just enough for him to free himself when I leave. "I've got to go," I explain, pulling on my clothes, "and you need to sleep."

"Will I see you again?"

"I meant to stay in Scotland longer; there was someplace in the Hebrides I wanted to go, but . . . I don't think I can go there now. I've got to get back to the States instead. But yes, eventually, you will see me again. For now, sleep, and we'll meet in your dreams."

I bend to kiss his brow, and his breath goes deep with sleep. I have that power. No need for him to see me leave the way I most enjoy. From the deep flannel pocket of my Inverness coat, I retrieve a ruby and place it on the bedside table. Then I open the window, lean over the sill, and shift.

Were David still conscious, he would see my edges shimmer and dissolve, the gray silhouette of my form smudging as if enveloped by the firth's incessant fog. He would see that gray outline disperse, trail through the window, a sentient mist, and recoalesce in midair.

Yes, of course, a huge bat, condor-sized. I have confused many night-wandering biologists who search their brains, their taxonomies, trying to explain that wingspan. Conspicuous, yes. Back home in West Virginia, hunting season would prove to be a major annoyance if hunters stalked by night. The few who've peppered me in dusk's first violet have soon, shrieking fools, borne my weight on their backs.

Tonight I skim over the firth—there is time yet. Nick, that big stupid boy, the one with the thick arms and military crewcut, the one who tried to charge me when we first met, Nick waits for me in Holyrood House, waits to hide me in that long-abandoned tower room. He likes his back flogged, and he is, he boasts, a master at constructing afternoon teas. How he will pine when I return to Appalachia, my adopted mountain home. How shallow will seem his days. Perhaps Her Majesty will soon return to Edinburgh and give him something interesting to do. Perhaps she will appreciate his watercress sandwiches.

Licking my teeth, I savor David still. The musk of his cock and ass, the salt of his armpits, blood and semen. Salinity come so far from Mara, the Mother, the sea. Tomorrow he will wonder at his weakness, will marvel at the bruises my teeth have left on his neck, nipples, buttocks and penis, will bear them for days like royal purple, a warrior's badge of pride. I have turned endurance into celebration, Angus, this night of May Eve, so far removed from your death. But now, before I sleep, as I soar above Calton Hill and dip about the tower of the Tolbooth Kirk, I owe it to you to remember. My memory is your cenotaph.

The local Christians said the standing stones were haunted, which was fine for Angus and me. Such folklore meant that no one went there, meant that we could meet amidst the stones, celebrate the Old Gods without disturbance, celebrate our love.

I'd known Angus McCormick since childhood. He and his family, members of our clan, herded their cattle and tended their sparse crops near that end of Mull closest to Iona. Iona, where the old kings were buried, where Columba landed, determined to see no more of Ireland, and began to spread his pestilence throughout the Highlands.

Well, I'm being unfair. Those early Celtic monks were gentle souls, I gather, but by the time I came of age in Lochbuie, in the early 1700s, Christianity was as narrow and grim in Scotland as it is in much of Appalachia these days of the early 21st century. My grandmother, who taught me the old faith, also taught me to hide it. The witch burnings were not at all remote, and to this day, on Edinburgh's Castle Hill, I leave roses by the memorial built to remember those burnt at that very spot.

And I knew to hide as well my feelings for Angus. God, how handsome he looked, striding behind the plow in spring, picking berries with me in midsummer, practicing our swordplay, or lounging in the blooming heather of early autumn. Behind that rough exterior was the kindest of hearts.

If you find a white sprig of heather amidst all the purple, you will have great good fortune, they say. I had found my white heather, that first night we spent together. Huddled in the barn, we curled close in the hay, in the dark, while cold rain—those incessant rains of the Hebrides—dripped off the eaves. What began as a shared display of battle scars became what we'd both guiltily dreamed of for years.

"Here, beneath my ribs. Feel," Angus invited me, gently taking my hand and pressing it to his side. He was always braver than I. "And here, across the right thigh." With shaking hands I touched him, with strong hands he peeled off my kilt. At last, as the storm crashed outside, at last I could run my fingers over his red-gold belly hair, his beard, the thick muscles shaped by hard farm work.

For many years of shared adventure, we'd managed to conceal our passion from others, politely shrugging off our parents' pleas to wed local lassies. After such sustained luck, perhaps, that Beltane night of 1730, Angus and I were overconfident, a little drunk on mead, slipping from Castle Moy, my family's ancient seat, and heading for the standing stones.

It was a beautiful night, a night far too lovely for death, for what unmoored soul could leave that soft wind off the loch, the scent of early flowers, the circling stars? Amidst the stones, stripped to nothing but our kilts, about a small flickering firepit we called air, fire, water and earth. We felt the gods inside us, the mating of heaven and earth, the coming of summer. In the wet grass, I knelt before Angus, choking and gasping beneath the folds of wool as he hammered my face, his red curls flaming against my mouth. In the wet grass, he shouldered my legs and rode into me hard, just as the gods are said to couple on that night.

The small warning sounds that would normally make us start apart were drowned by our groanings. And then they appeared in the firelight. They'd followed; they'd watched it all. Enemies of Angus's father, an old quarrel. Shouting Bible verses, they surrounded us. One excuse would have been enough for them: witches celebrating the Sabbat. "Thou shalt not suffer a witch to live!" But one man riding another? "Thou shalt not lie with mankind as with womankind!" Our dirks were out of reach; there were too many of them. I felt a boot in my jaw, another in my belly, and then a blade in my ribs, a blade in my back.

The fire had died to gray-ashed embers when I awoke. Between my shoulder blades and ribs, deep wounds throbbed. Angus lay naked at the foot of one stone. I crawled to him, gasping. I shook him, pressed my lips to his, to the deep slashes in his sides. The streaks of dried blood were dull black in the starlight.

"He is dead," said a voice, "and soon shall you follow him." I turned, none too quickly, for the pain of my wounds made me faint-headed. A shadow stepped from behind the stone. The silhouette of a warrior, in great kilt, with long hair and a bushy beard, old-style claymore hanging at his side. "Yes, boy, you are dying." *Boy?* I thought stupidly, *I am thirty, I have fought many battles. Fought many battles with Angus by my side.*

Angus. What could this stranger do for me? "Go away, old one." Dazed, I turned from him. Gingerly I touched my side, felt the blood patiently welling, then lay beside Angus, stroking his mud-caked hair. Light began to fill my eyes, as if the stars had descended and had begun to hive about me. It was harder and harder to breathe. *Vincere vel mori.* To conquer or die, the family motto. Dying beside a man I'd loved so much would be fitting, I thought, kissing Angus's closed eyelids. My only regret would be that his murderers would go unpunished. What pleasure could be left for me now on this earth but driving my claymore through their hearts?

"I can give you the power to survive this, Derek. I can give you the power to take your revenge. Will you come with me?" Oh, hell. I rolled over and looked up at him. "How do you know my name? How do you hear what I think?" He bent over me. In the dark I could see him smile, I could see his white teeth. He stroked my chest, pushed the black hair out of my eyes.

"Will you come with me?" he asked again. I nodded. What had I to lose? Bending, he lifted me, my proud warrior's bulk, as if I were insubstantial and hollow-boned as a bird. My head fell against his hard shoulder, he kissed my brow, great beard tickling my cheek, and carried me off into the dark.

* * *

Nick does what I tell him, in return for regular abuse. Tomorrow he will deal with the details, canceling the trip to Mull. He grows petulant, knowing how soon I will return to America. In the few minutes before sleep comes, I slap him around and briefly feed on him, which proves sufficient distraction for us both. If I cannot gather the courage to return to Mull, I decide, as I crawl into my coffin this morning of May Day, I will taste Edinburgh's delights a bit longer.

Angus, heather grows over your grave, there in the Maclaine cemetery above the loch, where all my family rest. The gorse grows golden on the surrounding slopes, sheep amble across the country roads, waves roll with a deep susurrus up the long slope of the shore. I do not need to be there to know these things. I should have been buried beside you.

Instead, I am here, in Canongate Kirkyard with this nervous boy. I've ripped open the front of his black T-shirt and maneuvered him against the graveyard's high wall. He's beginning to realize he's in danger, that I'm far stronger than he. I can smell his sweat. Within the minute, I will taste it.

Ensign Ewart's was crowded, as usual. I allowed myself a pint of heavy, just to look normal. The guitarist was singing "Barbara Allen." Oh, sad, the sort of song they love back in my West Virginia mountains. "From his heart grew a red, red rose." Well, I had a true lover's knot in mind, watching one tall young man getting drunk at the bar. One beer after another, a thirst to match mine. The night was hot for May, and the black T-shirt he'd no doubt carefully picked earlier that evening was doing its job, nicely highlighting a keystone-tapered torso and tribal tattoos spilling down his arms. Scruffy punk. Pierced eyebrows. Head shaved smooth, face clean-shaven save for a thick tuft of hair jutting just beneath his lower lip. The sort of edgy beauty that exudes arrogance, the sort I love to conquer, the kind of pride he'll soon regret.

It took little effort, a few glances over the vague maelstroms of tobacco smoke, to get his attention, to touch that place in his mind. Easy with the cocky and overconfident. Hubris, they should know better. But then most grimy pierced street punks don't read Aeschylus.

Now he's thinking twice about having offered me a cigarette, having followed me out, followed me down the long ramp of the Royal Mile and into the dark and isolated realm of this cemetery. His eyes skip from my smile to the graveyard's entrance. A goodly ways away. He licks his incongruous Cupid's bow lips. The tatters of his shirt hang from his waist like a storm-torn black flag.

"This is the grave of Clarinda," I explain, momentary tour guide, pointing to the plaque with its pretty silhouette of a woman's head. Before the grave, red roses are blooming profusely. From one stem I pluck a long thorn.

"Uh, guy, I wanna be paid first." What greed, what bravado.

I tug off the remnant of his T-shirt and toss it onto the ground. I run one finger over the black spikes of the tattoo spilling down his right arm. Tongues of black flame edged with red. I push him back against the rough wall.

"Clarinda, do you know who she was? The muse of Robert Burns. I met him once."

"Burns? Uh, football player, right? About that money . . . ?"

"No, rock star. His greatest hit was 'My Love is Like a Red Red Rose.' Can you sing that one? In Dumfries, I've seen his signature cut in glass." I run the tip of the thorn along the thin line of hair that ridges his pale belly and disappears into the top of his jeans.

"Hey, watch it! Look, I don't get fucked, y'know. You can blow me, though, for fifteen pounds. Uh, twenty, 'cause you've ruined my shirt."

"I think I'll do what I please," I growl. "And you won't be needing a new shirt." His head slams back against the wall before he knows what's happening. Stunned, he falls to his knees.

I pull off my belt, wrap it around his neck. He begins to cry. Delicious, this tough kid, pierced ears and eyebrows, shaved head, scuffed Doc Marten's, with a child's tears streaming down his face. Wrapping the belt around my right hand, I slowly lift him to his feet and lick the salt from his cheeks.

"God, man! Please!" He's mewling like a colicky brat now.

I backhand him once, then tug him forward with the makeshift leash, shove him over a waist-high grave marker, and jerk his pants down to his ankles. Now he's screaming as I slam into him, or would be screaming if my hand weren't clamped tightly over his mouth. His cheek and chin stubble tickle my palm.

I ride him till he passes out, then pitch him onto the grass. Into the black flames snaking down his right forearm I sink my teeth. Just a tinge of ink, then the blood, edged with the hoppy remnant of beer. I take my time, drawing ruby ropes from his veins the way a spider draws from its own those deadly filaments of silver. Like eating the petals of a red, red rose. One after another, till only the golden stamens are left.

His heart slows and stops like a clock someone forgot to wind. When they find him tomorrow, the letter D will have been cut into his brow with a thorn. Graveyard graffiti. Some over-imaginative police detective will probably deduce Dracula.

I rarely allow myself the luxury of killing. Usually in cities I happen to be passing through, where urban anonymity makes it easier to escape detection. Usually the cruel and the vicious, the ones who use their looks or their lies to manipulate. And, once in a great while, those so beautiful that I am maddened and I must possess them utterly. After three hundred years I have developed the self-control to sip, not gulp. The bagpiping street busker I took my last night in Edinburgh will wake, chilled with dawn, in the shadow of St. Giles Cathedral, a little bruised, a little woozy, remembering nothing. I had to have him. He stood on High Street, bare-chested in workboots and kilt, piping in the dusk, and the pipes made my eyes moist. *"For me and my true love will never meet again, on the bonnie bonnie banks of Loch Lomond."* I hum the tune to myself as I take the night train to London.

Steven is my London houseboy. He's short, endearingly so, the sort I love to lift into my arms when I drink from him. His beard is bushy, his ass is furry, he talks a lot about computers. So efficient, keeping the flat near Kensington Gardens ready for me at all times, though, truth be told, I get to London only once or twice a year. Too much busyness and noise. Though I cannot bring myself to return to Mull, my country roots are still too strong to tolerate cities for long, and so tonight, while I am prowling the Barbican for an acquiescent theater-goer during *Macbeth*'s intermission, Steven is booking an Atlantic passage for me. I want to smell, touch and taste the Appalachian spring.

The ship leaves from Southhampton, a mid-afternoon disembarkation I miss. When I rise at dusk, Steven is waiting, having guarded me all day. Dropping his Dostoyevsky, he shows me proudly about the fine stateroom he's booked for us. There are a small balcony from which to watch the stars, a suite in which to entertain what guests I might lure up for a nightcap, a bowl of roses from our own Kensington garden on the mantelpiece. In the fridge, along with the champagne, paté, and brie Steven dotes on, there are several bottles of pinot noir mixed with blood, so as to stave off hunger for a while if the hunt becomes inconvenient in such a hermetic environment. And in the bedroom, angled across the bed, a naked man, lying on his side.

He's about fifty, bulkily built, with a slate-gray beard and silver-gray hair lightly dusting his chest, curling thickly across his beer-belly. His hands are cuffed behind his back. He's sleeping—unconscious rather. In a crumpled pile on the carpet is an orange stoker's jumper, stained at the knees with grease. I am amazed.

"What is this, the complimentary basket of fruit?" I joke. "How did you do this?"

"I've learned a few things from you, Derek. Think about all those books on Celtic mythology, Scottish poetry, herbalism"—here a wide grin—"I've had to entertain myself with while you slept. *The Brothers Karamazov* is a welcome change of pace."

"This is Dimitri, I gather. Fetch the champagne and light the candelabra."

Steven watches from the armchair as I slap the man awake. In the candlelight he grins lazily, drunkenly, held in my arms. I nuzzle his beard: soft as the thistle seeds wild birds scatter in their excitement, gray as those clouds snagged in autumn on Mull's highest peaks. He smells like oil, like tobacco and day-old sweat. When I beckon, Steven moves to the side of the bed and begins to feed on our guest in his own way while I drink from the stoker's neck. Just a little. No harm. Later he'll wake in a cleaning closet down the hall, groggy, head throbbing, remembering nothing, cursing his own foolish overindulgence.

He's passed out again. I catch the last few drams in the two-handled drinking goblet we Scots call a quaich before lowering him to the mattress and solicitously—how caring I can be when the mood strikes me, when a man is so desirable—covering him with a blanket. Steven cleans opals from our stoker's thigh with his tongue, kisses me creamily, then rises to pop the champagne.

On the balcony, against the moonlight the golden flutes of cham-

pagne go pink, the very hue of wild red raspberries in the field below
my West Virginian farmhouse. It's like sipping restlessness itself, this
constant stream of bubbles rising like cathedral spires, like the Light-
Bearer's ambition. Side by side, Steven and I drink. Somewhere in the
mid-Atlantic, I muse, the curlicue wake of this ship might cross the
line of a wake centuries dispersed, the wake of the *Persephone*. I can almost see that immigrant ship, pitching as it did over the water, on its
way to America.

How eager I was to leave Scotland and the memories of Angus. I
came with many of my folk, dispossessed Scots braving the sea, dock-
ing in Philadelphia's harbor, discovering the best lands of Pennsylvania
already spoken for. Down the Great Wagon Road the cart bumped,
and on it the heavy box in which I slept, guarded by John and Ewan,
Angus's brothers. I had avenged their family, and they were loyal.
Accompanying me all their lives, they helped me penetrate the fron-
tier and erect Mount Storm, my fortress of a farmhouse in the Potomac
Highlands. When the Shawnee came, they unsheathed their claymores.
When the Cherokee came, they bartered. I never fed on them. They
farmed my land; they married well, lovely Cherokee women. One of their
descendants protects me still.

John and Ewan. It was hard to see them age, their heads of long hair
go gray, their warrior's muscles weaken. It was hard to visit their graves
in the night, after their families left, to sit by the fresh mounds of
earth and whisper them to sleep. Sometimes, in September, when the
ironweed is thick in the pasture and the fog said to herald a beautiful
day begins to weave itself among the trees near daybreak, I can see
them, young as when we first descended the Shenandoah, lifting their
swords by the lines of corn and grinning at me.

Manhattan. Tonight when I rise, Steven is reading Chekhov. He's
been on a Russian literary tear ever since that month in St. Petersburg.
There's a little silver on his temples tonight. Premature. He has years
of beauty left. I slip off the kilt I usually sleep in, pull on leather bar
garb—black jeans, white A-shirt, black leather jacket, black Durangos—
then move to the windows overlooking Central Park. There's a warm
drizzle smearing the city's lights. During these few days in New York, I

have phone calls to make, a publishing empire to nudge along. One can accumulate much wealth, given several centuries, especially when the right people die at the right time. This evening, however, I prefer to focus on pleasure, not business.

"You're seeing Dale tonight?"

"Yes," he sighs, clearly enamoured. "I'm meeting him in the Village, in that French place we like. God, he's, er, gifted."

I smile, open the window, and begin to shift. "One of these nights you'll have to share," I warn, the last word grading into a bat-growl as I glide out over the street far below, then loop around several towers in the fine rain. *Oh Westron wind, when will thou blow / The small rain down can rain?* Drones within are still humped over desks in the florescent glare, and I bump at a few windows just for the spite of it. One man spills his coffee in his lap, a woman begins running in hysterical circles at the sight of my red eyes, before hunger pulls me from this game and I head for the Lure.

When I return to the Potomac Highlands, I will have to resist any urge to drain a man completely—a diet of sorts—for murder is too much trouble to cover up there, in West Virginia's small towns and close-knit communities. But Manhattan is another matter. I will glut myself for the few nights I have left in New York.

And the Lure is like a buffet table, crowded tonight with the usual clientele. Men in chaps, tanktops, leather jackets and vests. Tattooed, bare-chested, pierced. Leashed boys being led about by daddies. I sit on a stool near the pool table and pull out a cigar. A boy sits beside me, with a bald head, muscle shirt and denim cut-offs so short his multi-pierced cock obligingly pops out with every other movement. He has his lighter out in an instant, ready to serve. I blow smoke in his face and dismiss him.

Dark corners, or red-lit. Thick with the scent of unwashed armpits, poppers, beer, cigars. If this is Hell, I can see why Lucifer chose to fall. Myself am hell. Indeed. But the torment is so easily—if temporarily—escaped. Tonight what I want's the bartender.

I have a penchant for bartenders. In leather bars they're almost always delectable and compulsively shirtless. This one is about twenty-five, with high cheekbones the dim lights above him throw into relief. He has a flattop, big sideburns that angle sharply across his cheeks, and a close-cropped brown goatee. No one relishes more than I the recent proliferation of goatees. Of course he's bare-chested, and pale, almost as pale as early spring's bloodroot bloom. Between his nipples, a diamond-shaped patch of hair. Around his thick neck, a studded dog collar. Around his moderately muscled upper arms, black leather bands.

This one is too good to live.

I take a draw off my cigar, stare at him till he turns his head, hands fumbling with bills and beers. "Whatever single malt you have," I say. When he hands the glinting glass to me, our fingers brush, and I can see his death.

I will not speak to him again, save to order another Scotch, for there are many witnesses here. I will follow him after closing, take enough blood to evoke a faint, then carry him—how's that for a silhouette against the moon, were there a moon tonight?—back to the penthouse. He'll keep nicely, tied to a chair and ball-gagged in the soundproof room. As young and strong as he is, he'll survive for several nights, struggling for the first few feedings, wrists bloodied with his efforts to escape, drool running down his goateed chin. By the end, he'll be sagging in the ropes, whimpering, so weak he submits. I cherish the whimpering, when a lover's manhood is broken, when his tears taste as rich as his blood or semen. I love it when he lies near death, splayed across my lap, head cradled in the crook of my arm, and our eyes meet before I bend over him one last time.

It only takes a few nights in Manhattan before I lose my patience. Despite the harvest of urban pulchritude, the urban abrasions are too much. What sounds were there in Lochbuie but the bees hovering about Scotch broom, the tinkle of sheep bells, that long sleepy roll of the sea up the shores of the loch? Here, despite what powers I possess, there is too much beyond my control. Traffic, crowds, the urine-yellow glare of streetlights, smell of garbage and exhaust. The inexhaustible banalities of the badly bred, exchanged on cell phones in the bookstore, in the opera, in the concert.

And those damned car stereos. As if my sensitivity weren't assailed enough. Finally, on Christopher Street, I mist into a car pausing at a stop sign, its sides throbbing with rap. The driver turns and chokes with shock. "When I first heard rap, I began to relax," I state matter-of-factly, "knowing then that the art of the West could degenerate no further." Reaching over, I slam his head—ridiculous brat, pimply teenager—against the steering wheel till blood spouts from his nose. "Keep your poor taste out of public space. It's your civic duty." Another slam against the wheel—the horn chirps—and now a snap of cartilage. A boxer's nose might improve his looks. The car glides, stately as the *Titanic*, into a fire hydrant. I slam my fist through the stereo and the dog-humping stops. In the aftermath of that auditory garbage, the quiet that follows seems like the silence of mountain pastures. The lesson on manners over—this time, at least—I shimmer/fade, then drift toward the Hudson. First time, I'm guessing, that Christopher Street has experienced a fog bank that could snicker.

In West Virginia, no doubt, the new leaves have already lost their gold and are jading into summer. The irises Bob has carefully planted for my pleasure are already collapsing in on themselves like toothless octogenarian mouths. Tomorrow, I will return to my mountain, where the nights are silent and flecked with fireflies, where the only faces I meet are those I love.

The train to Washington, D.C., then a van hissing down rainy interstates and up bumpy backroads. From the uneasy sleep of my travel I sense the series of movements that take me home.

When I lift the lid of my coffin—solid still, after these several centuries—I can smell, beyond the damp foundations of the house, the hills cooling with dusk, the high grass of late spring, and my throat tightens with pleasure.

Bob is standing nearby. When he sees me rise, he smiles. And what a smile. His face transforms, from the usual shy pout he habitually bears to as close as I get to noontime heat. He's wearing nothing but jeans, just the way I like my caretakers. Ink-black goatee, hairline receding just a bit, and fur matted all over, from his pierced nipples to his shoulders and the small of his back. No wonder he once posed for *Bear Magazine*.

"God, I'm glad you're finally home," he effuses, pulling me into a hug before tugging me toward the sliding panel of this secret cellar room. Upstairs, two glasses of port await, and he seizes them before shouldering me about the house.

"You've got to see what I've done with this place while you were in Scotland!" he chatters, full of improvements to report. "The back parlor is painted—sort of a mushroom—I love that Martha Stewart paint. I replaced a few chair rails, had the chimney cleaned. Got a new armchair for the tower room. Tried to put the cats on a diet, but it didn't work. And I've planted a butterfly garden and a wildflower garden. You just missed the bluebells. The bloodroot blooms—sorry, I know they're your favorite—are long gone. But the royal ferns are unfurling, and the clambering roses are thick with buds."

That about sums up Robert McCormick. He's big, furry, and burly, the sort that would look great straddling a Harley and looking mean, the sort that you know would want it rough, would hurt you if you wanted it. But he's also as sweetly domestic as they come. The house is immaculate, simply but beautifully appointed. The lawn is carefully landscaped. He has shelves of cookbooks and, with my permission, invites a small and trustworthy coterie of Bear buddies up once in a while for complex feasts, which, unfortunately, I cannot share, though on Burns Night I do manage a few bites of haggis just for auld lange syne. His apparent contradictions are typical of so many leathermen and Bears I know, so many butch mountaineer queers. With what ease and grace they alternate between toughness and tenderness, between the wild and the civilized. If, over after-dinner Bärenjäger, I were to bring up yang and yin, Apollo and Dionysos, their eyes might glaze over—"Derek, you're being a professor again!"—but they embody that balance nevertheless.

Descendant of John and Ewan, and just as protective, just as industrious, for years Bob has kept up the old farmhouse his ancestors helped me build. Mount Storm was ambitious to begin with, but a few centuries of renovation have made it even larger.

In the cellar, there is the usual series of dusty and heavily laden shelves common to rural homes: row after row of Ball jars full of beans, tomatoes, pickled beets, and chowchow Bob has canned, like any devoted amateur farmer. Incongruously, there's also a well-equipped dungeon, complete with exposed ceiling beams, sling and St. Andrew's Cross, for those guests who want rough play. And behind a secret panel lies the room where I sleep during the day, in the coffin my father had carved for me so long ago.

On the ground floor, there's a big porch—we Appalachians are inveterate porch-sitters—with the usual rocking chairs, where Bob and I rock some evenings, watch the lightning bugs, and smoke cigars. A patio's in the back, reached through French doors, full of night-blooming plants that Bob has chosen for my nocturnal pleasure. There's a huge kitchen he's insisted on expanding, and a roomy study, with desk, laptop, printer, and walls of books collected over centuries. A living room, full of the sort of antiques Bob takes pleasure in scouring West Virginia for, with, at one end, a picture window overlooking German Valley and, at the other, the original stone fireplace John and Ewan helped me build back in the 1700s. Over the mantel hangs my old claymore, the one with which I fought many battles while I was still human, while I still had Angus at my side.

Upstairs in the back are Bob's bedroom, a few guest rooms, the ritual room for Sabbat-celebrations in inclement weather, when the stone circle out back would prove too exposed to the elements. And, in the very front of the house, my bedroom, where, of course, I choose to feed occasionally rather than sleep. Here are an obligatory four-poster, built strong to withstand struggles both mock and earnest, and another great window overlooking the valley. Here also is a small locked door leading to tight corkscrew stairs which ascend to the tower room, my one concession to the Gothic, my one architectural echo of my family's castle at Lochbuie.

No one else ever comes to the tower. Not even my furry caretaker. From the windows I watch the moon rise over the Alleghenies' black ridges as if its silver shield rose over the sea. The mountains are like waves, if waves could be frozen, made suddenly solid in their crests and their troughs. Sometimes my airy solitude is as sweet as any hairy man's blood or semen. Sometimes I light a candle, sip Drambuie alone, the taste of Scotland's heather-honey, and I long for Angus to touch me again. Sometimes I think of the key, here in my prison. Sometimes, with a momentary perverse whimsy, I consider staying in the tower to face the rising sun. But it is a whim that passes long before Homer's rosy-fingered dawn stains the horizon and the eastern clouds look like bloody thumbprints. Life is still too sweet, there is too much beauty left to be tasted.

Now Bob leads me outside to admire the new beds of poppies and foxgloves, and, farther off, the vegetable garden, larger than ever, with its rows of half-runners, potatoes, peas, and pepper plants. In the woods beyond the barn, the black locusts are blooming, their butterscotch scent mingling with the aroma of honeysuckle, the honeysuckle I won't let Bob tear down. He's definitely Apollo when it comes to landscaping. Such a neoclassicist sometimes: everything neatly ordered, every weed eradicated, no matter how lovely its serendipitous bloom. I'm a romantic, of course, like anyone addicted to intensity, to thirst. I love the way the wilderness sprawls. Inside and out.

A full Flower Moon is rising through the eastern line of pines. I wrap one arm around his furry shoulders. "Considering the size of the white oak leaves—far larger than squirrel ears—I assume you have the corn in. Planted pecker-deep, as usual?"

Bob laughs, patting the front of his jeans. "Yes," he drawls, "and I've been patiently waiting for you to get home so you could help me insure a good crop in the time-honored way." In the months I've been in Europe, I've missed the soft-toned, rough-edged accents of these Southern mountains, the accent that has subsumed my own Scots burr after several hundred years here.

Bob leads me by the hand to the garden's far end, where corn plants sprout like tiny fountains. He peels off his jeans, turns to me, then swats one thigh. "Could you do something about the bugs? The winter here was mild, and they're already fierce."

I nod, wave my hand, focus for a second: "Git!" It's what we mountaineers say to pests. Not as dramatic as dismissing a pack of wolves, but for our present purposes, a practical skill.

He helps me off with my shirt, then strokes my left shoulder. "I love the new tattoo. Stag horns and beard. The Celtic god Cernunnos?"

I nod again. "Yep. Got it in Edinburgh."

"Uh, how do you . . . I mean, if swords and bullets don't have an effect?"

"It's in the choice, Bob. Like choosing to spread leather wings. I choose to be marked."

"Well, you don't have to worry about sunlight fading your tattoos," he laughs.

"True enough. This tattoo artist was very sexy and very smart. We talked about Kirkegaard and Nietzsche for an hour and a half. *Der Ubermensch, c'est moi?* The aesthetic versus the ethical. God, it's great when the pretty ones turn out to be bright," I sigh, tweaking his chin.

There's that noon-sun grin again. I gently tug one nipple ring—gold against his thick chest hair like that moon rising through the black limbs of pines—then lower him into the dry dirt between the rows of corn.

Angus, here is some remnant of you, blood as salty as the moon-sap I lapped from your thighs, your kilt folds falling over my shoulders, your hands gripping my head. *For me and my true love will never meet again.* Here is the blood I never tasted in life. The blood I wiped from your face by the standing stones, the blood that soaked into the soil and took your breath with it.

Even vampires have nightmares. In this one I'm in the graveyard on the hill above the loch. I'm naked, lying in the grass, watching the slow revolutions of the stars over Scotland. Then I hear him speak my name.

It's Angus. He's sitting on his gravestone, the one I've never had the courage to visit. He's wearing his kilt, the red/black/bluegreen tartan of the clan, and short boots. No shirt, his muscles as big as they were in life. His beard's a little longer, and still red-gold. His legs are spread, and I can see his pale cock in the darkness beneath his kilt. Between his calves, the name and dates carved on the stone are almost illegible after centuries of Hebridean rain.

"New scars, see? Touch them." I do, running my fingers along their raised ridges, scars curved as the scythe blades we used to clear off the hay, scars over his ribs, in the curly hair above his heart.

"Look, they're ripe." He holds out two earthenware bowls full of berries. One bowl of red berries, one of white. "I've been waiting for you. I've been saving them for you." He proffers the white berries. They seem to squirm.

"I want the red ones," I beg. I pluck one, crush it between thumb and forefinger, and mark his forehead with a ruddy rune. I crush another, reach beneath his kilt to anoint, then stroke, his cock. But when I kiss his lips, his beard scalds my face. I pull back. Red-gold. Color of the dawn. I turn to see the sky brightening over the eastern mountain.

"Stay here and eat the white berries with me," Angus pleads.

But I am racing away, toward the shadows of the Maclaine mausoleum. The dew is cold on my feet. The mausoleum door is locked. I am fumbling with it when the spear of the sun strikes me between the shoulder blades.

I start awake and bang my head on the coffin lid.

All my senses tell me it is noon. Bob is whistling somewhere, no doubt pulling lamb's quarter and raceweed from the Anaheim peppers and the strawberry plants.

It's a lie, a dream sent from the Gates of Ivory, not Horn. I've lived long enough to know that, if Angus waits for me, he waits not in the grave, but in the body of a man walking this earth.

The first of June, and I'm looking for *Swann's Way*. David had a copy in his room in Edinburgh but was in no position to discuss it with a sock crammed in his mouth. The title of the newest translation is *In Search of Lost Time*, a phrase we'll all have to get used to. It's a series I've put off for almost a century—along with some of the plumper novels of Thomas Mann—but tonight I'm in the mood to tackle Proust.

The several hours of tortuous car travel between Mount Storm and Charleston, the state capital, are reduced dramatically as the bat flies, to adapt a regional phrase. I can really move when I have a mind to. Up German Valley and over the sheer sandstone outcrop of Seneca Rocks—where I once snagged a solitary rock-climber who lingered too long in the lavender dusk. Then, veering southwest, watching the sparse lights of rural homes twinkle below, a few tiny communities here and there spangling the riverbanks. Oh, bless the darkness gliding beneath me, the black-wooded hills still free of human nuisance.

A couple hours' flight, and the Kanawha Valley curves below me now, its great ditch cutting through the center of the state. Tonight, as always, it's edged with interstate traffic, simmering with the lights of

Marmet, Malden, Belle, and the gleam of uremic chemical factories. Far too populous for my taste. I follow the river northwest to Charleston, where the lights thicken and spread by the black band of the Kanawha River. On the topmost spire of the golden Capitol dome I perch briefly, steeling myself. Like Byron's Childe Harold, I'm likely to overboil in the hot throng, but, amidst the annoyances of this city, there's a good bookstore, even a leather bar.

In an alley I land and recompose a human image: the usual jeans and boots, plus a Maclaine of Lochbuie T-shirt Bob found for me at a Highland festival. Capitol Street is pretty enough, lined with sycamores and honey locust trees. The buildings' handsome original facades were exposed several years back, when folk finally mustered enough sense to remove the ugly 1960s' "improvements." Outside Eppson Books, a few toughs congregate. Perhaps some junk food later?

For now, there it is in the fiction section, *Swann's Way*, the fat Modern Library paperback. Thomas Wolfe would envy me. As an undergraduate, he stood in the stacks of the Harvard library, despairing that he would never have the time, no matter how long he lived, to read all those books. I, on the other hand, have all the time in the world.

There's a gay poet I want to read as well. Allen Ferrell. I've seen his name in *RFD*, a gay magazine Bob receives. Yes, I have insisted on an isolated existence, high in the mountains, far from most humanity—partly for my own protection, partly from deepening misanthropy. Such solitude has grown easier as my appetites have lessened in ferocity over the centuries. But Bob has insisted on keeping us in touch with the outside world through magazine subscriptions, television, stereo, phone and cable modem, and I have indulged him. The coffee-table in the living room constantly hosts odd juxtapositions. Magazines like *Martha Stewart Living*, *Bound and Gagged*, *Appalachian Journal*, and *Drummer* are neatly stacked cheek by jowl beside an edition of Juvenal, a book on Wicca, a volume of poetry by Mark Doty, a Scottish cookbook. The stereo alternates between Puccini and Steve Earle, Joni Mitchell, Rachmaninoff, and Tim McGraw. Occasionally, when Bob begs, even a little Broadway. "Educated hillbillies," Bob calls us. "Ridge-runner Rump-rangers." The phrase would make a nice T-shirt, a gift for Bob's next birthday.

Ferrell's latest book is *Risk*, which I find in the Local Authors section. As I pluck it from the shelf, a deep voice behind me says, "You like him? I just finished that book. It's good stuff, but pretty morose! He can sure squeeze music out of unrequited love, though."

I turn my head, look down, and suppress a growl of lust. He's about 5 foot 8, about 35 years old. Thick brown hair to his shoulders, hazel eyes, thick eyebrows meeting werewolf-fashion over the bridge of his nose. Bushy biker goatee, grading into several days' worth of stubble. Hillbilly-length sideburns. His T-shirt—"Fuck Mountaintop Removal, Fuck Arch Coal" it blares—is taut over a meaty chest, taut over that little curve of belly I've come to relish on many mountain men, that belly which so often bespeaks an enthusiasm for beer, country food and the occasional box of doughnuts.

"I've seen Ferrell read here. Sort of sexy. Big chest, shaved head, graying beard. Looks a little like you might look in ten years' time. If he weren't married, I'd jump him. His lover has a great ass."

This is the sort of guy I want to punish and protect. What is it about the little ones, the short, stocky, beefy ones, that makes me ache to tie them tight, hurt them hard, drink them deep, then protect them from the world?

"You're the silent type? Big ole guy like you, shy?" He grabs my hand and pumps it with polite good-old-boy enthusiasm. His grip is strong. His forearms are thick, and that thickness ascends into almost disproportionate biceps before disappearing into the sleeves of his shirt. "Howdy, I'm Matt. Matthew Taylor. That's my name out on the chalkboard out front. Did you come just to browse queer hillbilly poetry? Or to hear me sing my infamous queer-hillbilly songs? You missed the first set, but we're on again in ten minutes."

"Uh, Derek." Almost three hundred years old, and still tongue-tied around ones this hot. "Derek, uh, Maclaine," I manage, silently cursing myself. My Kind are supposed to be suave, debonair, mysterious. Tonight, perhaps, I'll manage mysterious only because there's so much blood rushing to my dick that my brain and vocal chords have stopped functioning.

"Well, hell, Derek, good to meet you. Let's have us some wine. Eppson Books here serves wine this time of night. You gonna buy that poetry book? C'mon. Bring it along and I'll show you the tastiest parts before I hit the stage again."

He's given me no time to intone sonorously, "I don't drink . . . wine." Already he's heading for the café, and, stunned, I'm trailing obediently behind him, snuffling the wake of his scent. Hayfields at night, the cumin seeds Bob toasts for his Indian meals. The last remnant of this morning's Old Spice losing its battle with his natural armpit musk.

"Now I ain't much of a wine snob like some of my buddies here in the audience, but this here vintage is tasty enough," Matt exclaims, ordering us both pinot noir and then seating us at one of the café tables. "Better than that elderberry syrup my uncle used to make," he promises, taking a gulp.

Even his accent makes me hard, that accent the outside world has so often mocked but which I've come to find appealing after centuries in these mountains. Yes, it's often fused with fundamentalist rant and conservative rhetoric, but more often it's an accent wrapped around words of welcome, of good country manners and neighborly concern. So I must remind myself, misanthrope that I am. Sometimes the human world surprises me.

As it has tonight. "Now this one"—I can relax, no need to muster sufficient composure to speak, because he's not leaving room for me to wedge a word in—"this poem is hot. Dripping wax on nipples. *Yeeow!* Ain't tried that. Yet. And this one . . ." he enthuses on, as we bend over the book together. This close, beneath the stubble extending down his neck, I can see his carotid artery throb.

"Okay, buddy, time for the band to go on again," Matt exclaims, checking his wristwatch. "Hang around, and maybe we'll play something you know."

Is he always this on, I wonder, or have several cappuccinos served as a prelude to this wine? Before the front windows of the bookstore's café, stools and microphones stand, and soon he and the other two members of his band are seated, situated, tuned up, and ready to begin.

Matt props his wineglass on the windowsill, checks his Martin's bass string one more time, then bends so close to the microphone I think he's going to take the thing into his mouth. "Howdy, folks," he drawls huskily, and I'm suddenly hoping that the depth of his voice is directly correlated to the abundance of his body hair. "Thanks for staying. We're the Ridgerunners, and we're gonna stuff this set with some folk ballads. So old they're anonymous, so fuck you, ASCAP! This one's called 'round here 'The House Carpenter,' but in the British Isles, where the thing came from, courtesy of those Scots-Irish ancestors of ours, it's called 'The Demon Lover.'"

Luckily I do not have a mouth full of wine, else I might spew it across the table. How rich. Matt might as well be chanting an invocation, not singing a ballad. Invoking his future, his fate. Character is fate, the scholars say of *Oedipus*. So, sometimes, is physique.

> "Well met, well met, my own true love
> Well met, well met," said he.
> "I've just returned from the salt, salt sea,
> And it's all for the love of thee."

Something in the curve of his brow reminds me of Angus, something in the curve of those big biceps, in the way his thick hair frames his face. And his voice is like a good single malt from Islay, rough-edged with peat smoke, an undertone of honey.

I'm sounding like the write-up on the back of a Scotch bottle, I realize, shuddering at the first symptoms of infatuation. Matt's finger-picking the chords with surprising delicacy for such a beefy boy—I love the minor nines—and his buddies follow skillfully along with banjo and fiddle, moving through the familiar stanzas. It's a song I used to hum as I prowled the mountains during America's Civil War. Those were the years I loved and then lost Mark Carden, the soft-spoken Confederate soldier I met one summer evening at the Glen Ferris Inn. Those were the years I entertained myself by hunting down troops of Yankees, pilfering them from their bivouac campfires, youth by dirty youth. One could get away with so much during a war. Feasts without caution or concern. Feeding was so much simpler then.

I'm pulled back from my bloody nostalgia by the song's last stanzas, and Matt's baritone roughens with the denouement. The woman's left her husband, the house carpenter, and abandoned her child, all to run off with her old lover. Now his ship's sinking, and the silly wench has suddenly noticed, a little too late, that her lover's feet are cloven.

"What banks, what banks before us now
As white as any snow?"
"Those are the banks of heaven, my love,
Where all God's chosen go."

"What banks, what banks before us now
As black as any crow?"
"Those are the banks of hell, my love,
Where you and I must go."

The fiddle draws out a last mournful note, the banjo fades away, and now it's only Matt, finger-picking slowly and sadly—waves are curling creamily over the deck, the regretful woman is led by the hand up a beach of finely ground black volcanic sand—before he comes to a stop.

The crowd applauds and shouts. For a moment, I'm too distracted by the imprint of Matt's nipples against his T-shirt to notice that the audience is almost entirely composed of gay men and lesbians. This little trio of musicians seems to have a coterie of groupies, a good bunch of them Bears and Leather types. Two or three are just the kind of men I like to strip to the waist and tie to my four-poster. Normally, I'd be delighted at such a potential harvest, but tonight there's something about Matt that pulls my roving eyes back to focus on him.

"Thanks, guys. Guess she chose the wrong squeeze. I can relate. Stick to those House Carpenters, you can count on 'em.

"Lemme do one of my own songs now. This one's called 'The Scent of 'Shine.' It's dedicated to another Demon Lover: my ex-boyfriend Thom. Broke my heart, but at least I got a few songs out of 'im before he left."

The banjo player starts the tune this time, a rollicking country beat much different from the lugubrious ballad they just finished. Matt joins in, strumming without a pick.

*   *   *

The elderberry's bloomin' by the river bank.
I'm drivin' my pickup truck alone.
Love these high-summer hillbilly backroads.
Got to forget you, got to get on home.

The genre's familiar, almost to the point of cliché: lonely highways and pickup trucks, plus the simple chord progressions typical of country music. But there are no "hound dawgs" yet, and there is that lyrical reference to the elderberry bloom. And, well, I want him, so I'm predisposed to like what he sings.

Loved the scent of 'shine on your lips,
Licked apple pollen from your beard.
The taste of you was heaven, all right.
The loss of you, the hell I feared.

Licked pollen from a beard? Now, that stretches the genre a bit. Something delectable about a meaty, goateed butch boy up there twanging away in the best country-folk tradition and singing love songs full of tasty gay details like licking beards. In a public place, too, here in Bible Belt West Virginia. No wonder he said earlier that he was infamous.

Matt's had his own Angus, it suddenly occurs to me. And now, in memory's sudden distracting mist, his lyrics are beginning to fade, till all I'm hearing is the tone of his voice, increasingly rough-edged with emotion. All I'm seeing is Angus again, naked at the foot of the standing stone, bloodied in the grass, his face as gray as the ashes of the Beltane fire.

Then, suddenly, the vision shifts, and it's Matt, crumpled on gray pavement, blood oozing from his mouth. I can smell Matt's blood.

Applause again. I shake the mist from my head—talk about woolgathering. I've missed the last half of the song.

His audience is howling with enthusiasm, obviously delighted to find their lives—difficult amalgam of Appalachian and queer—reflected in his music. Two women near the front are especially enthusiastic. A good-looking lesbian couple, one ash-blonde, one a brunette with high cheekbones. Something familiar about the dark one, I'm thinking, before my eyes return longingly to Matt's face.

Matt's grinning and wincing at the same time, sucking on his right thumb. "Glad you all liked that one. I'll bet that dumb bastard Reverend Rodney Bates would love it too, eh, folks?" Several of the Bears jeer contemptuously. "Well, talk about sheddin' blood for your art: I got so carried away with that song, I cut my damn strummin' thumb on my strings. Time to get out the pick."

This is the way a bee feels approaching an orchard, I'm willing to guess. My teeth lengthen and throb. I want Matt naked in my lap and that juicy thumb in my mouth. The thumb to start with, as if I were some sort of huge, suckling, demonic child. Then the rest, inch by musky inch. This one, oh, this one I want to tie tight and top slowly. This man could be more than dinner. If his blood tastes as good as he looks, I may well be on my way toward serious addiction.

Loving a mortal? I've done that before. It's madness. Better to put my faith in that which moths, thieves and rust cannot steal. Better love mountains at night, the moon slipping behind clouds, the scent of honeysuckle, the precious safety of my solitude. Who knows better than I how fragile the human form is, how easily the skin breaks, the heart stops?

"The loss of you, the hell I feared." Oh yes. I've been through that too many times in the last couple hundred years. Again I see Matt broken on the pavement. There are bruises on his face. I bend to him, lift his face to mine. He is not breathing.

The band completes its second set with a few more ballads, a couple more country-queer love songs, then they announce a break and are cascaded with yee-haws, rebel yells, and applause. To my delight, Matt, after unshouldering his guitar, heads straight for my table.

"Well, guy, how'd you like us? You seemed to recognize that 'Demon Lover' thang, 'cause I saw your head bobbin'. Did you like my Hillbilly Homosexual tunes? The local Baptists are all up in arms over 'em."

Where did this ache come from? I haven't felt tenderness this dangerous, this deep, for centuries.

I want to practice detachment. Toss a glamor over him, lead him into an alley, take a few healthy swallows of blood as intoxicating as mountain-brewed moonshine. Then get out of here. Back to Mount Storm, back to the familiar, the domestic. Back to the ease of indifference.

But there are his nipples again. Top-hats, Steven used to call them when we cruised the leather bars of London together. They're hard, stippling the front of his T-shirt atop the fine swell of his pec mounds. And, yes, of course, as if I weren't in enough trouble—yes, what a fetish, I'm clearly obsessed—love these hirsute boys—David, Steven, Bob—there's a curl of hair poking over the collar of Matt's shirt. Dark smoke roiling off an underground mine fire, rising through a fissure in the hills.

I'm almost hissing with hunger, ready to tear the front of that T-shirt apart and sink my teeth into his chest, feel the blood pump, systole and diastole, into my mouth.

Luckily for both of us, he has no idea how close he is to death, how easily he might find himself drained utterly dry, the short duration of his life made even shorter. Like some wayward insect, hanging, sad dried husk bound about with silver cord, in a barn-rafter spider's web. Found in a dirty eddy of the Kanawha River, eyes staring at the sky, neck gashed open.

No. Too fine to finish so quickly. As a Scot, I should know. Don't gulp the best single malt. Sip it slowly, frugally. Who knows when you might find such richness again?

There is this tenderness too, standing between him and his death at my hands. I want, somehow simultaneously, two exact opposites. To hold him down and drink till his heart stops. To lift him into my arms, gently nuzzle his goatee, and defend him from any who wish him harm.

What is he going on about now? The boy does love to chatter. A well-placed bandana will remedy that, if I ever finagle him onto the four-poster at Mount Storm. "So, yeah, I guess I've paid a little bit of a price for the public honesty," he's explaining. "It's a little frightening."

Something important here? I begin to listen, tearing my eyes away from the darkness curling over the top of his shirt. "Price? What do you mean?"

"Man, you're on another planet. Did that little glass a' wine go to your head? Want another? Well, yeah, the guy's name is Rodney Bates. He's a preacher in Belle, upriver just a ways. I think it's 'cause of him that I'm gettin' the phone calls."

"Phone calls?" I manage confusedly.

"Guy, I just mentioned the calls a minute ago. You really must be drunk. Now you really do have to have another glass, just so's I can have an excuse to drive you home!"

He grins at his own naughty turn of phrase, pauses, then looks at me with just a touch of uncertainty from beneath his bushy eyebrows. A few seconds of silence settle over our table. The first time this evening I've seen him showing anything but macho bluster. The first time he's shut up.

He wants me, I realize, and he's not sure the feeling's returned. My God, the blabbermouth is insecure beneath all that swagger and chatter. Too endearing. It's the crassly overconfident ones I like to kill. What color is his hair? I can't come up with the right word for it.

Beneath the table, I rub the tip of my boot up his calf and he jumps. Our eyes lock. He looks truly startled. I reach for that place in his mind, so as to pull a little manipulative mesmerism, but there's no need. He's already hooked.

"Drive me home? That can probably be arranged. Eventually." I smile and stroke my beard. "What about the phone calls?"

He's grinning again, relieved at the apparent reciprocity of lust. "Well," he continues, rushing off into another spurt of garrulity, "a couple weeks after me and my band—that's Ken on fiddle, he's from Montgomery, we call him Montgomery Muscles, and that's Jonathan on banjo, he's a NASCAR fanatic, and he's got the sweetest little tattoo on his . . ."

"The phone calls," I prompt him. Damn, where's a ball gag when you need one? If he weren't so sexy, I would have been out of here a long time ago.

"Oh yeah, well, after my band and me decided we were tired of changin' the pronouns in our country songs, tired of sparin' the delicate feelin's of the good folk of Charleston, WV—and we play all over too—at Pipestem and Lost River and—yeah, yeah, stop growlin', you make me nervous—well, we came out, so to speak, just about six months ago. Started to put some gay love songs in our sets, stuff I write. Well, most folk were fine about it; we're not all rabid Bible-thumpers 'round here . . ."

"I know. I'm a West Virginian."

"No shit? Yeah, you do seem sorta local. But sorta foreign at the same time."

"I get that a lot. Scotland originally."

"Ummmm, you wear a kilt?"

"Yep. Occasionally. Tell me about the phone calls within the next minute, and maybe someday I'll wear it for you."

"Yeah? Is it true what they say about . . ."

"Yes. It's true. Nothing beneath."

"Not even a jockstrap? Now *that* would be a hot combination . . ."

"True. Within the next minute, or no kilt."

"Okay, dammit. So the *Charleston Gazette*, that's the local paper, runs a story on us. 'Ridgerunners Break the Stereotypes.' " All about how we're the first band 'round here to combine country and folk and queer. Got to admit it's an unusual combination. Interviewed us, ran a picture. Good excuse to buy a new leather vest for the photo shoot! And check out these new boots! Ariats!"

"Very sexy. Your minute is up. No kilt."

"Oh, shit. C'mon!"

"One more minute." I love playing with men's minds. Auburn hair, almost long enough for a ponytail. The goatee is lighter, a sandy brown. The forearm hair is lighter still, already bleached by the sun. I'm guessing he drives a pickup truck. I'm guessing he's like Bob, fond of mucking around in vegetable gardens. I'm guessing if I politely expressed a desire to string him up in my Mount Storm dungeon, he wouldn't put up much of a fuss. Many big furry boys like it a little—or a lot—perverse.

"Well, it was after the story ran that the phone calls started. Real hateful. 'Fucking fag, we're gonna get you, we're gonna bust your head, we're gonna frail you dead.' "

"Frail?"

"You know, frail. Like, 'Junior, if you don't straighten up, I'm gonna frail you with a stick.' Beat, strike. It's a word we use down home in Summers County. Well, anyway, I don't mind admittin' I'm a little scared. I know I've got me a decent set of muscles"—he leans back and proudly crosses his hands behind his head, showing off his biceps and just a peek of armpit hair—"but, hell, those bastards always travel in packs. Came out of here th'other week after a set with the boys, and someone'd slashed my pickup tires."

Pickup. Exactly. I can see him driving up Gauley Mountain a little too fast, taking the sharp angle of Chimney Corner with a screech of tires, blasting Steve Earle's "I Ain't Ever Satisfied" on the tape deck. He's shirtless. He's got a WVU Mountaineers baseball cap cocked on his head. It's hot, high noon, the windows are rolled down, and he can smell the new bloom of multiflora rose. There are twin trickles of sweat running down his sides.

I haven't seen the light of high noon since 1730.

Concentrate, Derek. Focus on something besides your fangs.

"So," I marshall my attention, "who's Rodney Bates? What does he have to do with the threatening calls?"

"Oh, that mother*fucker!* I know he's to blame. At least indirectly. He's a fire-and-brimstone type out at Belle, preaches every Sunday about what abominations we queers are. Says we're bound to 'fry in Hell like sausage patties.' He's always appearin' at town meetin's to block hate-crime legislation. His congregation crowds in with 'im. Buncha holier-than-thou idiots. Talk about a rich crop of eighth-grade educations! He writes letters to the editor as larded with Bible quotations as a cheap pork chop is with fat. All about how gays and lesbians are predators and pedophiles, all that ignorant shit, y'know? And about how the Ridgerunners are bad role models, tryin' to recruit kids with satanic music. Makes me wanna barf.

"Big problem is, ever since Bates started his regular rants, gay-bashin' incidents 'round here have really picked up. Just last week there was a teenaged kid—real bright kid, an actor in some local productions—that got beat up in an alley by a buncha thugs. Got hurt pretty bad. He said they were quotin' Leviticus while they frailed him with two-by-fours. Now ain't that pretty? A bunch of big guys quotin' the Bible while they outnumber some skinny high-school kid. There's some *real* men for ya.

"The same bunch went after Ken the other night outside The Tap Room, that's the Bear and Leather bar. But he's pretty big, and he kicked a couple of their asses before cops came around the corner just in time. We're callin' 'em the Leviticus Locusts. Or the Leviticus Lice, or Leviticus Lowlifes, take your pick. I'm guessin' that it's only a matter of time before I run into 'em, what with my reputation, so I've been workin' out a lot on my punching bag and gettin' my buddy Jonathan the banjo player to teach me a little Tae Kwon Do. Right now, though"— he grins sheepishly—"I know just enough martial arts to make me dangerous to myself. Th'other day, Jonathan was tryin' to teach me to kick the punchin' bag, and I landed on my ass. Still got a bruise. Too many nights drinkin' beer, too many intimate mornin's at Krispy Kreme," he laughs, patting his modest belly.

You think your ass is bruised now, I think wickedly, blithely. *Just wait. I'm guessing that your buttocks are furry and plump and . . .*

Now that image comes again. I have no penchant for Second Sight, despite my Celtic blood. Why am I seeing these things?

Matt's on the pavement. There's a pool of blood spreading around his head. A streetlight glints on broken glass. A two-by-four lies beside him, dark with blood. There's blood in my beard too. But it's not Matt's blood. It's mine. My own damned tears, salty as the Hebridean sea. I haven't wept for decades.

Look around. Where am I? There's an office across the street. It looks familiar. Big plate-glass windows. Absurd office furniture inside, plastic, futuristic. Lava lamps, for Herne's sake. And a street sign says . . .

"Where'd you go, man?" Matt is rubbing the back of my hand. "You sure drift off sometimes. Look, about drivin' you home, look, I think you're hot, but—hell, I cain't help but flirt with a big guy like you, you're just my type—but I, uh . . . ."

Again that sudden stammering shyness. Sometimes a man's weakness melts me as irresistibly as his strength. "But you're not over Thom, right? The guy in your songs?"

"Yeah. The Little Prick, I call him. Ferret Boy. God, he could lie. He already had a lover, but I was six months into it before I found that out. When they moved to Encino, boy, was I relieved. Especially when a friend told me Encino is, like, the *asshole* of California!"

"I understand. I'd just as soon take this slowly too." I reach over and run my fingers through his goatee. Bushy enough to be braided like a Viking's. Matt returns the gesture, shyly stroking the silver on my bearded chin with his right forefinger. God, my fangs hurt. Nearby, a fat middle-aged woman clucks her tongue and herds her children out of the café.

"Ha! See that? Just as well. I cain't stand children anyway."

"We agree on many things, Matt. They're damned ill-bred these days. Right now I've got to leave. I haven't had dinner tonight, and I'm famished. But here's my e-mail address"—I hurriedly scratch it on a napkin, then rise—"so keep in touch and maybe one night you can see my kilt. Meanwhile," I add, " be careful of the Leviticus Locusts."

"Hey, guy, you got the weak trembles? Me too. Let's go up the street to that late-night barbeque place. You game?"

But I've already dropped a few bills on the tabletop to cover the wine and headed toward the door. Matt's confused by my abrupt exit, no doubt, but breathing in his scent for the last hour, then feeling his fingers in my beard . . .

I've got to feed soon.

Easy enough on a Saturday night. I slip into the shadows of an alley just off Quarrier Street, then shift. Above the leaves of the Bradford pear trees I hover, looking for the toothsome and the solitary. This fire in my gut, the hunger pangs, as if I'd swallowed embers—it makes me impatient, a little surly. I'm so hungry I can for the most part ignore the sudden twinge of moral ambiguity I feel, realizing that I'm a threat lurking in the dark, just like those swine who brought their clubs down on a queer kid's thin shoulders.

Then someone familiar strides below. Joe, the hottest cop in town, patrolling the neighborhood. I've had him many times before. Always worth a repeat. Bald head, red-blond goatee, cocky as hell. High black-leather boots, Nautilus-tightened physique. I give him a little psychic nudge, and he steps into the very alley where I transformed myself. He lights up a cigarette and leans back, one booted foot propped against the wall. Closes his blue eyes and inhales.

When he opens his eyes, I am there before him. He jumps and gives a precious little yelp, before I slam one hand over his mouth and with the other shove him back against the wall, holding him there with the weight of my body.

He smells like beer. I love the fear in his eyes, but that fear and the

struggle that accompanies it fade fast. He remembers me. Because I
let him remember. And he remembers the pleasure. Beneath my palm,
I can feel his lips slowly form a smile. "Bad boy, drinking on the job," I
whisper. His eyes grow dreamy now. Beneath the pressure of my hand
he manages to nod his head, and so I unzip his uniform top and run
my fingers through that outrageously thick carpet, as dark as his beard
is blond. I squeeze one nipple between my thumb and forefinger, his
erection stiffens against my thigh, and now I tilt his head back and
press my lips to the excited drumming in his throat.

I make it back to Mount Storm an hour before dawn, hunger nicely
quenched. True, I did drink a little too deeply, and Joe's likely to have
to take a day off work due to that pesky twenty-four-hour bug he
comes down with sometimes. In the tower room, I sit in the dark, rocking in the new chair my sweet boy Bob bought for me. I try to name
the constellations that straddle the eastern horizon—Angus used to
teach me the names of the stars over Scotland—but that vision of
Matt dead in the alley still fades in and out, especially now that I am
drowsy with overindulgence.

Bates. And those bashers, shouting Leviticus while they bludgeoned
that high-school kid. The men who surrounded Angus and me the last
night of our lives together, they were shouting Bible verses, probably
the very same. They were more monosyllabic when I tracked them
down later, in those first nights of my new life, when I silenced their
shrieks forever.

Rising from my nest the next evening, I hear groans nearby. Sliding
back the secret door to the cellar crypt, I slip down the corridor to the
dungeon. Bob's bent over a sawhorse, getting tastily rammed by a boy
I recognize. Kurt, a big farmer from down Helvetia-way, who's been
driving up a lot lately to play with Bob. Or perhaps this particular passion has evolved past play. One of these days, I reflect sadly, my handsome caretaker's going to fall in love and leave me here on this
mountaintop to keep up the place myself.

As much as I would love to watch these boys going at it, I have more pressing things to do: Internet research. Bob, bless him, has taught this eighteenth-century Luddite a few things about computers.

The Charleston Gazette on-line files are full of rancid bits about Reverend Bates. "All homosexuals are child molesters," he keeps insisting obsessively. "Why should hate-crime legislation give them special rights and condone their sin?" he whines. Yes, there, inevitably, is a quotation from Leviticus, and there is his exhortation to his followers: "Pluck out Satan's perverted minions across the Mountain State." If that isn't an incitement to sanctimonious violence, I don't know what is. The Leviticus Locusts, as Matt and his musician buddies call them, might very well be taking Bates's sermons as their call to arms.

I'm pleased to find a picture of the man embedded amidst his printed blatherings. Knowing what he looks like will be useful for future reference, in case I'm bored some evening and decide to feed him to a pack of wild dogs. He looks just the way I expected. No wonder these devout types rail about the sins of this world, I reflect bitchily— they're all too damned ugly to harvest its joys. He's an oleaginous mooncalf, pure and simple. Porcine eyes, an almost terrifying pompadour. And as for his girth, well, "bloatacious" is the word begging to be coined. It's clear from his copious jowls and monstrous gut that his idea of Blessed Eternity is likely to be an endless helping of Spam.

Snarling with contempt, I read on. Here's an article about the wealthiest member of Bates's congregation. Jim Cofferdilly, who grew up in Belle, is now, through perverse flukes of inheritance, the owner of a small fortune in coal-industry money. Under Bates's influence, Cofferdilly—"Imagine a childhood bearing that name!" I smirk—has begun a campaign to erect huge wooden crosses all over West Virginia and other Appalachian states. These crosses, claims the article, are built to remind onlookers "of the glory of God and the sinfulness of humanity."

Reminders of the stupidity of humanity, perhaps. Reminders of the pestiferous ubiquity of flesh-hating faiths in Appalachia. Batwinging over West Virginia, I have occasionally seen these crosses and wondered what fool erected them. Always they appear in clumps of three, besmirching the mountains here and there, planted like toadstools in pastures and along interstates. One trio even sits on a rocky islet near Gauley Bridge, where the Gauley River joins the waters of the New.

Once I perched atop the central cross of that set, chewed at the wood with my bat fangs a bit, then spat upon it and flew off, goaded by the demands of appetite to seek more edible diversions.

Up to now, they have almost amused me, those pathetic crosses, for seeing them, I have been reminded of the small chapel on Mull, where the last of Angus's murderers took refuge. There were three crosses there too, carved into the front of the chapel. They crumbled as the chapel crumbled. I watched that fire for a long time. It warmed me; it stilled my rage.

One more computer search, a bit broader this time: hate crimes in West Virginia in the last few years. The statistics, I soon discover, support Matt's suspicions. Ever since Bates took over the position of minister in the Belle Apostolic Holiness Free Will Nazarene Charismatic Church of Christ, attacks against gay and lesbian folk have escalated significantly. A lesbian couple was attacked while hiking in Coonskin Park. Two gay men were beaten senseless when they exited a drag show at the Grand Palace. Near Fairmont, a young black man was struck by a car driven by two men who then backed over the body several times to make sure their work was done.

The blood I drained from Joe the Hot Cop is too sweet to lose and by now is thoroughly absorbed, else I might vomit last night's feast on the hardwood floor.

There's usually a bit of a breeze at Mount Storm. We're situated high on a ridge, and even in August the valley's heat never climbs this far. I'm wearing nothing but my kilt tonight, and that Allegheny breeze plays with the hair on my chest and legs, then slips under the green tent of my hunter's tartan to tease my cock.

Kilts are the garb of warriors, the kind of garment I wore my entire human life. I'm used to them; they wrap me in a sense of security as I sleep. They remind me of my youth, of my family and of Angus. Not of his death, but of the lovemaking we shared, the battles we fought, shoulder to shoulder, the battles we won. Even now, thousands of miles and centuries away from Mull, here at Mount Storm I wear a kilt several times a week. When I'm not going out—always wise for My

Kind not to call attention to ourselves. And always when I'm feeling warlike.

Tonight I feel warlike.

After just about breaking the sawhorse with the enviable vigor of their sodomy, Bob and his farmer have retired to Bob's bedroom—for a cuddle-fest, I'm guessing—and I'm sitting on the back patio watching a waning half-moon give midnight a focus. The nicotiana Bob's planted in my Edinburgh absence are getting tall. Soon they will bloom as whitely as this moon and pour out their summer scent. I'm sipping Drambuie and smoking a cigar, remembering that bartender from the Lure, the way he'd grunted against the ropes. Sweet futile struggle I sat and watched for hours.

Stroking the fine wool of my clan tartan, I'm also remembering a Viennese anthropologist I wooed once, for a good part of the year 1897. Why rush a meal with all of eternity to enjoy? It's one of my many mottos. And I loved the Hapsburgs' Vienna. One night over a bottle of Grüner Veltliner, as we lounged about his apartment near the Hofburg, he told me that he'd once written a monograph about mountain folk in the Scottish Highlands and the Bavarian Alps, in which he'd also included a few references to Appalachia. Like many refined European masochists, Friedrich was fascinated by my rough edges, and I laid the mountain accent on thick for his erotic benefit. Unlike the historian Arnold Toynbee, Friedrich didn't conclude that Appalachians were neo-barbarians, though he was fond enough of my barbarian tactics in bed. But he did say that mountain folk often evince a clan mentality.

"You, Derek, are a case in point. Ruthless to your enemies, indifferent to strangers, hotly devoted to your friends, family, lovers."

I'd told Friedrich a bit about my history but had neglected to mention that my immediate family was over a century dead. "Devoted to me, eh?" he added hopefully, pushing my willing head toward his crotch. Not as devoted as he'd hoped, though it was hard to leave behind his *fin de siècle* Vandyke, those conversations braided with strands of philosophy, anthropology, and literature, those smooth buttocks I often topped with the rich cream Austrians call *Schlagober*, as if Friedrich's ass were a kind of white-chocolate Sachertorte.

Listen. Appetite is selfish, and I am all about appetite. But Friedrich was right. Once as a man and now as a vampire, I am more than simple hunger. What was it that led Angus and me into those claymore-swinging battles if not a sense of honor and that inescapable sense of devotion that Friedrich would have called clan mentality? These are my people, and they come first for me. I will defend them. I will avenge them. The thistle is one of Scotland's national symbols—beautiful, but prickly and hardy, dangerous to touch, a fistful of thorns. *Nemo Me Impune Lacessit* is the Scottish motto: No one provokes me with impunity.

My cigar's burnt down to a nub. The moon's setting. I run a finger over the scars I received the last night of my life and think of how shyly I'd stroked Angus's scars that first night together in the barn. I am no hero. Too self-absorbed for that. I am an occasional killer. Again I remember that bartender I kept bound to a chair for almost a week, the way he shuddered as he died, before Steven body-bagged him and carried him down to the cellar furnace. Bates and his self-appointed Crew of Light may range as they will. But if he and his impinge directly on my world, on the men whose beauty assuages my hunger and inspires my tenderness—men like Bob, Matt, even Joe the Hot Cop—I will make him pay. I will string him up the way hill farmers string up hogs in late autumn, slicing open their scalded bellies and letting the entrails spill out like pink and gray balloons.

The return address is wvridgebear@yahoo.com. Matt's less verbose electronically. "Hey, Hot Guy! Great to meet you the other night. Want to get together sometime? How about the West Virginia Pride Parade this weekend? Drop me a line."

Outside the study, even though it's dark, there's a mockingbird chirping and cackling, its own Tower of Babel, a confusion of languages. Bob has Kurt and a few other pagan Bears over to share some Kingfisher beer, kheema and paranthas while they plan the summer solstice celebration coming up in another week. I can smell the curry and hear the deep laughter from the kitchen. In a few minutes I will join them.

How handsome they all are, how desirable. But none of them moves me the way Matt does. Luckily. That's a depth of feeling I discover in myself only once or twice a century. Vulnerability in the midst of a dungeon scene is one thing, but the heart's vulnerability is another. How easily a human life ends. How much I wanted to walk into the sun after the last of Angus's killers was destroyed, after I sifted through the chapel's ruins and scattered the bastard's burnt bones, when my vengeance was complete, when suddenly my hatred was no longer a sufficient excuse to survive.

Midsummer. I've been preparing for the holiday, rereading the Wiccan texts. On the summer solstice, the divine twin brothers fight for the love of the Goddess, and the Oak King, God of the Waxing Year, falls beneath the sword of the Holly King, God of the Waning Year. Then the days begin to shorten, the nights begin to lengthen, the power of the sun begins to fade. On midsummer, Hercules, the tribal king, representative of the Oak God, is sacrificed.

In my mythology, those twins are wrestling lovers, not rivals. And each of the men I feed upon is, for me, briefly, an embodiment of the Sacrificed King whose meaning Christians have so neatly borrowed. With a silver quaich I catch my own communion, from a quaich I drink the liquid that drives their hearts.

Rising from the temptation of Matt's e-mail message, I stroll to one bookcase and pull down Robert Graves's *The White Goddess*. "Hercules on the Lotus" is the chapter I read again and again. Midsummer, the Sacred King, drunk on mead, is led into the circle and bound to a lopped oak, T-shaped. Wrists, ankles, neck roped together in the five-fold bond. Beaten, blinded, flayed. Then his blood is carefully gathered and sprinkled upon the people to insure strength and fertility, and his body is devoured.

Now, I'll leave cannibalism to my werewolf cousins, and I'll leave out the blinding, flaying, and hacking into joints, but devouring beauty is what gives meaning to my breath, what makes my existence worth extending.

When I close my eyes, I can see Matt bound like Hercules to that cross I've erected for midsummer in the stone circle out back. Torches are flickering around us, and fireflies, and in the darkness beyond the firelight there's the steady beat of a drum. He's groaning, drunk. The rope binding his neck, wrists, and ankles is so taut that his head's bent back, and all he can see are stars. He's groaning as I take his cock between my lips and rake the shaft with my fangs, groaning and trembling as I take my sharp-bladed *sgian dhubh* and slowly, carefully, make a small cut in his side. The blood wells up like lava. It runs down his flank, gathers into dark droplets like midnight rain on twigs, and, before the famished earth can swallow it, I catch those drops on my tongue, as if my mouth were the Holy Grail.

"Derek, c'mon in," Bob's calling. "Help us plan the solstice celebration. We've only got a week left." I stare at the computer screen for another thirty seconds, then turn it off. In the kitchen, a small circle of Bears sits at the table. They cheer when I walk in. "Woof! Here's our kilted wonder!" jokes Kurt, softly punching me on the shoulder and offering me a beer.

It's the colors I miss. Imagine seeing color only by electric light, firelight, moonlight or candlelight. I have never seen these hills I love by the light of the sun. Always they are black or blue-gray, as I gaze at them from the tower room or arch over them in the form of a bat. Always dark, save for those times I wake from a dream of Mull, remembering the way afternoon shadows spread over the pastures, the way morning dew glittered in a spider's web, the way the hills colored with heather purple in early autumn. Then I leap from my coffin and rush upstairs, desperate to see the reds and greens and blues of Bob's garden, colors fading in those few minutes left between the sun's disappearance over the horizon and the ineluctable descent of night.

I want to see office workers jogging along the Kanawha River during their lunch breaks, college boys washing their cars in the summer heat, farmers hoeing their corn or glistening with sweat as they gather the hay. I want to see Matt perspiring in a pair of cut-offs as he cuts his grass; Matt clad in nothing but silk boxers, dozing away the afternoon in a hammock; Matt in jeans, cowboy boots and tight tanktop as he strides through downtown Charleston during the Pride Parade. I want to walk beside him in the light. I want to see the sun rise over Seneca Rocks, the sun turn the surface of the New River a polished brass, feel high-summer light warm the carven marble of my face.

This regret is not the yearning for another life, a past life, my human life. I do not regret the choices I have made or what I have become. It is simply the regret of any soul bound to one body, one identity. This is what we all regret: that there are always limits, that we cannot have it all.

As much as I want Matt tied to that cross for midsummer, I am afraid to see him again. I have not met a man who so arouses me in many decades. I am afraid of utterly devouring him, of becoming so crazed when I finally hold him in my arms that I will drain him in one draught.

The St. John's wort is blooming in the meadows, Bob's garden is coming in. Midsummer night passes without a sacrifice, willing or otherwise. I lead the coven in its lighthearted ritual within our circle of stones, those stones that remind me a little too much of the place where Angus died. The bonfire sends showers of sparks swirling into the night sky. The oak Tau-shaped cross looms before us, an empty emblem. We are calling the quarters, invoking the Gods, celebrating the zenith of the light. Afterward Bob sits everyone down to a feast of liebfraumilch, new peas and potatoes, wilted lettuce, brown beans, cornbread, and strawberry pie. For the sake of Bob's buddies, who know nothing of my true nature, I plead dyspepsia, think of Hercules, and sip a little glass of mead while they tuck into the meal with their country-hearty appetites.

A few weeks pass. The summer humidity descends. I track down amnesiac snacks in Elkins, Helvetia, Lost River. Matt drops me another tentative line: "Hey Derek, what are you up to? Hoped I'd see you at the Pride Parade. Want to meet at the Blossom for dinner sometime? My band will be performing at the bookstore day after tomorrow at eight p.m. Come on by."

I compose a reply, then delete it.

It's mid-July when Bob and Kurt wander into the kitchen one evening holding hands. Bob flashes a silver thumb ring. "Check out what Kurt got me!" Later I find them curled up together on the living room couch, watching *Interview with the Vampire*. I can't help but join them, just for the sake of Brad Pitt's lips. "Man, Louis could bite *me!*" groans Kurt as the tormented Catholic vampire stalks the night, and Bob and I exchange surreptitious grins, knowing that what Kurt doesn't know can't hurt him. As I watch them together, it's suddenly clear to me that their sex play has indeed led to something serious. Bob nestles his head in Kurt's lap, and Kurt strokes his head with an almost reverential gentleness. Occasionally, when Bob looks up at Kurt, I see adoration in Bob's brown eyes.

Kurt's headed up to bed, Bob's locking up, and I return to the study for another intimate evening with Nietzsche and Proust. I'm pouring myself a little port—just the color of that biker blood I sipped in Buckhannon last night—and wondering what a madeleine tastes like when Bob appears in the study's open door.

"Hey, Derek, I was wondering if I could leave you here alone for a week? Some of Kurt's friends are renting a house in Rehoboth Beach, and I was hoping that—"

"You bet," I reply. "I'll manage fine. Get a tan for me."

"I will, I promise!" he replies eagerly, clearly relieved by my response. "I may even get a henna tattoo. I can hire someone to keep the garden up, if—"

"I don't mind weeding lettuce by starlight. Don't worry about it."

Proust is a slow read. I'm about to take a break by checking e-mail, then think better of it. Instead I take my port onto the front porch, sit on the front step, and look out over the Potomac Highlands, slopes rising and falling like the chart of a heart. I listen to Bob and Kurt making love yet again, tugging on myself beneath my kilt till their moans reach a climax and then shift eventually to snores. I stay on the porch step till dewfall, then walk around back, moist grass tickling my toes. A tree frog is chirping somewhere. In the stone circle I sit cross-legged, leaning against the base of the cross, and masturbate.

Back to back, Angus and I have fought our way almost to the top of the crag, but the soldiers keep coming. We can only hold them back for so much longer. Behind us, I hear the sea far below.

Then the slope beneath our feet levels out. I look back and choke. There are only a few flat and rocky yards between us and the edge.

One of the soldiers lunges at me with his bayonet, but I dodge and plunge my dirk into his belly. He shrieks and flails, topples backward, taking a few of his comrades with him, but they are rapidly replaced by others. Angus is muttering curses. He swings his great two-handed claymore and clears a momentary swath before the gap fills with more redcoats.

I have read enough history to know of the Sacred Band of Thebes. The army composed of male lovers, whose passion for one another gave them courage. What warrior would be a coward in his lover's eyes? But Angus and I are only two, not a band.

"We've got to jump, Derek!" Angus shouts, swinging his sword again.

I look back once. The sky is a misty rose-orange, the hue it takes after a storm over the sea. Again I hear the waves crashing below. Does the sea run deep here, a blue-gray depth that would receive us, buoy us up? Or is that the sound of waves breaking against rocks that would rend us?

I run another redcoat through, shove him down the slope to dislodge yet more of his shouting companions, then look at Angus. Even in this extremity I notice with pride how thick his arms are. His right shoulder has been slashed and runs with blood.

He meets my eyes. He knows I am afraid. He takes out another swath of soldiers, then turns to me. "We can't be cowards, Derek," he gasps. "You know how to swim. I taught you. I know this coast. Trust me."

I nod. We turn toward the edge of the cliff. Mist is gathering over the sea at our feet. Behind us, a sudden silence falls. When I look over my shoulder, I see that the horde of soldiers has frozen. As if Angus and I had just peacefully ascended the slope of an Arcadian sculpture garden.

Angus drops his sword and grabs my right hand. I rest my left on his bloodied shoulder. For a few seconds, we look into one another's eyes. "Got to go forward," he grins, giving me a quick kiss before pulling me over the edge.

* * *

Damn it! Again I'm gingerly rubbing my forehead, which has just slammed against the coffin lid. I've been watching too many of Bob's adventure films. It's a clichéd cross between *Braveheart* and any number of Westerns.

There's no one in the house. Bob left for Rehoboth this morning. He and Kurt will probably spend the entire week fucking and never make it to the beach, I reflect jealously, settling back into the darkness and arranging the tartan blanket about me.

Matt's cornered. There are five of them brandishing clubs and jagged-edged beer bottles. He takes out two, his big fists hammering their stupid faces, before two others grab his arms and hold him against a yellow-brick wall. He curses and spits, struggles and kicks.

Why am I watching this without trying to help? Because it's not quite dark, I realize. There's a shaft of sun spilling over the scene, that last orange arrow the sun releases before dusk descends. I'm cowering in this tabernacle of shadows, shadows which are expanding toward Matt and his attackers, but not fast enough. The light recedes with maddening slowness.

I inch forward. Only a few more feet, the darkness in this alley will be complete, and then I will break their windpipes between my fingers, snap their sternums like stovewood.

The quotation's from Romans this time—"receiving that recompense of their error which was meet!"—as the ostensible leader shoves a hunting knife into Matt's belly. He hangs there in his captors' arms, stunned for about five seconds, the blood gushing over his T-shirt and belt, down the front of his jeans. Then, by God, he's cursing them again. They drop him to the pavement, kick him a few times, then scuttle off down the alley. "God *damn* you!" he shouts after them, one last curse before he rolls on his side and begins gasping.

The sun's gone. Too late. I fall to my knees before him. Not again. Not again. He looks up at me dimly. "Too damned late, Derek." I lie beside him on the pavement, pull his back against my chest, and kiss the back of his neck, counting his last breaths.

The sun will find us together at dawn.

*   *   *

I do not leap awake this time. I lie there in the darkness of my coffin, breathing heavily, wiping the sweat from my mustache. A few
crickets are chirping in the basement. The field mice Bob can't seem
to get rid of are gnawing potatoes in the root cellar.

I get up, straighten my kilt, and order the mice out. Upstairs, all is
dark, save for the desk lamp in my study, which Bob has left on.
Complete silence, just the way I like it. I walk from empty room to
empty room. I leaf through one of Bob's Leather magazines, pick up
and put down Nietzsche's *Beyond Good and Evil*. Then I remember my
promise to keep up the garden in Bob's absence.

"The damned raceweed, the damned lamb's quarter, the damned
crabgrass," I'm muttering to myself as I bend and pluck black weeds that
are no doubt bright green by day. "Weeding lettuce by starlight. Sounds
like an unusual country song. Maybe Matt could write it for me."

Discounting the usual slew of questions from those who run the
publishing company in my absence, there's only one message on my
Yahoo account today:

> *Damn, Derek,*
> *Great to get your note. I'd just about given up on you. Come*
> *on down to the bookstore tomorrow night. Jonathan and Ken*
> *and me will play you a few songs.*
> *Gonna wear your kilt? Woof, woof!*
> *Bearhugs, Matt*
> *P.S. Thanks for the song title. Maybe I'll even work up some*
> *lyrics by then.*

I'm afraid to meet Matt while I'm hungry, so I mist into Joe the Hot
Cop's apartment on the way to Eppson Books and silently materialize.
He's already sprawled in jockey shorts across the bed, snoring softly—
must have worked a late shift last night. There's a black sunburst tattooed on his left shoulder, which I bend down to gently touch. Now
I'm easing down onto the bed behind him, and before he realizes
what's happening, I've wrapped my arms around his arms, my legs
around his legs. Again I clamp one hand over his goateed mouth, os-

tensibly to silence that first shocked shout, but actually because we both enjoy it. He grunts in surprise, writhes with resistance against my grasp. Then, blinking his long-lashed blue eyes, he's suddenly and happily oriented to his surroundings. Instead of struggling, he begins to lap my palm and grind his ass against my groin. I rub my beard along the top of his shiny bald scalp for a good minute before tugging down his briefs, moistening both of us with spit, roughly pulling his head back, baring my fangs, and simultaneously entering him at both ends.

I've missed the first set again. By the way Matt's face lights up when I enter the café, I can tell he was convinced I'd stood him up. There's no place to sit, so I snap a mental finger, as it were, and immediately a teenaged boy with spiky hair leaves his seat and wanders confusedly from the room.

"Now, folks, you all've got to forgive this next one. It's sorta sappy. Reminds me of Robert Burns a little, and that reminds me of Scotland and a sexy Scot I've been pinin' over. It's an old folk song called 'The Lover's Farewell.' I've been playin' it a lot this summer, feelin' all pathetic and blue. Boy, celibacy can really make a man whine."

"Testify, brother!" pipes in Jonathan the banjo player. Several men in the crowd guffaw. "Aaarooo!!" one blond-bearded cutup howls like a blue-tick hound.

"Git that bird-dawg outta here!" Matt laughs. "Anyway, with any luck, after tonight, with that hot Scot around, maybe I'll lay off the sad songs for a while." Matt looks at me, his band buddies grin, and I try to look innocent. I'm very glad I *didn't* wear my kilt tonight.

Matt's Martin guitar starts in, a slow strum. E-minor, one of my favorites. We Highlanders are supposed to be melancholy. "Dour" is the word folk always use. And hell, he's got another tight T-shirt on, "West Virginia Mountaineers." No surprise, he's a football fan.

> Fare thee well, my own true love,
> Fare thee well for a while.
> I'm goin' back where I came from
> But I'll come back again
> Even if I go ten thousand mile.

Bright day will turn to night,
The rocks melt in the sun.
The fire will die and turn to ash,
The chilly sea will burn.

Great Herne, the boy *is* a sentimentalist. He seems a little embarrassed and won't meet my eyes now. He's hunched over his guitar, fellating that microphone the way he does, his thick brown hair falling over his eyes. Thank the gods I fed first.

Oh don't you see that mournin' dove
A-cryin' on the trumpet vine?
It's mournin' the loss of its own true love
And tonight I mourn for mine.

The last chord's another minor nine. It sounds like the autumn mist looked, drifting down Mull's glens that day Angus and I argued, a few years before he died, that day he left for Craignure without me, and I thought it was over between us.

The usual whooping applause from another audience of Bears, plus, to my surprise, a few drag queens, one with a tiara a good two feet tall. How does she go out in public without being bludgeoned, I wonder, reminded that butch boys don't have a patent on courage. For a few minutes I'm fondly remembering the Stonewall Inn, its ass-kicking queens, before Jonathan's banjo starts into "The Unquiet Grave" and I sit back to listen.

"Sorry I didn't have 'Weeding Lettuce by Starlight' ready for you," Matt apologizes as he sits heavily in the chair I offer him, his last set over. "Maybe we can work your garden together sometime. I got me a little patcha things out on my back patio here in Charleston, and back home my Daddy has a huge garden down by the Greenbrier River, so I got some experience in pickin' off potato beetles and such like."

"Well, you'd have to do it shirtless," I demand. I'd forgotten how he smells. Musky, spicy. I want to know how his armpits taste.

"Hell, that goes without sayin'. I work out. I like to show it off!" He laughs.

"Excellent," I reply, tenting my fingers. "All my farm workers wear nothing but jockstraps and work boots. It's just like a Zeus video," I joke. "And there's a houseboy position that might be opening up soon. Meanwhile, want some wine?"

I'd like to see him tipsy. We all know it's only a matter of time before a well-built drunken gay boy starts to take his clothes off. And I like blood when it's edged with alcohol, though it does make for a ragged flight pattern afterward. Imagine a bat with a three-foot wingspan weaving over the mountains as zigzag-erratic as birds grown drunk on poke berries.

"Nah, no wine. I want somethin' harder. You got farm workers, eh? Where you live anyway?"

"A good bit from here. A 'fur piece,' as the phrase goes. Up near Spruce Knob."

"Jeez, man, you drive all that way just to hear us play?" Matt exclaims, clearly flattered.

"It didn't take me as long to get here as you might think."

"I live up in Fort Hill. Nice neighborhood, sorta quiet, except for a goddamn poodle on Hayes. Great view over the river and the city. Five, ten minutes from here. Uh, wanna come up? I, uh, got some beer, some Bärenjäger, some Scotch, some Franklin County moonshine . . ."

"Single malt Scotch?" I quiz, creasing my brow with a connoisseur's doubt.

"Yep."

"If it's single malt, you bet." Having just fed, I can trust myself not to kill him.

"Where you parked?"

I was afraid he'd ask that. "Ummm, a goodly walk from here," I lie. "Could you give me a lift?"

"If you don't mind Tim McGraw CDs—now talk about woofy!—and a dirty pickup truck."

He leads the way down Capitol Street, clears beer bottles and Krispy Kreme boxes off the passenger's seat of his Chevy S-10, and we're off.

* * *

It's a split-level on Sheridan Circle, with a two-car garage and two shrieking cats that follow us up the stairs to the living room. "The big gray one's Tubbus, 'cause he's so big. He's a terrible table-beggar. Th'other's Snowball, who came with the name. I kinda wanted to call him Arcticus, or somethin' high-falutin' like his attitude," Matt explains, pouring each of us Isle of Jura straight up, then taking a healthy swig. "How you like the view?"

I'm not in a position to tell him that I get an even higher perspective of this city's lights with some leather-winged regularity. Below, Charleston's buildings glint yellow and blue, and traffic streams over the I-64 bridge.

"The weeping mulberry in the front yard there I call 'Cousin It.' Y'know, from *The Addams Family?* Lemme show you the roses out back. And the new viburnum bushes I just planted. Oh, and the fuchsias."

He's chattering again, this time about vegetation—hot pokers and day lilies and Cleome and the Home and Garden channel—but by now his garrulity only charms me, gives me a sense of power. His desire for me makes him nervous, I sense, and while I myself always withdraw into aloof silence when I'm anxious, he tries to defuse the tension by expatiating about whatever's at hand. How many Scotches before he makes a pass?

I get the landscaping tour, a discourse on the furniture, and now we're listening to Joni Mitchell—the boy's got taste—lounging on the couch and sipping a second Scotch in the dark, looking out over the distant city lights. Matt knocks back his drink, tugs off his Ariat boots and then goes on for a bit about the D.C. leather bars he gets to once in a rare while. Shirtless Night at the Green Lantern, Jockstrap Night at the Eagle, and so on.

On his fifth Scotch, he suddenly falls silent. I wait. Joni's singing "The Last Time I Saw Richard." *All romantics meet the same fate someday. . . .*

"Uh, Derek?" I can hear his heart beating. His terror is flattering.

"Yes, Matt?" I say evenly.

"Look, like I said the night we met, I'm still a little damaged, and I'm not ready for anything heavy, but, uh, I really want you, but, could we just cuddle for a while? Like I said . . ." He's slurring his consonants a little.

"We should take it slow, I know. That's fine," I reply. I have my own reason for taking it slow. Someone needs to be alive to feed the cats tomorrow morning.

Matt gives a shaky sigh and scoots toward me on the couch. He leans his head against my shoulder. "It's just that Thom really tore me up, and I'm scared." . . . *roses and kisses and pretty men to tell you all those pretty lies.*

"Sometimes men hurt men without meaning to, Matt." I should know. I brush the dark hair off his forehead. Beneath my fingertips I can feel the solidity of his skull. How many years does he have left? I think of those damned dreams, his blood on the pavement.

"Man. You're so gentle. It's been a while since a man's touched me."

As hot as he is, I find that hard to believe. He's shaking; this big guy is actually on the verge of tears. I turn his head to mine and kiss him. Briefly, softly, not the way I want to. Our mustaches brush. *Only a dark cocoon before I get my gorgeous wings and fly away.*

"Take your T-shirt off, Matt. No sex. Let's just lie here together."

He obeys. In the darkness of this room high above the city, I can see the deeper dark of hair matting his chest and belly. His torso is beautiful, just the sort I savor most, the beefy curves of a weightlifter with a big appetite. I brush my palm ever so lightly across the tuft curling in the pit of his neck. His warmth is intoxicating.

He looks down shyly, then up at me questioningly, yearningly, so I tug my shirt over my head too, then stand to pull off my own boots.

Now I'm sitting beside him. He reaches over to me with half-hesitant wonder and caresses my cold tattoos, first the black barbed wire around my upper right arm, then the dark face of the Horned God on my left shoulder. I kiss him again, as chastely as I can. My fangs are killing me.

"Derek, you feel real cold. You wanna blanket?"

"Sure."

He tugs an afghan off the back of the couch.

"Derek? I'm real drunk."

As am I, on the heat of him. "That's fine, Matt. Sleep it off." I stretch beside him on the couch, start stroking his head, and he drifts off almost instantly. With my right forefinger I smooth out his bushy werewolf eyebrows.

Five Scotches just to muster sufficient courage to touch another man. Next time I visit Zane in California, I reflect evilly, I'll have to track down his ex-lover Thom in the Asshole of Encino. Feed him to Zane. Now there's a vampiress who'll tear up the little prick. She'd stretch out his dying for a couple of weeks.

I want to do to Matt what I did to Joe the Hot Cop earlier this evening, but I still don't trust myself, and so, after listening to Matt snore awhile—it really does sound like a handsaw working over storm-fallen tree limbs—after playing with Matt's nipples, after nuzzling the thick hair veiling the nape of his neck, after patting his hirsute belly—damnation, it's hard to leave—I carefully rise so as not to wake him and tuck the edges of the afghan about his big frame. His cats, territorial, immediately leap up and position themselves about him as I shimmer/fade and mist under the door.

In the shadow of the porch I'm gathering a bat form when I notice the yapping. It's around three a.m., and some bad-mannered swine down the hill has left his dog out to bark all night and keep the neighbors up. Spreading my wings, I rise about Matt's mulberry tree and glide over the neighborhood toward the noise. It's the poodle Matt mentioned irritably in the café. Before the wretched yapper knows what's happening, I've snatched him up in my claws and sailed over the edge of the cliff fronting Fort Hill. The creature squeaks and whines, much to my pleasure. I contemplate the freeway below, but Fifi might hit the windshield of some hapless trucker. I have a fondness for truckers, their roadside stops and sleeping cabins. No, instead I squeeze the effete brute's head till it pops like a cherry tomato. Ah, the honied silence. The fluffy corpse drops several hundred feet to make a tiny splash in the black waters of the Elk River. Matt will sleep well tonight.

"These here are what a buddy of mine calls Shitberry Trees. Ginkgos. They were around when the dinosaurs lived here. The berries really stench up this street come November."

We're strolling down by the Kanawha River. It's hot and muggy, only a few nights before Lammas, and Matt's sweating through his black tanktop, his usual maddening musk. I've managed to convince him that last week, after leaving him to sleep, I simply hitched a ride

into downtown to return to my car. He claims to be a little juberous—
that's Summers County dialect for "dubious"—but, distracted by a
line of ginkgos, now he's going on about his enthusiasm for botany,
reminiscing about his student days in forestry at West Virginia University
and describing his job at a nearby state park. Tonight, though, the nervous babble has been replaced by slower, more measured speech, as if
he knows there's something between us he can trust, as if, after our
bare-chested nap together, he can now relax, having had some proof
that his feelings are returned.

"Damn, I'm ripe," Matt gingerly admits.

"I like it." I smile, nuzzling his armpit.

"Y'know, Derek, you don't sweat. Don't you ever sweat?"

"Only when I'm frightened. And when I'm fucking, but you'll find
that out as soon as you're ready."

"Gittin' there." Matt grins, dropping his eyes sheepishly.

It's like Keats' Grecian urn, I think. Frozen forever on the edge of
consummation. The tension is delicious, and I intend to draw it out as
long as Matt needs to wait. Meawhile, there's Joe the Hot Cop, plus
that smooth-assed farmer, a cousin of Kurt's, I've found near Helvetia,
and that truck stop along I-81 I make it to occasionally. No need to
starve while I'm waiting.

There's no one about, so we hold hands as we walk along the river. If
some intolerant type or Leviticus Locust were to loudly disapprove, I
might stave in some ribs, twist a few necks the way farmers dispatch
chickens, but that would reveal more to Matt than would be wise.

All evening I've cleverly fended off Matt's questions about my past.
"Where'd you grow up? How old are you? Got any siblings?" This is
the danger of intimacy with a mortal. How can I tell him what I really
am? Friedrich the Viennese anthropologist found out and had another
monograph in mind. I had to stop that. Now I try to imagine Matt's re-
actions to the truth, and all I can see is his handsome face distorting
with disbelief and then horror, his silhouette disappearing in the distance.

I have tried to remain detached. I have failed. I should have fed on
him that first night, then forgotten him.

Matt turns to me suddenly, grabs my face in his hands, and kisses
me. Hard. His tongue slips between my lips for just a second, too fast

to savor, before he pulls away, as if he's surprised himself, and points down the riverbank.

"Now y'see that wildflower? It's called joe-pye weed. When you see this'un, and ironweed, well, y'know summer's comin' to a close."

I squeeze his hand, then drop it as a nighttime jogger pants by.

"Derek, I don't get why we can't meet up this weekend. I got some vacation time comin'. I thought Saturday we could drive up to Hawk's Nest State Park, up over Gauley Mountain, maybe see the old mill at Babcock. They got some great cheeses and pepperoni rolls down at Capitol Market. We could have a picnic." Now Matt's the one with reason to be impatient.

Mid-August. The Kanawha Valley has gotten even muggier. Matt's instigated a romantic little adventure tonight. Dressed in nothing but olive-drab shorts and short work boots—Come Fuck Me Boots, I call them, the kind worn in just about every Leather video—we're sitting in the gardens of Terra Salis, a greenhouse business in Malden, only a few miles from Charleston. The nursery is closed, the employees gone home, but one of the workers, an old buddy of Matt's, has lent him a key. We've sneaked in after hours just to sit together in the deep and private darkness of this sycamore grove.

Behind us, an occasional car hums along Route 60. Above us, the canopy of leaves rustles in the breeze. A fountain's splashing somewhere. Crickets are fiddling autumn's slow approach. Across the Kanawha, a train rumbles by.

A trucker's death last night is what's saving Matt's life tonight. They've probably already found him naked in the sleeper compartment of his rig, covered with bruise-bites, bound from shoulders to ankles with bungee cords, a wide piece of duct tape across his mouth. Another murder along I-81. His name was Darius, of all things. Couldn't have been more than 25. I fucked him as he died.

Trying to restrain myself around Matt is making me more and more vicious. Maybe another trip to New York or London is in order, places where I may murder more freely.

For now, however, we're enjoying some bare-chested necking on this bench set between concrete urns of ferns. I'm playing with Matt's nipples, squeezing his pecs. He's unzipped my shorts and is rubbing the bulge in my briefs. Our conversation is fragmentary, sentences squeezed in between bouts of tongue-wrestling and beard-nuzzling. Occasionally I burrow a finger into his armpit or into his underwear, then lick off the sweat and the scent. If Matt notices my prominent canines as his tongue researches my mouth, he isn't saying. They keep inching slowly out, I keep willing them to retract. I don't want this beautiful man to know what kind of monster he's fallen in love with.

Considering how much bolder our caresses have become over the last couple of meetings, my guess is Matt's about ready to shuck all his lingering fears; he's about ready to give himself to me completely. As if I were a healer, not a destroyer. Ready to place in my arms his naked, powerful, fragile body, as solemnly as a priest lays on the altar the viaticum. Delicate white wafer. Color of moonlight, the skin of groin or buttocks, skin untouched by the aging sun. Watch the priest lift that wafer, snap it into fragments. This is your body, broken for me.

I've been using some version of the same tired excuse for centuries. "Can't meet you tomorrow. Work to do, research. How about tomorrow night?" Lately, it's been my publishing company, though truth is I've hired folk so efficient and independent I only have to give them input every few weeks.

I'm beginning to seem elusive to him with all my excuses. This will whet his appetite for a good while. We all love the chase, we're all intrigued by a mystery. But the elusive becomes the tiresome soon enough.

"Or how about Canaan Valley and Blackwater Falls? We could rent a cabin for the weekend, if they're not all filled up. Or we could camp out. I got a decent-sized tent." The more excited he gets with his plans for the future, the grimmer I feel. "Or, hey, Derek!" he exclaims, really going now. "Let's stay at that super gay guest house at Lost River! Man, it's great. Lots of sexy D.C. boys. Big pool, big breakfasts. And"—he pauses for just a second—"big beds."

I'm in such a slough of sadness at this point I miss the significance of this string of vacation suggestions. Raising one eyebrow, I stare at him. "You mean . . ."

He kisses my bare shoulder, the face of the Horned God. He grips my hand with his, and his is trembling. "Yep. I'm ready. I want to spend the night with you. I want you to tie me to one of those big beds at Lost River and hurt me good. I wanna feel you inside me, Derek. Or, hell, I wanna tie you down and feel myself inside you. Whatever you want."

Herne in Heaven. I can already see him, grunting and bucking, spread-eagled on the bed, while I ride his ass, while I tug aside his thick brown hair and bury my fangs in his carotid, gulping his life the way he gulps Scotch. I'll kill him. I'll kill him as surely as darkness follows day.

I jerk away, run my tongue over my fang teeth. I suppress a growl. What have I done? How could I let it get this far?

"Derek? What's wrong? Don't you want what I want? I thought . . ."

Matt grabs my shoulders and slowly turns me around to face him. Now we're both terrified. Now it's my turn to drop my eyes. I twist away again, drop my elbows onto my knees, wipe my brow and my mustache. Matt reaches over and again grabs my moist hand.

"Man, you're cold. Hell, you're sweating!"

"Matt," I lie lamely, "I think I'm a little sick." I've got to get away from him.

"Well, shit, I guess *so.* You're clammy. Let's get you back up to my place and I'll put you to bed."

"No, Matt, I can't spend the night. I've got to get home to Mount Storm."

"*Hell* no! That's gotta be a four-hour drive! You look like you're gonna faint. You got to stay with me tonight. No hanky-panky. I just wanna take care of you."

Caught in my own lie. Fool. Damned fool. Come daybreak he'd rise to find a smouldering skeleton in his bed.

"I have a, uh, conference call tomorrow morning. Got to get back for that." I push back the bloodlust and compose myself. "I feel better, really. Let's head back to town now. I'm parked near the library. Drop me off at the corner of Quarrier and Capitol, okay?"

For the first time, I deliberately manipulate his mind, so as to disperse his doubts, so as to force him to believe me. Mildly dazed, he nods, pulls out his keys, and leads the way to his truck.

* * *

This is the Tap Room, Charleston's Leather and Bear bar. My London houseboy Steven would call it, after *AbFab*, "an underground shame hole," but that's par for the course in West Virginia, where just about all the gay venues are stuck away in shabby neighborhoods and seedy buildings. But the music's good, the clientele's friendly, the bartenders are efficient and flirtatious. For a few seconds I almost feel as if I belong, just another big bearded guy sucking down beer and cruising other big bearded guys. Except, of course, I'm an undead killer, bearing the mark of Cain which Lord Byron found so fascinating. Slayer of his brother, denied peace for eternity.

That's two truckers I've killed this month. Bob has come into my study and dropped the newspapers on my desk. He's begged me to be careful.

I've met Matt here tonight so that I could break it off. Again and again I muster my courage, again and again I pick through the bevy of excuses I've fabricated to explain why we can't see one another any longer. But he's too damned desirable. He's wearing black jeans and cowboy boots, a black leather vest over his otherwise bare chest. I've also dressed for the context: army pants, biker boots, gray muscle shirt. Matt stands by my elbow, laughing with his friends. He's so proud to be with me, so happy to have a big man at his side rather than being "That Poor Bastard Who Got Dumped by That Weasel Thom." Every now and then he reaches down to squeeze my ass, reaches up to tweak my nipples or tug my hoop earring.

His Bear buddies Dwight and Daryl have drifted off, and we're sitting on a set of dark inner stairs where customers often go to make out, when Matt swigs the last of his beer and pulls something from his back pants pocket. "Got something for you in D.C.," he announces, winking, holding up a silver-studded black leather band.

"A cock ring?"

"Well, you *can* wear it on your wrist, for bar display." He snaps it around my right wrist, then promptly unsnaps it. "Or, yeah, for more private moments . . ." Now he's unbuttoning the front of my pants. He's pulling down the zipper, gently pulling my cock and balls out, snapping the band around them.

"Yep, that's pretty." He falls to his knees before me, hefts up my hardening cock and brushes his thick goatee over my scrotum.

My thighs begin to quake. How can I leave this man? How can I contribute to the damage his heart has already endured? How can I make love to him without consuming him completely, without sucking up his life the way desert dunes suck up rain?

Matt's worked his tongue halfway up my shaft when we're interrupted. A couple of guys passing in the corridor below stop and stare, then begin to urge us on. "Yeeow! Nice meat. Woof! Give us a show, boys!"

Ignoring them, Matt looks up at me, smiling broadly. "Damn, Derek, you taste good! I'm fuckin' crazy about you. Let's go to my place."

I don't think that would be wise, but we've got to get out of here, or I'm going to face-fuck him in this stairwell and then go for one of several arteries, and all with an eager audience. Already, attracted by our onlookers' loud enthusiasm, other men have wandered over.

"Sorry, guys! Show's over," Matt laughs, stuffing my cock back down my pants, zipping me up, and grabbing my hand. "Get thee to a bathhouse! Take thyself in hand!" he advises, shouldering them aside. We're past the bar, out the entrance and up the steps in four seconds.

His truck's parked just down the street, but instead of fishing out his keys, he's pushing me up against the building's yellow-brick wall and kissing me roughly. Tugging up my muscle shirt, he starts in on my nipples with his fingers. "C'mon, Derek, goddamn it, we've waited long enough. I'm tired of bein' teased. I wanna hear you yelp," Matt hisses, pinching harder. "I'm gonna make these babies sore. One or th'other of us is gonna get screwed tonight, and one or th'other of us is gonna have a hard time walkin' tomorrow."

His brutality surprises and delights me. I didn't think he had it in him. I nod and close my eyes, leaning against the wall and relishing the discomfort. When I begin to groan, Matt claps his right hand over my mouth just the way I love to hand-gag Joe the Hot Cop, and now with his left hand he's squeezing my buttocks and working his fingers into the cloth-covered cleft of my ass as best he can. Hell, I think, he'd be a lot safer on top. What we need is some padded silver handcuffs. . . .

Matt abruptly pulls me from the wall, swings me around, and pushes me face forward over the hood of a parked Jeep. Pretty damned strong for a guy so short. The boy's acting like he's going to rape me right here.

It's then, as Matt's slapping my ass with the back of his hand and muttering, "I'm gonna give it to you good, buddy," that I see the plate glass window across the street.

Absurd futuristic office furniture. Those damned nightmares.

Now, suddenly shaken from the haze of erotic distraction, I hear the sounds Angus and I missed that night amidst the standing stones.

I heave myself off the truck hood and spin around. There are five of them.

All barely out of their teens. One's fat. One's square-headed, about six foot five, a sort of fundamentalist Frankenstein's monster. One's blond, with chubby cherubic cheeks. One's bald. One's got oily red hair and buckteeth. Shuffling holler homophobes, pious troglodytes. The Leviticus Locusts.

But big. And armed. I take stock: broken beer bottle, a pipe, two-by-fours, and a hunting knife. The knife from the dream. The one I saw driven into Matt's belly.

"You're that faggot singer!" the fat one shouts, pointing at Matt. "We been lookin' for you."

"Goddamn queers. We're gonna make you pay!" the tall one snarls.

"Sinners! 'Men with men working that which is unseemly!' " yells the bald one. Christian skinhead? At least he has sufficient mind to memorize Bible verses.

They're advancing quickly, fanning around us, raising their weapons. I push Matt behind me. How do I tear this flock of fools apart without revealing to Matt that I'm more than human?

Dialect pushes through in times of crisis. "Git, Matt! Go fetch help!" I beg, but he's having none of that. He's as brave as Angus was.

"*Shit*, no! I ain't leavin' you here! C'mon, you motherfuckers! You big dumb Bible-thumping *bastards*! You all the ones been callin' me with all those threats? I'm gonna break your fuckin' teeth!"

Matt's self-defense coach would be proud. He's leapt forward and slammed his fist into the fat one's jaw, then swung around and slammed his boot heel into the knee of the blond kid. Both opponents hit the pavement hard and lie there yelping, clearly unaccustomed to such an ass-kicking queer. I'm guessing their past prey has exclusively been small women and skinny high-school boys.

"Thou shalt not lie with mankind as with womankind!" howls the bald one, swinging a pipe at my head.

A bad choice for him. I recognize the last words I heard in Lochbuie's standing stones before the knives descended and I blacked out. Those evil words that filled the last seconds of Angus's life.

I seize the pipe in midair. Wrenching it from him, I grab him by the arm. My mouth opens, fangs extended, and I hiss, full of the panther's hatred, the tiger's, the serpent's, all the fearful things of this earth.

He's screaming as my fingers dig deeper into his arm. I shove the pipe down his throat, smash in his skull with the back of my fist, then toss him to the ground.

God, that was fun. Sometimes malice gets me harder than blood-drinking. The rich pleasures of being God's scourge. But now I'm distracted from self-satisfaction by the Frankenstein's monster, who throws one arm around my throat from behind and lifts me off the asphalt.

I sink my fangs, now almost unmanageably long, into his biceps. He yowls, dropping me. I turn, slam a fist into his solar plexus and he drops to his knees.

Behind me, Matt's shouting obscenities. No time to play with this one. I will not lose Matt the way I did Angus. Cupping the cretin's mushmelon head in my hands, I twist his neck with a sweet snap.

My hot little hillbilly has been doing a good job. All three of his attackers have split and bloody lips, but by the time I turn from my kill they've regrouped. The rabbit-toothed one and the fat one have grabbed Matt's arms and are shoving him up against the brick wall of the bar.

He's struggling and panting. He's bare-chested now, his leather vest torn off in the scuffle. There's blood running down his face and welling thickly from a knife gash in his right forearm. The blond kid—face like a Sunday-school teacher—grips that hunting knife under-handed, waving it in the air for a few seconds of what seems like uncertainty before the blade lunges forward.

Toward Matt's belly. That warm belly I stroked our first Scotch-sodden night together on his couch. That little beer-and-doughnuts spare tire from whose thick fur I fully intend to lap semen as soon as possible.

I'm between them in a split second. The blade pierces me just above the navel. The force of it slams me back against Matt, whose head snaps back and —I can hear the crack—connects with brick.

I bend double for only three heartbeats, clenching my fists and gritting my teeth—yes, certainly it hurts—before raising my eyes to the knife-wielding cherub and breaking into a broad smile. He stares, losing his grip on the knife handle. His buddies, equally stunned, drop Matt, who slides unconscious onto the dirty parking lot. Thank Cernunnos, I can hear his heartbeat.

By now I would have thought that all this noise would have summoned help from the bar, but the music inside must be far too loud. Very good. There will be no witnesses.

We Scots are known for our fine venison dishes. We know how to dress a deer.

Straightening up, I pull the knife from my innards and grip the cherub's neck with my other hand. "Now keep still," I say sweetly. "This will only hurt a minute." I drive the blade into his midsection, jerk upward till the steel meets his sternum. He gasps once, his eyes roll back in his head, and I toss him aside. A minute's worth of breath is all he has left.

The fat one has soiled himself, much to my amusement, though at this point I might wish not to have such keen senses. Wrinkling my nose, I seize him by the jaw, slam his head against the brick wall. Once, twice, thrice. And now the brain pan splits, like milkweed pods in November.

One left. The bucktoothed boy. He has one use left on this earth before the maggots have at him.

He falls to his knees beside Matt's prone form. Oh, what a cowardly keening. What a wringing of hands.

With his oily hair, I lift him to his feet. "Oh Christ!" he moans.

"There's your Christ," I snarl, pointing to Matt. "Another beautiful innocent the soldiers tried to crucify. Not this time." My voice softens. "What's your name, boy?"

He manages "Robbie" between sobs.

"Robbie, I want to know who told you to do this. Who encouraged you to attack two men you've never met before?"

Now he's soiled himself as well. Nasty creature.

"I cain't tell," he whines. "Oh Jesus!"

"Robbie, have you read Shakespeare? *Titus Andronicus?*"

He shakes his head mutely.

"Villains raped a lovely girl, then cut off her hands and cut out her tongue, just so she couldn't report them. I think tonight I'll do all that to you. Unless you tell me who sent you."

With one hand I lift him in the air, his feet kicking like an insect's. I stroll with him across the alley, throw him down onto his belly, and bend to retrieve the knife from his compatriot's entrails.

Matt's moaning behind me, coming to. Got to make this fast.

"Robbie," I purr, "ever had a big queer's big cock up your ass? No? Well, relax. I'm not going to besmirch myself. Instead I'll use this knife."

That does it. "Reverend Bates," the kid sobs. "Reverend Bates!"

"Full name, please. Just to banish any doubts."

"Rodney Bates! Preacher down in Belle. 'Got to destroy Satan's perverted servants,' he said. Preached it every Sunday."

"And I'll spare you more of his long-winded sermons." I implement my promise immediately, planting one knee between his shoulder blades and drawing the knife across his windpipe.

By the time I lift Matt into my arms, he's regaining consciousness. "Derek?" He blinks at me confusedly. "What happened?"

"We slaughtered them, Matt. You're hurt, and I'm taking you home with me. Meanwhile,"—I kiss his bloody brow—"you've got to sleep." And he does.

Now to destroy as much evidence as possible. *Come,* I call silently into the night. *Come from your dark nests in the earth. Aid me now. Aid this priest of the Lord of the Beasts.*

Nothing for a full minute. Nighttime silence pockmarked with the usual sounds of the city. A helicopter heading for the roof of a downtown hospital. A car with a bad muffler grumbling down Quarrier Street.

Then a faint skittering, like October leaves wind-blown over sidewalks. The sound thickens and thickens, and then all about me they pour, a twitching molasses, from grates and broken brick foundations and sewer drains. They swirl about my feet, seethe over the alley floor and break like waves over the scattered forms of my enemies. The boys' white skin dims and disappears, like a moon devoured by snow clouds.

I leave the rats to their feast. Were Matt to awake in midair, he might immediately slip back into senselessness, finding himself clamped carefully in the claws of a monstrous bat while, hundreds of feet below, the lights of the Kanawha Valley stream swiftly by and then fade away.

By the time I reach Mount Storm, I'm almost wishing I liked skinny, hairless twinkie boys instead of bulky Leatherbears. Matt's a talonful after the first twenty miles. I lower him gently into the dewy grass of the front lawn, then shift into human form before tearing into the farmhouse shouting for Bob.

Those Cherokee ancestors of Bob's knew a lot about herbal medicine, and so does he. Soon enough we've carried Matt up to the master bedroom and stripped him of his boots and dirty jeans. We've washed off the blood and grime, cleaned the cuts on his head, poulticed and bandaged the shallow knife wound on his forearm, and tucked him beneath my bear-claw quilt. Matt awakens just long enough to grumble, "Jesus, Derek, stop coddlin' me. You remind me of my nanny," before slipping off again.

I light a candle in the window, change into my kilt, then sit in a rocking chair by the bed and watch Matt sleep. To the gods of war I offer up my thanks, and to the gods of healing. Over the darkness of German Valley, framed by the big front window, the Corn Moon rises, spilling benedictions over Matt's brow. To the Queen of Heaven I add my praise, and to the Horned One, my patron deity, God of the Wild Hunt, the wild night, and the wild beauty of men.

Matt's snoring steadily now, and in the moonlight I bend to my knees beside the bed and kiss his bushy chin. I pull the covers back from his naked body, kiss his bandaged forearm and his many bruises. I kiss his throat, kiss the pelted swell of muscle over his heart, kiss his belly and the tip of his limp cock.

How easily I could have lost him. As easily and as swiftly as I'd lost Angus.

What a miracle, that a killer could find in himself so deep a capacity for love.

I pull the quilt back over Matt's moonlit form, then leave the bedroom, closing the door quietly behind me. I stride downstairs, turn into the living room, and, from its place above the mantelpiece, take down my claymore.

On the front porch I sit atop the steps, one of my habitual musing places, legs spread, the usual mountain breezes tickling the hair of my inner thighs. The moonlight glints off the long blade of my claymore as I polish it with a soft cloth. The crickets are louder than ever. There's a cool edge to the night. September's not far away.

I ran them through with this sword, the men who murdered Angus. Oh, how surprised they all were to see me again. How they'd blubbered and begged, before I slipped this long blade through their guts, lopped off their heads, and left them to sate the grateful ravens or feed the chapel fire.

Along one edge of the sword I run a thumb. The blood wells up and I lap it off. Still as sharp as ever. More than sufficient to gut a pig.

When the mountains fade into violet dusk, I rise, hurrying from the secret room and striding upstairs, anxious to see how Matt's recuperating.

"Yeeow, there it is!" Matt whoops as I stride into the lamplit bedroom. He's propped up in bed with what appears to be an after-dinner dram of Bob's prized peach moonshine. Sipping it from a Ball jar, for Hertha's sake. On the floor beside the bed, there are an empty bottle of Clos du Bois merlot and empty dishes on a tray. The scents of recently gobbled blue-cheese scalloped potatoes and filet mignon fill the room. There's a small fire going on the hearth, pushing off the chilly high-altitude air. Bob's rocking away in the rocking chair, grinning his high-noon grin, clearly a little soused. Matt's flushed with alcohol as well, bare-chested and bandaged, quilt pulled up to his waist, staring at me with naked lust.

Oh yes, I realize, looking down at myself. He hasn't seen the kilt yet. And that's all I'm wearing.

"Daddy, you look great!" Matt's clearly recovering at a record pace. He pats the side of the bed eagerly.

"Oh, yum!" He knocks back the last of the moonshine as I sit by him, then starts squeezing my biceps, brushing my beard, stroking my tartan, and burrowing one hand beneath my kilt.

"All right, invalid. We'll get to that later," I smile, retrieving his exploratory fingers. "Mr. Bob, looks like you've been feasting the patient."

"Yep, and he's been flirting with me something fierce. Glad you got back from the office when you did, or I'd have had to ravish him." Matt and Bob exchange salacious smiles. Apparently they've already begun to develop a casual erotic camaraderie, that playful and free-floating desire I've seen so often among Leatherbears. Light years away from the clutching insecurities of monogamy.

Fine with me. I love them both. Normally, no more possessive than they, I might pour myself some of that moonshine, sit back and watch them go at it for a while, then join in. Tonight, however, I have important details to arrange.

"Mercy, boys! Met just last night and already you're buddies looking to play. Later. Matt, you settle down," I command. "You're bruised and bandaged, remember? Time enough to get frisky later. For now, try to get some sleep, and I'll be back soon to check on you."

"Yeah, yeah, Derek. Coddle away." Matt slips obediently beneath the quilt.

"And Bob, you come with me. I have a few questions for you."

Bob tweaks Matt's right ear, clicks off the bedside lamp, then silently follows me from the room, shutting the door behind him.

In the privacy of my downstairs study, Bob grimly hands me *The Charleston Gazette*. Front page headlines, of course. "Half-eaten Bodies Found in Parking Lot near Tap Room. Victims' identities as yet unknown."

"Hide the newspapers from him. Try to keep him from watching the TV news. I don't want him to know about all this yet."

"You mean he doesn't . . . ?" Bob mutters amazedly.

"No. He was either embroiled by the thick of battle or unconscious when I killed them. He doesn't know what I am. And I need some time to tell him. He's got to stay here where it's safe until I finish off what

threat remains. Strap him to the St. Andrew's Cross if you have to"—
Bob smacks his lips—"yeah, yeah, that'd be a chore, I know, but however you do it, keep him here."

Matt's standing naked by the window when I return to the dark
bedroom. In the quivering firelight I can make out wide shoulders, a
few feathering wings of hair across his lats, a round and hirsute ass. He
hears me enter and turns, silhouetted against the view of moonlit
mountains, his limp cock swinging softly. His body is shadowed with
fur, from his neck to his ankles. His shoulders, arms and chest curved
with muscle.

Theophany. The Horned God descended into human form. I want
to fall to my knees with reverence and take every inch of him into my
mouth. The landscape of his body, as lovely as the great dark sweep of
mountains behind him: what is more deserving of worship, of praise?
His is a beauty I could have lost irrevocably.

And suddenly, reminded of how close he came to death, with a flood
of relief this blessed hope hits: perhaps now I have the self-control to
love him without myself becoming the instrument of his destruction.

"Damn, Derek, you got a sweet place here."

"Thanks. Thought I told you to sleep," I croak, throat tight with joy.
I'm trying to memorize his nakedness, the cherished details. In the
dim room, the whiteness of his bandage gleams.

"Man, I'm fine. Cain't sleep. I did that most of the day. Look, I
gotta call work. I'm due to work at the park tomorrow. I haven't told
you this, but, well, my boss is a conservative Baptist, and he's heard
about my queer music, and, well, there ain't any laws in West Virginia
that protect gays from employment discrimination, and, hell, I *cain't*
miss work tomorrow. He might use it as an excuse to fire me."

"You're still a little banged up, Matt. I'd like you to stay here for a
few days and recuperate some more. I'll call your boss and explain."

"Derek, I don't think he'd . . ."

"I can be very persuasive, I promise. In fact, perhaps I'll visit him in
person." With a mental nudge, I dismiss the anxiety from his mind,
just as easily as, tomorrow night, I will convince his boss that Matt is
the best employee in the park and richly deserves a little time off.

Tonight we have sweeter things to focus on. There is nothing sepa-
rating us now but this hesitant silence and a few dim feet of bedroom.

"A little, uh, more moonshine?" I ask, suddenly awkward, meeting
Matt's dark eyes.

"Well, sure, if you'll join me," Matt replies with a shy smile.

Bob has thoughtfully left the liquor on the bedside table, along with
an extra sipping jar, and I pour for us. Matt's shivering a little when I
hand him his drink, as much from the coldness of the room as from
the erotic tension. "Come here by the fire, Matt. You must be chilly,
despite all that tasty pelt." Snatching big throw pillows from the bed, I
toss them onto the floor before the hearth, then pull the huge quilt off
the bed and wrap it around his shoulders.

We're sitting cross-legged before the fire now, quietly sipping our
moonshine, watching the chestnut oak crumble in the andirons. "Hey,
big man, bet you're cold too. Git *in* here," Matt invites, opening the
quilt to me. I slide over and he arranges the blanket about our bare
shoulders.

"Hell, you're icy. Come 'ere!" He wraps one big arm around me and
pulls me closer. God, his skin is glowing like a furnace. His blood is
coursing like magma. The familiar spicy scent of his body wafts over
me, and I nuzzle his neck through a thick veil of chestnut hair.

"We've waited long enough, Matt," I whisper, turning to him and
kissing him on the mouth, softly, then deeply, savoring the fiery taste
of peaches. Now my fingers are blindly fumbling through his chest hair
till I find his stiff nipples. "Those are the On Buttons," he pants, arch-
ing his big chest into my hands, and I flick the nubs with my fingernails, then work each thick pectoral muscle hard beneath my palms.
By now his erection is bobbing in his lap, and the front of my kilt is
tenting considerably.

Matt's pushing me back onto the pillows now, muttering, "Man,
I've been achin' to do this," as he pulls up my kilt and his head disappears. In the wooly darkness beneath the tartan fabric, he chews my
balls a little before deep-throating me. I lie back against the pillows,
one hand cupping the back of his head, with the other tipping the jar
of moonshine to my lips, watching the firelight joust with shadows
across the broad plain of his back.

Now I increase the pressure on the back of his head till his nose meets my pubic hair, and now he's gagging on the length of me. I let him choke and gasp for a few seconds before I jerk him up by the hair. His red face pops out of the tartan tabernacle, gasping, eyes wide, goateed lips glistening with spit.

"Damn, guy, you sure know how to treat a man," he sighs, as I drag him up beside me before rolling on top of him and forcing his wrists to the floor above his head. Kissing him is like burying my face in a stick of butter. I enter him as deeply as the length of my tongue will allow. In between mouthfuls, he's full of butch challenge, his wounds forgotten. "Ha! You wanna wrestle, eh? I got prizes for that in college. We'll see who ends up on top!"

He slips out from under me and seizes me around the waist. For ten sweaty minutes, I let him flip me around—he knows all the moves—and I've been slammed onto the floor in a series of tight holds before eluding the last of them, throwing him over onto his belly and locking his arms behind him in my own wrestler's grip.

What a struggle, the pillows flying across the hardwood floor, his ass bumping against my hard cock as he thrashes around beneath me, laughing and gasping and cussing before his struggles finally subside.

"Goddamn, Derek, how'd you get so strong?" Matt pants. "Okay, okay, you win! Guess I'm the Boy tonight."

I release him, then slip a pillow beneath him and cross his wrists behind his back. "That's the sweetest thing about fighting for top, Matt. No one really loses. Now keep your hands together."

"Yes, sir!" He knows the drill.

For a few seconds I'm thinking of David, that delicious student in Edinburgh, and wishing him a long, fulfilling life, as I tug several neatly coiled lengths of cotton rope from the bottom drawer of the armoire. Matt looks up at me with bright eyes, right hand clenching his left wrist. He's humping the pillow almost imperceptibly.

"I like it tight," he prompts, and I oblige, straddling his ass and roping his wrists together, careful not to disturb the bandage. Considerate Bottom, he arches his arms up, away from the sweat-moist small of his back, so I can more easily and efficiently bind him. Tugging him to his knees, I tie the ends around his belly a few times, then with more lengths I cinch his elbows together and—sacrificial aesthetic—crisscross white rope all about his upper arms and torso.

"Guess you got me where you want me, huh?" Matt grins. How many months have I waited to see him like this? On his knees and helpless, both of us in love with his helplessness. "Now whatcha gonna do to me, big man?" He's almost mocking, daring me to test his limits.

"Shut up, Matt," I growl, dipping my cock in the jar of moonshine, then feeding fiery flesh to him till he's choking again beneath my kilt. As soon as I pull out, between gasps for air he's goading me again. "C'mon, Derek. Don't you think I can take it? This is child's play. If you can't hurt me right, you'd better let *me* take charge. *I'll* show you how it ought—"

"I told you to be quiet, Matt. If you don't shut up, I'll shut you up," I snarl, rooting through the armoire's toy drawer. I love it when they fight back, when they challenge me, when they ask for it, when their macho defiance conceals a deep need to be forced. Considering what a little hellion he was in the parking lot brawl, I figured he'd give me a tasty fight in bed.

"Oh, yeah?" he's jeering, twisting around in his bonds. "Wait'll I get out of these, I'll give you a good hard . . ."

Between rebellious syllables I push the rubber bit between his teeth. I take my time securing it, letting him fight like an irritable horse. He's growling and shaking his head, trying to force it out, but soon enough I have the straps tightly buckled behind his head.

I stand over him. Still on his knees, he looks up at me, blinking, mouth working around the gag. He shakes his head hard, like a rain-drenched dog, long hair tossing about his face, then manages a distorted "Goddammit" before dropping his eyes to the floor in momentary defeat.

"Go ahead, Matt. You're a big strong guy. Maybe I didn't manage the knots well enough. Struggle for a while, try to escape. If you can get loose, then you're Top for the rest of the evening."

What I want's a muscle show, and Matt gives it to me. Against the restraining web of the ropes, his chest, shoulders and arms are flexing and bulging and straining every which way. Four-letter Anglo-Saxon words force themselves in a long litany—moist consonants bent at the edges—past the rubber bit. Sweat pours down his violently twisting sides and back, lacquered in the dying firelight.

I prop myself up on a pillow and stretch out on the bed, sipping moonshine, watching and smiling. Occasionally, Matt pauses to get his breath, and it's then that our eyes lock—mine calm, his flashing with frustration, shame, and a sheepish rapture—before he's off again, cussing and thrashing. I can hear his heart pumping savagely, the blood coursing through him. He's wild to get loose and hoping like hell that he can't.

He keeps up the bid to escape for a good fifteen minutes, with gasping breaks. By now drool is soaking his goatee. I'm guessing his knees are sore as hell and his wrists chafed raw. He gives a long sigh, half despair and half satisfaction, and settles his ass back on his calves. His big shoulders slump, his head bows. He knows he's beaten. In the sudden silence, a silver drop of saliva gathers on his chin before slowly stringing to the floor.

I take no passion in crushing the weak. What delights me is conquering the strong.

The bedsprings creak as I rise. I fall to my knees beside him. I lift his chin, lap the gag-inspired drool from it, and gaze into his eyes. "That's it? You're done?" He nods, and I bend close, till our chins touch, our noses bump. Matt's eyes are obsidian mirrors, and in them I see not only my own mastery but the exhausted peace his struggles and his futility have allowed.

Again I run my tongue over his spit-wet goatee, then take a good handful of his thick hair and slowly pull his head to one side. I can wait no longer.

This is the practical advantage of sadomasochistic sex, the way it sidesteps suspicion. When I sink in my teeth, what my lovers feel is only another in a series of ecstatic wounds. Just another jet bead in a rosary of rope-burns and bruises, to be counted and admired in the morning light, by those who survive. Bruises that say *Remember my touch. Remember.*

I lick his neck softly, spreading the anesthetic saliva, rake one fang-tip over his goose-pimpling skin, then bite down. He jumps with the shock, and I wrap my arms around his roped-tight torso. His blood is still racing from his exertion, and the rusty taste of it hits the back of my throat like a tiny red geyser.

Human metaphors? Yes, yes, easy enough. Squeezing purple juice from tiny wine grapes, shattering the wax cells of the honeycomb, crushing the ripeness of pomegranate seeds between your teeth.

I'm gulping him the way he nervously gulped Scotch that first evening in Fort Hill. He's groaning, his drool is running down my tattooed shoulder. I reach down to grip his cock, and he thrusts into my palm. Once, twice. He's tensing, just this side of release, so with a thumb I press his perineum, blocking the blood flow and easing him down. At the same time, I pull out. I want this lovemaking to last, just as I want his life to last.

I have only to imagine him dead—at my hands, at the hands of those alley Calibans—to achieve control over my hunger. This is a feast, an orchard, an arbor, I will husband and harvest with care, for as many decades as time and reciprocity will allow.

Matt's clearly dizzy from the sudden blood loss when I jerk him to his feet, so I lift him into my arms. His head falls against my shoulder. "You all right?" He nods.

"That's 'Yes, sir.' " I am master of his movement, master of his speech.

"Yeth Thirr," he slurs. Eyes closed, he gives his head a little shake, fighting back the faintness.

I carry him to the window and stand for a minute, feeling his breath against my skin, looking out at the night. No more fireflies. Lammas and its Corn Feast well over, the autumn equinox on its way. Any day now the black walnut trees will glow yellow and begin dropping leaves the way the prematurely balding lose hair.

Now I sit on the edge of the bed, holding him still in my arms. I brush my beard over Matt's face, kiss his bruised cheek—rough with stubble, a cornfield in autumn—and his eyelids—soft as cornsilk. "You are my sacrifice, you are the Christ in the Corn," I whisper. He nods, more from obedience than comprehension.

John Barleycorn. Body of the god made into bread, into beer. Body of the god devoured. How does the song go? I sing a few stanzas:

> *They've hired men with the scythes so sharp*
> *To cut him off at the knee,*
> *They've rolled him and tied him by the way*
> *Serving him most barbarously.*

They've hired men with the sharpest hooks
Who've pricked him to the heart,
And the loader, he has served him worse than that,
For he's bound him to the cart.

Onto the broad bed I gently lower Matt onto his side. My mouth is moist with his blood, and my body is raging for more. Just a soupçon. Bob will keep him in bed tomorrow, fry him up some iron-rich liver and onions, perhaps a mite of haggis. Enrich the earth, prepare the soil for another cautiously gleaned crop.

The fire's coated with gray ash. I step over to stoke the last embers, then light votive candles around the room. I unbuckle my kilt and neatly drape it over the rocking chair. "Roll over onto your belly, Matt," and he obeys. The hunger's rising in me, black and blinding tide I fight back, as I prop his groin on a pillow, spread his legs, and rope his ankles to the bedposts.

If I weren't so ravenous, I'd stand above him and study him for hours: the white ropes circling his wrists and arms, the soft hair pooling like midnight rain in the small of his back, the mossy cleft of his buttocks, the muscles of his calves as he tests the cords securing his feet. From the bedside table I take a candle, hold it above him and tip it. He winces and grunts as the hot wax stings his skin. Across his buttocks I trace a D.

Now I lie atop him, and the cooling wax seals my loins to his ass. He groans, chewing and slurping on rubber. I nuzzle his ear. "You want more, Matt? You want me inside you?" His head bobs with eager affirmation. He grinds his buttocks against my crotch.

"Please?" I coax, wiping more spit from his chin.

"Pleeth, thirr." How I relish the garbled speech of a man whose mouth is forced full.

Breaking our waxen seal, I slide my lips down his spine. Between my sharp canines, I lightly nip his furry cheeks before pressing them apart with my palms and working the very tip of my tongue inside him.

Matt cries out as best he can, pushing his ass back against my beard. Within the knots, his hands are clenching and unclenching. I pull out and flick my tongue along wet arabesques of hair before working in again. He bucks back, opens himself a fraction more, and I bury my face deeper. I want to enter him just as deeply as this love for him has pierced me.

He's sobbing something completely unintelligible by the time I desist, something with the tone of a plea. Straddling the small of his back, I bend over him and, muttering love words in Gaelic, I kiss the bunched muscles of his back. I stroke auburn hair from his sweaty brow, gently work the bit around in his mouth, then moisten the palm of my hand with the drool soaking his goatee. Now I slide off him, and, kneeling between his spread thighs, I sink my teeth into my own right wrist. Blood wells up and drips into my left palm, mixing with his spit to make a viscous fluid I then smooth into the crack of his ass. When I touch the center of his tightness, he starts to whimper and presses his face into the sheets.

"Slow and easy, I promise." I bend down to taste that chrism of his saliva and my blood, then enter him with a finger. "Relax, Matt," I whisper, kissing his buttocks and sliding in another slow finger, then another.

"Feel good?" He nods. "Ready?" He nods. I can smell both fear and exultation.

Moistening myself, I stretch out along the moist and fuzzy length of him, then begin to slide in. He grunts with pain, and I stop, keeping perfectly still for several minutes, feeling the taut ring of his heartbeat pulsing around me. Then he nods again, and I continue.

Sacred giving space, fern-edged grotto of the gods. Clench of storm-wet satin. Fistful of coal-heat, blossom of the blood-rose summer-eased open. Now I'm inside completely. In giving me his manhood, he's only confirmed it.

I slip my arms around his chest, slide out and then in again. He's growling now, grinding against me, ready to get it rough, so I begin to slam him hard, thrusts he meets in perfect time, with muffled shouts thrashing in my grasp, tossing his head from side to side.

His heartbeat's seismic, shaking me to my bones. Suddenly I sink my fangs into the thick muscles of his right shoulder. It's a small pang he doesn't even notice in the midst of the brutal hammering he's getting. Before I know it, we're both on the edge, and as Matt grunts and humps the pillow and his ass clenches about my spasming cock, I drink mouthful after syrupy mouthful, one dark rivulet escaping to bedew my beard and drip over his back.

He shakes and gasps one more time, collapses on the bed, breathing hard, and then goes limp. Atop him, I withdraw my fangs and drowse in my own delight for a good minute before realizing that he's a little too still.

"Matt?" I nip one ear. Nothing. I've gone too far. Aradia, he's passed out.

Pulling out, I unbind his ankles, roll him over and check his vital signs. Breathing a little shallow, but heart still strong. Damn it, Derek. I unbuckle the gag, unknot his wrists and arms, then climb into bed beside him. Pulling the bear-claw quilt over us, I cup his cold body in the curve of my own.

I thought I had more control over my thirst. I thought he was safe from me.

By the time the birds begin, the votive candles have burnt out, and jocund day stands tiptoe, etc. That's Bob's frigging rooster now, emitting his deep-jungle cries. I slip out of bed, tuck Matt in warmly—his breathing is back to normal—and pull on my kilt. I'm almost out the door when I hear him croak, "Derek?"

He's only half-conscious, and confused. "You had a little too much to drink, Matt, and I got a little too rough. Go back to sleep."

"Where you goin'? Come back to bed. Ain't it real early yet? *Man*, I feel wiped out. I don't rightly recall . . ."

"It's that popskull moonshine, Matt. Must have been a bad batch. Listen, I have to drive to D.C. today for business," I lie. Centuries of deception have made me the smoothest liar I've ever known. "Bob'll take care of you till I get back."

"Derek, you were wonderful. I ain't never been topped like that. C'mon over here and hug on me awhile."

"I have to go. Tell Bob to get out some of his Cherokee salve for those rope burns."

The first glimmer of dawn is seeping into the room, and the skin of my bare chest is stinging. *Sleep*, I command, before rushing downstairs, scrawling a note for Bob and dashing for the cellar door.

* * *

"Jesus, you're a monster!" Matt's standing over my coffin, staring at me in horror. "You tried to kill me!" Candlelight plays across his handsome face, twisted now with disgust.

I rise, shaking my head, and he backs away. "I didn't mean to hurt you, Matt! You've got to believe me."

The rest of them are standing around the room. The Leviticus Locusts. That bloated preacher, who's rubbing pomade into the lopsided rain cloud of hair breaking over his brow.

"Here, Matthew, you must save your own soul," intones Reverend Bates, patting his hair one last time before handing Matt a fat, sharp stake. The Locusts close in, seizing me, holding me down. Rats drop from their shirt sleeves and scuttle into my coffin.

"Lo, though I walk through the Valley of the Shadow of Death," Bates is droning in a bored tone.

Matt steps forward, runs his fingers regretfully through the hair on my chest before taking the mallet from Bates and placing the tip of the stake on my left nipple.

Worse ways to die than at the hands of a gorgeous man. I should have told him I loved him, I muse with a sudden calm, as my death's delivered, long overdue.

"Fucking Hammer film!" My language is getting as crass as Matt's. "Where's the cliché police?"

Just overhead, someone's pacing in my study. Not a good sign. The sun, my senses tell me, has about five minutes before it slips entirely behind the hill, so I slip from the secret room, head through the cellar and up the stairs. Just inside the darkness, I wait.

Now. Safe. I pull open the door. Bob's sitting at the kitchen table with his head in his hands. Hearing the door creak, he looks up. Panicked. "Matt . . ." he begins, then shakes his head.

"What the hell?!" I shout, suddenly sick with fear. "He was just a little weak when I left him this morning. You can't mean that . . ."

"No, he's in the study. But . . ."

I turn, flying down the hall. Matt's pacing back and forth in front of my desk, in his jeans and a T-shirt he must have borrowed from Bob. He stops abruptly and swings around to face me. His fists are clenched.

"Matt, what's wrong?"

He glares at me. "I hate a liar, Derek."

"What are you talking about?"

"I got tired of stayin' in bed, as woozy as I was most of the morning. I came down here to find a book to read till you got back from—where'd you say?—D.C.? Bob was out in the garden. Thought I'd check my e-mail. Thought you wouldn't mind. Guess what I found?"

Goddamned computer. "What?" Derek, banish that quiver from your voice.

"Messages from Charleston friends, all worried about me. Hadn't seen me since the corpses were discovered."

"Corpses?" I'm trying to look confused, but the thought of losing him is paralyzing the normally facile muscles of my face.

"Yeah, the corpses. Rats ate most of 'em. In the parkin' lot right outside the Tap Room. No one knows who they are—were—for sure, but folk think they're some kids from Belle who didn't come home th'other day. Members of Reverend Bates's church. Yep, we know, don't we, Derek? We know who they are."

I stare at him. A blood-dew starts up on my palms. I drop my eyes.

"You're a killer, Derek! Why'd you kill them?"

"I . . . They were trying to murder us, Matt! They would have staved our heads in without a second thought. I really care for you. I'd do anything to make you safe."

"How'd you get the rats to eat them, Derek? I ain't *never* heard of folk bein' chewed up by rats. Not so thoroughly. Pretty damned convenient for you, I'd say."

"Matt, please, I . . ."

"Oh, and, Derek? What was blood doin' on the bedsheets this mornin'? *My* blood, I'm guessin'. I mean, I like it rough, and last night I got it rough, and I loved it, sure as shootin'. Shit, you're the best goddamn lay I ever had, but"—now he's pulling the T-shirt over his head and throwing it on the floor—"what the hell are *these?!*"

He's pointing to—what else?—the scabby fang marks on his right shoulder and on the side of his neck.

"Now I sorta remember you bitin' me in the midst of that good hot fuck, but these cain't be your teeth marks. Hell, looks like a damn snakebite!"

He pauses, glaring at me, waiting for answers. I silently drop my eyes, suddenly ashamed of my own appetites.

"And another thang. You never went to D.C., man. I've been watchin' the road up this mountain all damn day. That Jeep has been sittin' in the driveway the whole time. Where the hell *were* you? Has anything you've ever said to me been the truth?

"You know what I think?" he says, his voice lower, almost confidential, as, eyes cautiously fixed on me, he retrieves his T-shirt. "I think you're some kinda psycho. This ain't no hangover I'm feelin'. I think last night, after I passed out, you pulled some kinda awl from under the bed and bled me like a pig. This mornin', when I woke, when I thought about the way you made love to me last night, givin' it to me just the way I've always dreamed of gettin' it, I thought, 'Jesus, I could love this guy. I could eat this guy up. I could chew on this guy's dick forever.' But now, Derek . . ."

Matt turns from me, suddenly a little short of breath. He leans weakly against the desk and stares out the window, toward the ripening apple orchard. "I want Bob to drive me back to Charleston. Now. I got a life to get back to."

"Matt, I want to explain." I either tell him the truth, manipulate his mind, kill him, or let him leave without answers, most likely never to return.

As if I could kill him in cold blood. And as for mind control, I want a lover, not a slave.

"Derek, you must be some kind of sick fuck, and I guess I'm damn lucky to be alive today. Or are you plannin' to finish the job you started last night?" He turns toward me now, in a defensive posture, his eyes snapping around the room for something heavy to brandish.

"Will you listen to me?" It's been a good century since Derek Maclaine has begged. I move toward him. I want to fall on my knees and wrap my arms around his waist and press my face into his little beer belly.

"Get away from me, Derek. Don't touch me." That's fear in his eyes now. "Are you gonna let me leave or not?" He's picking up a letter opener.

I step back from the study door. My head's hanging the way his did last night after his long and sweaty bid to escape.

As he strides past me, there's that musk-scent again, that scent that always makes me want to lick his skin. He's weaving as I follow him down the hall—this stress combined with last night's blood loss is taking its toll—and he almost stumbles over the edge of the front hall carpet. Bob's standing before the front door, arms crossed, eyebrows raised. My guess is he's got a knife in his boot.

"Bob, Matt wants to go back to Charleston. Will you drive him?"

Bob's eyes widen with disbelief. I'm letting him go? With memory obviously intact? I can tell he's thinking about those sunken unmarked graves in the woods out back.

"Yep, sure, Derek," Bob mutters, stepping away from the door.

At the top of the front porch steps, Matt turns. "By the way, you can relax about one thang. I ain't talkin' to the cops. With my reputation as the big queer singer, and them rat-gobbled boys bein' Bates's gay-bashin' cronies, well, I reckon I'd be in as much hot water as you. Oh, and, Derek? Stay the hell away from me."

He's off the porch before I can respond. He wobbles a little as he heads for the driveway, and Bob grabs one arm to support him. Sekhmet knows Bob has practice escorting good-looking men who are dazed with blood loss.

In the tower room, I watch the headlights of Bob's Jeep descending the dark side of the mountain. No appetite tonight. No need for a feeding jaunt. Instead, I sit in candlelight and rock. I pray to the Horned One. I remember the wet curls of hair between Matt's buttocks. I remember Angus, who left me still loving me, who lent me the names of the stars.

The Harvest Moon, then Mabon. For what harvests I have been permitted, I give thanks. Bob and his little Bear-coven share an Appalachian feast of corn on the cob, fried green tomatoes, half-runners, and country ham, while I claim my usual indigestion and sip supposedly medicinal Merlot. After dinner, they light beeswax tapers amidst the standing stones and arrange the altar. I sit in the cricket-nervous night outside the circle, glad to watch the ritual but with no desire to participate. Tonight, the autumnal equinox, the darkness and the light are wrestling equals. It is a balance only the seasons achieve, and briefly at that.

I cannot bring myself to return to Charleston, so I fly east once a week instead. No more trucker deaths along I-81, however. Sadness has eroded my hunger. When I bury my teeth in a man now, I think of Matt's frightened, outraged face. *You're a killer, Derek.* In the sleeper cabins, I drink from them carefully, and when they pass out from blood loss or slip into the sleepy exhaustions after orgasm, I hold them in my lethal arms and stroke them with the tenderness I had hoped to shower on Matt. I listen to the breathing it would be so easy for me to end.

On e-mail, the usual queries and weekly reports from the publishing house. Never a note from Matt.

Bob's contacts keep him informed of relevant news. Matt's kept his word. No witnesses have come forward. The bashers' bodies have been identified through dental records. No explanation yet as to why the rats devoured them. Another mystery, bound to be preserved in local folklore along with such West Virginian legends as the Mothman, the Lady of Bluestone Lake, the turnpike's ghostly hitchhiker, and the Braxton County Terror.

Every night I think about bat-winging my way to Charleston. I fear for him. I want to shadow him in the night, protect him from whatever dangers remain. I want to hover above his bed, a moonlit mist, and guard his sleep. I want to bury my face in his chest hair. *Derek, stay the hell away from me.*

Perhaps I should go to Manhattan soon. Spend the winter there. Or return to Vienna. Or Zermatt, that storybook village. Or Santorini. Or Provincetown, so peaceful off season. The whole world will be my distraction.

Eventually. Something keeps me here. I cannot leave just yet. I want to see autumn in Appalachia. The crimson seeds of redtop grass. The burnt-orange immolations of the sugar maple, that great bonfire the leaves achieve in their dying. The scarlet of the staghorn sumac. The first frost, its crystalline rat teeth gnawing the last of the tomato vines. The sound of Canada geese mustering over German Valley, heading south in wavery alphabets.

Mid-October. Bob's standing by my coffin when I rise this evening. Always an indicator of trouble. He's been into the moonshine.

I raise one worried eyebrow as I clamber out. It's hell to get out of a coffin on a dais. No undead dignity there.

"They caught up with him, Derek," Bob mumbles.

"What are you talking about?" My guts suddenly feel like a bag of gravel, stretched and sagging as an oriole's nest.

"Matt. It's in the *Gazette* today. He and his band members got jumped in an alley after another Eppson Books performance. There were ten of them this time. Matt and Ken broke a few heads, but they were beaten pretty badly before that Tae Kwon Do banjo-picking buddy of theirs cleaned up the entire alley. Ken's not so bad—his family took him home to Montgomery to recover. Matt's in the hospital in Charleston."

There's a cold rain coming down tonight, and I streak through it like a black comet, gnashing my fangs with impatience and rage. Beneath me the Alleghenies slip by in a wet black blur.

The Kanawha Valley's clotted with fog, a convenient veil through which I flap about the hospital, peering into windows, snuffling the air, till I find him and slip, gray mist a few shades darker than tonight's drizzle, into his room.

The usual complex apparatus. Medicine was so much simpler—and inadvertently murderous—when I was first alive. Little bouncing lights and beeps. Tubes, a bag of glucose, humming machines I cannot name. Matt's got a bandage wrapped around his head. One arm's in a sling. He's fast asleep. Someone's left a floor lamp on. The bed across the room is, thankfully, empty.

Solid again, I bend over his bed. There's a big tuft of fur curling over the top of his hospital smock. I reach down and stroke it with my fingertips.

Rivulets of blood in my beard, damn it, diluted with brine. It's the only way a warrior should weep—when there are no witnesses. I can't help but smile at my own archaic sense of honor.

Matt sighs once, rolls his head against the pillow. His eyes open.

I freeze. It was a mistake to touch him. I'd forgotten those long eyelashes. I'd forgotten how full his lips are, framed by that great goatee, half-hidden by his thick mustache.

"Derek?" He must be too drugged to be afraid.

"It's just a dream, Matt." I'm lying again. Centuries-old habits are hard to break. I need to pull a mist-shift fast and get out of here.

"No, it ain't," he whispers, grabbing my hand. "You're here. Why are you here?"

"I know, I'm sorry, look, I know you told me to s-stay away, but"— I'm sputtering now, like some inarticulate adolescent—"I had to, uh, I had to see how you were."

Matt tries to sit up, winces—"Goddamn!"—and lies back down.

"Derek," he begins again, eyes glazed with medications that have left him somehow limply relaxed though still lucid, "I been waitin' for you."

"Why?"

"'Cause I figured you'd be lookin' to kill me."

I pull my hand from his. "I could never hurt you, Matt." I want to believe that's true. I want him to believe that's true.

"Derek, you got blood on your face."

"Those are tears."

"You cry red? Look, man, be honest with me. Did you really kill those guys that night? I still cain't believe it."

I sigh. "Yes."

"And that was my blood on the sheets? Why did you bleed me?"

I can't bring myself to answer, but somehow he makes the intuitive leap.

"Jesus, Derek, did you *drink* my blood?"

"Yes." I can't meet his eyes.

He's silent for a full minute, head turned to watch rain beat against the dark hospital window. He swallows hard.

"So, like, you're . . . what? A psychopath? So why ain't you gonna kill me, now I know all this stuff?"

"Because I . . ." It's been too long since I've had any reason to say that word to a man. I try again. "Because I care about you. A lot."

"You kill folks and you *care* about me?"

"Look, someone I knew a long time ago told me about clan mentality among mountain people. For my family, I fight to the death, and I do my best to destroy my enemies. You're a hillbilly too, Matt. You should understand. Hatfields and McCoys, and all that. This is just an extreme form . . ."

"Extreme, huh?" He coughs out a dry laugh. "*I'd* say. And family? I don't know if I wanna be a member of your family, Derek."

A little blood-brine is trickling into my mouth. Cursing silently, I wipe my face. No tears before witnesses. "Those men the other night, the ones whose hate sent you to this hospital bed. Wouldn't you have killed one of them if you had to?"

He hesitates. "Well, yeah. In fact," he admits, with a touch of pride and a touch of shame, "Jonathan tells me a couple of the guys I whipped before I went down are in this here hospital. One of the fucker's in a coma."

He's a little confused now—the neat edge of morality's been tattered with pinking shears—and I edge forward. How badly I want to kiss him.

"No, no, no, Derek. You stay over there. I don't trust you any farther than I could lob a three-legged steer."

Good Goddess, the sheet over his crotch is rising. The boy's more confused than I am. I can stand this no longer. The suspicion in his eyes is too painful. Besides, I have another visit to make tonight. And I can hear a nurse just outside the door.

"All right. Do me one favor," I plead. "Close your eyes. For three seconds. Count 'em. I cain't do anything to you in three seconds." My accent's thickening again, as it does when I'm frightened, angry or amorous. "And hear that? A nurse is right out in the hall."

He glares at me. "Please?" I'm about ready to whine. He shrugs, gives me one second's glance redolent of "You touch me and I'll whip your ass!" then closes his eyes.

The nurse, an obese blonde with teeteringly high hair, wheels in the medicine tray, stops by Matt's bed, and flaps her hand in the air. "Mr. Taylor!" she scolds. "What is all this smoke? Are you hidin' a cigar in here?"

There's not much to Belle. It's one of a string of small towns along the Kanawha River, along the railroad track. Full of good, kind people, for the most part, the kind of Christians I've learned to admire. Rain is tearing down by the time I shift forms in a phone booth like some sort of demonic Superman and start flipping the wrinkled pages. And here are the addresses, both Bates's residence and his church, the lengthily named Belle Apostolic Holiness Free Will Nazarene Charismatic Church of Christ. As far as I know, they don't handle snakes like the folks up in Scrabble Creek and down in Jolo. I wonder what they'd do if a slithering mass of copperheads were to join tonight's service through the unfortunate accident of a cracked back door?

No time for fun, Derek, I chide myself, batting off again.

Bates lives in a hovel with a sway-backed roof and white aluminum siding. Got to give it to him, he's truly not interested in the pleasures and vanities of this world. He's also evaded the sinful entrapments, the inconvenient handicaps, of an aesthetic sense. I can't help but smirk, hovering over his plastic collection of yard art, a garish assortment of nailed-down saviors, angels, and haloed farm animals. Of course he's far too holy to besmirch his lawn with decadent Halloween decorations.

The windows are dark. It *is* Sunday night, I realize. I can hear a big dog baying in the backyard, a nasty pit bull by the sound and reek of it, and one bat-fang catches on the lower lip of a grin as I contemplate slashing the beast to shreds and leaving what's left on the front stoop just to give Bates something to worry about. But I haven't fed lately— Joe the Hot Cop tied to a chair would be just right tonight—and I've got to find Bates and reconnoiter a bit before getting back to Mount Storm before dawn. Gutting the dog will have to wait. For hatred's gourmets, revenge is a feast to be served in many courses.

I've jetted over just a couple blocks of rain-slick rooftops before I hear the pious whooping of what a big sign proclaims is indeed the Belle Apostolic, Etc. Church. It's a white cinderblock rectangle with a stubby steeple, and it sounds like it's packed with people. I land on the dripping gutter, wrap my talons around the rotting metal, swing upside down and peer in the window.

A lavender-haired woman on the little podium up front is howling away, grimacing her apple-doll face, and slamming at her guitar as if she were trying to punish it. I'm just about ready to swoop off again so as to save my hypersensitive ears when she abruptly stops. An expectant silence falls, and the man himself shuffles down the aisle and ascends to the pulpit. I'd recognize that done-lopped-over belly, lax jowls and greased, dyed-black, Swaggart-style pompadour anywhere. It's as if someone just struck oil on his forehead.

"Brothers and sisters, my text tonight is from Romans," he begins. Oh, hell, I've heard all this before. I want to play. There has got to be a nasty nest of copperheads snoozing near here, or . . .

The gutter suddenly sags a little beneath me. *Derek.* I swivel my head. She's hanging by the next window over, only a few feet away, in an identical position. A bat fully as large as I.

Great Herne. I haven't seen another vampire in years.

Friendly, I think. She's grinning. Suddenly she swings forward and bumps the window. Hard. A woman inside screams. Another bump, then another. The glass cracks, then shatters. The bat opens her maw and hisses.

Okay, I should enjoy this game. There's a skinny man with thick spectacles sitting at the end of the pew, just inside my window. I slam my muzzle against the glass, and it splinters. Shards fly into the man's lap. I swing forward again, snarling and spitting. He shrieks like a disappointed drag queen denied a coveted crown, leaps to his feet and heads for the door.

When I turn toward my mysterious compatriot, more than ready to follow such a showwoman's lead, she flips up and off the gutter like a gymnast—a gymnast with leather wings, snout and claws, that is—and streaks off.

Faster than I am. My strength is low tonight. I was so looking forward to roping Joe the Hot Cop to an armchair, but I've got to see who she is and what she wants.

She's heading up the Kanawha River toward Montgomery. We pass the locks at London, the misty lights of West Virginia Tech, Glen Ferris and the broken white horseshoe of Kanawha Falls. At the mouth of the Gauley River, she circles that leaf-bushy islet with its crown of miserable Cofferdilly crosses before heading northeast toward clearer skies.

Vixen! Hell-harlot! Slow down! By the time we flap past Elkins, an hour later, I'm fagged considerably, and it's only when we've reached the great outcrop of Seneca Rocks that she slows down, circles over the valley in a palpable rapture of flight, and finally settles onto the high-est pinnacle.

I land beside her, and simultaneously we shift: a gasping man and a statuesque woman with an amused smile.

"I gather you've fed tonight," I pant.

"Indeed. Quite sweetly, thank you. A sumptuous Charleston tri-athlete named Robin. Sorry to lead you on such a long and merry chase, but I assumed you wouldn't mind it if we ended up here, a few miles from your home. And," she adds, gesturing over the starlit sweep of the valley below, "I do love a dramatic setting for a dramatic situa-tion."

Her hair is short and dark—one version of the most recent lesbian cut—her eyes deep-set, her cheekbones Slavic-high. There's an Eastern European lilt to her voice.

"Poland, actually. Krakow. It's still as lovely as when I walked its streets in the 1400s. I take Lara there occasionally. She loves to buy Polish glass."

Twice as old. No wonder she's stronger than I am. And a mind-reader, of course. I was never too good at that.

"My name's Cynthia. Yes, I know where you live. I've soared by a few times. I saw you first at Eppson Books, when Matthew Taylor and his Ridgerunners were performing."

The lesbian couple in the audience. "Yes, I remember."

"I like Matt. He's adorable, really. Brave little soul. If I fed on men, I'd borrow a taste of him occasionally. As it is . . . well, Derek Maclaine, I've been wanting to meet you for a while now. We have several things in common."

"Other than bat-winging and blood-drinking? I can guess one other area of shared enthusiasm: you're a descendant of Carmilla, so to speak? A frightful invert? Bent on eroding the sacred landscape of the American family?"

"Correct," she smiles. "I love a well-educated vampire, and you do have their amusing rhetoric down nicely. Yes, I'm a lesbian. My lover Lara runs the post office in Charleston. She's human, so I understand some of what you must have been going through with Matthew. Especially since last week; while I was enjoying a petite snack at Black-water Falls, Lara narrowly escaped a couple of pig-eyed thugs who are no doubt connected to the men who've landed Matthew in the hospital. She's quite out, a vocal member of the West Virginia Gay and Lesbian Coalition. She's spoken before the Charleston city council and the state legislature on the topic of hate crimes, so she's apparently ended up on Reverend Bates's list. As for Lara's attackers, she—how would your potty-mouthed mountaineer put it?—flattened their nuts. Scrambled their eggs. Such a natural weakness in the male armor. Irresistible."

"So"—it's all beginning to fit together, and it's too delicious to believe—"you were spying on Bates too?"

"Well, of course," she says, eyes narrowing. "I have decided not to turn Lara. She is, therefore, mortal with a mortal's inescapable fragility. Bates and his kennel of mangy followers threaten to take her from me. I intend, to use the pious warthog's phrase, to pluck them out." In the darkness her fangs glint as she smiles at the thought of such pleasure. "One by one. And I thought you might relish giving me a hand."

By now we're stretching out side by side on a narrow ledge of sandstone, talking in the dark. A shooting star arcs over and disappears. A cold wind curls over the summit of this great stegosaur-back of stone. I try to imagine spending the coming winter in Mount Storm without Matt.

"Cynthia, did you hear about the . . ."

"Oh, yes. Rats can be useful, though they leave a bit of a mess. Prefer cats myself. Bobcats, actually. I have two in particular I'm fond of. Delphi and Astraea. A rapist down in Beckley, well, that's a story for another time. Do go on."

"Yes. Though I have a sexy little friend who fudges police papers occasionally or drops embarrassing evidence down the sewer, I'd like to avoid a murder investigation or another well-publicized and inexplicable rodent buffet. And we mustn't make the reverend a martyr, as much as I would love to shove my claymore through him . . ."

"Oh, yes. Scotland. Lovely country."

". . . and watch him wriggle. So what do you suggest?"

Cynthia stretches, then tucks her hands behind her head. "We certainly must concentrate on Bates first. Lara compares organizations like his to the multiflora rose. Not an entirely appropriate metaphor,

Jeff Mann

since the blossoms have a lovely scent, and, having spied on Bates for the last several nights, I've become more than acquainted with his stink, especially when he's up there sweating behind the pulpit. Lara says you can't just lop off the thorny tentacles. The only way to eradicate such a spreading pest is to cut up the root. And that's going to be easier than you might imagine."

I can hear her licking her lips.

"And why is that, Mizz Cynthia?"

"Oh, Bates has such a nasty secret. Remember how I said I love a well-read vampire? You should recognize this reference. Derek, my dear, Bates is a Humbert Humbert."

By the next service, the dedicated congregation of the Belle Apostolic, Etc. Church has managed to rustle up some plywood to replace their broken windows. "Devil's work," they are muttering from pew to pew, comparing notes on the glass-shattering terrors that assailed them the previous evening.

And now Bates waddles up to the pulpit. He begins ranting about the dark things of the night sent to frighten good Christians from their holy purpose. By the time an odd mist behind the last pew, thoroughly bored, begins to disperse, the preacher has started on the God-sent blessings of mountaintop removal, the foul errors of environmentalists, and the many murders committed by abortion clinics. A widely ranging sermon, to be sure, punctuated by the staccato gasps peculiar to his ilk. "And the Lard has tole me—hah!—we must rise up—hah!—an' stop the baby-killin' monsters—hah!"

His pet's a square-framed pit bull, as I'd suspected the previous night. A vicious dog for a vicious man. As soon as I take human form in Bates's backyard, the baying animal is on me. I could command it to stop, but instead I slam my forearm between its jaws, poke out its eyes with my free forefinger, then toss its yelping body into the mud. Caution forbids me to eviscerate the master, but I have no such compunction concerning the dog. Its belly parts neatly beneath my fingers. Its agony makes me smile. I hang it by its own intestines from the plastic antlers of Bates's yard-art deer, and the darkness of the soil beneath it deepens with blood.

The back door is nothing. Its cheap hinges snap instantly. I would invest in more formidable locks, had I a secret as dangerous as his. Well, of course I do, and my secret room at Mount Storm is not only well-hidden but bolted with steel. Inside Bates's saintly shack are over-heated air, cheap paneling, a few framed and no-doubt-mail-order degrees, a ratty armchair, and other furnishings I have no time to notice. The howls of the dying dog—I simply couldn't resist, I hate the brutes—might attract notice, so I work fast.

First, I wash my hands in the kitchen sink. No need to sully the precious souvenir. And the manila folder is precisely where Cynthia predicted it would be: hidden in what passes for a study, behind a bookcase full of broken-backed religious tomes. Grinning, I check the folder's contents, then slip it into the inside pocket of my black duster. On the refrigerator I leave a note—"Thanks for the photographs!"—then leave the way I came.

The dog is silent now. No lights on in the surrounding trailers—they must all be wedged into the church pews down the street. Orion is straddling the ridge across the river. There's a pin oak in the adjoining yard, and for a minute or two I listen to wind hissing through the tree's stubbornly remaining leaves before taking to the air with my prize.

When I rise tonight, I find a big fire burning in the living room's sandstone hearth. Cold nights come early in altitudes as high as Mount Storm's. Carly Simon's singing, *"Do the walls come down when you think of me? Do you let me in?"* Bob and Kurt are in the kitchen crimping pie dough and baking butternut squash. I join them for a glass of pinot noir before strolling out into the darkness.

The earth is mustering its last efforts: winter squash, kale, mustard greens, turnips, and pumpkins. The corn is cut and shocked. The leaves of chestnut oak and sugar maple are raked and spread onto the fallow plots. On the field's edges, purple asters and goldenrod gather, shuddering in the cold breeze. Soon it will be Samhain, Feast of the Final Harvest.

A week has passed since I stole the folder from Bates's hovel, a folder since safely tucked away in my coffin. Angus's killers got off too easily. Young and enraged as I was, I killed them quickly. But several centuries have taught me how to extend my pleasures in the realms of both love and hate. For a week Bates has been living with the knowledge that someone knows his worst secret. He has been hoist on his own guts, so to speak, not unlike his late hound.

Cynthia, that consummate spy, has come by Mount Storm a couple of times to report on his condition. He's cancelled his sermons, pleading illness, pacing his study till the wee hours. *Cast into the outer darkness, where there is much weeping and wailing and gnashing of teeth.* She has also reported that Matt's been released from the hospital.

I run my fingers along a sharp-edged brown leaf which flutters like a flag from a twine-bound shock of corn. *They've rolled him and tied him by the way, / Serving him most barbarously.* I wrap my arms around the shock and bury my face in the brittle stalks. They smell like old paper, not flesh. I want to press my lips to his wounds. For once I want to be the healer, not the pestilence.

"Derek?"

She's come. I look up to see her standing beside me, her brow creased with bemusement.

A trifle embarrassed, I leave off my embrace and straighten up. "We're having a Halloween celebration next week, Cynthia. Will you come? Bring Lara."

"Certainly. That would be lovely. Are you ready?"

"Not quite. I need to fetch my kilt and claymore. And the pictures."

"He will come back to you," Cynthia whispers. "Meanwhile, other pleasures await."

I break into a broad smile, half hope and half malice, then lope off toward the house.

"Oh, Reverend," Cynthia's gushing into the stolen cell phone. "Ah jus' cain't tell you mah name. Jus' call me Cindy Lou. But Ah have this envelope. Ah think it's yours. Some bad men stole it from you, but by the Lawd's grace, Ah've recovered it. Yes, Ah'm a membah of your church. No, no, no thanks are needed. Ah jus' thank Gawd Ah could hep you in your time a' need."

She's really laying it on thick. Blanche Dubois with canines. Bates is probably desperately searching his musty memory, trying to recall when a Mississippi belle ever attended his services. All she needs is an ink-black hoop skirt.

"Well, yais, th' pitchers are a little odd. Ah *did* look at 'em. What sort of preevert did you wrest 'em from? Yais, yais, Ah understand. Oh, Lawd, no! I dint show 'em to anybody else! Ah haven't tole a soul! Well, why don't you meet me and fetch 'em? No, no, thas too public. Why don't you meet me here? Ah live near Ansted. As a mattah of fact, les us meet at Hawk's Nest. Up here on Gauley Mountain? How 'bout the ovahlook? How long will it take you?"

I can tell by the smirk on her face that she's about to explode, and she's barely hung up before she bursts into laughter.

"Ah have always depended on the genitals of strangahs!" she manages before the Dixie act evaporates and the Polish lilt returns. "He'll be here soon. A normal driver would take almost an hour to get here from Belle, but he sounds fairly agitated, and I suspect he'll be risking several speeding tickets. My, that was fun. I always wanted to act."

Striding to the stone wall edging the precipice, she drops the phone. We listen to it bounce several times on rocks jutting from the cliff face before it shatters into pieces a long ways down. The tinny echo reverberates and dies. Now there is no sound but the New River shushing over stones many hundreds of feet below, the wind rustling the last oak leaves above our heads. Before us, beneath the newly waning Blood Moon, the black Alleghenies unscroll beneath autumn's constellations, our distant and patient witnesses.

Waiting in the moonlight, I try to imagine the two men, the one I love and the one I hate.

Matt's asleep. It's late, and the painkillers knocked him out hours ago. His arm's still in a cast. He's slumped across his bed in a pair of boxer briefs. Yellow-brown bruises scatter his body, an afghan entwines him. His cats sleep on either side of him. Now a nightmare shakes him awake, a menace he fled from. Was it the Leviticus Locusts he dreamed of, or was it me?

Bates is driving fast down Route 60. The dead ash-gray vines of kudzu spill over the roadside slopes. Coal cars rumble along the railroad tracks, lights gleam from the factory windows of Alloy. He's sweating, despite the cold October night. My guess is he has a gun, so as to insure that his holy reputation remains intact. He no doubt intends to pray for her soul when he sends that treacle-tongued belle to her Maker.

DO NOT THROW OBJECTS OVER OVERLOOK says the posted sign. Those Civilian Conservation Corps men were fine workers in stone, building a walled semicircle atop the rock, giving future generations this sweeping view of the river and wooded mountains.

It is a view Reverend Rodney Bates is in no state of mind to appreciate, however, as he bursts from the forest edge and stumbles down the flight of stone stairs leading to the overlook. The park's officially closed at ten p.m., but rules never deter the desperate.

What does he see? Nothing at first. Edging the precipice, a stone wall, topped with a rail of short iron spikes. Several pay-for-a-better-view binoculars, mounted on posts. The wind's died down for the moment, and there's nothing to hear but the distant New River, second oldest in the world, white water's eternal song.

"Cindy Lou? Honey, where are you?" he calls shakily. Suddenly he's in a panic, afraid that she and the incriminating evidence won't show up.

From the woods behind him a screech owl starts up, the auditory equivalent of an icicle sliding down his spine, bumping each vertebra as it goes. He turns toward the sound, and there she is.

Not at all the vacuous, pastel-frocked blonde he's expected. No woman who's attended his services has ever worn her hair so short, has ever worn black pants and a leather jacket which dully gleams with moonlight. In the darkness her eyes seem to emit a faint greenish glow. She's sitting on a stone bench built into the wall behind him, and the coveted and crucial manila envelope is lying on the bench beside her.

"Are you Cindy Lou?" Bates stammers, disbelieving, backing up, fumbling in his shapeless raincoat's pocket. As massive as he is, he suddenly feels threatened by this small woman who rises from the bench and faces him.

"Ah, Reverend, at last you've come. I am indeed Cindy Lou. Or, rather, Cynthia. I've come to discuss literature with you. And politics."

"Listen, missy, I don't know who you are," Bates mutters, clearly confused. "You ain't one of my parishioners. But you've got to give me that folder."

"Well, no, Reverend. Actually, these will be going to *The Charleston Gazette*. Now, in the novel *Lolita*, Vladimir Nabokov paints a convincing portrait of . . ."

"Shut up!" Bates demands, and—yes, as I expected—pulls out a pistol. Anyone ruthless enough to encourage the Leviticus Locusts isn't above using a little God-sanctioned violence to save his pious public image. "That's right, little lady," he threatens. "We still got the right to bear arms in this country. Now hand over the folder." With jowls so Jell-o-jiggly, it must be hard to muster a threatening appearance, but Bates is doing the best he can. After all, she's a mere woman—clearly fallen, from her unfeminine outfit—and he's the right hand of God.

"Mercy, you're not a literature buff? Well, then, how about Hobbes? You see, Reverend Bates, this," Cynthia declaims, sweeping her hand in a semicircle to include the woodlands, the edge of the overlook and the moonlit mountains beyond, "this is much like the State of Nature that Hobbes spoke of. Where lives often turn out to be solitary, poor, nasty, brutish, and short. Some, not short enough." She's edging toward him now, and he's backing up, despite his brandished gun. "By the way, Reverend, your beastly thugs attacked my lover. Have you ever heard of Lara Martin?"

"Or Matthew Taylor?"

At the sound of another voice, Bates's head jerks up. What he sees now is meant to be alarmingly incongruous: a dark-bearded man in a black jerkin and kilt standing at the top of the stone steps descending to the overlook. As if the membrane between the centuries had ruptured, and the present were suddenly flooded by images of the past. Threatening images, more to the point, for the kilted man is drawing a sword and descending those steps.

For such a pulpit verbosity, Bates is speechless. Mesmerized by the approaching moon-glint of such a sharp length of steel, he backs away. The sounds he's making resemble the sputter of bacon frying in its own fat. By the time I've reached the bottom of the stairs and he remembers his gun, Cynthia has yanked it from his grasp.

The stone wall is nudging his chubby back now, the tip of my claymore is gently prodding one of his myriad chins. The wind picks up;

Bates swallows loudly. The moon is enveloped by a brief cloud, ember smothered by ash, then bursts into chalk-white flame again.

"What did Poe say about revenge, Cynthia?" I ask, keeping my eyes on the porcine preacher's sweaty face. "This idiot wouldn't know. He thinks it's sufficient to read only the Bible." Bates moans, and I give him just the slightest poke with my sword.

"Oh, let's see, you mean in 'The Cask of Amontillado'? Revenge is perfect when, number one, the swine you punish knows that it is you who are responsible for his destruction, and number two, you destroy him with impunity."

"Yes. Thank you." I nod politely in her direction, then meet my foe's watery stare.

"I loved a man once, Bates. A man with big shoulders and a red-gold beard. Men like you killed him. I love a man now, a man with a deep hillbilly baritone and a rich crop of chest hair. Your followers tried to kill him." With the traumas Bates's bloated body is about to endure, I can allow myself one tiny slice. Just a snick. I twist my wrist, and beneath the steel sword-tip a small red crescent opens on his neck. He wails, just about the sound his dog made when I uncoiled its guts like baling twine.

I can't resist some ritual formality. "I consign you to the forest compost, to the maws of the buzzard, the rat, the shrew and the maggot. Let this bulk you have so patiently accumulated feed the earth whose divinity you have denied."

The urge to grasp the hilt with both hands and sweep off his head is maddeningly strong, but Cynthia and I have agreed: no investigation, no martyr. Just as Bates is wincing beneath the certainty of a death-blow, I step back, sheathe my sword, and retreat to the right side of the overlook.

He blinks wildly, slumps back against the wall, and sighs. His mumbled prayers appear to have been answered.

"Heeeere, kitty, kitty, kitty!" It's the sound many a housewife bearing a plate of cat food has falsettoed out the back door. "Yes, Derek, you mustn't sully your steel on vermin blood," Cynthia adds, stepping to the other side of the overlook, a look of anticipation gleaming on her face.

All three of us are staring at the steps now, or, rather, at the dark forest at the top of those stairs, where a rustling has begun. Veering closer and closer, the sound of feet bounding through carpets of fallen leaves.

The Blood Moon is a willing spotlight, glittering off eyes as green as Cynthia's. They hesitate at the top of the stairs, as if aware of their own fatal magnificence, as if waiting for the proper introduction.

Cynthia obliges. "This is Delphi, Reverend," she announces sweetly, "who prophesizes doom for the guilty. And this is Astraea, in whom we behold the Goddess of Justice."

One bobcat and then the other screeches—the sound an infant might make before it is devoured. Together, snarling, they bound down the stairs, and together, teeth bared, they circle the fat man with the greasy pompadour.

Bates makes a dash for the stairs, but Astraea heads him off. He stumbles in our direction, but I draw my sword and smile. Shrieking, he turns and does exactly what we want him to do, moving in the only direction he has left: he grips the spikes atop the stone wall edging the cliff and tries to heave himself over.

Halfway up, he hangs suspended, his feet kicking ineffectually, and for a moment it looks as if I'll have to give him a hand. That's a big load for an out-of-shape fanatic to hoist. But a few swipes of Delphi's claws across his capacious backside and he's over the top.

I'm expecting a final scream trailing off into the distance, followed by a significant spine-splintering thump, but instead there's more sputtering and mumbling. Across the wall, amazingly, Bates's face is still visible.

I sheathe my claymore again, stride over, and look down, the cats snarling and pacing about my legs. There's a tiny ledge between the overlook wall and the precipice, about a foot across, on which Bates is balancing. Quite a feat, considering the size of that belly. His pudgy, sweat-greased fingers clasp the wall-top spikes. Prayers all run out, he's utterly silent, save for an overweight panting.

And I will have a more immediate vengeance after all. The gesture is appropriate, one used by faith healers on television. "Heal," they howl, slamming their palms against the supposed sufferers' foreheads.

Angus's blood seeping into the soil beneath the standing stones, Matt's blood streaking his temples. Unsmiling, I shove the heel of my hand against Bates's brow and launch him out toward the treetops.

Like the cell phone before him, he strikes a few outcrops before there
is that last satisfying thud and the screaming abruptly stops.

The girls in the photographs are all younger than sixteen. They are
all naked, and each one of their faces is flushed with shame. Some of
the photographs are stuck together, the *Charleston Gazette* reporter
gingerly notes as he shuffles through them. Who left the manila folder
on his desk? He has no idea.

Tourists taking in the overlook vista at Hawk's Nest State Park notice the circling buzzards first. Probably a dead deer, someone notes, as
a carrion reek rises from the woods below. Mountain breezes briefly
disperse the stink. Then the odor crowds in again, and tourists flee the
cliff edge in disgust. Pity the poor park ranger ordered to investigate.

Why did they decide to come forward? ask the social workers.
Because of the dreams, the girls admit. In their dreams, a dark lady
told them it was safe to tell the truth. He was their preacher; they
looked up to him. Then he touched them. He took pictures of them.
He told them the devil would drag them to hell if they told.

"So, La Clairvoyante, you sent me dreams as well then?" I ask Cynthia
at the Halloween feast.

It's taken Bob and Lara only one week to become best buddies, enthusiastic swappers of recipes and gossip. The big candlelit kitchen of
Mount Storm is full of the rich scents of their culinary collaborations:
roast pork, baked acorn squash, cabbage rolls, Scottish stuffed chicken,
bacon-braised kale, maple-nut biscotti. After the Samhain ritual, Bob,
Kurt, Lara, and a host of pagan Bears are celebrating the season in grand
and fattening style, while I treat Cynthia to some Clos du Bois merlot
by the fireside.

"I do have a precognitive streak. I knew Matt was in danger. I could
see what his fate would be, without someone's intervention. Sending
you visions seemed to me to be the most graceful—and vivid—way to
nudge you. Images are often so much more convincing than words.
And I knew you'd relish being his Knight in Ebony Armor."

I refold the several *Gazettes* we've been snickering over. GIRLS COME

FORWARD. INCRIMINATING PHOTOS IN POLICE POSSESSION. MINISTER'S
BODY FOUND IN WOODS: APPARENT SUICIDE. And, in smaller print, "Belle
Church Suffers Invasion of Copperheads," accompanied by a priceless
photo of the reptiles swarming out the front door of the rapidly emp-
tied church.

"Oh, yes, a knight he'll have nothing further to do with." I sip my
merlot and sigh, rubbing my silvering beard. Lately I haven't had
much appetite, and, without a recent meal, my age is catching up to
me.

"I know, I know, you're obsessed with that boy's goatee and chest
hair. What a fur fetishist! Matched only by your passion for sado-
masochism!" Cynthia teases, then falls silent. A hard wind is worrying
the edges of the old house, whining about the eaves and rattling the
casements. By Yule the snows will have set in.

"And by Yule, you will have heard from him, Derek," she whispers.

"You! Missy! Get out of my mind!" I knock back the last gulp of
wine, toss another log on the fire, and pace a bit before asking with
what must sound like a child's voice, "Really?"

"Mark my words." Cynthia is all confidence. "Meanwhile, I have a
charming lark planned that should distract you till you have that beefy
guitarist around to rope and ravish again. Do you remember the
ridiculous name Cofferdilly?"

Dark water swirls silently around the base of the great boulder, here
at the foot of Gauley Mountain, at the confluence of the Gauley and
the New. Both streams are swollen with weeks of cold November rains.

This island I once visited before, during one of my many solitary
wingings over the state. Tonight I am not alone. Cynthia is with me,
and two axes, which we are sharpening with whetstones as another autumnal drizzle begins, speckling our leather jackets.

"It's turning to sleet, I think." I'm working with slow, patient
strokes, the way my father taught me. Cynthia's axe is double-headed,
appropriately. A labrys.

"Heavy frost due in this weekend. It will take its cue from your
beard, I think. Are you on a starvation diet, Derek? Your hair is quite
gray."

I smile sheepishly, run my fingers through the fur on my face. "I plan to meet a biker down in Lost River in a couple of weeks. That should spruce me up. Are you ready?"

"Oh, yes. I've been touching myself for weeks at the thought of this. Now please take your time. This is work to relish."

Cynthia swings first. The steel sinks deep into the cheap wood, and soon she's got an expert notch going in the side of the cross. It creaks and topples over. I follow suite with the second. We take leisurely turns on the largest of the trio, bringing it down with only a few strokes apiece. The crossbeams we break into fragments with our bare hands and toss out over the water piece by piece.

The shards, painted yellow and light blue, are swept downriver, toward Kanawha Falls and Charleston, toward the Ohio and the Mississippi, toward the Gulf of Mexico.

We sit on the rock in silence for a few minutes, watching the midnight river rush by. On the far shore, lights have come up in a few houses, someone's shouting. Roused by the sounds of our axes, I gather. What I wouldn't give to see their faces in the morning, gazing across the water at a great boulder returned to its original state. For faith, the unadorned earth should be sufficient fact.

"Next week? That set of crosses near Buckhannon?" Cynthia asks, tugging affectionately on my beard. "Then we can start on the others along I-79."

"It's a date." As we rise to gather up our axes, the drizzle becomes a downpour.

It is the season of Death, and I am one of the dead. The winds that beat down upon Mount Storm are freezing now, though I do not feel discomfort as I sleep in my chilly coffin or sit alone in starlight among the standing stones. Frost forms slowly on the windows at night, and I am there to study that patient art, to watch the coming winter sketch ferns and flowers on the glass. The nights are longer and longer, and in the tower room I rock, marking the moons as they come and go. Sometimes I descend, to sit by the fire fueled by logs Bob and Kurt have felled and split. I sip Tobermory single malt, the waters of Mull distilled into fire. I brush my snowy beard across the back of my hand and try to remember the scents of the men I have loved.

Imagine them, the millennia of Yule celebrations, scattered across continents and centuries. The great holiday marked by Stonehenge and Newgrange, by the rough dolmens of Mystery Hill. The return of the sun. When the God of the Waning Year is vanquished by the God of the Waxing Sun. When the gray days begin to lengthen.

Bob and Kurt have gathered mistletoe with its seminal berries, holly with its blood-drops, clubfoot moss and white pine to decorate the mantelpiece. Bob and Lara are pulling out hand-scrawled family recipes for mulled wine and stollen, for crown roast, for Polish hunter's stew and Scottish shortbread.

By Yule, she'd said. But less than a week remains, and my hope is running out.

In my fireside dreams, Matt is the Lord of Light. He who was sacrificed in high summer is now the Yule priest, and it is I, manifestation of darkness, who am wrestled naked to my knees, then bound to the cross amidst the standing stones. When I close my eyes, I can feel the silver chains about my neck, wrists and ankles, the wood of the cross against my bare shoulders. A leather strap across my brow binds my head back, and all I can see are stars. Scorpio and Sagittarius. And Orion the Hunter. Hunter become the prey.

I shift in the chains, and the links clink together softly. I suck in cold air, exhale, and my breath draws a gray veil across the constellations. Frost, like the weight of years, is silently silvering my black chest hair. There's a drum throbbing somewhere, and the flicker of torches. The smell of heaped snow. And the scent of Matt, standing beneath me. Matt, who brushes his goatee across my belly and hipbones, gently bites my flanks, then takes me between his lips. I grunt and shove into him. I bite down on my tongue, and my own blood fills my mouth.

Long Nights Moon, they call it, riding above German Valley. It fights its way through snow clouds tonight. A blizzard predicted for the Potomac Highlands, with even more storms on the way. Bob's stocked in provisions and has corn chowder simmering. From my study window, I watch the pines bend beneath hard wind before pouring out some Scotch and turning on the computer.

Only two days are left till Yule. For weeks, the e-mail I've hopefully checked every evening has consisted of nothing but notes from my New York publishing minions.

I'm thinking about spring in San Francisco when the message comes up.

> *Derek,*
> *We got to talk. I'll be at the Glen Ferris Inn till Saturday morning. Job retreat. Can you meet me tomorrow night? The dining room at 8?*
> *Matt*

Bob is in the study in three breaths. He's never heard a vampire yell yeee-haw.

I leave the snowstorm behind at Elkins, and by a quarter to eight, I'm flapping over the rock Cynthia and I recently cleaned of crosses and soaring downriver. There, below, almost immediately, spreads the curved susurrus of Kanawha Falls, white in the moonlight, and beside it stand the columns and yellow-lit windows of the inn.

I'm in a hopeful and playful mood tonight, so I dive-bomb a family in the inn's snow-scattered parking lot. The children scream, the woman herds them toward the car, the man fumbles with his keys. They're inside with admirable rapidity. I bump the windshield once or twice, showing my long teeth, before bidding them adieu as they rocket out of the parking lot and down Route 60.

Outside one window and then another I hover, searching. There he is. Through the steamed glass of the dining room, I can see Matt sitting alone in the corner. He's drinking red wine, brooding. A candle on his table flickers across his face. He finishes his glass and orders another. He needs to be half-drunk to face me.

How handsome he is. What purpose has my life save devouring

beauty? Literally, metaphorically. Whatever is possible, whatever is allowed. There's a several-days' shadow of stubble across his cheeks. His hair is longer than before, spilling over his shoulders. His goatee is even bushier. The sleeves of his rag-wool sweater are rolled up, and his forearms are thick with muscle. He buries his face in his hands for several seconds, then brushes his hair back from his eyes and takes another swallow.

The parking lot is now pleasingly free of witnesses, so there I shift before striding in among the pillars of the front porch and through the door. I haven't been here for over a hundred years. What a picture Mark Carden was, peeling off his gray wool uniform in that room upstairs.

The dining room is dim and almost empty. An elderly waitress, the aroma of fried seafood, a few quiet tables of hotel guests. Busy wallpaper, antique furniture, Christmas lights and plastic greenery strung along the mantelpiece.

"Matt."

He looks up. His face flushes. His heart is pounding, and, by Cernunnos, his scent is the same. It makes my head swim.

"Derek. Sit down," he says, looking away, grabbing his glass and knocking back what's left of his wine.

I slip off my black duster and slide into a chair. Our knees bump. He jumps and moves his leg away.

There's a mist smearing my vision. The cataracts of lust. I should have fed earlier this evening. The appetite I've lacked for months has come rushing back. I mustn't touch him tonight, even if he invites me, but, considering his body language, there's not much likelihood of that.

I try to meet his eyes, with no success. "Matt, why did you want to see me?"

He hesitates, staring at his empty glass, and sighs. "Don't know. I've been dreamin' about you every night. In some of 'em, you kill me. With an ice pick, with an awl, with your bare hands. In others, you're fuckin' me. No. Makin' love to me. Real rough, and then real tender. I wake up to . . . well, I've been runnin' through the Kleenex. So I figured the only way I could make sense of thangs was to see you again."

The waitress pauses by our table. "No, no, ma'am. No more wine.

Just put it on my room tab, okay? Derek, I gotta get some air. Let's go outside."

I'm relieved and amazed that he would consider being alone with me. Matt rises unsteadily and shoulders on his leather jacket. I pull on my duster, and we're out the door.

The garden behind the inn overlooks the river. The flowerbeds are dusted with day-old snow and full of the withered stalks of last summer's blooms. Above us loom a bare-limbed sycamore and a black walnut. In the darkness just upriver, the Kanawha Falls continue their constant subdued rushing, the same sound I drowsed to upstairs with Mark in my arms. Long, long ago.

Matt sits down on a small concrete bench and almost immediately rises.

"*Shit*, that's cold! I don't need ice on my ass."

The moon, veiled till now, slips from behind a cloud, and for the first time tonight, Matt looks me full in the face. His eyes widen with shock.

"Derek, what's happened to you? Your beard is *white!*"

I turn from him, touch the smooth white bark of the sycamore beside me, then settle heavily onto the bench, my wintry flesh matching the concrete chill for chill.

"Let me explain that circuitously. I'm glad you asked me to meet you here. I have some pleasant memories of this inn. Many years ago I spent a few sweet nights here with a soldier. That room right up there. I loved him almost as much as I love you."

Matt stares at me. He groans and turns abruptly toward the river, takes a few strides forward. For a second, I fear he's going to jump in rather than contemplate being loved by a killer. But then he stops and, back to me, stands in silence.

The moon disappears again, swallowed by what must be snow clouds, to judge by the scent of this brisk breeze sweeping over the garden.

Matt shivers and turns his collar up against the cold. "You love me?" The tone of his voice is a mixture of strained disbelief, and oddly, relief, as if something's been decided.

"Yes. Yes, I love you. Yes, I drank your blood. Yes, given your permission, I will strip you, tie your hands behind your back, make love to you and then drink your blood again."

He turns toward me. Light from the inn windows illuminates that combination of emotions I've come to expect after three centuries: terror and longing.

"Did you hear that, Matt?" I ask softly. "With your permission. I will not hurt you."

"You really think I'd let you touch me again? After you killed those guys in that alley?"

"I did that to protect you. You might as well know I also disposed of Bates. Again, to protect you. Because of him, you almost died. I made it look like suicide. He needed killin'—that's the Southern expression, I think. I'll kill anyone who threatens me and those I love."

"Jesus, you killed Bates?!" he gasps. I can't tell whether he's horrified or impressed. He shakes his head and looks out toward the falls' distant white curtain. "Man, you've been busy." Then, softly, begrudgingly, "Cain't say I'm sorry Bates is dead, though."

Matt kicks at a fallen sycamore twig, then mutters, "So what about that guy you mentioned? The soldier you slept with here. You still love him?" There's the tiniest edge of jealousy to the question, and that gives me hope.

"As much as one can love the deceased. Mark Carden is long gone. He was a Confederate soldier. He died at the Battle of Chickamauga in 1863. And I . . . I died in Scotland, in the year 1730."

"You're insane, Derek." He faces me again, eyes wide, and starts backing up.

And I'm losing my patience. "It's a little bit more complicated than that. Watch."

The shimmer begins around my head, then cascades over my shoulders. Next my figure goes translucent, and the edges dissolve. Now Matt is alone, save for the sound of the falls and an eldritch mist which eddies around him before drifting over to the trunk of the sycamore and slowly regaining human form.

I'll give it to him. He's as brave as he was in that alley, tearing into those punks. Instead of running away as fast as he can, he stands stock-still, his face as pale as mine. Then his knees begin to quiver and he sits on the bench, its cold forgotten for the moment.

"Sorry to be such a show-off. It was the fastest way to convince you."

"So you're what? A ghost?" he manages shakily. "No, shit, I should know better than anyone how solid you are. You . . . my blood on the sheets, that night at your farm . . . you didn't use an awl, did you?"

"If I may?" I cock my head quizzically.

He nods uncertainly. I swore I wouldn't touch him, but the temptation is too great. I stride over, sit beside him, and gently take one clenched fist into my hands. The heat of his skin is a shock in this wintry garden, and I can feel him suppress a flinch as my cold flesh touches his. I kiss a knuckle, brush my bearded chin over the back of his hand. I unclasp his tense fingers, bend down, and gently press the sharp tip of one extended fang against the ball of his thumb.

"My God," he whispers. Instead of recoiling, he runs his index finger over one fang and then the other. I can't resist licking his finger, sucking on it a second before pulling away.

"My beard is white because I haven't fed for a good while. I am, after all, three hundred years old. Blood keeps me young."

Matt's looking at me with wonder now. I can smell the cheap wine on his breath. "Goddamn, what *is* this? Some kind of hillbilly *Dark Shadows?* So, the sunlight . . . and bats? Coffins, and . . ."

"Yes, much of the folklore's true. I can run through your questions later, if you'd like. If there's to be a later. That's the only question I have."

Matt rests his elbows on his knees, cups his forehead in his hands, and mutters, "Are you wantin' to change me, Derek? You know, into . . . Can you do that?"

"I can," I admit. "But I never have. Not in all these years. I would never do such a thing without your consent. And I'm afraid this . . . chemistry between us might be cancelled. What we feel when we touch, it's the play between darkness and light, the tension between winter and summer, the sparks that leap between polarities. If you became what I am, we might lose that. I don't want to lose that."

"What do you want from me then?" He wraps his arms around himself and shivers. The wind is rising. Somewhere I can hear pellets of old snow skittering across a crust of ice.

"What do I want from you? You're beautiful, Matt." Reaching up, I steal a quick stroke of his thick hair. "I want to touch you. Passionately and often. I had a lover when I was human. His name was Angus. He was my brother-in-arms, my companion. What I had with him I want with you. Not marriage, not monogamy. That's like trying to store lava in Tupperware. And if I fed on you solely, you wouldn't last long. Neither would I, if I had to live with the knowledge that I'd killed you."

Now I'm risking a hand on his knee. "Yes, I'm a monster. But when I touch you, I'm also human. I want you in my bed, warm and hairy and naked and willing. I want to have another night like the one we shared in Mount Storm. If there's a next time," I promise shame-facedly, "my thirst won't get the better of me. Warrior's honor. I want a night like that, and then another, and another. For as long as our mutual appetite lasts."

Matt's utterly silent for about five seconds before he groans, "Oh hell," turns, takes my head in his hands and kisses me hard, just as the first fat flakes of snow start falling over the Kanawha Valley. By the time my stunned heart has started a faint undead beat again and we've managed to wrap our arms around big shoulders and bulky coats, his teeth are beginning to chatter.

"Damn, I'm freezing," Matt laughs, pulling free, jumping up and shaking his ass. "These leather jackets are sure hot to look at, but they're damned cold to wear this time of year."

Rising, I recover from my shocked flood of relief fast enough to be gallant. "We'll warm one another. Come in here," I whisper, shrugging off my duster before wrapping it and then my arms around him. He leans his head against mine, and the gratitude almost chokes me. His trust in me—unearned, undeserved—is a kind of Grace.

"I'm terrified," Matt admits quietly, his breath hot against my face.

I nod, incapable of speech for a long moment, before muttering, "Tomorrow's the winter solstice, Matt. We're having a party up at Mount Storm. Bob's hot buttered rum really takes off that mountain chill. And with this weather, we might be fortunate enough to be snowed in. Want to come up?"

Another thoughtful silence before he replies, "Yeah, I think so. Maybe I'll help Bob chop wood while you sleep. As long as I get Top for a change." He grins, tugging on the stainless-steel hoop in my icy left ear. "Chainin' you up would, uh, well, I'd feel safer. And I got lots more questions you got to answer."

The brief steam of his breath spirals off down the wind. I think of the cross amidst the standing stones, and, grinning, I open my mouth to catch snow like defeated stars on my tongue.

I nod. "It's a deal. Whatever helps you learn to trust me. Want to go in now?" The windows of the inn are orange with inviting lamplight.

"Not yet, Derek. This coat of yours helps. And I like to watch the snow. Have since I was a kid down in Summers County."

Flakes are coming faster now, slanting across the river. The Kanawha Falls roar on, a sound bound to outlive us both, human and vampire. I hold Matt tighter, brush my beard against his cheek, against the miracle of his heat. Together we watch as dead grass at our feet grows pale, as cold white crystals are cast from the sky and swallowed by the dark waters of the river.